DEBBIE MACOMBER

A Christmas Message

mira

MIX
Paper from
responsible sources
FSC® C021394
FSC
www.fsc.org

PLEASE RECYCLE
THIS PRODUCT IS RECYCLABLE

Recycling programs
for this product may
not exist in your area.

mira™

ISBN-13: 978-0-7783-8822-7

A Christmas Message

Copyright © 2020 by Harlequin Books S.A.

Christmas Letters
First published in 2006. This edition published in 2020.
Copyright © 2006 by Debbie Macomber

Call Me Mrs. Miracle
First published in 2010. This edition published in 2020.
Copyright © 2010 by Debbie Macomber

All rights reserved. No part of this book may be used or reproduced in
any manner whatsoever without written permission except in the case of
brief quotations embodied in critical articles and reviews.

This is a work of fiction. Names, characters, places and incidents are
either the product of the author's imagination or are used fictitiously.
Any resemblance to actual persons, living or dead, businesses, companies,
events or locales is entirely coincidental.

This edition published by arrangement with Harlequin Books S.A.

For questions and comments about the quality of this book,
please contact us at CustomerService@Harlequin.com.

Mira
22 Adelaide St. West, 40th Floor
Toronto, Ontario M5H 4E3, Canada
www.Harlequin.com

Printed in Lithuania

Also available from Debbie Macomber and MIRA

Blossom Street

The Shop on Blossom Street
A Good Yarn
Susannah's Garden
Back on Blossom Street
Twenty Wishes
Summer on Blossom Street
Hannah's List
"The Twenty-First Wish"
    (in *The Knitting Diaries*)
A Turn in the Road

Cedar Cove

16 Lighthouse Road
204 Rosewood Lane
311 Pelican Court
44 Cranberry Point
50 Harbor Street
6 Rainier Drive
74 Seaside Avenue
8 Sandpiper Way
92 Pacific Boulevard
1022 Evergreen Place
Christmas in Cedar Cove
    (*5-B Poppy Lane* and
    A Cedar Cove Christmas)
1105 Yakima Street
1225 Christmas Tree Lane

The Dakota Series

Dakota Born
Dakota Home
Always Dakota
Buffalo Valley

The Manning Family

The Manning Sisters
    (*The Cowboy's Lady* and
    The Sheriff Takes a Wife)

The Manning Brides
    (*Marriage of Inconvenience* and
    Stand-In Wife)
The Manning Grooms
    (*Bride on the Loose* and
    Same Time, Next Year)

Christmas Books

A Gift to Last
On a Snowy Night
Home for the Holidays
Glad Tidings
Christmas Wishes
Small Town Christmas
When Christmas Comes
    (now retitled *Trading
    Christmas*)
There's Something About Christmas
Christmas Letters
The Perfect Christmas
Choir of Angels
    (*Shirley, Goodness and Mercy*,
    Those Christmas Angels and
    Where Angels Go)
Call Me Mrs. Miracle

Heart of Texas

Texas Skies
    (*Lonesome Cowboy* and
    Texas Two-Step)
Texas Nights
    (*Caroline's Child* and
    Dr. Texas)
Texas Home
    (*Nell's Cowboy* and
    Lone Star Baby)
Promise, Texas
Return to Promise

CONTENTS

CHRISTMAS LETTERS

To Katherine Orr
Better known as K.O.
for her encouragement and support
through the years

Prologue

Zelda O'Connor Davidson
76 Orchard Avenue
Seattle, Washington
Christmas, 2006

Dear Family and Friends:

Merry Christmas, everyone!

Let me warn you—this Christmas letter won't be as clever as last year's. My sister, Katherine (whom you may know better as K.O.), wrote that one for me but, ironically, she hasn't got time to do this year's. Ironic because it's due to the popularity of that particular letter that she's managed to start a little business on the side—writing Christmas letters for other people! (She offered to write mine, of course, but I know that between her work doing medical transcriptions, her job search and her Christmas letters, it would be a real stretch to find the time.)

So, here goes. The twins, Zoe and Zara, have recently turned five. They're looking forward to starting kindergarten next September. It's hard to believe our little girls are almost old enough for school! Still, they keep themselves (and us!) busy. So do our assorted pets—especially the dogs, two Yorkies named Zero and Zorro.

I'm still a stay-at-home mom and Zach's still working as a software programmer. This year's big news, which I want to share with all of you, has to do with a wonderful book I read. It changed my family's life. It's called *The Free Child* and it's by Dr. Wynn Jeffries. My sister scoffs at this, but Dr. Jeffries believes that children can be trusted to set their own boundaries. He also believes that, as parents, we shouldn't impose fantasies on them—fantasies like Santa Claus. Kids are capable of accepting reality, he says, and I agree! (See page 146 of *The Free Child*.)

So, this Christmas will be a different kind of experience for us, one that focuses on family, not fantasy.

Zach and the girls join me in wishing all of you a wonderful Christmas. And remember, a free child is a happy child (see page 16).

Love and kisses,

Zelda, Zach, Zoe and Zara

(and a wag of the tail from Zero & Zorro)

Chapter One

It *was* him. Katherine O'Connor, better known as K.O., was almost positive. She squinted just to be sure. He looked identical to the man on the dust jacket of that ridiculous book, the one her sister treated like a child-rearing bible. Of course, people didn't really look like their publicity photos. And she hadn't realized the high and mighty Dr. Wynn Jeffries was from the Seattle area. Furthermore, she couldn't imagine what he was doing on Blossom Street.

She'd never even met him, but she distrusted him profoundly and disliked him just as much. It was because of Dr. Jeffries that she'd been banned from a local bookstore. She'd had a small difference of opinion with the manager on the subject of Wynn's book. Apparently the bookseller was a personal friend of his, because she'd leaped to Dr. Jeffries's defense and had ordered K.O. out of the store. She'd even suggested K.O. take her future book-purchasing business elsewhere, which seemed unnecessarily extreme.

"K.O.," Bill Mulcahy muttered, distracting her. They sat across from each other at the French Café, filled to capacity during the midmorning rush. People lined up for coffee, and another line formed at the bakery counter. "Did you get all that?" he asked.

"Sure," K.O. said, returning her attention to him. "Sorry—I thought I saw someone I knew." Oh, the things she was willing to do for some extra holiday cash. One witty Christmas letter written on her sister's behalf, and all of a sudden K.O. was the most sought-after woman at her brother-in-law's office. They all wanted her to write their Christmas letters. She'd been shocked to discover how much they'd willingly plunk down for it, too. Bill Mulcahy was the third person she'd met with this week, and his letter was the most difficult so far. Leno or Letterman would've had a hard time finding anything amusing about this man's life.

"I don't know what you're going to write," Bill continued. "It's been an exceptionally bad year. As I explained earlier, my son is in a detention home, my daughter's living with her no-good boyfriend and over Thanksgiving she announced she's pregnant. Naturally, marriage is out of the question."

"That *is* a bit of a challenge," K.O. agreed. She widened her eyes and stared again at the man who waited in the long line at the cash register. It *was* him; she was convinced of it now. The not-so-good doctor was—to put it in appropriately seasonal terms—a fruitcake. He was a child psychologist who'd written a book called *The Free Child* that was the current child-rearing rage.

To be fair, K.O. was single and not a mother. The only child-rearing experience she'd had was with her identical twin nieces, Zoe and Zara, whom she adored. Until recently, anyway. Overnight the five-year-olds had become miniature monsters and all because her sister had followed the "Free Child" rules as set out by Dr. Jeffries.

"My wife," Bill said, "is on the verge of a breakdown."

K.O. pitied the poor woman—and her husband.

"We've written Christmas letters for years and while life wasn't always as perfect as we—well, as we implied…" He let the rest fade away.

"You painted the picture of a model family."

"Yes." Bill cleared his throat and offered her a weak smile. "Patti, that's my wife, chose to present a, shall we say, rosier depiction of reality." He exhaled in a rush. "We never included family pictures and if you met my son, you'd know why. Anyone looking at Mason would know in a minute that this kid isn't a member of the National Honor Society." He released his breath again and shook his head sadly. "Mason's into body piercing," Bill added. "He pierced his eyebrows, his nose, his lips, his tongue, his nipples—"

K.O. stopped him before he went any lower. "I get it."

"You probably don't, but that's lucky for you. Oh, and he dyed his hair green."

"Green?"

"He wears it spiked, too, and he…he does this thing with paint." Bill dropped his voice.

K.O. was sure she'd misunderstood. "I beg your pardon?"

"Mason doesn't call it paint. It's some form of cosmetic he smears across his face. I never imagined that my son would be rummaging through his mother's makeup drawer one day."

"I suppose that is a bit disconcerting," K.O. murmured.

"I forget the actual significance of the black smudges under his eyes and across his cheeks," Bill said. "To me it looks like he's some teenage commando."

Yes, this letter would indeed be a challenge. "Have you

thought about skipping your Christmas letter this year?" K.O. asked hopefully.

"Yeah, I'd like to, but as I said, Patti's emotional health is rather fragile. She claims people are already asking about our annual letter. She's afraid that if we don't send it the same as we do every year, everyone will figure out that we're pitiful parents." His shoulders drooped. "In other words, we've failed our children."

"I don't think you've necessarily *failed*," K.O. assured him. "Most teenagers go through a rebellious stage."

"Did you?"

"Oh, sure."

"Did you pierce anything?"

"Well, I had my ears pierced...."

"That's not the same thing." He peered at her earrings, visible through her straight blond hair, which she wore loosely tied back. "And you only have one in each ear—not eight or ten like my son." He seemed satisfied that he'd proved his point. "Then you'll write our Christmas letter and smooth over the rough edges of our year?"

K.O. was less and less confident that she could pull this off. "I don't know if I'm your person," she said hesitantly. How could she possibly come up with a positive version of such a disastrous year? Besides, this side job was supposed to be fun, not real work. It'd begun as a favor to her sister and all of a sudden she was launching a career. At some stage she'd need to call a halt—maybe sooner than she'd expected.

Her client shifted in his seat. "I'll pay you double what you normally charge."

K.O. sat up straight. Double. He said he'd pay double? "Would four days be enough time?" she asked. Okay, so she could be bought. She pulled out her Day-Timer, checked her schedule and they set a date for their next meeting.

"I'll give you half now and half when you're finished."

That seemed fair. Not one to be overly prideful, she held out her hand as he peeled off three fifty-dollar bills. Her fingers closed around the cash.

"I'll see you Friday then," Bill said, and reaching for his briefcase, he left the French Café carrying his latte in its takeout cup.

Looking out the windows with their Christmas garland, she saw that it had begun to snow again. This was the coldest December on record. Seattle's normally mild climate had dipped to below-freezing temperatures for ten days in a row. So much for global warming. There was precious little evidence of it in Seattle.

K.O. glanced at the coffee line. Wynn Jeffries had made his way to the front and picked up his hot drink. After adding cream and sugar—lots of both, she observed—he was getting ready to leave. K.O. didn't want to be obvious about watching him, so she took a couple of extra minutes to collect her things, then followed him out the door.

Even if she introduced herself, she had no idea what to say. Mostly she wanted to tell him his so-called Free Child movement—no boundaries for kids—was outright lunacy. How could he, in good conscience, mislead parents in this ridiculous fashion? Not that she had strong feelings on the subject or anything. Okay, so maybe she'd gone a little overboard at the bookstore that day, but she couldn't help it. The manager had been touting the benefits of Dr. Jeffries's book to yet another unsuspecting mom. K.O. felt it was her duty to let the poor woman know what might happen if she actually followed Dr. Jeffries's advice. The bookseller had strenuously disagreed and from then on, the situation had gotten out of hand.

Not wanting him to think she was stalking him, which she supposed she was, K.O. maintained a careful distance. If his office was in Seattle, it might even be in this neighborhood. After the renovations on Blossom Street a few years ago, a couple of buildings had been converted to office space. If she could discreetly discover where he practiced, she might go and talk to him sometime. She hadn't read his book but had leafed through it, and she knew he was a practicing child psychologist. She wanted to argue about his beliefs and his precepts, tell him about the appalling difference in her nieces' behavior since the day Zelda had adopted his advice.

She'd rather he didn't see her, so she dashed inconspicuously across the street to A Good Yarn, and darted into the doorway, where she pretended to be interested in a large Christmas stocking that hung in the display window. From the reflection in the window, she saw Dr. Jeffries walking briskly down the opposite sidewalk.

As soon as it was safe, she dashed from the yarn store to Susannah's Garden, the flower shop next door, and nearly fell over a huge potted poinsettia, all the while keeping her eyes on Dr. Jeffries. He proved one thing, she mused. Appearances were deceiving. He looked so…so normal. Who would've guessed that beneath that distinguished, sophisticated and—yes—handsome exterior lay such a fiend? Perhaps *fiend* was too strong a word. Yet she considered Wynn Jeffries's thinking to be nothing short of diabolical, if Zoe and Zara were anything to judge by.

No way!

K.O. stopped dead in her tracks. She watched as Wynn

Jeffries paused outside her condo building, her very own building, entered the code and strolled inside.

Without checking for traffic, K.O. crossed the street again. A horn honked and brakes squealed, but she barely noticed. She was dumbfounded.

Speechless.

There had to be some mistake. Perhaps he was making a house call. No, that wasn't right. What doctor made house calls in this day and age? What psychologist made house calls *ever?* Besides, he didn't exactly look like the compassionate type. K.O. bit her lip and wondered when she'd become so cynical. It'd happened around the same time her sister read Dr. Jeffries's book, she decided.

The door had already closed before she got there. She entered her code and stepped inside just in time to see the elevator glide shut. Standing back, she watched the floor numbers flicker one after another.

"Katherine?"

K.O. whirled around to discover LaVonne Young, her neighbor and friend. LaVonne was the only person who called her Katherine. "What are you doing, dear?"

K.O. pointed an accusing finger past the elegantly decorated lobby tree to the elevator.

LaVonne stood in her doorway with her huge tomcat, named predictably enough, Tom, tucked under her arm. She wore a long shapeless dress that was typical of her wardrobe, and her long graying hair was drawn back in a bun. When K.O. had first met her, LaVonne had reminded her of the character Auntie Mame. She still did. "Something wrong with the elevator?" LaVonne asked.

"No, I just saw a man…" K.O. glanced back and noticed that the elevator had gone all the way up to the penthouse suite. That shouldn't really come as a shock. His book sales being what they were, he could easily afford the penthouse.

LaVonne's gaze followed hers. "That must be Dr. Jeffries."

"You know him?" K.O. didn't bother to hide her interest. The more she learned, the better her chances of engaging him in conversation.

"Of course I know Dr. Jeffries," the retired accountant said. "I know everyone in the building."

"How long has he lived here?" K.O. demanded. She'd been in this building since the first week it was approved for occupation. So she should've run into him before now.

"I believe he moved in soon after the place was renovated. In fact, the two of you moved in practically on the same day."

That was interesting. Of course, there was a world of difference between a penthouse suite and the first-floor, one-bedroom unit she owned. Or rather, that the bank owned and she made payments on. With the inheritance she'd received from her maternal grandparents, K.O. had put a down payment on the smallest, cheapest unit available. It was all she could afford at the time—and all she could afford now. She considered herself lucky to get in when she did.

"His name is on the mailbox," LaVonne said, gesturing across the lobby floor to the mailboxes.

"As my sister would tell you, I'm a detail person." It was just the obvious she missed.

"He's a celebrity, you know," LaVonne whispered conspiratorially. "Especially since his book was published."

"Have you read it?" K.O. asked.

"Well, no, dear, I haven't, but then never having had children myself, I'm not too concerned with child-raising.

However, I did hear Dr. Jeffries interviewed on the radio and he convinced me. His book is breaking all kinds of records. Apparently it's on all the bestseller lists. So there must be *something* to what he says. In fact, the man on the radio called Dr. Jeffries the new Dr. Spock."

"You've got to be kidding!" Jeffries's misguided gospel was spreading far and wide.

LaVonne stared at her. "In case you're interested, he's not married."

"That doesn't surprise me," K.O. muttered. Only a man without a wife and children could possibly come up with such ludicrous ideas. He didn't have a family of his own to test his theories on; instead he foisted them on unsuspecting parents like her sister, Zelda, and brother-in-law, Zach. The deterioration in the girls' behavior was dramatic, but Zelda insisted this was normal as they adjusted to a new regimen. They'd "find their equilibrium," she'd said, quoting the book. Zach, who worked long hours, didn't really seem to notice. The twins' misbehavior would have to be even more extreme to register on him.

"Would you like me to introduce you?" LaVonne asked.

"No," K.O. responded immediately. Absolutely not. Well, maybe, but not now. And not for the reasons La-Vonne thought.

"Do you have time for tea?" LaVonne asked. "I wanted to tell you about the most recent class I attended. Fascinating stuff, just fascinating." Since her retirement, LaVonne had been at loose ends and signed up for a variety of workshops and evening classes.

"I learned how to unleash my psychic abilities."

"You're psychic?" K.O. asked.

"Yes, only I didn't know it until I took this class. I've learned so much," she said in wonder. "So much. All these years, my innate talent has lain there, unused and unful-filled. It took this class to break it free and show me what I should've known all along. *I can see into the future.*" She spoke in a portentous whisper.

"You learned this after one class?"

"Madame Ozma claims I have been blessed with the sight. She warned me not to waste my talents any longer."

This *did* sound fascinating. Well…bizarre, anyway. K.O. would have loved to hear all about the class, but she really needed to start work. In addition to writing Christmas let-ters—which she did only in November and December—she was a medical transcriptionist by training. It paid the bills and had allowed her to put herself through college to obtain a public relations degree. Now she was searching for a job in PR, which wasn't all that easy to find, even with her degree. She was picky, too. She wanted a job with a salary that would actually meet her expenses. Over the years she'd grown accustomed to a few luxuries, like regu-lar meals and flush toilets.

Currently her résumé was floating around town. Any-time now, she was bound to be offered the perfect job. And in the meanwhile, these Christmas letters gave her some useful practice in creating a positive spin on some unprom-ising situations—like poor Bill Mulcahy's.

"I'd love a cup of tea, but unfortunately I've got to get to work."

"Perhaps tomorrow," LaVonne suggested.

"That would be great."

"I'll call upon my psychic powers and look into your fu-ture if you'd like." She sounded completely serious.

"Sure," K.O. returned casually. Perhaps LaVonne could let her know when she'd find a job.

LaVonne's eyes brightened. "I'll study my class notes and then I'll tell you what I *see* for you."

"Thanks." She reached over and scratched Tom's ears. The big cat purred with pleasure.

With a bounce in her step, LaVonne went into her condo, closing the door with a slam that shook her Christmas wreath, decorated with golden moons and silver stars. K.O. headed for her own undecorated door, which was across the hall. Much as she disapproved of her sister's hero, she could hardly wait to tell Zelda the news.

Chapter Two

K.O. waited until she'd worked two hours straight before she phoned her sister. Zelda was a stay-at-home mom with Zoe and Zara, who were identical twins. Earlier in the year Zelda and Zach had purchased the girls each a dog. Two Yorkshire terriers, which the two girls had promptly named Zero and Zorro. K.O. called her sister's home the Land of Z. Even now, she wasn't sure how Zelda kept the girls straight, let alone the dogs. Even their barks sounded identical. *Yap. Yap* and *yap* with an occasional *yip* thrown in for variety, as if they sometimes grew bored with the sound of their own yapping.

Zelda answered on the third ring, sounding frazzled and breathless. "Yes?" she snapped into the phone.

"Is this a bad time?" K.O. asked.

"Oh, hi." The lack of enthusiasm was apparent. In addition to everything else, Dr. Jeffries's theories had placed a strain on K.O.'s relations with her younger sister.

"Merry Christmas to you, too," K.O. said cheerfully. "Can you talk?"

"Sure."

"The girls are napping?"

"No," Zelda muttered. "They decided they no longer need naps. Dr. Jeffries says on page 125 of his book that children should be allowed to sleep when, and only when, they decide they're tired. Forcing them into regimented nap-and bedtimes, is in opposition to their biological natures."

"I see." K.O. restrained the urge to argue. "Speaking of Dr. Jeffries…"

"I know you don't agree with his philosophy, but this is the way Zach and I have chosen to raise our daughters. When you have a family of your own, you can choose how best to parent your children."

"True, but…"

"Sorry," Zelda cried. It sounded as if she'd dropped the phone.

In the background, K.O. could hear her sister shouting at the girls and the dogs. Her shouts were punctuated with the dogs' yapping. A good five minutes passed before Zelda was back.

"What happened?" K.O. asked, genuinely concerned.

"Oh, nothing."

"As I started to say, I saw Dr. Jeffries."

"On television?" Zelda asked, only half-interested.

"No, in person."

"Where?" All at once she had Zelda's attention.

"On Blossom Street. You aren't going to believe this, but he actually lives in my building."

"Dr. Jeffries? Get out of here!"

Zelda was definitely interested now. "Wait—I heard he moved to Seattle just before his book was published." She took a deep breath. "Wow! You really *saw* him?"

"Uh-huh."

"Oh, my goodness, did you talk to him? Is he as handsome in person as he is in his photo?"

Feeling about him the way she did, K.O. had to consider the question for a moment. "He's fairly easy on the eyes." That was an understatement but looks weren't everything. To her mind, he seemed stiff and unapproachable. Distant, even.

"Did you tell him that Zach and I both read his book and what a difference it's made in our lives?"

"No, but..."

"K.O., could you... Would it be too much to get his autograph? Could you bring it on the fifteenth?"

K.O. had agreed to spend the night with the twins while Zelda and Zach attended his company's Christmas party. Her sister and brother-in-law had made arrangements to stay at a hotel downtown, just the two of them.

"All the mothers at the preschool would *die* to have Dr. Jeffries's autograph."

"I haven't met him," K.O. protested. It wasn't like she had any desire to form a fan club for him, either.

"But you just said he lives in your building."

"Yes."

"Are you sure it's him?"

"It looks like him. Anyway, LaVonne said it was."

Zelda gave a small shout of excitement. "If LaVonne says it's him, then it must be. How could you live in the same building as Dr. Jeffries and not know it?" her sister cried as though K.O. had somehow avoided this critical knowledge on purpose. "This is truly amazing. I've *got* to have his autograph."

"I'll...see what I can do," K.O. promised. This was not good. She'd hoped to find common ground with her sister, not become a...a go-between so Zelda could get her hero's autograph. Some hero! K.O.'s views on just about everything having to do with parenting were diametrically opposed to those purveyed by Dr. Wynn Jeffries. She'd feel like a fraud if she asked for his autograph.

"One more thing," Zelda said when her excitement had died down. "I know we don't agree on child-rearing techniques."

"That's true, but I understand these are your daughters." She took a deep breath. "How you raise them isn't really any of my business."

"Exactly," Zelda said emphatically. "Therefore, Zach and I want you to know we've decided to downplay Christmas this year."

"Downplay Christmas," K.O. repeated, not sure what that meant.

"We aren't putting up a tree."

"No Christmas tree!" K.O. sputtered, doing a poor job of hiding her disapproval. She couldn't imagine celebrating the holiday without decorating a tree. Her poor nieces would be deprived of a very important tradition.

"I might allow a small potted one for the kitchen table." Zelda seemed a bit doubtful herself. She *should* be doubtful, since a Christmas tree had always been part of their own family celebration. The fact that their parents had moved to Arizona was difficult enough. This year they'd decided to take a cruise in the South Pacific over Christmas and New Year's. While K.O. was happy to see her mother and father enjoying their retirement, she missed them enormously.

"Is this another of Dr. Jeffries's ideas?" K.O. had read enough of his book—and heard *more* than enough about his theories—to suspect it was. Still, she could hardly fathom that even Wynn Jeffries would go this far. Outlaw Christmas? The man was a menace!

"Dr. Jeffries believes that misleading children about Santa does them lasting psychological damage."

"The girls can't have Santa, either?" This was cruel and unusual punishment. "Next you'll be telling me that you're doing away with the tooth fairy, too."

"Why, yes, of course. It's the same principle."

K.O. knew better than to argue with her sister. "Getting back to Christmas…" she began.

"Yes, Christmas. Like I said, Zach and I are planning to make it a low-key affair this year. Anything that involves Santa is out of the question."

Thankfully her sister was unable to see K.O. roll her eyes.

"In fact, Dr. Jeffries has a chapter on the subject. It's called 'Bury Santa Under the Sleigh.' Chapter eight."

"He wants to bury Santa Claus?" K.O. had heard enough. She'd personally bury Dr. Jeffries under a pile of plowed snow before she'd let him take Christmas away from Zoe and Zara. As far as she was concerned, his entire philosophy was unacceptable, but this no-Santa nonsense was too much. Here was where she drew her line in the snow—a line Wynn Jeffries had overstepped.

"Haven't you been listening to *anything* I've said?" Zelda asked.

"Unfortunately, I have."

Her doorbell chimed. "I need to go," K.O. told her sister. She sighed. "I'll see what I can do about that autograph."

"Yes, please," Zelda said with unmistakable gratitude. "It would mean the world to me if you could get Dr. Jeffries's autograph."

Sighing again, K.O. replaced the receiver and opened the door to find her neighbor LaVonne standing there. Although *standing* wasn't exactly the right word. LaVonne was practically leaping up and down. "I'm sorry to bother you but I just couldn't wait."

"Come in," K.O. said.

"I can't stay but a minute," the retired CPA insisted as she stepped over the threshold, clutching Tom. "I did it!" she exclaimed. "I saw the future." She squealed with delight and did a small jig. "I saw the future of your love life, K.O. It happened when I went to change the kitty litter."

"The…kitty litter." That was fitting, since it was where her love life happened to be at the moment. In some kind of toilet, anyway.

"Tom had just finished his business," LaVonne continued, gazing lovingly at her cat, "and there it was, plain as day."

"His business?" K.O. asked.

"No, no, the future. You know how some people with the *gift* can read tea leaves? Well, it came to me in the kitty-litter box. I know it sounds crazy but it's true. It was right there in front of me," she said. "You're going to meet the man of your dreams."

"Really?" K.O. hated to sound so disappointed. "I don't suppose you happened to see anything in the kitty litter about me finding a job?"

LaVonne shook her head. "Sorry, no. Do you think I should go back and look again? It's all in the way it's arranged in the kitty litter," she confided. "Just like tea leaves."

"Probably not." K.O. didn't want to be responsible for her neighbor sifting through Tom's "business" any more than necessary.

"I'll concentrate on your job prospects next."

"Great." K.O. was far more interested in locating full-time employment than falling in love. At twenty-eight she wasn't in a rush, although it *was* admittedly time to start thinking about a serious relationship. Besides, working at home wasn't conducive to meeting men. Zelda seemed to think that as a medical transcriptionist K.O. would meet any number of eligible physicians. That, however, hadn't turned out to be the case. The only person in a white coat she'd encountered in the last six months had been her dentist, and he'd been more interested in looking at her X-rays than at her.

"Before I forget," LaVonne said, getting ready to leave. "I'd like you to come over tomorrow for cocktails and appetizers."

"Sure." It wasn't as if her social calendar was crowded. "Thanks."

"I'll see you at six." LaVonne let herself out.

"Concentrate on seeing a job for me," K.O. reminded her, sticking her head in the hallway. "The next time you empty the litter box, I mean."

LaVonne nodded. "I will," she said. As she left, she was mumbling to herself, something K.O. couldn't hear.

The following morning, K.O. set up her laptop on a window table in the French Café, determined to wait for Dr. Jeffries. Now she felt obliged to get his autograph, despite her disapproval of his methods. More importantly, she had to talk to him about Christmas. This clueless man was destroying Christmas for her nieces—and for hundreds of thousands of other kids.

She had no intention of knocking on his door. No, this had to seem unplanned. An accidental meeting. Her one hope was that Wynn Jeffries was hooked on his morning latte. Since this was Seattle, she felt fairly certain he was.

Nearly everyone in the entire state of Washington seemed to be a coffee addict.

In an effort to use her time productively, K.O. started work on the Mulcahy Christmas letter, all the while reminding herself that he was paying her double. She had two ideas about how to approach the situation. The first was comical, telling the truth in an outlandish manner and letting the reader assume it was some sort of macabre humor.

Merry Christmas from the Mulcahys, K.O. wrote. She bit her lip and pushed away a strand of long blond hair that had escaped from her ponytail. *Bill and I have had a challenging year. Mason sends greetings from the juvenile detention center where he's currently incarcerated. Julie is pregnant and we pray she doesn't marry the father. Bill, at least, is doing well, although he's worried about paying for the mental care facility where I'm receiving outpatient therapy.*

K.O. groaned. This *wasn't* humorous, macabre or otherwise. It was difficult to turn the Mulcahys' disastrous year into comedy, especially since the letter was purportedly coming from them.

She deleted the paragraph and tried her second approach.

Merry Christmas from the Mulcahys, and what an— interesting? unexpected? unusual?—*year it has been for our lovely family.* K.O. decided on eventful. *Bill and I are so proud of our children, especially now as they approach adulthood. Where have all the years gone?*

Mason had an opportunity he couldn't turn down and is currently away at school. Our son is maturing into a fine young man and is wisely accepting guidance from authority figures. Our sweet Julie is in her second year of college. She and her boyfriend have decided to deepen their rela-

*tionship. Who knows, there might be wedding bells—and
perhaps even a baby—in our daughter's future.*

So intent was she on putting a positive spin on the sad
details of Bill Mulcahy's year that she nearly missed Wynn
Jeffries. When she looked up, it was just in time to see Dr.
Jeffries walk to the counter. K.O. leaped to her feet and
nearly upset her peppermint mocha, an extravagance she
couldn't really afford. She remained standing until he'd collected his drink and then straightening, hurried toward him.

"Dr. Jeffries?" she asked, beaming a winsome smile.
She'd practiced this very smile in front of the mirror before job interviews. After her recent cleaning at the dentist's, K.O. hoped she didn't blind him with her flashing
white teeth.

"Yes?"

"You are Dr. Jeffries, Dr. Wynn Jeffries?"

"I am." He seemed incredibly tall as he stood in front of
her. She purposely blocked his way to the door.

K.O. thrust out her hand. "I'm Katherine O'Connor. We
live in the same building."

He smiled and shook her hand, then glanced around her.
He seemed eager to escape.

"I can't tell you what a surprise it was when LaVonne
pointed out that the author of *The Free Child* lived in our
building."

"You know LaVonne Young?"

"Well, yes, she's my neighbor. Yours, too," K.O. added.
"Would you care to join me?" She gestured toward her table
and the empty chairs. This time of day, it was rare to find
a free table. She didn't volunteer the fact that she'd set up
shop two hours earlier in the hope of bumping into him.

He checked his watch as if to say he really didn't have time to spare.

"I understand *The Free Child* has hit every bestseller list in the country." Flattery just might work.

Wynn hesitated. "Yes, I've been most fortunate."

True, but the parents and children of America had been most *un*fortunate in her view. She wasn't going to mention that, though. At least not yet. She pulled out her chair on the assumption that he wouldn't refuse her.

He joined her, with obvious reluctance. "I think I've seen you around," he said, and sipped his latte.

It astonished her that he knew who she was, while she'd been oblivious to his presence. "My sister is a very big fan of yours. She was thrilled when she heard I might be able to get your autograph."

"She's very kind."

"Her life has certainly changed since she read your book," K.O. commented, reaching for her mocha.

He shrugged with an air of modesty. "I've heard that quite a few times."

"Changed for the *worse,*" K.O. muttered.

He blinked. "I beg your pardon?"

She couldn't contain herself any longer. "You want to take Santa away from my nieces! *Santa Claus.* Where's your heart? Do you know there are children all over America being deprived of Christmas because of *you?*" Her voice grew loud with the strength of her convictions.

Wynn glanced nervously about the room.

K.O. hadn't realized how animated she'd become until she noticed that everyone in the entire café had stopped talking and was staring in their direction.

Wynn hurriedly stood and turned toward the door, probably attempting to flee before she could embarrass him further.

"You're no better than...than Jim Carrey," K.O. wailed. She meant to say the Grinch who stole Christmas but it was the actor's name that popped out. He'd played the character in a movie a few years ago.

"Jim Carrey?" He turned back to face her.

"Worse. You're a...a regular Charles Dickens." She meant Scrooge, darn it. But it didn't matter if, in the heat of her anger, she couldn't remember the names. She just wanted to embarrass him. "That man," she said, stabbing an accusatory finger at Wynn, "wants to bury Santa Claus under the sleigh."

Not bothering to look back, Wynn tore open the café door and rushed into the street. "Good riddance!" K.O. cried and sank down at the table, only to discover that everyone in the room was staring at her.

"He doesn't believe in Christmas," she explained and then calmly returned to the Mulcahys' letter.

Chapter Three

The confrontation with Wynn Jeffries didn't go well, K.O. admitted as she changed out of her jeans and sweater later that same afternoon. When LaVonne invited her over for appetizers and drinks, K.O. hadn't asked if this was a formal party or if it would be just the two of them. Unwilling to show up in casual attire if her neighbor intended a more formal event, K.O. chose tailored black slacks, a white silk blouse and a red velvet blazer with a Christmas tree pin she'd inherited from her grandmother. The blouse was her very best. Generally she wore her hair tied back, but this evening she kept it down, loosely sweeping up one side and securing it with a rhinestone barrette. A little lip gloss and mascara, and she was ready to go.

A few minutes after six, she crossed the hall and rang LaVonne's doorbell. As if she'd been standing there waiting, LaVonne opened her door instantly.

K.O. was relieved she'd taken the time to change. Her neighbor looked lovely in a long skirt and black jacket with any number of gold chains dangling around her neck and at least a dozen gold bangles on her wrists.

"Katherine!" she cried, sounding as though it'd been weeks since they'd last spoken. "Do come in and meet Dr. Wynn Jeffries." She stepped back and held open the door and, with a flourish, gestured her inside.

Wynn Jeffries stood in the center of the room. He held a cracker raised halfway to his mouth, his eyes darting to and fro. He seemed to be gauging how fast he could make his exit.

Oh, dear. K.O. felt guilty about the scene she'd caused that morning.

"I believe we've met," Wynn said stiffly. He set the cracker down on his napkin and eyed the door.

Darn the man. He looked positively gorgeous, just the way he did on the book's dust jacket. This was exceedingly unfair. She didn't *want* to like him and she certainly didn't want to be attracted to him, which, unfortunately she was. Not that it mattered. She wasn't interested and after their confrontation that morning, he wouldn't be, either.

"Dr. Jeffries," K.O. murmured uneasily as she walked into the room, hands clasped together.

He nodded in her direction, then slowly inched closer to the door.

Apparently oblivious to the tension between them, La-Vonne glided to the sideboard, where she had wine and liquor bottles set on a silver platter. Sparkling wineglasses and crystal goblets awaited their decision. "What can I pour for you?" she asked.

"I wouldn't mind a glass of merlot, if you have it," K.O. said, all the while wondering how best to handle this awkward situation.

"I do." LaVonne turned to Wynn. "And you, Dr. Jeffries?"

He looked away from K.O. and moved to stand behind the sofa. "Whiskey on the rocks."

"Coming right up."

"Can I help?" K.O. asked, welcoming any distraction.

"No, no, you two are my guests." And then as if to clear up any misconception, she added, "My *only* guests."

"Oh," K.O. whispered. A sick feeling attacked the pit of her stomach. She didn't glance at Wynn but suspected he was no more pleased at the prospect than she was.

A moment later, LaVonne brought their drinks and indicated that they should both sit down.

K.O. accepted the wine and Wynn took his drink.

With her own goblet in hand, LaVonne claimed the overstuffed chair, which left the sofa vacant. Evidently Dr. Jeffries was not eager to sit; neither was K.O. Finally she chose one end of the davenport and Wynn sat as far from her as humanly possible. Each faced away from the other.

"Wynn, I see you tried the crab dip," LaVonne commented, referring to the appetizers on the coffee table in front of them.

"It's the best I've ever tasted," he said, reaching for another cracker.

"I'm glad you enjoyed it. The recipe came from Katherine."

He set the cracker down and brushed the crumbs from his fingers, apparently afraid he was about to be poisoned.

K.O. sipped her wine in an effort to relax. She had a feeling that even if she downed the entire bottle, it wasn't going to help.

"I imagine you're wondering why I invited you here this evening," LaVonne said. Phillip, her white Persian, strolled regally into the room, his tail raised, and with one powerful thrust of his hind legs, leaped into her lap. La-

Vonne ran her hand down the length of his body, stroking his long, white fur. "It happened again," she announced, slowly enunciating the words.

"What happened?" Wynn asked, then gulped his drink.

Dramatically, LaVonne closed her eyes. "The sight."

Obviously not understanding, Wynn glanced at K.O., his forehead wrinkled.

"LaVonne took a class this week on unleashing your psychic abilities," K.O. explained under her breath.

Wynn thanked her for the explanation with a weak smile.

LaVonne's shoulders rose. "I have been gifted with the sight," she said in hushed tones.

"Congratulations," Wynn offered tentatively.

"She can read cat litter," K.O. told him.

"That's not all," LaVonne said, raising one hand. "As I said, it happened again. This morning."

"Not with the litter box?" K.O. asked.

"No." A distant look came over LaVonne as she fixed her gaze on some point across the room.

Peering over her shoulder, K.O. tried to figure out what her neighbor was staring at. She couldn't tell—unless it was the small decorated Christmas tree.

"I was eating my Raisin Bran and then, all of a sudden, I knew." She turned slightly to meet K.O.'s eyes. "The bran flakes separated, and that was when two raisins bobbed to the surface."

"You saw...the future?" K.O. asked.

"What she saw," Wynn muttered, "was two raisins in the milk."

LaVonne raised her hand once more, silencing them. "I saw the *future*. It was written in the Raisin Bran even more clearly than it'd been in the cat litter." She pointed a finger at K.O. "Katherine, it involved *you*."

"Me." She swallowed, not sure whether to laugh or simply shake her head.

"And you." LaVonne's finger swerved toward Wynn. Her voice was low and intent.

"Did it tell you Katherine would do her utmost to make a fool of me at the French Café?" Wynn asked. He scooped up a handful of mixed nuts.

As far as K.O. was concerned, *nuts* was an appropriate response to her neighbor's fortune-telling.

LaVonne dropped her hand. "No." She turned to K.O. with a reproachful frown. "Katherine, what did you do?"

"I…" Flustered, she looked away. "Did…did you know Dr. Jeffries doesn't believe in Santa Claus?" There, it was in the open now.

"My dear girl," LaVonne said with a light laugh. "I hate to be the one to disillusion you, but there actually *isn't* a Santa."

"There is if you're five years old," she countered, glaring at the man on the other end of the sofa. "Dr. Jeffries is ruining Christmas for children everywhere." The man deserved to be publicly ridiculed. Reconsidering, she revised the thought. "He should be censured by his peers for even *suggesting* that Santa be buried under the sleigh."

"It appears you two have a minor difference of opinion," LaVonne said, understating the obvious.

"I sincerely doubt Katherine has read my entire book."

"I don't need to," she said. "My sister quotes you chapter and verse in nearly every conversation we have."

"This is the sister who asked for my autograph?"

"Yes," K.O. admitted. Like most men, she concluded, Dr. Jeffries wasn't immune to flattery.

"She's the one with the children?"

K.O. nodded.

"Do you have children?"

LaVonne answered for her. "Katherine is single, the same as you, Wynn."

"Why doesn't that surprise me?" he returned.

K.O. thought she might have detected a smirk in his reply. "It doesn't surprise me that you're single, either," she said, elevating her chin. "No woman in her right mind—"

"My dears," LaVonne murmured. "You're being silly."

K.O. didn't respond, and neither did Wynn. "Don't you want to hear what I saw in my cereal?"

Phillip purred contentedly as LaVonne continued to stroke his fluffy white fur.

"The future came to me and I saw—" she paused for effect "—I saw the two of you. Together."

"Arguing?" Wynn asked.

"No, no, you were in love. Deeply, deeply in love."

K.O. placed her hand over her heart and gasped, and then almost immediately that remark struck her as the most comical thing she'd ever heard. The fact that LaVonne was reading her future, first in cat litter and now Raisin Bran, was ridiculous enough, but to match K.O. up with Wynn— It was too much. She broke into peals of laughter. Pressing her hand over her mouth, she made an effort to restrain her giggles.

Wynn looked at her curiously.

LaVonne frowned. "I'm serious, Katherine."

"I'm sorry. I don't mean to be rude. LaVonne, you're my friend and my neighbor, but I'm sorry, it'll never happen. Never in a million years."

Wynn straightened. "While Katherine and I clearly don't see eye to eye on any number of issues, I tend to agree with her on this."

LaVonne sighed expressively. "Our instructor, Madam

Ozma, warned us this would happen," she said with an air of sadness. "Unbelievers."

"It isn't that I don't believe you," K.O. rushed to add. She didn't want to offend LaVonne, whose friendship she treasured, but at the same time she found it difficult to play along with this latest idea of hers. Still, the possibility of a romance with just about anyone else would have suited her nicely.

"Wynn?" LaVonne said. "May I ask how you feel about Katherine?"

"Well, I didn't officially meet her until this morning."

"I might've given him the wrong impression," K.O. began. "But—"

"No," he said swiftly. "I think I got the right impression. You don't agree with me and I had the feeling that for some reason you don't like me."

"True…well, not exactly. I don't know you well enough to like *or* dislike you."

LaVonne clapped her hands. "Perfect! This is just perfect."

Both K.O. and Wynn turned to her. "You don't really know each other, isn't that correct?" she asked.

"Correct," Wynn replied. "I've seen Katherine around the building and on Blossom Street occasionally, but we've never spoken—until the unfortunate incident this morning."

K.O. felt a little flustered. "We didn't start off on the right foot." Then she said in a conciliatory voice, "I'm generally not as confrontational as I was earlier today. I might've gotten a bit…carried away. I apologize." She did feel guilty for having embarrassed him and, in the process, herself.

Wynn's dark eyebrows arched, as if to say he was pleasantly surprised by her admission of fault.

"We all, at one time or another, say things we later regret," LaVonne said, smiling down on Phillip. She raised her eyes to K.O. "Isn't that right, Katherine?"

"Yes, I suppose so."

"And some of us," she went on, looking at Wynn, "make hasty judgments."

He hesitated. "Yes. However in this case—"

"That's why," LaVonne said, interrupting him, "I took the liberty of making a dinner reservation for the two of you. Tonight—at seven-thirty. An hour from now."

"A dinner reservation," K.O. repeated. Much as she liked and respected her neighbor, there was a limit to what she was willing to do.

"It's out of the question," Wynn insisted.

"I appreciate what you're doing, but…" K.O. turned to Wynn for assistance.

"I do, as well," he chimed in. "It's a lovely gesture on your part. Unfortunately, I have other plans for this evening."

"So do I." All right, K.O.'s plans included eating in front of the television and watching *Jeopardy,* and while those activities might not be anything out of the ordinary, they did happen to be her plans.

"Oh, dear." LaVonne exhaled loudly. "Chef Jerome Ray will be so disappointed not to meet my friends."

If Wynn didn't recognize the name, K.O. certainly did. "You know Chef Jerome Ray?"

"Of Chez Jerome?" Wynn inserted.

"Oh, yes. I did his taxes for years and years. What most people don't realize is that Jerome is no flash in the pan, if you'll excuse the pun. In fact, it took him twenty years to become an overnight success."

The Seattle chef had his own cooking show on the Food

Network, which had become an immediate hit. His techniques with fresh seafood had taken the country by storm. The last K.O. had heard, it took months to get a reservation at Chez Jerome.

"I talked to Jerome this afternoon and he said that as a personal favor to me, he would personally see to your dinner."

"Ah…" K.O. looked at Wynn and weighed her options.

"Dinner's already paid for," LaVonne said in an encouraging voice, "and it would be a shame to let it go to waste."

A nuked frozen entrée and *Jeopardy,* versus one dinner with a slightly contentious man in a restaurant that would make her the envy of her friends. "I might be able to rearrange my plans," K.O. said after clearing her throat. Normally she was a woman of conviction. But in these circumstances, for a fabulous free dinner, she was willing to compromise.

"I think I can do the same," Wynn muttered.

LaVonne smiled brightly and clapped her hands. "Excellent. I was hoping you'd say that."

"With certain stipulations," Wynn added.

"Yes," K.O. said. "There would need to be stipulations."

Wynn scowled at her. "We will *not* discuss my book or my child-rearing philosophies."

"All right," she agreed. That sounded fair. "And we'll… we'll—" She couldn't think of any restriction of her own, so she said, "We refuse to overeat." At Wynn's frown, she explained, "I'm sort of watching my weight."

He nodded as though he understood, which she was sure he didn't. What man really did?

"All I care about is that the two of you have a marvelous dinner, but I know you will." LaVonne smiled at them both. "The raisins have already assured me of that." She studied her watch, gently dislodged Phillip and stood. "You'll need to leave right away. The reservation's under my name," she said and ushered them out the door.

Before she could protest or comment, K.O. found herself standing in the hallway with Wynn Jeffries, her dinner date.

Chapter Four

If nothing else, K.O. felt this dinner would afford her the opportunity to learn about Wynn. Well, that and an exceptional dining experience, of course. Something in his background must have prompted a child-rearing ideology that in her opinion was completely impractical and threatened to create a generation of spoiled, self-involved brats. Although she didn't have children of her own, K.O. had seen the effect on her nieces ever since Zelda had read that darn book. She was astonished by how far her sister had been willing to go in following the book's precepts, and wondered if Zach understood the full extent of Zelda's devotion to *The Free Child*. Her brother-in-law was quite the workaholic. He was absorbed in his job and often stayed late into the evenings and worked weekends.

Chez Jerome was only a few blocks from Blossom Street, so K.O. and Wynn decided to walk. She retrieved a full-length red wool coat from her condo while Wynn waited outside the building. The moment she joined him, she was hit by a blast of cold air. A shiver went through her, and she hunched her shoulders against the wind. To her surprise, Wynn changed places with her, walking by the curb, outside the shelter of the buildings, taking the brunt of the wind. It was an old-fashioned gentlemanly action and one she hadn't expected. To be fair, she didn't know *what* to expect from him. With that realization came another. He didn't know her, either.

They didn't utter a single word for the first block.

"Perhaps we should start over," she suggested.

Wynn stopped walking and regarded her suspiciously. "You want to go back? Did you forget something?"

"No, I meant you and me."

"How so?" He kept his hands buried in the pockets of his long overcoat.

"Hello," she began. "My name is Katherine O'Connor, but most people call me K.O. I don't believe we've met."

He frowned. "We did earlier," he said.

"This is pretend." Did the man have to be so literal? "I want you to erase this morning from your memory and pretend we're meeting for the first time."

"What about drinks at LaVonne's? Should I forget that, too?"

"Well." She needed to think this over. That hadn't been such a positive experience, either. "Perhaps it would be best," she told him.

"So you want me to act as if this is a blind date?" he asked.

"A blind date," she repeated and immediately shook her head. "I've had so many of those, I need a Seeing Eye dog."

He laughed, and the sound of it was rich and melodious. "Me, too."

"You?" A man this attractive and successful required assistance meeting women?

"You wouldn't believe how many friends have a compulsion to introduce me to *the woman of my dreams*."

"My friends say the same thing. *This* is the man you've been waiting to meet your entire life. Ninety-nine percent of the time, it's a disaster."

"Really? Even you?" He seemed a little shocked that she'd had help from her matchmaking friends.

"What do you mean *even you?*"

"You're blond and beautiful—I thought you were joking about those blind dates."

She swallowed a gasp of surprise. However, if that was the way he saw her, she wasn't going to argue.

He thrust out his hand. "Hello, Katherine, my name is Jim Carrey."

She laughed and they shook hands. They continued walking at a leisurely pace, and soon they were having a lively conversation, exchanging dating horror stories. She laughed quite a few times, which was something she'd never dreamed she'd do with Wynn Jeffries.

"Would you mind if I called you Katherine?" he asked.

"Not at all. Do you prefer Wynn or Dr. Jeffries?"

"Wynn."

"I've heard absolutely marvelous things about Chez Jerome," she said. Not only that, some friends of K.O.'s had recently phoned to make dinner reservations and were told the first available opening was in May.

"LaVonne is certainly full of surprises," Wynn remarked. "Who would've guessed she had a connection with one of the most popular chefs in the country?"

They arrived at the restaurant, and Wynn held the door for her, another gentlemanly courtesy that made her smile. This psychologist wasn't what she'd expected at all. After hearing his theories about Christmas, she'd been sure he must be a real curmudgeon. But in the short walk from Blossom Street to the restaurant, he'd disproved almost every notion she'd had about him. Or at least about his personality. His beliefs were still a point of contention.

When Wynn mentioned LaVonne's name to the maître d', they were ushered to a secluded booth. "Welcome to Chez Jerome," the man said with a dignified bow.

K.O. opened her menu and had just started to read it when Jerome himself appeared at their table. "Ah, so you are LaVonne's friends."

K.O. didn't mean to gush, but this was a real honor. "I am so excited to meet you," she said. She could hardly wait to tell Zelda about this—even though her sister would be far more impressed by her meeting Wynn Jeffries than Jerome.

The chef, in his white hat and apron, kissed her hand. The entire restaurant seemed to be staring at them and whispering, wondering who they were to warrant a visit from the renowned chef.

"You won't need those," Jerome said and ostentatiously removed the tasseled menus from their hands. "I am preparing a meal for you personally. If you do not fall in love after what I have cooked, then there is no hope for either of you."

Wynn caught her eye and smiled. Despite herself, K.O. smiled back. After a bit of small talk, Jerome returned to the kitchen.

Once the chef had gone, Wynn leaned toward her and teased, "He makes it sound as if dinner is marinated in Love Potion Number Nine." To emphasize the point, he sang a few lines from the old song.

K.O. smothered a giggle. She hated to admit it, but rarely had she been in a more romantic setting, with the elegant linens, flattering candlelight and soft classical music. The mood was flawless; so was their dinner, all four courses, even though she couldn't identify the exact nature of everything they ate. The appetizer was some kind of soup,

served in a martini glass, and it tasted a bit like melted
sherbet. Later, when their waiter told them the soup featured sea urchin, K.O. considered herself fortunate not to
have known. If she had, she might not have tasted it. But,
in fact, it was delicious.

"Tell me about yourself," she said to Wynn when the
soup dishes were taken away and the salads, which featured frilly greens and very tart berries, were delivered.

He shrugged, as though he didn't really have anything
of interest to share. "What would you like to know?"

"How about your family?"

"All right." He leaned back against the luxurious velvet
cushion. "I'm an only child. My mother died three years
ago. My father is Max Jeffries." He paused, obviously waiting to see if she recognized the name and when she didn't,
he continued. "He was a surfer who made a name for himself back in the late sixties and early seventies."

She shook her head. Surfing wasn't an activity she knew
much about, but then she really wasn't into sports. Or exercise, either. "My dad's the captain of his bowling team,"
she told him.

He nodded. "My parents were hippies." He grinned.
"True, bona fide, unreconstructed hippies."

"As in the Age of Aquarius, free love and that sort of
thing?" This explained quite a bit, now that she thought
about it. Wynn had apparently been raised without boundaries himself and had turned out to be a successful and even
responsible adult. Maybe he figured that would be true of
any child raised according to his methods.

Wynn nodded again. "Dad made it rich when he was
awarded a patent for his surfboard wax. Ever heard of
Max's Waxes?" He sipped his wine, a lovely mellow pinot
gris. K.O. did, too, savoring every swallow.

"I chose my own name when I was ten," he murmured.

It was hardly necessary to say he'd lived an unconventional life. "Why did you decide on Wynn?" she asked, since it seemed an unusual first name.

"It was my mother's maiden name."

"I like it."

"Katherine is a beautiful name," he commented. "A beautiful name for a beautiful woman."

If he didn't stop looking at her like that, K.O. was convinced she'd melt. This romantic rush was more intense than anything she'd ever experienced. She wasn't even prepared to *like* Wynn, and already she could feel herself falling for this son of a hippie. In an effort to break his spell, she forced herself to look away.

"Where did you grow up?" she asked as their entrées were ceremoniously presented. Grilled scallops with wild rice and tiny Brussels sprouts with even tinier onions.

"California," he replied. "I attended Berkeley."

"I lived a rather conventional life," she said after swooning over her first bite. "Regular family, one sister, two parents. I studied to become a medical transcriptionist, worked for a while and returned to college. I have a degree in public relations, but I'm currently working from home as a transcriptionist while looking for full-time employment. I'd really like to work as a publicist, but those jobs are rare and the pay isn't all that great." She closed her eyes. "Mmm. I think this is the best meal I've ever had." And she wasn't referring *just* to the food.

He smiled. "Me, too."

A few minutes later, he asked, "Your sister is married with children?"

"Identical twin girls. Zoe and Zara. I'm their godmother." When she discussed the twins, she became animated, telling him story after story. "They're delightful," she finally said. Dessert and coffee arrived then. An unusual cranberry crème brûlée, in honor of the season, and cups of exquisite coffee.

"So you like children?" Wynn asked when they'd made serious progress with their desserts.

"Oh, yes," she said, then added a qualifier, "especially well-behaved children."

His eyebrows arched.

Seeing how easy it was to get sidetracked, she said, "I think children are a subject we should avoid."

"I agree." But Wynn's expression was good-natured, and she could tell he hadn't taken offense.

Even after a two-and-a-half-hour dinner, K.O. was reluctant to leave. She found Wynn truly fascinating. His stories about living in a commune, his surfing adventures—including an encounter with a shark off the coast of Australia—and his travels kept her enthralled. "This has been the most wonderful evening," she told him. Beneath the polished exterior was a remarkable human being. She found him engaging and unassuming and, shock of shocks, *likeable*.

After being assured by Jerome that their meal had already been taken care of, Wynn left a generous tip. After fervent thanks and a protracted farewell, they collected their coats. Wynn helped K.O. on with hers, then she wrapped her scarf around her neck.

When they ventured into the night, they saw that snow had begun to fall. The Seattle streets were decorated for the season with sparkling white lights on the bare trees. The scene was as festive as one could imagine. A horse-drawn carriage passed them, the horse's hooves clopping on the pavement, its harness jingling.

"Shall we?" Wynn asked.

K.O. noticed that the carriage was traveling in the opposite direction from theirs, but she couldn't have cared less. For as long as she could remember, she'd wanted a carriage ride. "That would be lovely." Not only was Wynn a gentleman, but a romantic, as well, which seemed quite incongruous with his free-and-easy upbringing.

Wynn hailed the driver. Then he handed K.O. into the carriage before joining her. He took the lap robe, spread it across her legs, and slipped his arm around her shoulders. It felt like the most natural thing in the world to be in his embrace.

"I love Christmas," K.O. confessed.

Wynn didn't respond, which was probably for the best, since he'd actually put in writing that he wanted to bury Santa Claus.

The driver flicked the reins and the carriage moved forward.

"It might surprise you to know that I happen to feel the same way you do about the holidays."

"But you said—"

He brought a finger to her lips. "We agreed not to discuss my book."

"Yes, but I *have* to know...."

"Then I suggest you read *The Free Child.* You'll understand my philosophies better once you do. Simply put, I feel it's wrong to mislead children. That's all I really said. Can you honestly object to that?"

"If it involves Santa, I can."

"Then we'll have to agree to disagree."

She was happy to leave that subject behind. The evening was perfect, absolutely perfect, and she didn't want anything to ruin it. With large flakes of snow drifting down

and the horse clopping steadily along, the carriage swaying, it couldn't have been more romantic.

Wynn tightened his arm around her and K.O. pressed
her head against his shoulder.

"I'm beginning to think LaVonne knows her Raisin
Bran," Wynn whispered.

She heard the smile in his voice. "And her cat litter,"
she whispered back.

"I like her cats," he said. "Tom, Phillip and…"

"Martin," she supplied. The men in her neighbor's life
all happened to be badly spoiled and much-loved cats.

The carriage dropped them off near West Lake Center. Wynn got down first and then helped K.O. "Are you
cold?" he asked. "I can try to find a cab if you'd prefer not
to walk."

"Stop," she said suddenly. All this perfection was con-
fusing, too shocking a contrast with her previous impres-
sions of Dr. Wynn Jeffries.

He frowned.

"I don't know if I can deal with this." She started walking at a fast pace, her mind spinning. It was difficult to
reconcile this thoughtful, interesting man with the hard-
hearted destroyer of Christmas Zelda had told her about.

"Deal with *what?*" he asked, catching up with her.

"You—you're wonderful."

He laughed. "That's bad?"

"It's not what I expected from you."

His steps matched hers. "After this morning, I wasn't
sure what to expect from you, either. There's a big difference between the way you acted then and how you've been
this evening. *I* didn't change. You did."

"I know." She looked up at him, wishing she understood

what was happening. She recognized attraction when she felt it, but could this be real?

He reached for her hand and tucked it in the crook of his arm. "Does it matter?" he asked.

"Not for tonight," she said with a sigh.

"Good." They resumed walking, more slowly this time. She stuck out her tongue to catch the falling snow, the way she had as a child. Wynn did, too, and they both smiled, delighted with themselves and each other.

When they approached their building on Blossom Street, K.O. was almost sad. She didn't want the evening to end for fear she'd wake in the morning and discover it had all been a dream. Worse, she was afraid she'd find out it was just an illusion created by candlelight and gorgeous food and an enchanting carriage ride.

She felt Wynn's reluctance as he keyed in the door code. The warmth that greeted them inside the small lobby was a welcome respite from the cold and the wind. The Christmas lights in the lobby twinkled merrily as he escorted her to her door.

"Thank you for one of the most romantic evenings of my life," she told him sincerely.

"I should be the one thanking you," he whispered. He held her gaze for a long moment. "May I see you again?"

She nodded. But she wasn't sure that was wise.

"When?"

K.O. leaned against her door and held her hand to her forehead. The spell was wearing off. *"I don't think this is a good idea."* That was what she'd *intended* to say. Instead, when she opened her mouth, the words that popped out were, "I'm pretty much free all week."

He reached inside his overcoat for a PDA. "Tomorrow?"

"Okay." How could she agree so quickly, so impulsively? Every rational thought told her this relationship wasn't going to work. At some point—probably sooner rather than later—she'd have to acknowledge that they had practically nothing in common.

"Six?" he suggested.

With her mind screaming at her to put an end to this *now,* K.O. pulled out her Day-Timer and checked her schedule. Ah, the perfect excuse. She already had a commitment. "Sorry, it looks like I'm booked. I have a friend who's part of the Figgy Pudding contest."

"I beg your pardon?"

"Figgy Pudding is a competition for singing groups. It's a fund-raising event," she explained, remembering that he was relatively new to the area. "I told Vickie I'd come and cheer her on." Then, before she could stop herself, she added, "Want to join me?"

Wynn nodded. "Sure. Why not."

"Great." But it wasn't great. During her most recent visit with Vickie, K.O. had ranted about Dr. Jeffries for at least ten minutes. And now she was going to be introducing her friend to the man she'd claimed was ruining America. Introducing him as her...*date?*

She had to get out of this.

Then Wynn leaned forward and pressed his mouth to hers. It was such a nice kiss, undemanding and sweet. Romantic, too, just as the entire evening had been. In that moment, she knew exactly what was happening and why, and it terrified her. She liked Wynn. Okay, *really* liked him. Despite his crackpot theories and their total lack of compatibility. And it wasn't simply that they'd spent a delightful evening together. A charmed evening. No, this had all the hallmarks of a dangerous infatuation. Or worse.

Wynn Jeffries! Who would've thought it?

Chapter Five

The phone woke K.O. out of a dead sleep. She rolled over, glanced at the clock on her nightstand and groaned. It was already past eight. Lying on her stomach, she reached for the phone and hoped it wasn't a potential employer, asking her to come in for an interview that morning. Actually, she prayed it *was* a job interview but one with more notice.

"Good morning," she said in her best businesslike voice.

"Katherine, it's LaVonne. I didn't phone too early, did I?"

In one easy motion, K.O. drew herself into a sitting position, swinging her legs off the bed. "Not at all." She rubbed her face with one hand and stifled a yawn.

"So," her neighbor breathed excitedly. "How'd it go?"

K.O. needed a moment to consider her response. La-Vonne was obviously asking about her evening with Wynn; however, she hadn't had time to analyze it yet. "Dinner was incredible," she offered and hoped that would satisfy her friend's curiosity.

"Of course dinner was incredible. Jerome promised me it would be. I'm talking about you and Wynn. He's very nice, don't you think? Did you notice the way he couldn't take his eyes off you? Didn't I tell you? It's just as I saw in the kitty litter and the Raisin Bran. You two are *meant* for each other."

"Well," K.O. mumbled, not knowing which question to answer first. She'd prefer to avoid them all. She quickly reviewed the events of the evening and was forced to admit one thing. "Wynn wasn't anything like I expected."

"He said the same about you."

"You've talked to him?" If K.O. wasn't awake before, she certainly was now. "What did he say?" she asked in a rush, not caring that LaVonne would realize how interested she was.

"Exactly that," LaVonne said. "Wynn told me you were nothing like he expected. He didn't know what to think when you walked into my condo. He was afraid the evening would end with someone calling the police—and then he had a stupendous night. That was the word he used— *stupendous.*"

"Really." K.O. positively glowed with pleasure.

"He had the look when he said it, too."

"What look?"

"The *look,*" LaVonne repeated, emphasizing the word, "of a man who's falling in love. You had a good time, didn't you?"

"I did." K.O. doubted she could have lied. She *did* have a wonderful evening. Shockingly wonderful, in fact, and that made everything ten times worse. She wanted to view Wynn as a lunatic confounding young parents, a grinch out to steal Christmas from youngsters all across America. How could she berate him and detest him if she was in danger of falling in love with him? This was getting worse and worse.

"I knew it!" LaVonne sounded downright gleeful. "From

the moment I saw those raisins floating in the milk, I knew. The vision told me everything."

"Everything?"

"Everything," LaVonne echoed. "It came to me, as profound as anything I've seen with my psychic gift. You and Dr. Jeffries are perfect together."

K.O. buried her face in her hand. She'd fallen asleep in a haze of wonder and awakened to the shrill ring of her phone. She couldn't explain last night's feelings in any rational way.

She wasn't attracted to Wynn, she told herself. How could she be? The man who believed children should set their own rules? The man who wanted to eliminate Santa Claus? But she was beginning to understand what was going on here. For weeks she'd been stuck inside her condo, venturing outside only to meet Christmas-letter clients. If she wasn't transcribing medical records, she was filling out job applications. With such a lack of human contact, it was only natural that she'd be swept along on the tide of romance LaVonne had so expertly arranged for her.

"Wynn told me you were seeing him again this evening," LaVonne said eagerly.

"I am?" K.O. vaguely remembered that. "Oh, right, I am." Her mind cleared and her memory fell into place like an elevator suddenly dropping thirteen floors. "Yes, as it happens," she said, trying to think of a way out of this. "I invited Wynn to accompany me to the Figgy Pudding event at West Lake Plaza." She'd *invited* him. What was she thinking? *What was she thinking?* Mentally she slapped her hand against her forehead. Before this afternoon, she had to find an excuse to cancel.

"He's very sweet, isn't he?" LaVonne said.

"He is." K.O. didn't want to acknowledge it but he was.

He'd done it on purpose; she just didn't know *why*. What was his purpose in breaking down her defenses?

She needed to think. She pulled her feet up onto the bed and wrapped one arm around her knees. He *had* been sweet and alarmingly wonderful. Oh, he was clever. But what was behind all that charm? Nothing good, she'd bet.

"I have more to tell you," LaVonne said, lowering her voice to a mere whisper. "It happened again this morning." She paused. "I was feeding the boys."

K.O. had half a mind to stop her friend, but for some perverse reason she didn't.

"And then," LaVonne added, her voice gaining volume, "when I poured the dry cat food into their bowls, some of it spilled on the floor."

"You got a reading from the cat food?" K.O. supposed this shouldn't surprise her. Since LaVonne had taken that class, everything imaginable provided her with insight— mostly, it seemed, into K.O.'s life. Her love life, which to this point had been a blank slate.

"Would you like to know how many children you and Wynn are going to have?" LaVonne asked triumphantly.

"Any twins?" K.O. asked, playing along. She might as well. LaVonne was determined to tell her, whether she wanted to hear or not.

"Twins," LaVonne repeated in dismay. "Oh, my goodness, I didn't look that closely."

"That's fine."

LaVonne took her seriously. "Still, twins are definitely a possibility. Sure as anything, I saw three children. Multiple births run in your family, don't they? Because it might've been triplets."

"Triplets?" It was too hard to think about this without her

morning cup of coffee. "Listen, I need to get off the phone. I'll check in with you later," K.O. promised.

"Good. You'll give me regular updates, won't you?"

"On the triplets?"

"No," LaVonne returned, laughing. "On you and Wynn. The babies come later."

"Okay," she said, resigned to continuing the charade. Everything might've been delightful and romantic the night before, but this was a whole new day. She was beginning to figure out his agenda. She'd criticized his beliefs, especially about Christmas, and now he was determined to change hers. It was all a matter of pride. *Male* pride.

She'd been vulnerable, she realized. The dinner, the wine, Chef Jerome, a carriage ride, walking in the snow. *Christmas*. He'd actually used Christmas to weaken her resolve. The very man who was threatening to destroy the holiday for children had practically seduced her in Seattle's winter wonderland. What she recognized now was that in those circumstances, she would've experienced the same emotions with just about any man.

As was her habit, K.O. weighed herself first thing and gasped when she saw she was up two pounds. That fabulous dinner had come at a price. Two pounds. K.O. had to keep a constant eye on her weight, unlike her sister. Zelda was naturally thin whereas K.O. wasn't. Her only successful strategy for maintaining her weight was to weigh herself daily and then make adjustments in her diet.

Even before she'd finished putting on her workout gear, the phone rang again. K.O. could always hope that it was a potential employer, but caller ID informed her it was her sister.

"Merry Christmas, Zelda," K.O. said. This was one

small way to remind her that keeping Santa away from Zoe and Zara was fundamentally wrong.

"Did you get it?" Zelda asked excitedly. "Did you get Dr. Jeffries's autograph for me?"

"Ah…"

"You didn't, did you?" Zelda's disappointment was obvious.

"Not exactly."

"Did you even *talk* to him?" her sister pressed.

"Oh, yes, we did plenty of that." She recalled their conversation, thinking he might have manipulated that, too, in order to win her over to his side. The dark side, she thought grimly. Like Narnia without Aslan, and no Christmas.

A stunned silence followed. "Together. You and Dr. Jeffries were together?"

"We went to dinner…."

"You went to dinner with Dr. Wynn Jeffries?" Awe became complete disbelief.

"Yes, at Chez Jerome." K.O. felt like a name-dropper but she couldn't help it. No one ate at Chez Jerome and remained silent.

Zelda gasped. "You're making this up and I don't find it amusing."

"I'm not," K.O. insisted. "LaVonne arranged it. Dinner was incredible. In fact, I gained two pounds."

A short silence ensued. "Okay, I'm sitting down and I'm listening really hard. You'd better start at the beginning."

"Okay," she said. "I saw Wynn, Dr. Jeffries, in the French Café."

"I already know that part."

"I saw him again." K.O. stopped abruptly, thinking better of telling her sister about the confrontation and calling him names. Not that referring to him as Jim Carrey and

Charles Dickens was especially insulting, but still… "Anyway, it's not important now."

"Why isn't it?"

"Well, Wynn and I agreed to put that unfortunate incident behind us and start over."

"Oh, my goodness, what did you do?" Zelda demanded. "What did you say to him? You didn't embarrass him, did you?"

K.O. bit her lip. "Do you want to hear about the dinner or not?"

"Yes! I want to hear *everything*."

K.O. then told her about cocktails at LaVonne's and her neighbor's connection with the famous chef. She described their dinner in lavish detail and mentioned the carriage ride. The one thing she didn't divulge was the kiss, which shot into her memory like a flaming dart, reminding her how weak she really was.

As if reading her mind, Zelda asked, "Did he kiss you?"

"Zelda! That's private."

"He did," her sister said with unshakable certainty. "I can't believe it. Dr. Wynn Jeffries kissed my sister! You don't even like him."

"According to LaVonne I will soon bear his children."

"What!"

"Sorry," K.O. said dismissively. "I'm getting ahead of myself."

"Okay, okay, I can see this is all a big joke to you."

"Not really."

"I don't even know if I should believe you."

"Zelda, I'm your sister. Would I lie to you?"

"Yes!"

Unfortunately Zelda was right. "I'm not this time, I swear it."

Zelda hesitated. "Did you or did you not get his auto-graph?"

Reluctant though she was to admit it, K.O. didn't have any choice. "Not."

"That's what I thought." Zelda bade her a hasty farewell and disconnected the call.

Much as she hated the prospect, K.O. put on her sweats and headed for the treadmill, which she kept stored under her bed for emergencies such as this. If she didn't do some-thing fast to get rid of those two pounds, they'd stick to her hips like putty and harden. Then losing them would be like chiseling them off with a hammer. This, at least, was her theory of weight gain and loss. Immediate action was re-quired. With headphones blocking outside distractions, she dutifully walked four miles and quit only when she was confident she'd sweated off what she'd gained. Still, a day of reduced caloric intake would be necessary.

She showered, changed her clothes and had a cup of cof-fee with skim milk. She worked on the Mulcahys' Christ-mas letter, munching a piece of dry toast as she did. After that, she transcribed a few reports. At one o'clock LaVonne stopped by with a request.

"I need help," she said, stepping into K.O.'s condo. She carried a plate of cookies.

"Okay." K.O. made herself look away from the delec-table-smelling cookies. Her stomach growled. All she'd had for lunch was a small container of yogurt and a glass of V8 juice.

"I hate to ask," LaVonne said, "but I wasn't sure where else to turn."

"LaVonne, I'd do anything for you. You know that."

Her friend nodded. "Would you write my Christmas letter for me?"

"Of course." That would be a piece of cake. Oh, why did everything come down to food?

"I have no idea how to do this. I've never written one before." She sighed. "My life is pitiful."

K.O. arched her brows. "What do you mean, pitiful? You have a good life."

"I do? I've never married and I don't have children. I'm getting these Christmas letters from my old college friends and they're all about how perfect their lives are. In comparison mine is so dull. All I have are my three cats." She looked beseechingly at K.O. "Jazz up my life, would you? Make it sound just as wonderful as my girlfriends' instead of just plain boring."

"Your life is *not* boring." Despite her best efforts, K.O. couldn't keep her eyes off the cookies. "Would you excuse me?"

"Ah...sure."

"I'll be back in a minute. I need to brush my teeth."

Her neighbor eyed her speculatively as K.O. left the room.

"It's a trick I have when I get hungry," she explained, coming out of the bathroom holding her toothbrush, which was loaded with toothpaste. "Whenever I get hungry, I brush my teeth."

"You do what?"

"Brush my teeth."

Her friend regarded her steadily. "How many times have you brushed your teeth today?"

"Four...no, five times. Promise me you'll take those cookies home."

LaVonne nodded. "I brought them in case I needed a bribe."

"Not only will I write your letter, I'll do it today so you can mail off your cards this week."

Her friend's eyes revealed her gratitude. "You're the best."

Ideas were already forming in K.O.'s mind. Writing La-Vonne's Christmas letter would be a snap compared to finishing Bill Mulcahy's. Speaking of him… K.O. glanced at her watch. She was scheduled to meet him this very afternoon.

"I've got an appointment at three," she told her friend. "I'll put something together for you right away, drop it off, see Bill and then stop at your place on my way back."

"Great." LaVonne was still focused on the toothbrush. "You're meeting Wynn later?"

She nodded. "At six." She should be contacting him and canceling, but she didn't know how to reach him. It was a weak excuse—since she could easily ask LaVonne for his number. Actually, she felt it was time to own up to the truth. She wanted to see Wynn again, just so she'd have some answers. *Was* she truly attracted to him? *Did* he have some nefarious agenda, with the intent of proving himself right and her wrong? Unless she spent another evening with him, she wouldn't find out.

"Are you…" LaVonne waved her hand in K.O.'s direction.

"Am I what?"

LaVonne sighed. "Are you going to take that toothbrush with you?"

"Of course."

"I see." Her neighbor frowned. "My psychic vision didn't tell me anything about that."

"No, I don't imagine it would." K.O. proceeded to return to the bathroom, where she gave her teeth a thorough brushing. Perhaps if Wynn saw her foaming at the mouth, he'd know her true feelings about him.

Chapter Six

K.O. had fun writing LaVonne's Christmas letter. Compared to Bill Mulcahy's, it was a breeze. Her friend was worried about how other people, people from her long-ago past, would react to the fact that she'd never married and lacked male companionship. K.O. took care of that.

Merry Christmas to my Friends, K.O. began for La-Vonne. *This has been an exciting year as I juggle my time between Tom, Phillip and Martin, the three guys in my life. No one told me how demanding these relationships can be. Tom won my heart first and then I met Phillip and how could I refuse him? Yes, there's a bit of jealousy, but they manage to be civil to each other. I will admit that things heated up after I started seeing Martin. I fell for him the minute we met.*

I'm retired now, so I have plenty of time to devote to the demands of these relationships. Some women discover love in their twenties. But it took me until I was retired to fall into this kind of happiness. I lavish attention and love on all three guys. Those of you who are concerned that I'm taking on too much, let me assure you—I'm woman enough to handle them.

I love my new luxury condo on Blossom Street here in Seattle. And I've been continuing my education lately, enhancing my skills and exploring new vistas.

K.O. giggled, then glanced at her watch. The afternoon had escaped her. She hurriedly finished with a few more details of LaVonne's year, including a wine-tasting trip to the Yakima Valley, and printed out a draft of the letter.

The meeting with Bill Mulcahy went well, and he paid her the balance of what he owed and thanked her profusely. "This is just perfect," he said, reading the Christmas letter. "I wouldn't have believed it, if I wasn't seeing it for myself. You took the mess this year has been and turned it all around."

K.O. was pleased her effort had met with his satisfaction.

LaVonne was waiting for her when she returned, the Christmas letter in hand. "Oh, Katherine, I don't know how you do it. I laughed until I had tears in my eyes. How can I ever thank you?"

"I had fun," she assured her neighbor.

"I absolutely insist on paying you."

"Are you kidding? No way." After everything LaVonne had done for her, no thanks was necessary.

"I love it so much, I've already taken it down to the printer's and had copies made on fancy Christmas paper. My cards are going out this afternoon, thanks to you."

K.O. shrugged off her praise. After all, her friend had paid for her dinner with Wynn at Chez Jerome and been a good friend to her all these months. Writing a simple letter was the least she could do.

K.O. had been home only a short while when her doorbell chimed. Thinking it must be LaVonne, who frequently stopped by, she casually opened it, ready to greet her neighbor.

Instead Wynn Jeffries stood there.

K.O. wasn't ready for their outing—or to see him again. She needed to steel herself against the attraction she felt toward him.

"Hi." She sounded breathless.

"Katherine."

"Hi," she said again unnecessarily.

"I realize I'm early," he said. "I have a radio interview at 5:30. My assistant arranged it earlier in the week and I forgot to enter it into my PDA."

"Oh." Here it was—the perfect excuse to avoid seeing him again. And yet she couldn't help feeling disappointed.

He must've known, as she did, that any kind of relationship was a lost cause.

"That's fine, I understand," she told him, recovering quickly. "We can get together another time." She offered this in a nonchalant manner, shrugging her shoulders, deciding this really was for the best.

His gaze held hers. "Perhaps you could come with me," he said.

"Come with you?" she repeated and instantly recognized this as a bad idea. In fact, as bad ideas went, it came close to the top. She hadn't been able to keep her mouth shut in the bookstore and had been banned for life. If she had to listen to him spout off his views in person, K.O. didn't know if she could restrain herself from grabbing the mike and pleading with people everywhere to throw out his book or use it for kindling. Nope, attending the interview with him was definitely *not* a good plan.

When she didn't immediately respond, he said, "After

the interview, we could go on to the Figgy Pudding thing you mentioned."

She knew she should refuse. And yet, before she could reconsider it, she found herself nodding.

"I understand the radio station is only a few blocks from West Lake Plaza."

"Yes…" Her mouth felt dry and all at once she was nervous.

"We'll need to leave right away," he said, looking at his watch.

"I'll get my coat." She was wearing blue jeans and a long black sweater—no need to change.

Wynn entered her condo and as she turned away, he stopped her, placing one hand on her arm.

K.O. turned back and was surprised to find him staring at her again. He seemed to be saying he wasn't sure what was happening between them, either. Wasn't sure what he felt or why… Then, as if he needed to test those feelings, he lowered his mouth to hers. Slowly, ever so slowly… K.O. could've moved away at any point. She didn't. The biggest earthquake of the century could've hit and she wouldn't have noticed. Not even if the building had come tumbling down around her feet. Her eyes drifted shut and she leaned into Wynn, ready—no, more than ready—*eager* to accept his kiss.

To her astonishment, it was even better than the night before. This *couldn't* be happening and yet it was. Fortunately, Wynn's hands were on her shoulders, since her balance had grown unsteady.

When he pulled away, it took her a long time to open her eyes. She glanced up at him and discovered he seemed as perplexed as she was.

"I was afraid of that," he said.

She blinked, understanding perfectly what he meant. "Me, too."

"It was as good as last night."

"Better," she whispered.

He cleared his throat. "If we don't leave now, I'll be late for the interview."

"Right."

Still, neither of them moved. Apparently all they were capable of doing was staring at each other. Wynn didn't seem any happier about this than she was, and in some small way, that was a comfort.

K.O. forced herself to break the contact between them. She collected her coat and purse and was halfway to the door when she dashed into the bathroom. "I forgot my toothbrush," she informed him.

He gave her a puzzled look. "You brush after every meal?" he asked.

"No, before." She smiled sheepishly. "I mean, I didn't yesterday, which is why I have to do it today."

He didn't question her garbled explanation as she dropped her toothbrush carrier and toothpaste inside her purse.

Once outside the building, Wynn walked at a fast pace as if he already had second thoughts. For her part, K.O. tried not to think at all. To protect everyone's peace of mind, she'd decided to wait outside the building. It was safer that way.

By the time they arrived at the radio station, K.O. realized it was far too frigid to linger out in the cold. She'd wait in the lobby.

Wynn pressed his hand to the small of her back and guided her through the impressive marble-floored lobby toward the elevators.

"I'll wait here," she suggested. But there wasn't any seating or coffee shop. If she stayed there, it would mean standing around for the next thirty minutes or so.

"I'm sure they'll have a waiting area up at the station," Wynn suggested.

He was probably right.

They took the elevator together, standing as far away from each other as possible, as though they both recognized the risk for potential disaster.

The interviewer, Big Mouth Bass, was a well-known Seattle disk jockey. K.O. had listened to him for years but this was the first time she'd seen him in person. He didn't look anything like his voice. For one thing, he was considerably shorter than she'd pictured and considerably...rounder. If she had the opportunity, she'd share her toothbrush trick with him. It might help.

"Want to sit in for the interview?" Big Mouth asked.

"Thank you, no," she rushed to say. "Dr. Jeffries and I don't necessarily agree and—"

"No way." Wynn's voice drowned hers out.

Big Mouth was no fool. K.O. might've imagined it, but she thought a gleam appeared in his eyes. He hosted a live interview show, after all, and a little controversy would keep things lively.

"I insist," Big Mouth said. He motioned toward the hallway that led to the control booth.

K.O. shook her head. "Thanks, anyway, but I'll wait out here."

"We're ready for Dr. Jeffries," a young woman informed the radio personality.

"I'll wait here," K.O. said again, and before anyone could argue, she practically threw herself into a chair and grabbed a magazine. She opened it and pretended to read, sighing with relief as Big Mouth led Wynn out of the waiting area. The radio in the room was tuned to the station, and a couple of minutes later, Big Mouth's booming voice was introducing Wynn.

"I have with me Dr. Wynn Jeffries," he began. "As many of you will recall, Dr. Jeffries's book, *The Free Child,* advocates letting a child set his or her own boundaries. Explain yourself, Dr. Jeffries."

"First, let me thank you for having me on your show," Wynn said, and K.O. was surprised by how melodic he sounded, how confident and sincere. "I believe," Wynn continued, "that structure is stifling to a child."

"*Any* structure?" Big Mouth challenged.

"Yes, in my opinion, such rigidity is detrimental to a child's sense of creativity and his or her natural ability to develop moral principles." Wynn spoke eloquently, citing example after example showing how structure had a negative impact on a child's development.

"No boundaries," Big Mouth repeated, sounding incredulous.

"As I said, a child will set his or her own."

Just listening to Wynn from her chair in the waiting room, K.O. had to sit on her hands.

"You also claim a parent should ignore inappropriate talk."

"Absolutely. Children respond to feedback and when we don't give them any, the undesirable action will cease."

Big Mouth asked a question now and then. Just before the break, he said, "You brought a friend with you this afternoon."

"Yes…" All the confidence seemed to leave Wynn's voice.

"She's in the waiting area, isn't she?" Big Mouth continued, commenting more than questioning. "I gathered, during the few minutes in which I spoke to your friend, that she doesn't agree with your child-rearing philosophy."

"Yes, that's true, but Katherine isn't part of the interview."

Big Mouth chuckled. "I thought we'd bring her in after the break and get her views on your book."

"Uh..."

"Don't go away, folks—this should be interesting. We'll be right back after the traffic and weather report."

On hearing this, K.O. tossed aside the magazine and started to make a run for the elevator. Unfortunately Big Mouth was faster than his size had led her to believe.

"I... I don't think this is a good idea," she said as he led her by the elbow to the control booth. "I'm sure Wynn would rather not..."

"Quite the contrary," Big Mouth said smoothly, ushering her into the recording room, which was shockingly small. He sat her next to Wynn and handed her a headset. "You'll share a mike with Dr. Jeffries. Be sure to speak into it and don't worry about anything."

After the traffic report, Big Mouth was back on the air.

"Hello, Katherine," he said warmly. "How are you this afternoon?"

"I was perfectly fine until a few minutes ago," she snapped.

Big Mouth laughed. "Have you read Dr. Jeffries's book?"

"No. Well, not really." She leaned close to the microphone.

"You disagree with his philosophies, don't you?"

"Yes." She dared not look at Wynn, but she was determined not to embarrass him the way she had in the French Café. Even if they were at odds about the validity of his Free Child movement, he didn't deserve to be publicly humiliated.

"Katherine seems to believe I'm taking Christmas away from children," Wynn blurted out. "She's wrong, of course. I have a short chapter in the book that merely suggests parents bury the concept of Santa."

"You want to *bury Santa?*" Even Big Mouth took offense at that, K.O. noticed with a sense of righteousness.

"My publisher chose the chapter title and against my better judgment, I let it stand. Basically, all I'm saying is that it's wrong to lie to a child, no matter how good one's intentions."

"He wants to get rid of the Tooth Fairy and the Easter Bunny, too," K.O. inserted.

"That doesn't make me a Jim Carrey," Wynn said argumentatively. "I'm asking parents to be responsible adults. That's all."

"What does it hurt?" K.O. asked. "Childhood is a time of make-believe and fairy tales and fun. Why does everything have to be so serious?"

"Dr. Jeffries," Big Mouth cut in. "Could you explain that comment about Jim Carrey?"

"I called him that," K.O. answered on his behalf. "I meant to say the Grinch. You know, like in *How the Grinch Stole Christmas*. Jim Carrey was in the movie," she explained helplessly.

Wynn seemed eager to change the subject. He started to say something about the macabre character of fairy tales and how they weren't "fun," but Big Mouth cut him off.

"Ah, I see," he said, grinning from ear to ear. "You two have a love/hate relationship. That's what *really* going on here."

K.O. looked quickly at Wynn, and he glared back. The "hate" part might be right, but there didn't seem to be any "love" in the way he felt about her.

"Regrettably, this is all the time we have for today," Big Mouth told his audience. "I'd like to thank Dr. Jeffries for stopping by this afternoon and his friend Katherine, too. Thank you both for a most entertaining interview. Now for the news at the top of the hour."

Big Mouth flipped a switch and the room went silent. So silent, in fact, that K.O. could hear her heart beat.

"We can leave now," Wynn said stiffly after removing his headphones.

Hers were already off. K.O. released a huge pent-up sigh. "Thank goodness," she breathed.

Wynn didn't say anything until they'd entered the elevator.

"That was a disaster," he muttered.

K.O. blamed herself. She should never have accompanied him to the interview. She'd known it at the time and still couldn't resist. "I'm sorry. I shouldn't have gone on the air with you."

"You weren't given much choice," he said in her defense.

"I apologize if I embarrassed you. That wasn't my intention. I tried not to say anything derogatory—surely you could see that."

He didn't respond and frankly, she didn't blame him.

"The thing is, Katherine, you don't respect my beliefs."

"I don't," she reluctantly agreed.

"You couldn't have made it any plainer." The elevator doors opened and they stepped into the foyer.

"Perhaps it would be best if we didn't see each other again." K.O. figured she was only saying what they were both thinking.

Wynn nodded. She could sense his regret, a regret she felt herself.

They were outside the building now. The street was festive with lights, and Christmas music could be heard from one of the department stores. At the moment, however, she felt anything but merry.

The Figgy Pudding contest, which was sponsored by the Pike Market Senior Center and Downtown Food Bank as an annual fund-raiser, would've started by now and, although she didn't feel the least bit like cheering, she'd promised Vickie she'd show up and support her efforts for charity.

K.O. thrust out her hand and did her utmost to smile. "Thank you, Wynn. Last night was one of the most incredible evenings of my life," she said. "Correction. It was *the* most incredible night ever."

Wynn clasped her hand. His gaze held hers as he said, "It was for me, too."

People were stepping around them.

She should simply walk away. Vickie would be looking for her. And yet…she couldn't make herself do it.

"Goodbye," he whispered.

Her heart was in her throat. "Goodbye."

He dropped his hand, turned and walked away. His steps were slow, measured. He'd gone about five feet when he glanced over his shoulder. K.O. hadn't moved. In fact, she stood exactly as he'd left her, biting her lower lip—a habit she had when distressed. Wynn stopped abruptly, his back still to her.

"Wynn, listen," she called and trotted toward him. "I have an idea." Although it'd only been a few feet, she felt as if she was setting off on a marathon.

"What?" He sounded eager.

"I have twin nieces."

He nodded. "You mentioned them earlier. Their mother read my book."

"Yes, and loved it."

There was a flicker of a smile. "At least *someone* in your family believes in me."

"Yes, Zelda sure does. She thinks you're fabulous." K.O. realized she did, too—aside from his theories. "My sister and her husband are attending his company Christmas dinner next Friday, the fifteenth," she rushed to explain. "Zelda asked me to spend the night. Come with me. Show me how your theories *should* work. Maybe Zelda's doing it wrong. Maybe you can convince me that the Free Child movement makes sense."

"You want me to come with you."

"Yes. We'll do everything just as you suggest in your book, and I promise not to say a word. I'll read it this week, I'll listen to you and I'll observe."

Wynn hesitated.

"Until then, we won't mention your book or anything else to do with your theories."

"Promise?"

"Promise," she concurred.

"No more radio interviews?"

She laughed. "That's an easy one."

A smile came to him then, appearing in his eyes first. "You've got yourself a deal."

Yes, she did, and K.O. could hardly wait to introduce Zoe and Zara to Dr. Wynn Jeffries. Oh, she was sincere about keeping an open mind, but Wynn might learn something, too. The incorrigible twins would be the true crucible for his ideas.

K.O. held out her hand. "Are you ready for some Figgy Pudding?" she asked.

He grinned, taking her mittened hand as they hurried toward the Figgy Pudding People's Choice competition.

Chapter Seven

The Figgy Pudding People's Choice event was standing room only when Wynn and K.O. arrived. Vickie and her friends hadn't performed yet and were just being introduced by a popular morning-radio host for an easy-listening station. K.O. and Vickie had been friends all through high school and college. Vickie had married three years ago, and K.O. had been in her wedding party. In fact, she'd been in any number of wedding parties. Her mother had pointedly asked whether K.O. was ever going to be a bride, instead of a bridesmaid.

"That's my friend over there," K.O. explained, nodding in Vickie's direction. "The one in the Santa hat."

Wynn squinted at the group of ladies huddled together in front of the assembly. "Aren't they all wearing Santa hats?"

"True. The young cute one," she qualified.

"They're all young and cute, Katherine." He smiled. "Young enough, anyway."

She looked at Wynn with new appreciation. "That is such a sweet thing to say." Vickie worked for a local dentist as a hygienist and was the youngest member of the staff. The other women were all in their forties and fifties. "I could just kiss you," K.O. said, snuggling close to him. She looped her arm through his.

Wynn cleared his throat as though unaccustomed to such open displays of affection. "Any particular reason you suddenly find me so kissable?"

"Well, yes, the women with Vickie are…a variety of ages."

"I see. I should probably tell you I'm not wearing my glasses."

K.O. laughed, elbowing him in the ribs. "And here I thought you were being so gallant."

He grinned boyishly and slid his arm around her shoulders.

Never having attended a Figgy Pudding event before, K.O. didn't know what to expect. To her delight, it was enchanting, as various groups competed, singing Christmas carols, to raise funds for the Senior Center and Food Bank. Vickie and her office mates took second place, and K.O. cheered loudly. Wynn shocked her by placing two fingers in his mouth and letting loose with a whistle that threatened to shatter glass. It seemed so unlike him.

Somehow Vickie found her when the singing was over. "I wondered if you were going to show," she said, shouting to be heard above the noise of the merry-go-round and the crowd. Musicians gathered on street corners, horns honked and the sights and sounds of Christmas were everywhere. Although the comment was directed at K.O., Vickie's attention was unmistakably on Wynn.

"Vickie, this is Wynn Jeffries."

Her friend's gaze shot back to K.O. "Wynn Jeffries? Not *the* Wynn Jeffries?"

"One and the same," K.O. said, speaking out of the corner of her mouth.

"You've got to be joking." Vickie's mouth fell open as she stared at Wynn.

For the last two months, K.O. had been talking her friend's ear off about the man and his book and how he was ruining her sister's life. She'd even told Vickie about the incident at the bookstore, although she certainly hadn't confided in anyone else; she wasn't exactly proud of being kicked out for unruly behavior. Thinking it might be best to change the subject, K.O. asked, "Is John here?"

"John?"

"Your husband," K.O. reminded her. She hadn't seen Wynn wearing glasses before, but she hoped his comment about forgetting them was sincere, otherwise he might notice the close scrutiny Vickie was giving him.

"Oh, *John*," her friend said, recovering quickly. "No, he's meeting me later for dinner." Then, as if inspiration had struck, she asked, "Would you two like to join us? John got a reservation at a new Chinese restaurant that's supposed to have great food."

K.O. looked at Wynn, who nodded. "Sure," she answered, speaking for both of them. "What time?"

"Nine. I was going to do some shopping and meet him there."

They made arrangements to meet later and Vickie went into the mall to finish her Christmas shopping.

"I'm starving now," K.O. said when her stomach growled. Although she had her toothbrush, there really wasn't a convenient place to foam up. "After last night, I didn't think I'd ever want to eat again." She considered mentioning the two pounds she'd gained, but thought better of it. Wynn might not want to see her again if he found out how easily she packed on weight. Well, she didn't *really* believe that of him, but she wasn't taking any chances.

Which proved that, despite everything, she was interested. In fact, she'd made the decision to continue with this relationship, see where their attraction might lead, almost without being aware of it.

"How about some roasted chestnuts?" he asked. A vendor was selling them on the street corner next to a musician who strummed a guitar and played a harmonica at the same time. His case was open on the sidewalk for anyone who cared to donate. She tossed in a dollar and hoped he used whatever money he collected to pay for music lessons.

"I've never had a roasted chestnut," K.O. told him.

"Me, neither," Wynn confessed. "This seems to be the season for it, though."

While Wynn waited in line for the chestnuts, K.O. became fascinated with the merry-go-round. "Will you go on it with me?" she asked him.

Wynn hesitated. "I've never been on a merry-go-round."

K.O. was surprised. "Then you have to," she insisted. "You've missed a formative experience." Taking his hand, she pulled him out of the line. She purchased the tickets herself and refused to listen to his excuses. He rattled off a dozen—he was too old, too big, too clumsy and so on. K.O. rejected every one.

"It's going to be fun," she said.

"I thought you were starving."

"I was, but I'm not now. Come on, be a good sport. Women find men who ride horses extremely attractive."

Wynn stopped arguing long enough to raise an eyebrow. "My guess is that the horse is generally not made of painted wood."

"Generally," she agreed, "but you never know."

The merry-go-round came to a halt and emptied out on the opposite side. They passed their tickets to the attendant and, leading Wynn by the hand, K.O. ushered him over to a pair of white horses that stood side by side. She set her foot in the stirrup and climbed into the molded saddle. Wynn stood next to his horse looking uncertain.

"Mount up, partner," she said.

"I feel more than a little ridiculous, Katherine."

"Oh, don't be silly. Men ride these all the time. See? There's another guy."

Granted, he was sitting on a gaudy elephant, holding a toddler, but she didn't dwell on that.

Sighing, Wynn climbed reluctantly onto the horse, his legs so long they nearly touched the floor. "Put your feet in the stirrups," she coaxed.

He did, and his knees were up to his ears.

K.O. couldn't help it; she burst out laughing.

Wynn began to climb off, but she stopped him by leaning over and kissing him. She nearly slid off the saddle in the process and would have if Wynn hadn't caught her about the waist.

Soon the carousel music started, and the horses moved up and down. K.O. thrust out her legs and laughed, thoroughly enjoying herself. "Are you having fun yet?" she asked Wynn.

"I'm ecstatic," he said dryly.

"Oh, come on, Wynn, relax. Have some fun."

Suddenly he leaned forward, as if he were riding for the Pony Express. He let out a cry that sounded like sheer joy.

"That *was* fun," Wynn told her, climbing down when the carousel stopped. He put his hands on her waist and she felt the heat of his touch in every part of her body.

"You liked it?"

"Do you want to go again?" he asked.

The line was much longer now. "I don't think so."

"I've always wanted to do that. I felt like a child all over again," he said enthusiastically.

"A Free Child?" she asked in a mischievous voice.

"Yes, free. That's exactly what my book's about, allowing children freedom to become themselves," he said seriously.

"Okay." She was biting her tongue but managed not to say anything more. Surely there were great rewards awaiting her in heaven for such restraint.

"Would you like to stop at the bookstore?" he asked. "I like to sign copies when I'm in the neighborhood."

"You mean an autographing?" She hoped it wouldn't be at the same bookstore that had caused all the trouble.

"Not exactly an autographing," Wynn explained. "The bookseller told me that a signed book is a sold book. When it's convenient, authors often visit bookstores to sign stock."

"Sort of a drive-by signing?" she asked, making a joke out of it.

"Yeah." They started walking and just as she feared, they were headed in the direction of *the* bookstore.

As they rounded the corner and the store came into sight, her stomach tightened. "I'll wait for you outside," she said, implying that nothing would please her more than to linger out in the cold.

"Nonsense. There's a small café area where you can wait in comfort."

"Okay," she finally agreed. Once she'd made it past the shoplifting detector K.O. felt more positive. She was afraid her mug shot had been handed out to the employees and she'd be expelled on sight.

Thankfully she didn't see the bookseller who'd asked her to leave. That boded well. She saw Wynn chatting with a woman behind the counter. He followed her to the back of the store. Some of the tension eased from K.O.'s shoulder blades. Okay, she seemed to be safe. And she didn't have to hide behind a coffee cup. Besides, she loved to read and since she was in a bookstore, what harm would it do to buy a book? She was in the mood for something entertaining. A romantic comedy, she decided, studying a row of titles. Without much trouble, she found one that looked perfect and started toward the cashier.

Then it happened.

Wynn was waiting up front, speaking to the very bookseller who'd banished K.O. from the store.

Trying to be as inconspicuous as possible, K.O. set the book aside and tiptoed toward the exit, shoulders hunched forward, head lowered.

"Katherine," Wynn called.

With a smile frozen in place, she turned to greet Wynn and the bookseller.

"It's you!" The woman, who wore a name tag that identified her as Shirley, glared at K.O.

She timidly raised her hand. "Hello again."

"You two know each other?" Shirley asked Wynn in what appeared to be complete disbelief.

"Yes. This is my friend Katherine."

The bookseller seemed to have lost her voice. She looked from Wynn to Katherine and then back.

"Good to see you again," K.O. said. She sincerely hoped Shirley would play along and conveniently forget that unfortunate incident.

"It *is* you," Shirley hissed from between clenched teeth.

"What's this about?" Wynn asked, a puzzled expression on his face. "You've met before?"

"Nothing," K.O. all but shouted.

"As a matter of fact, we have met." Shirley's dark eyes

narrowed. "Perhaps your *friend* has forgotten. I, however, have not."

So it was going to be like that, was it? "We had a difference of opinion," K.O. told Wynn in a low voice.

"As I recall, you were permanently banned from the store."

"Katherine was *banned* from the store?" Wynn asked incredulously. "I can't believe she'd do anything deserving of that."

"Maybe we should leave now," K.O. suggested, and tugged at his sleeve.

"If you want to know," Shirley began, but K.O. interrupted before she could launch into her complaint.

"Wynn, please, we should go," she said urgently.

"I'm sure this can all be sorted out," he murmured, releasing his coat sleeve from her grasp.

Shirley, hands on her hips, smiled snidely. She seemed to take real pleasure in informing Wynn of K.O.'s indiscretion.

"This *friend* of yours is responsible for causing a scene in this very bookstore, Dr. Jeffries."

"I'm sure no harm was meant."

K.O. grabbed his arm. "It doesn't matter," she said, desperate to escape.

"Katherine does tend to be opinionated, I agree," he said, apparently determined to defend her. "But she's actually quite reasonable."

"Apparently you don't know her as well as you think."

"I happen to enjoy Katherine's company immensely."

Shirley raised her eyebrows. "Really?"

"Yes, really."

"Then you might be interested to know that your so-called friend nearly caused a riot when she got into an argument with another customer over *your* book."

Wynn swiveled his gaze to K.O.

She offered him a weak smile. "Ready to leave now?" she asked in a weak whisper.

Chapter Eight

K.O.'s doorbell chimed, breaking into a Satisfying dream. Whatever it was about seemed absolutely wonderful and she hated to lose it. When the doorbell rang again, the sound longer and more persistent, the dream disappeared. She stumbled out of bed and threw on her flannel housecoat.

Reaching the door, she checked the peephole and saw that it was LaVonne. No surprise there. Unfastening the lock, K.O. let her in, covering a yawn.

"What time did you get home last night?" her neighbor cried as she hurried in without a cat—which was quite unusual. "I waited up as long as I could for you." LaVonne's voice was frantic. "I didn't sleep a wink all night," she said and plopped herself down on the sofa.

K.O. was still at the front door, holding it open. "Good morning to you, too."

"Should I make coffee?" LaVonne asked, leaping to her feet and flipping on the light as she swept into the kitchen. Not waiting for a response, she pulled out the canister where K.O. kept her coffee grounds.

K.O. yawned again and closed the front door. "What

time is it?" Early, she knew, because her eyes burned and there was barely a hint of daylight through her living room windows.

"Seven-twenty. I didn't get you up, did I?"

"No, I had to answer the door anyway." Her friend was busy preparing coffee and didn't catch the joke. "How are the guys?" K.O. asked next. LaVonne usually provided her with daily updates on their health, well-being and any cute activities they'd engaged in.

"They're hiding," she said curtly. "All three of them." She ran water into the glass pot and then poured it in the coffeemaker.

Katherine wondered why the cats were in a snit but didn't have the energy to ask.

"You haven't answered my question," LaVonne said as the coffee started to drip. She placed two mugs on the counter.

"Which one?" K.O. fell into a kitchen chair, rested her arms on the table and leaned her head on them.

"Last night," LaVonne said. "Where were you?"

"Wynn and I were out—"

"*All* night?"

"You're beginning to sound like my mother," K.O. protested.

LaVonne straightened her shoulders. "Katherine, you hardly know the man."

"I didn't sleep with him, if that's what you think." She raised her head long enough to speak and then laid it down on her arms again. "We went out to dinner with some friends of mine after the Figgy Pudding contest."

"It must've been a very late dinner." LaVonne sounded as if she didn't quite believe her.

"We walked around for a while afterward and went out

for a drink. The time got away from us. I didn't get home until one."

"I was up at one and you weren't home," LaVonne said in a challenging tone. She poured the first cup of coffee and took it herself.

"Maybe it was after two, then," K.O. said. She'd completely lost track of time, which was easy to do. Wynn was so charming and he seemed so interested in her and her friends.

Vickie's husband, John, was a plumbing contractor. Despite Wynn's college degrees and celebrity status, he'd fit in well with her friends. He'd asked intelligent questions, listened and shared anecdotes about himself that had them all laughing. John even invited Wynn to play poker with him and his friends after the holidays. Wynn had accepted the invitation.

Halfway through the meal Vickie had announced that she had to use the ladies' room. The look she shot K.O. said she should join her, which K.O. did.

"That's really Wynn Jeffries?" she asked, holding K.O.'s elbow as they made their way around tables and through the restaurant.

"Yes, it's really him."

"Does he know about the bookstore?"

K.O. nodded reluctantly. "He does now."

"You didn't tell him, did you?"

"Unfortunately, he found out all on his own."

Vickie pushed open the door to the ladies' as K.O. described the scene from the bookstore. "No way," her friend moaned, then promptly sank down on a plush chair in the outer room.

K.O.'s face grew red all over again. "It was embarrassing, to say the least."

"Was Wynn upset?"

What could he say? "He didn't let on if he was." In fact, once they'd left the store, Wynn seemed to find the incident highly amusing. Had their roles been reversed, she didn't know how she would've felt.

"He didn't blow up at you or anything?" Vickie had given her a confused look. "This is the guy you think should be banned from practicing as a psychologist?"

"Well, that might've been a bit strong," she'd said, reconsidering her earlier comment.

Vickie just shook her head.

"He rode the merry-go-round with me," K.O. said aloud, deciding that had gone a long way toward redeeming him in her eyes. When she glanced up, she realized she was talking to LaVonne.

"He did what?" LaVonne asked, bringing her back to the present.

"Wynn did," she elaborated. "He rode the carousel with me."

"Until two in the morning?"

"No, before dinner. Afterward, we walked along the waterfront, then had a glass of wine. We started walking again and finally stopped for coffee at an all-night diner and talked some more." He seemed to want to know all about her, but in retrospect she noticed that he'd said very little about himself.

"Good grief," LaVonne muttered, shaking her head, "what could you possibly talk about for so long?"

"That's just it," K.O. said. "We couldn't *stop* talking." And it was even more difficult to stop kissing and to say good-night once they'd reached her condo. Because there was so much more to say, they'd agreed to meet for coffee at the French Café at nine.

LaVonne had apparently remembered that Katherine didn't have any coffee yet and filled her mug. "Just black," K.O. told her, needing a shot of unadulterated caffeine. "Thanks."

"Why were you waiting up for me?" she asked after her first bracing sip of coffee. Then and only then did her brain clear, and she understood that LaVonne must have something important on her mind.

"You wrote that fantastic Christmas letter for me," her neighbor reminded her.

"I did a good job, didn't I?" she said.

"Oh, yes, a good job all right." LaVonne frowned. "I liked it so much, I mailed it right away."

"So, what's the problem?"

"Well…" LaVonne sat down in the chair across from K.O. "It was such a relief to have something clever and… and exciting to tell everyone," LaVonne said, "especially my college friends."

So far, K.O. didn't see any problem at all. She nodded, encouraging her friend to get to the point.

LaVonne's shoulders sagged. "If only I'd waited," she moaned. "If only I'd picked up my own mail first."

"There was something in the mail?"

LaVonne nodded. "I got a card and a Christmas letter from Peggy Solomon. She was the president of my college sorority and about as uppity as they come. She married her college boyfriend, a banker's son. She had two perfect children and lives a life of luxury. She said she's looking forward to seeing me at our next reunion." There was a moment of stricken silence. "Peggy's organizing it, and she included the invitation with her card."

"That's bad?"

"Yes," LaVonne wailed. "It's bad. How am I supposed to

show up at my forty-year college reunion, which happens to be in June, without a man? Especially *now*. Because of my Christmas letter, everyone in my entire class will think I've got more men than I know what to do with."

"LaVonne, you might meet someone before then."

"If I haven't met a man in the last forty years, what makes you think I will in the next six months?"

"Couldn't you say it's such a tricky balancing act you don't dare bring any of them?"

LaVonne glared at her. "Everyone'll figure out that it's all a lie." She closed her eyes. "And if they don't, Peggy's going to make sure she tells them."

Another idea struck K.O. "What about your psychic powers? Why don't you go check out the litter box again?" On second thought, maybe that wasn't such a great idea.

"Don't you think I would if I could?" she cried, becoming ever more agitated. "But I don't see anything about myself. Trust me, I've tried. So far, all my insights have been about you and Wynn. A lot of good my newfound talent has done *me*. You're being romanced night and day, and I've just made a complete fool of myself."

"LaVonne..."

"Even my cats are upset with me."

"Tom, Phillip and Martin?" K.O. had never understood why her neighbor couldn't name her feline companions regular cat names like Fluffy or Tiger.

"They think *I'm* upset with *them*. They're all hiding from me, and that's never happened before."

K.O. felt guilty, but she couldn't have known about the college reunion, any more than LaVonne did. "I'm sure everything will work out for the best," she murmured. She wished she had more than a platitude to offer, but she didn't.

"At this point that's all I can hope for." LaVonne expelled

her breath and took another sip of coffee. That seemed to relax her, and she gave K.O. a half smile. "Tell me about you and Wynn."

"There's not much to say." And yet there was. She honestly liked him. Vickie and John had, too. Never would K.O. have guessed that the originator of the Free Child movement she so reviled would be this warm, compassionate and genuinely nice person. She would've been happy to settle for *one* of those qualities. Despite everything K.O. had done to embarrass him, he was attracted to her. And it went without saying that she found Wynn Jeffries compelling and smart and…wonderful. But she was afraid to examine her feelings too closely—and even more afraid to speculate about his.

"You've spent practically every minute of the last two days together," LaVonne said. "There's got to be something."

Shrugging, K.O. pushed her hair away from her face.

"You were with him until two this morning."

"And I'm meeting him at the café in about an hour and a half," she said as she glanced at the time on her microwave.

"So what gives?" LaVonne pressed.

"I like him," she said simply. K.O. hadn't been prepared to have any feelings for him, other than negative ones. But they got along well—as long as they didn't discuss his book.

Overjoyed by her confession, LaVonne clapped her hands. "I knew it!"

K.O. felt it would be wrong to let her friend think she really believed in this psychic nonsense. She'd cooperated with LaVonne's fantasy at first but now it was time to be honest. "Wynn said he asked you about me before you introduced us."

LaVonne looked away. "He did, but it was just in passing."

"He knew I lived in the building and had seen me around."

Her neighbor shifted in her seat. She cleared her throat before answering. "All right, all right, I was aware that he might be interested." She paused. "He asked me if you were single."

Really? Wynn hadn't told her that. "When was this?"

"Last week."

"Was it before or after you discovered your psychic talents?"

"Before."

Aha.

"Why didn't he just introduce himself?"

"I asked him that, too," LaVonne said. "Apparently he's shy."

"Wynn?"

LaVonne raised one shoulder. She frowned over at the phone on the counter. "You've got a message."

It'd been so late when she finally got to bed that K.O. hadn't bothered to check. Reaching over, she pressed the play button.

"K.O.," Zelda's voice greeted her. "Good grief, where are you? You don't have a date, do you?" She made it sound as if that was the last thing she expected. "Is there any chance it's with Dr. Jeffries? Call me the minute you get home." The message was followed by a lengthy beep and then there was a second message.

"Katherine," Zelda said more forcefully this time. "I don't mean to be a pest, but I'd appreciate it if you'd get back to me as soon as possible. You're out with Dr. Jeffries, aren't you?" Zelda managed to make that sound both accusatory and improbable.

Another beep.

"In case you're counting, this is the third time I've phoned you tonight. Where can you possibly be this late?"

No one ever seemed to care before, K.O. thought, and now her sister and LaVonne were suddenly keeping track of her love life.

Zelda gave a huge sigh of impatience. "I won't call again. But I need to confirm the details for Friday night. You're still babysitting, aren't you?"

"I'll be there," K.O. muttered, just as if her sister could hear. *And so will Wynn.*

Zelda added, "And I'd really like it if you'd get me that autograph."

"I will, I will," K.O. promised. She figured she'd get him to sign Zelda's copy of his book on Friday evening.

LaVonne drained the last of her coffee and set the mug in the sink. "I'd better get back. I'm going to try to coax the boys out from under the bed," she said with a resigned look as she walked to the door.

"Everything'll work out," K.O. assured her again—with a confidence she didn't actually feel.

LaVonne responded with a quick wave and left, slamming the door behind her.

Now K.O. was free to have a leisurely shower, carefully choose her outfit…and daydream about Wynn.

Chapter Nine

Wynn had already secured a window table when K.O. arrived at the French Café. As usual, the shop was crowded, with a long line of customers waiting to place their orders.

In honor of the season, she'd worn a dark-blue sweater sprinkled with silvery stars and matching star earrings. She hung her red coat on the back of her chair.

Wynn had thoughtfully ordered for her, and there was a latte waiting on the table, along with a bran muffin, her favorite. K.O. didn't remember mentioning how much she enjoyed the café's muffins, baked by Alix Townsend, who sometimes worked at the counter. The muffins were a treat she only allowed herself once a week.

"Good morning," she said, sounding a little more breathless than she would've liked. In the space of a day, she'd gone from distrust to complete infatuation. Just twenty-four hours ago, she'd been inventing ways to get out of seeing Wynn again, and now...now she could barely stand to be separated from him.

She broke off a piece of muffin, after a sip of her latte in its oversize cup. "How did you know I love their bran muffins?" she asked. The bakery made them chock-full of raisins and nuts, so they were deliciously unlike blander varieties. Not only that, K.O. always felt she'd eaten something healthy when she had a bran muffin.

"I asked the girl behind the counter if she happened to know what you usually ordered, and she recommended that."

Once again proving how thoughtful he was.

"You had one the day you were here talking to some guy," he said flippantly.

"That was Bill Mulcahy," she explained. "I met with him because I wrote his Christmas letter."

Wynn frowned. "He's one of your clients?"

"I told you how I write people's Christmas letters, remember?" It'd been part of their conversation the night before. "I'll write yours if you want," she said, and then thinking better of it, began to sputter a retraction.

She needn't have worried that he'd take her up on the offer because he was already declining. He shook his head. "Thanks, anyway." He grimaced. "I don't want to offend you, but I find that those Christmas letters are typically a pack of lies!"

"Okay," she said mildly. She decided not to argue. K.O. sipped her coffee again and ate another piece of muffin, deciding not to worry about calories, either. "Don't you just love Christmas?" she couldn't help saying. The sights and sounds of the season were all around them. The café itself looked elegant; garlands draped the windows and pots of white and red poinsettias were placed on the counter. Christmas carols played, just loudly enough to be heard. A bell-ringer collecting for charity had set up shop outside the café and a woman sat at a nearby table knitting a Christmas stocking. K.O. had noticed a similar one displayed in A Good Yarn, the shop across the street, the day she'd followed Wynn. Christmas on Blossom Street, with its gaily decorated streetlights and cheerful banners, was as Christmassy as Christmas could be.

"Yes, but I had more enthusiasm for the holidays before today," Wynn said.

"What's wrong?"

He stared down at his dark coffee. "My father left a message on my answering machine last night." He hesitated as he glanced up at her. "Apparently he's decided—at the last minute—to join me for Christmas."

"I see," she said, although she really didn't. Wynn had only talked about his parents that first evening, at Chez Jerome. She remembered that his parents had been hippies, and that his mother had died and his father owned a company that manufactured surfboard wax. But while she'd rattled on endlessly about her own family, he'd said comparatively little about his.

"He didn't bother to ask if I had other plans, you'll notice," Wynn commented dryly.

"Do you?"

"No, but that's beside the point."

"It must be rather disconcerting," she said. Parents sometimes did things like that, though. Her own mother often made assumptions about holidays, but it had never troubled K.O. She was going to miss her parents this year and would've been delighted if they'd suddenly decided to show up.

"Now I have to go to the airport on Sunday and pick him up." Wynn gazed out the window at the lightly falling snow. "As you might've guessed, my father and I have a rather...difficult relationship."

"I'm sorry." She wasn't sure what to say.

"The thing is," Wynn continued. "My father's like a big kid. He'll want to be entertained every minute he's here. He has no respect for my work or the fact that I have to go into the office every day." Wynn had told her he met with patients most afternoons; he kept an office in a medical building not far from Blossom Street.

"I'm sorry," she said again.

Wynn accepted her condolences with a casual shrug. "The truth is, I'd rather spend my free time with you."

He seemed as surprised by this as K.O. herself. She sensed that Wynn hadn't been any more prepared to feel this way about her than she did about him. It was all rather unexpected and at the same time just plain wonderful.

"Maybe I can help," K.O. suggested. "The nice thing about working at home is that I can choose my own hours." That left her open for job interviews, Christmas letters and occasional babysitting. "My transcription work is really a godsend while I'm on my job quest. So I can help entertain him if you'd like."

Wynn considered for a moment. "I appreciate your offer, but I don't know if that's the best solution." He released a deep sigh. "I guess you could say my father's not my biggest fan."

"He doesn't believe in your child-rearing ideas, either?" she teased.

He grinned. "I wish it was that simple. You'll know what I mean once you meet him," Wynn said. "I think I mentioned that at one time he was a world-class surfer."

"Yes, and he manufactures some kind of special wax."

Wynn nodded. "It's made him rich." He sighed again. "I know it's a cliché, but my parents met in San Francisco in the early 70s and I think I told you they joined a commune. They were free spirits, the pair of them. Dad hated what he called 'the establishment.' He dropped out of college, burned his draft card, that sort of thing. He didn't want any responsibility, didn't even have a bank account—until about fifteen years ago, when someone offered to mass-produce his surfboard wax. And then he grabbed hold with both hands."

K.O. wondered if he realized he was advocating his parents' philosophy with his Free Child movement. However, she didn't point it out.

"In the early days we moved around because any money Dad brought in was from his surfing, so the three of us followed the waves, so to speak. Then we'd periodically return to the commune. I had a wretched childhood," he said bleakly. "They'd called me Radiant Sun, Ray for short, but at least they let me choose my own name when I was older. They hated it, which was fine by me. The only real family I had was my maternal grandparents. I moved in with the Wynns when I was ten."

"Your parents didn't like your name?"

"No, and this came from someone who chose the name Moon Puppy for himself. Mom liked to be called Daffodil. Her given name was Mary, which she'd rejected, along with her parents' values."

"But you—"

"My grandparents were the ones who saw to it that I stayed in school. They're the ones who paid for my education. Both of them died when I was a college senior, but they were the only stable influence I had."

"What you need while your father is here," K.O. said, "is someone to run interference. Someone who can act as a buffer between you and your father, and that someone is me."

Wynn didn't look convinced.

"I want to help," she insisted. "Really."

He still didn't look convinced.

"Oh, and before I forget, my sister left three messages on my phone. She wants your autograph in the worst way. I thought you could sign her copy of *The Free Child* next Friday when—" It suddenly occurred to her that if Wynn's father was visiting, he wouldn't be able to watch the twins with her. "Oh, no," she whispered, unable to hide her disappointment.

"What's wrong?"

"I— You'll have company, so Friday night is out." She put on a brave smile. She didn't actually need his help, but this was an opportunity to spend time with him—and to prove that his theories didn't translate into practice. She might be wrong, in which case she'd acknowledge the validity of his Free Child approach, but she doubted it.

Wynn met her eyes. "I'm not going to break my commitment. I'll explain to my father that I've got a previous engagement. He doesn't have any choice but to accept it, especially since he didn't give me any notice."

"When does he arrive?" K.O. asked. She savored another piece of her muffin, trying to guess which spices Alix had used.

"At four-thirty," Wynn said glumly.

"It's going to work out fine." That was almost identical to what she'd told LaVonne earlier that morning.

Then it hit her.

LaVonne needed a man in her life.

Wynn was looking for some way to occupy his father.

"Oh, my goodness." K.O. stood and stared down at Wynn with both hands on the edge of the table.

"What?"

"Wynn, I have the perfect solution!"

He eyed her skeptically.

"LaVonne," she said, sitting down again. She was so sure her plan would work, she felt a little shiver of delight. "You're going to introduce your father to LaVonne!"

He frowned at her and shook his head. "If you're thinking what I suspect you're thinking, I can tell you right now it won't work."

"Yes, it will! LaVonne needs to find a man before her college reunion in June. She'd—"

"Katherine, I appreciate the thought, but can you honestly see LaVonne getting involved with an ex-hippie who isn't all that ex—and is also the producer of Max's Waxes?"

"Of course I can," she said, refusing to allow him to thwart her plan. "Besides, it isn't up to us. All we have to do is introduce the two of them, step back and let nature take its course."

Wynn clearly still had doubts.

"It won't hurt to try."

"I guess not…"

"This is what I'll do," she said, feeling inspired. She couldn't understand Wynn's hesitation. "I'll invite your father and LaVonne to my place for Christmas cocktails."

Wynn crossed his arms. "This is beginning to sound familiar."

"It should." She stifled a giggle. Turnabout was fair play, after all.

"Maybe we should look at the olives in the martinis and tell them we got a psychic reading," Wynn joked.

"Oh, that's good," K.O. said with a giggle. "A drink or two should relax them both," she added.

"And then you and I can conveniently leave for dinner or a movie."

"No…no," K.O. said, excitedly. "Oh, Wynn this is ideal! We'll arrange a dinner for *them*."

"Where?"

"I don't know." He was worrying about details too much. "We'll think of someplace special."

"I wonder if I can reach Chef Jerome and get a reservation there," Wynn murmured.

K.O. gulped. "I can't afford that."

"Not to worry. My father can."

"That's even better." K.O. felt inordinately pleased with herself. All the pieces were falling into place. Wynn would have someone to keep his father occupied until Christmas, and LaVonne might find a potential date for her class reunion.

"What are your plans for today?" Wynn asked, changing the subject.

"I'm meeting Vickie and a couple of other friends for shopping and lunch. What about you?"

"I'm headed to the gym and then the office. I don't usually work on weekends, but I'm writing a follow-up book." He spoke hesitantly as if he wasn't sure he should mention it.

"Okay." She smiled as enthusiastically as she could. "Would you like me to go to the airport with you when you pick up your father?"

"You'd do that?"

"Of course! In fact, I'd enjoy it."

"Thank you, then. I'd appreciate it."

They set up a time on Sunday afternoon and went their separate ways.

K.O. started walking down to Pacific Place, the mall where she'd agreed to meet Vickie and Diane, when her cell phone rang. It was Wynn.

"What day?" he asked. "I want to get this cocktail party idea of yours on my schedule."

"When would you suggest?"

"I don't think we should wait too long."

"I agree."

"Would Monday evening work for you?"

"Definitely. I'll put together a few appetizers and make some spiked eggnog. I'll pick up some wine—and gin for martinis, if you want." She smiled, recalling his comment about receiving a "psychic" message from the olives.

"Let me bring the wine. Anything else?"

"Could you buy a cat treat or two? That's in case La-Vonne brings Tom or one of her other cats. I want her to concentrate on Moon Puppy, not kitty."

Wynn laughed. "You got it. I'll put in a call to Chef Jerome, although I don't hold out much hope. Still, maybe he'll say yes because it's LaVonne."

"All we can do is try. And there are certainly other nice places."

Wynn seemed reluctant to end the conversation. "Katherine."

"Yes."

"Thank you. Hearing my father's message after such a lovely evening put a damper on my Christmas."

"You're welcome."

"Have fun today."

"You, too." She closed her cell and set it back in her purse. Her step seemed to have an extra bounce as she hurried to meet her friends.

Chapter Ten

Saturday afternoon, just back from shopping, K.O. stopped at LaVonne's condo. She rang the doorbell and waited. It took her neighbor an unusually long time to answer; when she did, LaVonne looked dreadful. Her hair was disheveled, and she'd obviously been napping—with at least one cat curled up next to her, since her dark-red sweatshirt was covered in cat hair.

"Why the gloomy face?" K.O. asked. "It's almost Christmas."

"I know," her friend lamented.

"Well, cheer up. I have great news."

"You'd better come inside," LaVonne said without any real enthusiasm. She gestured toward the sofa, although it seemed to require all the energy she possessed just to lift her arm. "Sit down if you want."

"Wouldn't you like to hear my good news?"

LaVonne shrugged her shoulders. "I guess."

"It has to do with you."

"Me?"

"Yup. I met Vickie and Diane at Pacific Place, and we had lunch at this wonderful Italian restaurant."

LaVonne sat across from her, and Martin automatically jumped into her lap. Tom got up on the chair, too, and leisurely stretched out across the arm. She petted both cats with equal fondness.

"I ordered the minestrone soup," K.O. went on to tell her, maintaining her exuberance. "That was when it happened." She'd worked out this plan on her way home, inspired by Wynn's joke about the olives.

"What?"

"I had a psychic impression. Isn't that what you call it? Right there with my two friends in the middle of an Italian restaurant." She paused. "It had to do with romance."

"Really?" LaVonne perked up, but only a little.

"It was in the soup."

"The veggies?"

"No, the crackers," K.O. said and hoped she wasn't carrying this too far. "I crumbled them in the soup and—"

"What did you see?" Then, before K.O. could answer, LaVonne held out one hand. "No, don't tell me, let me guess. It's about you and Wynn," her neighbor said. "It must be."

"No...no. Remember how you told me you don't have the sight when it comes to yourself? Well, apparently I don't, either."

LaVonne looked up from petting her two cats. Her gaze narrowed. "What did you see, then?"

"Like I said, it was about *you*," K.O. said, doing her best to sound excited. "You're going to meet the man of your dreams."

"I am?" She took a moment to consider this before her shoulders drooped once more.

"Yes, you! I saw it plain as anything."

"Human or feline?" LaVonne asked in a skeptical voice.

"Human," K.O. announced triumphantly.

"When?"

"The crackers didn't say exactly, but I felt it must be soon." K.O. didn't want to tell LaVonne too much, otherwise she'd ruin the whole thing. If she went overboard on the details, her friend would suspect K.O. was setting her up. She needed to be vague, but still implant the idea.

"I haven't left my condo all day," LaVonne mumbled, "and I don't plan to go out anytime in the near future. In fact, the way I feel right now, I'm going to be holed up in here all winter."

"You're overreacting."

Her neighbor studied her closely. "Katherine, you *really* saw something in the soup?"

"I did." Nothing psychic, but she wasn't admitting that. She'd seen elbow macaroni and kidney beans and, of course, the cracker crumbs.

"But you didn't take the class. How were you able to discover your psychic powers if you weren't there to hear the lecture from Madam Ozma?" she wanted to know.

K.O. crossed her fingers behind her back. "It must've rubbed off from spending all that time with you."

"You think so?" LaVonne asked hopefully.

"Sure." K.O. was beginning to feel bad about misleading her friend. She'd hoped to mention the invitation for Monday night, but it would be too obvious if she did so now.

"There might be something to it," LaVonne said, smiling for the first time. "You never know."

"True...one never knows."

"Look what happened with you and Wynn," LaVonne said with a glimmer of excitement. "The minute I saw those two raisins gravitate toward each other, I knew it held meaning."

"I could see that in the crackers, too."

This was beginning to sound like a church revival meeting. Any minute, she thought, LaVonne might stand up and shout *Yes, I believe!*

"Then Wynn met you," she burbled on, "and the instant he did, I saw the look in his eyes."

What her neighbor had seen was horror. LaVonne couldn't have known about their confrontation earlier that day. He'd clearly been shocked and, yes, horrified to run into K.O. again. Especially with the memory of her ranting in the café so fresh in his mind.

"You're right," LaVonne said and sat up straighter. "I shouldn't let a silly letter upset me."

"Right. And really, you don't even know how much of what your college friend wrote is strictly true." K.O. remembered the letter she'd written for Bill Mulcahy. Not exactly lies, but not the whole truth, either.

"That could be," LaVonne murmured, but she didn't seem convinced. "Anyway, I know better than to look to a man for happiness." LaVonne was sounding more like her old self. "Happiness comes from within, isn't that right, Martin?" she asked, holding her cat up. Martin dangled from her grasp, mewing plaintively. "I don't need a man to be complete, do I?"

K.O. stood up, gathering her packages as she did. Toys and books for the twins, wrapping paper, a jar of specialty olives.

"Thanks for stopping by," LaVonne said when K.O. started toward the door. "I feel a hundred percent better already."

"Keep your eyes open now," she told LaVonne. "The

man in the soup could be right around the corner." Or on the top floor of their condo building, she added silently.

"I will," her neighbor promised and, still clutching Martin, she shut the door.

Sunday afternoon Wynn came to K.O.'s door at three, his expression morose.

"Cheer up," she urged. "Just how bad can it be?"

"Wait until you meet Moon Puppy. Then you'll know."

"Come on, is your father really *that* bad?"

Wynn sighed deeply. "I suppose not. He's lonely without my mother. At loose ends."

"That's good." She paused, hearing what she'd said. "It's not good that he's lonely, but... Well, you know what I mean." LaVonne might seem all the more attractive to him if he craved female companionship. LaVonne deserved someone who needed her, who would appreciate her and her cats and her...psychic talents.

"You ready?" he asked.

"Let me grab my coat."

"You don't have to do this, you know."

"Wynn, I'm happy to," she assured him, and she meant it.

The airport traffic was snarled, and it took two turns through the short-term parking garage to find an available space. Thankfully they'd allotted plenty of time.

Wynn had agreed to meet his father at baggage claim. No more than five minutes after they'd staked out a place near the luggage carousel, a man wearing a Hawaiian shirt, with long dark hair tied in a ponytail, walked toward them. He didn't have a jacket or coat.

K.O. felt Wynn stiffen.

"Wynn!" The man hurried forward.

Wynn met his father halfway, with K.O. trailing behind,

and briefly hugged him. "Hello, Dad." He put his hand on K.O.'s shoulder. "This is my friend Katherine O'Connor. Katherine, this is my father, Moon Puppy Jeffries."

Moon Puppy winced. "Delighted to meet you, Katherine," he said politely. "But please, call me Max. I don't go by Moon Puppy anymore."

"Welcome to Seattle," K.O. said, shaking hands. "I'm sorry you didn't arrive to sunshine and warmer weather."

"Thank you. Don't worry, I've got a jacket in my bag."

In a few minutes Max had collected his suitcase and Wynn led the way to his car. "It's been unseasonably chilly," K.O. said, making small talk as they took the escalator to the parking garage. Max had retrieved his jacket by then.

At the car, Wynn took the suitcase from his father and stored it in the trunk. This gave K.O. an opportunity to study father and son. She glanced at Wynn and then back at his father. After the description Wynn had given her, she'd expected something quite different. Yes, Max Jeffries looked like an old hippie, as Wynn had said, but his hair was neatly trimmed and combed. He wore clean, pressed clothes and had impeccable manners. He was an older version of Wynn and just as respectable looking, she thought. Well, except for the hair.

"It was a surprise to hear you were coming for Christmas," Wynn commented when he got into the car.

"I figured it would be," his father said. "I didn't mention it earlier because I was afraid you'd find a convenient excuse for me not to come."

So Max Jeffries was direct and honest, too. A lot like his son. K.O. liked him even more.

They chatted on the ride into Seattle, and K.O. casually invited him for cocktails the following afternoon.

"I'd enjoy that," Wynn's father told her.

"Katherine wants to introduce you to her neighbor, La-Vonne."

"I see," Max said with less enthusiasm and quickly changed the subject. "I understand your book is selling nicely."

"Yes, I'm fortunate to have a lot of publisher support."

"He's writing a second book," K.O. said, joining the conversation. It pleased her that Max seemed proud of his son.

"So, how long have you two been seeing each other?" Max asked, looking at K.O.

"Not long," Wynn answered for them. His gaze caught K.O.'s in the rearview mirror. "We met through a psychic," he said.

"We most certainly did not." K.O. was about to argue when she realized Wynn was smiling. "We actually met through a mutual friend who believes she has psychic powers," she explained, not telling Max that her neighbor and this "psychic" were one and the same.

As they exited off the freeway and headed into downtown Seattle and toward Blossom Street, Max said, "I had no idea Seattle was this beautiful."

"Oh, just wait until nighttime," K.O. told him. It was fast becoming dark, and city lights had begun to sparkle. "There's lots to do at night. Wynn and I took a horse-drawn carriage ride last week and then on Friday night we went on a merry-go-round."

"My first such experience," Wynn said, a smile quivering at the edges of his mouth.

"Your mother and I never took you?" Max sounded incredulous.

"Never."

"I know I had some failings as a father," Max said despondently.

"Not getting to ride on a merry-go-round isn't exactly a big deal, Dad. Don't worry about it," Wynn muttered.

That seemed to ease his father's mind. "So what's on the agenda for tomorrow?" he asked brightly.

Wynn cast K.O. a look as if to say he'd told her so.

"I can take you on a tour of Pike Place Market," K.O. offered.

"That would be great." Max thanked her with a warm smile. "I was hoping to get a chance to go up the Space Needle while I'm here, too."

"We can do that on Tuesday."

Max nodded. "Do you have any free time, Wynn?" he asked.

"Some," Wynn admitted with obvious reluctance. "But not much. In addition to my appointments and writing schedule, I'm still doing promotion for my current book."

"Of course," Max murmured.

K.O. detected a note of sadness in his voice and wanted to reassure him. Unfortunately she didn't know how.

Chapter Eleven

Wynn phoned K.O. early Monday morning. "I don't think this is going to work," he whispered.

"Pardon?" K.O. strained to hear.

"Meet me at the French Café," he said, his voice only slightly louder.

"When?" She had her sweats on and was ready to tackle her treadmill. After shedding the two pounds, she'd gained them again. It wasn't much, but enough to send her racing for a morning workout. She knew how quickly these things could get out of control.

"Now," he said impatiently. "Want me to pick you up?"

"No. I'll meet you there in ten minutes."

By the time she entered the café, Wynn had already purchased two cups of coffee and procured a table. "What's wrong?" she asked as she pulled out the chair.

"He's driving me insane!"

"Wynn, I like your father. You made him sound worse than a deadbeat dad, but he's obviously proud of you and—"

"Do you mind if we don't list his admirable qualities

just now?" He brought one hand to his temple, as if warding off a headache.

"All right," she said, doing her best to understand.

"The reason I called is that I don't think it's a good idea to set him up with LaVonne."

"Why not?" K.O. thought her plan was brilliant. She had everything worked out in her mind; she'd bought the liquor and intended to dust and vacuum this afternoon. As far as she was concerned, the meeting of Max and LaVonne was destiny. Christmas romances were always the best.

"Dad isn't ready for another relationship," Wynn declared. "He's still mourning my mother."

"Shouldn't he be the one to decide that?" Wynn might be a renowned child psychologist but she believed everyone was entitled to make his or her own decisions, especially in matters of the heart. She considered it all right to lend a helping hand, however. That was fair.

"I can tell my father's not ready," Wynn insisted.

"But I invited him for drinks this evening and he accepted." It looked as if her entire day was going to be spent with Max Jeffries, aka Moon Puppy. Earlier she'd agreed to take him to Pike Place Market, which was a must-see for anyone visiting Seattle. It was always an entertaining place for tourists, but never more so than during the holiday season. The whole market had an air of festivity, the holiday mood infectious.

"What about LaVonne?" he asked.

"I'll give her a call later." K.O. hadn't wanted to be obvious about this meeting. Still, when LaVonne met Max, she'd know, the same way Wynn and K.O. had known, that they were being set up.

"Don't," he said, cupping the coffee mug with both hands.

"Why not?"

He frowned. "I have a bad feeling about this."

K.O. smothered a giggle. "Are you telling me you've found your own psychic powers?"

"Hardly," he snorted.

"Wynn," she said, covering his hand with hers in a gesture of reassurance. "It's going to work out fine, trust me." Hmm. She seemed to be saying that a lot these days.

He exhaled slowly, as if it went against his better judgment to agree. "All right, do whatever you think is best."

"I've decided to simplify things. I'm serving eggnog and cookies." And olives, if anyone wanted them. When she'd find time to bake she didn't know, but K.O. was determined to do this properly.

"Come around five-thirty," she suggested.

"That early?"

"Yes. You're taking care of arranging their dinner, right?"

"Ah... I don't think they'll get that far."

"But they might," she said hopefully. "You make the reservation, and if they don't want to go, then we will. Okay?"

He nodded. "I'll see what I can do." Wynn took one last swallow of coffee and stood. "I've got to get to the office." Slipping into his overcoat, he confided, "I have a patient this morning. Emergency call."

K.O. wondered what kind of emergency that would be— an ego that needed splinting? A bruised id? But she knew better than to ask. "Have a good day," was all she said. In his current mood, that was an iffy proposition. K.O. couldn't help wondering what Max had done to upset him.

"You, too," he murmured, then added, "And thank you for looking after Moon Puppy."

"His name is Max," K.O. reminded him.

"Maybe to you, but to me he'll always be the hippie surfer bum I grew up with." Wynn hurried out of the café.

By five that afternoon, K.O. felt as if she'd never left the treadmill. After walking for forty minutes on her machine, she showered, baked and decorated three dozen cookies and then met Wynn's father for a whirlwind tour of the Seattle waterfront, starting with Pike Place. She phoned LaVonne from the Seattle Aquarium. LaVonne had instantly agreed to drinks, and K.O. had a hard time getting off the phone. LaVonne chatted excitedly about the man in the soup, the man K.O. had claimed to see with her "psychic" eyes. Oh, dear, maybe this had gone a little too far....

Max was interested in absolutely everything, so they didn't get back to Blossom Street until after four, which gave K.O. very little time to prepare for *the meeting.*

She vacuumed and dusted and plumped up the sofa pillows and set out a dish of peppermint candies, a favorite of LaVonne's. The decorated sugar cookies were arranged on a special Santa plate. K.O. didn't particularly like sugar cookies, which, therefore, weren't as tempting as shortbread or chocolate chip would've been. She decided against the olives.

K.O. was stirring the rum into the eggnog when she saw the blinking light on her phone. A quick check told her it was Zelda. She didn't have even a minute to chat and told herself she'd return the call later.

Precisely at 5:30 p.m., just after she'd put on all her Christmas CDs, Wynn arrived without his father. "Where's your dad?" K.O. demanded as she accepted the bottle of wine he handed her.

"He's never on time if there's an excuse to be late,"

Wynn muttered. "He'll get here when he gets here. You noticed he doesn't wear a watch?"

K.O. had noticed and thought it a novelty. LaVonne wasn't known for her punctuality, either, so they had at least that much in common. Already this relationship revealed promise—in her opinion, anyway.

"How did your afternoon go?" Wynn asked. He sat down on the sofa and reached for a cookie, nodding his head to the tempo of "Jingle Bell Rock."

"Great. I enjoyed getting to know your father."

Wynn glanced up, giving her a skeptical look.

"What is it with you two?" she asked gently, sitting beside him.

Wynn sighed. "I didn't have a happy childhood, except for the time I spent with my grandparents. I resented being dragged hither and yon, based on where the best surf could be found. I hated living with a bunch of self-absorbed hippies whenever we returned to the commune, which was their so-called home base. For a good part of my life, I had the feeling I was a hindrance my father tolerated."

"Oh, Wynn." The unhappiness he still felt was at odds with the amusing stories he'd told about his childhood at Chez Jerome and during dinner with Vickie and John. She'd originally assumed that he was reflecting his own upbringing in his "Free Child" theories, but she now saw that wasn't the case. Moon Puppy Max might have been a hippie, but he'd imposed his own regimen on his son. Not much "freedom" there.

"Well, that's my life," he said stiffly. "I don't want my father here and I dislike the way he's using you and—"

"He's not using me."

He opened his mouth to argue, but apparently changed his mind. "I'm not going to let my father come between us."

"Good, because I'd feel terrible if that happened." This would be a near-perfect relationship—if it wasn't for the fact that he was Wynn Jeffries, author of *The Free Child.* And the fact that he hadn't forgiven his father, who'd been a selfish and irresponsible parent.

His eyes softened. "I won't let it." He kissed her then, and K.O. slipped easily into his embrace. He wrapped his arms around her and they exchanged a series of deep and probing kisses that left K.O.'s head reeling.

"Katherine." Wynn breathed harshly as he abruptly released her.

She didn't want him to stop.

"You'd better answer your door," he advised.

K.O. had been so consumed by their kisses that she hadn't heard the doorbell. "Oh," she breathed, shaking her head to clear away the fog of longing. This man did things to her heart—not to mention the rest of her—that even a romance novelist couldn't describe.

Wynn's father stood on the other side of the door, wearing another Hawaiian flowered shirt, khaki pants and flip-flops. From the way he'd dressed, he could be on a tropical isle rather than in Seattle with temperatures hovering just above freezing. K.O. could tell that Max's choice of clothes irritated Wynn, but to his credit, Wynn didn't comment.

Too bad the current Christmas song was "Rudolph," instead of "Mele Kaliki Maka."

K.O. welcomed him and had just poured his eggnog when the doorbell chimed again. Ah, the moment she'd been waiting for. Her friend had arrived. K.O. glided toward the door and swept it open as if anticipating Santa himself.

"LaVonne," she said, leaning forward to kiss her friend's cheek. "How good of you to come." Her neighbor had brought Tom with her. The oversize feline was draped over her arm like a large furry purse.

"This is so kind of you," LaVonne said. She looked startled at seeing Max.

"Come in, please," K.O. said, gesturing her inside. She realized how formal she sounded—like a character in an old drawing room comedy. "Allow me to introduce Wynn's father, Max Jeffries. Max, this is LaVonne Young."

Max stood and backed away from LaVonne. "You have a cat on your arm."

"This is Tom," LaVonne said. She glanced down lovingly at the cat as she stepped into the living room. "Would you like to say hello?" She held Tom out, but Max shook his head adamantly.

By now he'd backed up against the wall. "I don't like cats."

"What?" She sounded shocked. "Cats are magical creatures."

"Maybe to you they are," the other man protested. "I don't happen to be a cat person."

Wynn shared an I-told-you-so look with K.O.

"May I get you some eggnog?" K.O. asked, hoping to rescue the evening from a less-than-perfect beginning.

"Please," LaVonne answered just as "Have Yourself a Merry Little Christmas" began.

Eager for something to do, K.O. hurried into the kitchen and grabbed the pitcher of eggnog.

She heard Tom hiss loudly and gulped down some of her own eggnog to relax.

"Your cat doesn't like me," Max said as he carefully approached the sofa.

"Oh, don't be silly. Tom's the friendly one."

"You mean you have *more* than one?"

"Dad," Wynn said, "why don't you sit down and make yourself comfortable. You're quite safe. Tom is very well-behaved."

"I don't like cats," Max reiterated.

"Tom is gentle and loving," LaVonne said.

Max slowly approached the sofa. "Then why is he hissing at me?"

"He senses your dislike," LaVonne explained. She gave Max a dazzling smile. "Pet him, and he'll be your friend for life."

"See, Dad?" Wynn walked over to LaVonne, who sat with Tom on her lap. He ran his hand down Tom's back and the tabby purred with pleasure.

"He likes you," Max said.

"He'll like you, too, as soon as you pet him." LaVonne was still smiling happily, stroking the cat's head.

Max came a bit closer. "You live in the building?" he asked, making his way, step by careful step, toward La-Vonne.

"Just across the hall," she answered.

"Your husband, too?"

"I'm single. Do you enjoy cards? Because you're welcome to stop by anytime."

K.O. delivered the eggnog. This was going even better than she'd hoped. Max was already interested and LaVonne was issuing invitations. She recognized the gleam in the other man's eyes. A sense of triumph filled her and she cast a glance in Wynn's direction. Wynn was just reaching into his pocket, withdrawing a real-looking catnip mouse.

Relaxed now, Max leaned forward to pet Tom.

At that very moment, chaos broke out. Although La-Vonne claimed she'd never known Tom to take a dislike to anyone, the cat clearly detested Max. Before anyone could react, he sprang from her lap and grabbed Max's bare arm. The cat's claws dug in, drawing blood. He wasn't about to let go, either.

"Get him off," Max screamed, thrashing his arm to and fro in an effort to free himself from the cat-turned-killer. Wynn was desperately—and futilely—trying to distract Tom by waving the toy mouse. It didn't help.

"Tom, Tom!" LaVonne screeched at the top of her lungs. Blood spurted onto the carpet.

In a panic, Max pulled at Tom's fur. The cat then sank his teeth into Max's hand and Max yelped in pain.

"Don't hurt my cat," LaVonne shrieked.

Frozen to the spot, K.O. watched in horror as the scene unfolded. Wynn dropped the mouse, and if not for his quick action, K.O. didn't know what would have happened. Before she could fully comprehend how he'd done it, Wynn had disentangled Tom from his father's arm. LaVonne instantly took her beloved cat into her embrace and cradled him against her side.

At the sight of his own blood, Max looked like he was about to pass out. K.O. hurriedly got him a clean towel, shocked at the amount of blood. The scratches seemed deep. "Call 911," Max shouted.

Wynn pulled out his cell phone. "That might not be a bad idea," he said to K.O. "Cat scratches can get infected."

"Contact the authorities, too," Max added, glaring at LaVonne. He stretched out his good arm and pointed at her. "I want that woman arrested and her animal destroyed."

LaVonne cried out with alarm and hovered protectively over Tom. "My poor kitty," she whispered.

"You're worried about the *cat?*" Max said. "I'm bleeding to death and you're worried about your cat?"

Wynn replaced his phone. "The medics are on their way."

"Oh...good." K.O. could already hear sirens in the background. She turned off her CD player. Thinking she should open the lobby door, she left the apartment, and when the aid car arrived, she directed the paramedics. Things had gotten worse in the short time she was gone. Max and LaVonne were shouting at each other as the small living room filled with people. Curious onlookers crowded the hallway outside her door.

"My cat scratched him and I'm sorry, but he provoked Tom," LaVonne said stubbornly.

"I want that woman behind bars." Max stabbed his finger in LaVonne's direction.

"Sir, sir, we need you to settle down," instructed the paramedic who was attempting to take his blood pressure.

"While she's in jail, declaw her cat," Max threw in.

Wynn stepped up behind K.O. "Yup," he whispered. "This is a match made in heaven, all right."

Then, just when K.O. was convinced nothing more could go wrong, her phone started to ring.

Chapter Twelve

Don't you think you should answer that?" the paramedic treating Max's injuries asked.

K.O. was too upset to move. The romantic interlude she'd so carefully plotted couldn't have gone worse. At least Wynn seemed to understand her distress.

"I'll get it," Wynn said, and strode into the kitchen. "O'Connor residence," he said. At the way his eyes instantly shot to her, K.O. regretted not answering the phone herself.

"It's your sister," he said, holding the phone away from his ear.

Even above the racket K.O. could hear Zelda's high-pitched excitement. Her idol, Dr. Wynn Jeffries, had just spoken to her. The last person K.O. wanted to deal with just then was her younger sister. However, she couldn't subject Wynn to Zelda's adoration.

She took the phone, but even before she had a chance to speak, Zelda was shrieking, "Is it *really* you, Dr. Jeffries? Really and truly?"

"Actually, no," K.O. informed her sister. "It's me."

"But Dr. Jeffries is with you?"

"Yes."

"Keep him there!"

"I beg your pardon?"

"Don't let him leave," Zelda said, sounding even more excited. "I'm calling on my cell. I'm only a few minutes away." She took a deep breath. "I need to talk to him. It's urgent. Zach and I just had the biggest argument *ever,* and I need to talk to Dr. Jeffries."

"Zelda," K.O. cut in. "Now is not the best time for you to visit."

"Didn't you hear me?" her sister cried. "This is an emergency."

With that, the phone went dead. Groaning, K.O. replaced the receiver.

"Is something wrong?" Wynn asked as he stepped around the paramedic who was still looking after Max.

"It's Zelda. She wants—no, *needs*—to talk to you. According to her it's an emergency." K.O. felt the need to warn him. "She's already on her way."

"Now? You mean she's coming now?"

K.O. nodded. "Apparently so." Zelda hadn't mentioned what this argument with Zach was about. Three guesses said it had to do with Christmas and Wynn's theories. Oh, great. Her sister was arriving at the scene of a disaster.

"Are you taking him to the h-hospital?" LaVonne sobbed, covering her mouth with both hands.

"It's just a precaution," the medic answered. "A doctor needs to look at those scratches."

"Not that dreadful man!" LaVonne cried, pointing at Max. "I'm talking about my cat."

"Oh." The paramedic glanced at his companion. "Unfortunately, in instances such as this, we're obliged to notify Animal Control."

"You're hauling my Tom to…jail?"

"Quarantine," he told her gently.

For a moment LaVonne seemed about to faint. Wynn put his arm around the older woman's shoulders and led her to the sofa so she could sit down. "This can't be happening," LaVonne wailed. "I can't believe this is happening to my Tom."

"Your cat should be—"

Wynn cast his father a look meaningful enough to silence the rest of whatever Max had planned to say.

"I'm going to be scarred for life," Max shouted. "I just hope you've got good insurance, because you're going to pay for this. And you're going to pay big."

"Don't you dare threaten me!" LaVonne had recovered enough to shout back.

With his arm stretched out in front of him, Max Jeffries followed the paramedic out of the condo and past the crowd of tenants who'd gathered in the hallway outside K.O.'s door.

"That…that terrible man just threatened me," LaVonne continued. "Tom's never attacked anyone like this before."

"Please, please, let me through."

K.O. heard her sister's voice.

Meanwhile LaVonne was weeping loudly. "My poor Tom. My poor, poor Tom. What will become of him?"

"What on earth is going on here?" Zelda demanded as she made her way into the apartment. The second paramedic was gathering up his equipment and getting ready to leave. The blood-soaked towels K.O. had wrapped around Max's arm were on the floor. The scene was completely chaotic and Zelda's arrival only added to the mayhem.

"Your f-father wants to s-sue me," LaVonne stuttered,

pleading with Wynn. "*Do* something. Promise me you'll talk to him."

Wynn sat next to LaVonne and tried to comfort her. "I'll do what I can," he said. "I'm sure that once my father's settled down he'll listen to reason."

LaVonne's eyes widened, as though she had trouble believing Wynn. "I don't mean to insult you, but your father doesn't seem like a reasonable man to me."

"Whose blood is that?" Zelda asked, hands on her hips as she surveyed the room.

K.O. tried to waylay her sister. "As you can see," she said, gesturing about her, "this *really* isn't a good time to visit."

"I don't care," Zelda insisted. "I need to talk to Dr. Jeffries." She thrust his book at him and a pen. "Could you sign this for me?"

Just then a man wearing a jacket that identified him as an Animal Control officer came in, holding an animal carrier. The name Walt was embroidered on his shirt.

Wynn quickly signed his name, all the while watching the man from Animal Control.

LaVonne took one look at Walt and burst into tears. She buried her face in her hands and started to rock back and forth.

"Where's the cat?" Walt asked.

"We've got him in the bathroom," the paramedic said.

"Please don't hurt him," LaVonne wept. "Please, please…"

Walt raised a reassuring hand. "I handle situations like this every day. Don't worry, Miss, I'll be gentle with your pet."

"Dr. Jeffries, Dr. Jeffries." Zelda slipped past K.O. and climbed over LaVonne's knees in order to reach Wynn. She plunked herself down on the coffee table, facing him. "I really do need to talk to you."

"Zelda!" K.O. was shocked by her sister's audacity.

"Zach and I never argue," Zelda said over her shoulder, glaring at K.O. as if that fact alone should explain her actions. "This will only take a few minutes, I promise. Once I talk to Dr. Jeffries, I'll be able to tell Zach what he said and then he'll understand."

LaVonne wailed as Walt entered the bathroom.

K.O. heard a hiss and wondered if her shower curtain was now in shreds. She'd never seen a cat react to anyone the way Tom had to Wynn's father. Even now she couldn't figure out what had set him off.

"This'll only take a minute," Zelda went on. "You see, my husband and I read your book, and it changed everything. Well, to be perfectly honest, I don't know if Zach read the whole book." A frown crossed her face.

"LaVonne, perhaps I should take you home now," K.O. suggested, thinking it might be best for her neighbor not to see Tom leave the building caged.

"I can't leave," LaVonne said. "Not until I know what's happening to Tom."

The bathroom door opened and Walt reappeared with Tom safely inside the cat carrier.

"Tom, oh, Tom," LaVonne wailed, throwing her arms wide.

"Dr. Jeffries, Dr. Jeffries," Zelda pleaded, vying for his attention.

"Zelda, couldn't this wait a few minutes?" K.O. asked.

"Where are you taking Tom?" LaVonne demanded.

"We're just going to put him in quarantine," Walt said in a soothing voice.

"Tom's had all his shots. My veterinarian will verify everything you need to know."

"Good. Still, we're legally required to do this. I guarantee he'll be well looked after."

"Thank you," K.O. said, relieved.

"Can I speak to Dr. Jeffries now?" Zelda asked impatiently. "You see, I don't think my husband really did read your book," she continued, picking up where she'd left off. "If he had, we wouldn't be having this disagreement."

"I'll see LaVonne home," K.O. said. She closed one arm around her friend's waist and steered her out of the condo.

Wynn looked at Zelda and sent K.O. a beseeching glance.

"I'll be back as soon as I can," she promised.

He nodded and mouthed the word *hurry*.

K.O. rolled her eyes. As she escorted LaVonne, the sound of her sister's voice followed her into the hallway, which was fortunately deserted. It didn't take long to get LaVonne settled in her own place. Once she had Phillip and Martin with her, she was comforted, since both seemed to recognize her distress and lavished their mistress with affection.

When she returned to her condo, K.O. found that her sister hadn't moved. She still sat on the coffee table, so close to Wynn that their knees touched. Judging by the speed with which Zelda spoke, K.O. doubted he'd had a chance to get a word in edgewise.

"Then the girls started to cry," Zelda was saying. "They want a Christmas tree and Zach thinks we should get one."

"I don't believe—" Wynn was cut off before he could finish his thought.

"I know you don't actually condemn Christmas trees, but I didn't want to encourage the girls about this Santa thing, and I feel decorating a tree would do that. If we're going to bury Santa under the sleigh—and I'm in complete agreement with you, Dr. Jeffries—then it makes sense to downplay everything else having to do with Christmas, too. Certainly all the commercial aspects. But how do I handle the girls' reaction when they hear their friends talking about Santa?"

Wynn raised a finger, indicating that he'd like to comment. His request, however, was ignored.

"I feel as you do," Zelda rushed on breathlessly, bringing one hand to her chest in a gesture of sincerity. "It's wrong to mislead one's children with figures of fantasy. It's wrong, wrong, wrong. Zach agreed with me—but only in principle, as it turns out. Then we got into this big fight over the Christmas tree and you have to understand that my husband and I hardly ever argue, so this is all very serious."

"Where's Zach now?" K.O. asked, joining Wynn on the sofa.

As if to let her know how much he appreciated having her back, Wynn reached for her hand. At Zelda's obvious interest, he released it, but the contact, brief as it was, reassured her.

Zelda lowered her head. "Zach's at home with the girls. If you must know, I sort of left my husband with the twins."

"Zoe and Zara," K.O. said under her breath for Wynn's benefit.

"Despite my strong feelings on the matter, I suspect my husband is planning to take our daughters out to purchase a Christmas tree." She paused. "A *giant* one."

"Do you think he might even decorate it with Santa figurines and reindeer?" K.O. asked, pretending to be scandalized.

"Oh, I hope not," Zelda cried. "That would ruin everything I've tried so hard to institute in our family."

"As I recall," Wynn finally said. He waited a moment as if to gauge whether now was a good time to insert his opinions. When no one interrupted him, he continued. "I didn't say anything in my book against Christmas trees, giant or otherwise."

"Yes, I know that, but it seems to me—"

"It seems to *me* that you've carried this a bit further than advisable," Wynn said gently. "Despite what you and K.O. think, I don't want to take Christmas away from your children or from you and your husband. It's a holiday to be celebrated. Family and traditions are important."

K.O. agreed with him. She felt gratified that there was common ground between them, an opinion on which they could concur. Nearly everything she'd heard about Wynn to this point had come from her sister. K.O. was beginning to wonder if Zelda was taking his advice to extremes.

"Besides," he said, "there's a fundamental contradiction in your approach. You're correct to minimize the element of fantasy—but your children are telling you what they want, aren't they? And you're ignoring that."

K.O. wanted to cheer. She took Wynn's hand again, and this time he didn't let go.

"By the way," Zelda said, looking from Wynn to K.O. and staring pointedly at their folded hands. "Just when did you two start dating?"

"I told you—"

"What you said," her sister broke in, "was that Dr. Jeffries lived in the same building as you."

"I told you we went to dinner a couple of times."

"You most certainly did not." Zelda stood up, an irritated expression on her face. "Well, okay, you did mention the one dinner at Chez Jerome."

"Did you know that I'm planning to join Katherine this Friday when she's watching the twins?" Wynn asked.

"She's bringing you along?" Zelda's eyes grew round with shock. "You might've said something to me," she burst out, clearly upset with K.O.

"I thought I had told you."

"You haven't talked to me in days," Zelda wailed. "It's like I'm not even your sister anymore. The last I heard, you were going to get Dr. Jeffries's autograph for me, and you didn't, although I specifically asked if you would."

"Would you prefer I not watch the twins?" Wynn inquired.

"Oh, no! It would be an honor," Zelda assured him, smiling, her voice warm and friendly. She turned to face K.O. again, her eyes narrowed. "But my own sister," she hissed, "should've told me she intended on having a famous person spend the night in my home."

"You're not to tell anyone," K.O. insisted.

Zelda glared at her. "Fine. I won't."

"Promise me," K.O. said. Wynn was entitled to his privacy; the last thing he needed was a fleet of parents in SUVs besieging him about his book.

"I promise." Without a further word, Zelda grabbed her purse and made a hasty exit.

"Zelda!" K.O. called after her. "I think we need to talk about this for a minute."

"I don't have a minute. I need to get home to my husband and children. We'll talk later," Zelda said in an ominous tone, and then she was gone.

Chapter Thirteen

I'd better leave now, as well," Wynn announced, getting his coat. "Dad'll need me to drive him back from the emergency room." K.O. was glad he didn't seem eager to go.

For her part, she wanted him to stay. Her nerves were frayed. Nothing had worked out as she'd planned and now everyone was upset with her. LaVonne, her dear friend, was inconsolable. Zelda was annoyed that K.O. hadn't kept her updated on the relationship with Wynn. Max Jeffries was just plain angry, and while the brunt of his anger had been directed at LaVonne, K.O. realized he wasn't pleased with her, either. Now Wynn had to go. Reluctantly K.O. walked him to the door. "Let me know how your father's doing, okay?" she asked, looking up at him.

"Of course." Wynn placed his hands on her shoulders. "You know I'd much rather be here with you."

She saw the regret in his eyes and didn't want to make matters worse. "Thank you for being so wonderful," she said and meant it. Wynn had been the voice of calm and reason throughout this entire ordeal.

"I'll call you about my father as soon as I hear."

"Thank you."

After a brief hug, he hurried out the door.

After a dinner of eggnog and peanut butter on crackers, K.O. waited up until after midnight, but no word came. Finally, when she couldn't keep her eyes open any longer, she climbed between the sheets and fell instantly asleep. This surprised her; she hadn't anticipated sleeping easily or well. When she woke the following morning, the first thoughts that rushed into her mind were of Wynn. Something must have happened, something unexpected and probably dreadful, or he would've called.

Perhaps the hospital had decided to keep Max overnight for observation. While there'd been a lot of blood involved, K.O. didn't think any of the cuts were deep enough to require stitches. But if Max had filed a police report, that would cause problems for LaVonne and might explain Wynn's silence. Every scenario that roared through her head pointed to trouble.

Even before she made her first cup of coffee, K.O.'s stomach was in knots. As she headed into the kitchen, she discovered a sealed envelope that had been slipped under her door.

It read:

Katherine,
I didn't get back from the hospital until late and I was afraid you'd already gone to bed. Dad's home and, other than being cantankerous, he's doing fine, so don't worry on his account. The hospital cleaned and bandaged his arm and said he'd be good as new in a week or so. Please reassure LaVonne. The cuts looked worse than they actually were.
Could you stop by my office this afternoon? I'm at

*the corner of Fourth and Willow, Suite 1110. Does one
o'clock work for you? If you can't fit it into your schedule, please contact my assistant and let her know. Otherwise, I'll look forward to seeing you, then.*
Wynn

Oh, she could fit it in. She could *definitely* fit it in. K.O.
was ready to climb Mount Rainier for a chance to see
Wynn. With purpose now, she showered and dressed and
then, on the off chance Max might need something, she
phoned Wynn's condo.

His father answered right away, which made her wonder if he'd been sitting next to the phone waiting for a call.

"Good morning," she said, striving to sound cheerful
and upbeat—all the while hoping Max wasn't one to hold
grudges.

"Who is this?"

"It's K.O.," she told him, her voice faltering despite her
effort to maintain a cheery tone.

He hesitated as if he needed time to place who she might
be. "Oh," he finally said. "The woman from downstairs.
The woman whose *friend* caused me irreparable distress."
After another pause, he said, "I'm afraid I might be suffering from trauma-induced amnesia."

"Excuse me?" K.O. was sure she'd misunderstood.

"I was attacked yesterday by a possibly rabid beast and
am fortunate to be alive. I don't remember much after that vicious animal sank its claws into my arm," he added shakily.

K.O. closed her eyes for a moment. "I'm so sorry to
hear that," she said, going along with it. "But the hospital
released you, I see."

"Yes." This was said with disdain; apparently, he felt the

medical profession had made a serious error in judgment. "I'm on heavy pain medication."

"Oh, dear."

"I don't know where my son's gone," he muttered fretfully.

If Wynn hadn't told his father he was at the office, then K.O. wasn't about to, either. She suspected Wynn had good reason to escape.

"Since you live in the building…" Max began.

"Uh…" She could see it coming. Max wanted her to sit and hold his uninjured hand for the rest of the day.

"I do, but unfortunately I'm on my way out."

"Oh."

It took K.O. a few more minutes to wade through the guilt he was shoveling in her direction. "I'll drop by and check on you later," she promised.

"Thank you," he said, ending their conversation with a groan, a last shovelful of guilt.

K.O. hung up the phone, groaning, too. This was even worse than she'd imagined and she had a fine imagination. Max was obviously playing this incident for all it was worth. Irreparable distress. Rabid beast. Trauma-induced amnesia! Oh, brother.

Wanting to leave before Max decided to drop by, she hurried out the door and stopped at the French Café for a mocha and bran muffin. If ever she'd deserved one, it was now. At the rate her life was going, there wouldn't be enough peppermint mochas in the world to see her through another day like yesterday.

Rather than linger as she normally did, K.O. took her drink and muffin to go and enjoyed a leisurely stroll down Blossom Street. A walk would give her exercise and clear her mind, and just then clarity was what she needed. She admired the evergreen boughs and garlands decorating the storefronts, and the inventive variations on Christmas themes in every window. The weather remained unseasonably cold with a chance of snow flurries. In December Seattle was usually in the grip of gloomy winter rains, but that hadn't happened yet this year. The sky was already a clear blue with puffy clouds scattered about.

By the time she'd finished her peppermint mocha, K.O. had walked a good mile and felt refreshed in both body and mind. When she entered her building, LaVonne—wearing a housecoat—was stepping out of her condo to grab the morning paper. Her eyes were red and puffy and it looked as if she hadn't slept all night. She bent over to retrieve her paper.

"LaVonne," K.O. called out.

Her friend slowly straightened. "I thought I should see if there's a report in the police blotter about Tom scratching that...that man," she spat out.

"I doubt it."

"Is he...back from the hospital?"

"Max Jeffries is alive and well. He sustained a few scratches, but it isn't nearly as bad as we all feared." Wynn's father seemed to be under the delusion that he'd narrowly escaped with his life, but she didn't feel the need to mention that. Nor did K.O. care to enlighten LaVonne regarding Max's supposed amnesia.

"I'm so glad." LaVonne sounded tired and sad.

"Is there anything I can get you?" K.O. asked, feeling partially to blame.

"Thanks for asking, but I'm fine." She gave a shuddering sob. "Except for poor Tom being in jail..."

"Call if you need me," K.O. said before she returned to her own apartment.

The rest of the morning passed quickly. She worked

for a solid two hours and accomplished more in that brief time than she normally did in four. She finished a medical report, sent off some résumés by email and drafted a Christmas letter for a woman in Zach's office who'd made a last-minute request. Then, deciding she should check on Max Jeffries, she went up for a quick visit. At twelve-thirty, she grabbed her coat and headed out the door again. With her hands buried deep in her red wool coat and a candy-cane striped scarf doubled around her neck, she walked to Wynn's office.

This was her first visit there, and she wasn't sure what to expect. When she stepped inside, she found a comfortable waiting room and thought it looked like any doctor's office.

A middle-aged receptionist glanced up and smiled warmly. "You must be Katherine," she said, extending her hand. "I'm Lois Church, Dr. Jeffries's assistant."

"Hello," K.O. said, returning her smile.

"Come on back. Doctor is waiting for you." Lois led her to a large room, lined with bookshelves and framed degrees. A big desk dominated one end, and there was a sitting area on the other side, complete with a miniature table and chairs and a number of toys.

Wynn stood in front of the bookcase, and when K.O. entered the room, he closed the volume he'd been reading and put it back in place.

Lois slipped quietly out of the room and shut the door.

"Hi," K.O. said tentatively, wondering at his mood.

He smiled. "I see you received my note."

"Yes," she said with a nod. She remained standing just inside his office.

"I asked you to come here to talk about my father. I'm afraid he's going a little overboard with all of this."

"I got that impression myself."

Wynn arched his brows. "You've spoken to him?"

She nodded again. "I stopped by to see how he's doing. He didn't seem to remember me right away. He says he's suffering from memory loss."

Wynn groaned.

"I hate to say this, but I assumed that hypochondria's what he's really suffering from." She paused. "Either that or he's faking it," she said boldly.

Wynn gave a dismissive shrug. "I believe your second diagnosis is correct. It's a recurring condition of his," he said with a wry smile.

K.O. didn't know quite what to say.

"He's exaggerating, looking for attention." Wynn motioned for her to sit down, which she did, sinking into the luxurious leather sofa. Wynn took the chair next to it. "I don't mean to sound unsympathetic, but for all his easygoing hippie ways, Moon Puppy—Max—can be quite the manipulator."

"Well, it's not like LaVonne did it on purpose or anything."

There was a moment's silence. "In light of what happened yesterday, do you still want me to accompany you to your sister's?" he asked.

K.O. would be terribly disappointed if he'd experienced a change of heart. "I hoped you would, but if you need to bow out because of your father, I understand."

"No," he said decisively. "I want to do this. It's important for us both, for our relationship."

K.O. felt the same way.

"I've already told my father that I have a business appointment this weekend, so he knows I'll be away."

That made K.O. smile. This *was* business. Sort of.

"I'd prefer that Max not know the two of us will be together. He'll want to join us and, frankly, dealing with him will be more work than taking care of the kids."

"All right." Despite a bit of residual guilt, K.O. was certainly willing to abide by his wishes. She was convinced that once Wynn spent time with Zoe and Zara, he'd know for himself that his theories didn't work. The twins and their outrageous behavior would speak more eloquently than she ever could.

"I'm afraid we might not have an opportunity to get together for the rest of the week."

She was unhappy about it but understood. With his injuries and need for attention, Max would dominate Wynn's time.

"Are you sure your father will be well enough by Friday for you to leave?" she asked.

"He'd better be," Wynn said firmly, "because I'm going. He'll survive. In case you hadn't already figured this out, he's a little...immature."

"Really?" she asked, feigning surprise. Then she laughed out loud.

Wynn smiled, too. "I'm going to miss you, Katherine," he said with a sigh. "I wish I could see you every day this week, but between work and Max..."

"I'll miss you, too."

Wynn checked his watch and K.O. realized that was her signal to go. Wynn had appointments.

They both stood.

"Before I forget," he said casually. "A friend of mine told me his company's looking for a publicist. It's a small publisher, Apple Blossom Books, right in the downtown area, not far from here."

"They are?" K.O.'s heart raced with excitement. A small publishing company would be ideal. "Really?"

"I mentioned your name, and Larry asked if you'd be willing to send in a résumé." Wynn picked up a business card from his desk and handed it to her. "You can email it directly to him."

"Oh, Wynn, thank you." In her excitement, she hugged him.

That seemed to be all the encouragement he needed to keep her in his arms and kiss her. She responded with equal fervor, and it made her wonder how she could possibly go another three days until she saw him again.

They smiled at each other. Wynn threaded his fingers through her hair and brought his mouth to hers for another, deeper kiss.

A polite knock at the door was followed by the sound of it opening.

Abruptly Wynn released her, taking a step back. "Yes, Lois," he said, still looking at K.O.

"Your one-thirty appointment has arrived."

"I'll be ready in just a minute," he said. As soon as the door was shut, he leaned close, touching his forehead to hers. "I'd better get back to work."

"Me, too." But it was with real reluctance that they drew apart.

As K.O. left, glancing at the surly teen being ushered into his office, she felt that Friday couldn't come soon enough.

Chapter Fourteen

On Thursday afternoon, LaVonne invited K.O. for afternoon tea, complete with a plate of sliced fruitcake. "I'm feeling much better," her neighbor said as she poured tea into mugs decorated with cats in Santa costumes. "I've been allowed to visit Tom, and he's doing so well. In a couple of days, he'll be back home where he belongs." She frowned as if remembering Wynn's father. "No thanks to that dreadful man who had Tom taken away from me."

K.O. sat on the sofa and held her mug in one hand and a slice of fruitcake in the other. "I'm so pleased to hear Tom will be home soon." Her conscience had been bothering her, and for the sake of their friendship, K.O. felt the need to confess what she'd done.

"The best part is I haven't seen that maniac all week," LaVonne was saying.

K.O. gave her neighbor a tentative smile and lowered her gaze. She hadn't seen Max, either. Or Wynn, except for that brief visit to his office, although they'd emailed each other a couple of times. He'd kept her updated on his father and the so-called memory loss, from which Max had apparently made a sudden recovery. In fact, he now remembered a little too much, according to Wynn. But the wounds on his arm appeared to be healing nicely and Max seemed to enjoy the extra attention Wynn paid him. Wynn, meanwhile, was looking forward to the reprieve offered by their visit to Zelda's.

"I owe you an apology," K.O. said to LaVonne.

"Nonsense. You had no way of knowing how Tom would react to Mr. Jeffries."

"True, but…" She swallowed hard. "You should know…" She started again. "I didn't really have a psychic experience."

LaVonne set down her mug and stared at K.O. "You didn't actually see a man for me in the soup? You mean to say there *wasn't* any message in the cracker crumbs?"

"No," K.O. admitted.

"Oh."

"It might seem like I was making fun of you and your psychic abilities, but I wasn't, LaVonne, I truly wasn't. I thought that if you believed a man was coming into your life, you'd be looking for one, and if you were expecting to meet a man, then you just might, and I hoped that man would be Wynn's father, but clearly it wasn't…isn't." This was said without pausing for breath.

A short silence ensued, followed by a disappointed, "Oh."

"Forgive me if I offended you."

LaVonne took a moment to think this through. "You didn't," she said after a while. "I've more or less reached the same conclusion about my psychic abilities. But—" she smiled brightly "—guess what? I've signed up for another class in January." She reached for a second slice of fruitcake and smiled as Martin brought K.O. the catnip mouse Wynn had given Tom that ill-fated evening.

"Another one at the community college?" K.O. asked.

LaVonne shook her head. "No, I walked across the street into A Good Yarn and decided I'd learn how to knit."

"That sounds good."

"Want to come, too?" LaVonne asked.

Every time her friend enrolled in a new course, she urged K.O. to take it with her. Because of finances and her job search, K.O. had always declined. This time, however, she felt she might be able to swing it. Not to mention the fact that she owed LaVonne… "I'll see."

"Really?" Even this little bit of enthusiasm seemed to delight LaVonne. "That's wonderful."

"I had a job interview on Wednesday," K.O. told her, squelching the desire to pin all her hopes on this one interview. Apple Blossom Books, the publisher Wynn had recommended, had called her in almost immediately. She'd met with the president and the marketing manager, and they'd promised to get back to her before Christmas. For the first time in a long while, K.O. felt optimistic. A publishing company, even a small one, would be ideal.

"And?" LaVonne prompted.

"And…" K.O. said, smiling. "I'm keeping my fingers crossed."

"That's just great! I know you've been looking for ages."

"The Christmas letters are going well, too," she added. "I wrote another one this week for a woman in Zach's office. She kept thinking she had time and then realized she didn't, so it was a rush job."

"You might really be on to something, you know. A little sideline business every Christmas."

"You aren't upset with me about what I did, are you?"

K.O. asked, returning to her apology. "You've been such a good friend, and I wouldn't do anything in the world to hurt you."

"Nah," LaVonne assured her, petting Phillip, who'd jumped into her lap. "If anyone's to blame it's that horrible man. As far as I'm concerned, he's a fruitcake." That said, she took another bite of the slice she'd been enjoying.

Wynn had devised a rather complicated plan of escape. On Friday afternoon he would leave his office at three-thirty and pick K.O. up on the corner of Blossom Street and Port Avenue. Because he didn't want to risk going inside and being seen by his father, she'd agreed to wait on the curb with her overnight bag.

K.O. was packed and ready long before the time they'd arranged. At three, her phone rang. Without checking caller ID, she knew it had to be her sister.

"I can't believe Dr. Wynn Jeffries is actually coming to the house," she said and gave a shrill cry of excitement. "You can't *imagine* how jealous my friends are."

"No one's supposed to know about this," K.O. reminded her.

"No one knows exactly when he'll be here, but I did mention it to a few close friends."

"Zelda! You promised."

"I know, I know. I'm sorry, but I couldn't keep this to myself. You just don't understand what an honor it is to have Dr. Jeffries in my home."

"But…"

"Don't worry, no one knows it's this weekend," Zelda told her.

"You're *sure?*"

"I swear, all right?"

It would be a nightmare if a few dozen of Zelda's closest friends just happened to drop by the house unannounced. Unfortunately, K.O. didn't have any choice but to believe her.

"How are the girls?" K.O. asked, hoping the twins were up to their usual antics. She didn't want Zoe and Zara to be on their best behavior. That would ruin all her plans.

"They're fine. Well, mostly fine. Healthwise, they're both getting over ear infections."

Oh, dear. "You might've told me this before!" K.O. cried. Her mind shifted into overdrive. If the girls were sick, it would throw everything off. Wynn would insist their behavior was affected by how they were feeling.

"They've been on antibiotics for the last two weeks," Zelda said, breaking into her thoughts. "The doctor explained how important it is to finish the medicine, and they only have a couple of doses left. I wrote it all down for you and Dr. Jeffries, so there's no need to worry."

"Fine," K.O. said, relieved. "Anything else you're not telling me?"

Her sister went silent for a moment. "I can't think of anything. I've got a list of instructions for you and the phone numbers where we can be reached. I do appreciate this, you know."

K.O. in turn appreciated the opportunity to spend this time with the twins—and to share the experience with Wynn. At least they'd be able to stop tiptoeing around the subject of the Free Child movement.

"We have a Christmas tree," Zelda murmured as if she were admitting to a weakness of character. "Zach felt we needed one, and when I spoke to Dr. Jeffries last Monday he didn't discourage it. So I gave in, although I'm still not sure it's such a good idea."

"You made the right choice," K.O. told her.

"I hope so."

K.O. noticed the clock on her microwave and was shocked to see that it was time to meet Wynn. "Oh, my goodness, I've got to go. I'll see you in about thirty minutes."

K.O. hung up the phone and hurried to put on her long wool coat, hat and scarf. Grabbing her purse and overnight bag, she rushed outside. Traffic was heavy, and it was already getting dark. She'd planned to be waiting at the curb so when Wynn pulled up, she could quickly hop inside his car. Then they'd be on their way, with no one the wiser.

No sooner had she stepped out of the building than she saw Max Jeffries walking toward her. His cheeks were ruddy, as if he'd been out for a long stroll.

"Well, hello there, Katherine," he said cheerfully. "How are you this fine cold day?"

"Ah…" She glanced furtively around. "I'm going to my sister's tonight," she said when he looked pointedly at her small suitcase.

"Wynn's away himself."

"Pure coincidence," she told him and realized how guilty she sounded.

Max chuckled. "Business trip, he said."

She nodded, moving slowly toward the nearby corner of Blossom and Port. She kept her gaze focused on the street, fearing she was about to give everything away.

"I'm healing well," Max told her conversationally. "I had a couple of rough days, but the pain is much better now."

"I'm glad to hear it."

"Yes, me, too. I never want to see that crazy cat woman again as long as I live."

It demanded restraint not to immediately defend her

friend, but K.O. managed. "I see your memory's back," she said instead, all the while keeping a lookout for Wynn.

"Oh, yes, it returned within a day or two. In some ways," he sighed, "I wished it hadn't. Because now all I can think about is how that vicious feline latched on to my arm."

Not wanting to give Max an excuse to continue the conversation, K.O. threw him a vague smile.

"Have you ever seen so much blood in your life?" he said with remarkable enthusiasm.

"Uh, no," she murmured. Since it was her towels that had cleaned it up, she had to confess there'd been lots.

"My son seems to be quite taken with you," Max said next.

As badly as she wanted to urge Max to go about his business, K.O. couldn't ignore that particular comment. Not when Max dropped this little morsel at her feet—much as Martin had presented her with the catnip mouse. "He does? Really?"

Max nodded.

"He talks about me?"

"Hmm. It's more a question of what he doesn't say than what he does. He was always an intense child. As a youngster… Well, I'm sure you don't have time to go into that right now."

K.O. thought she could see Wynn's car. "I don't… I'm sorry."

"Take my word for it, Wynn's interested in you."

K.O. felt like dancing in the street. "I'm interested in him, too," she admitted.

"Good, good," Max said expansively. "Well, I'd better get back inside. Have a nice weekend."

"I will. Thank you." It did look like Wynn's car. His

timing was perfect—or almost. She hoped that when he reached the curb, his father would be inside the building.

Just then the front doors opened and out stepped La-Vonne. She froze in midstep when she saw Wynn's father. He froze, too.

K.O. watched as LaVonne's eyes narrowed. She couldn't see Max's face, but from LaVonne's reaction, she assumed he shared her resentment. They seemed unwilling to walk past each other, and both stood there, looking wildly in all directions except ahead. If it hadn't been so sad, it would've been laughable.

K.O. could see that it was definitely Wynn's car. He smiled when he saw her and started to ease toward the curb. At the same moment, he noticed his father and LaVonne and instantly pulled back, merging into traffic again. He drove straight past K.O.

Now LaVonne and Max were staring at each other. They still hadn't moved, and people had to walk around them as they stood in the middle of the sidewalk.

K.O. had to find a way to escape without being detected. As best as she could figure, Wynn had to drive around the block. With one-way streets and heavy traffic, it might take him ten minutes to get back to Blossom. If she hurried, she might catch him on Port Avenue or another side street and avoid letting Max see them together.

"I think my ride's here," she said, backing away and dragging her suitcase with her.

They ignored her.

"Bye," she said, waving her hand.

This, too, went without comment. "I'll see you both later," she said, rushing past them and down the sidewalk.

Again there was no response.

K.O. didn't dare look back. Blossom Street had never

seemed so long. She rounded the corner and walked some distance down Port, waiting until she saw Wynn's car again. Raising her arm as if hailing a taxi, she managed to catch his attention.

Wynn pulled up to the curb, reached over and opened the passenger door. "That was a close call," he murmured as she climbed inside.

"You have no idea," she said, shaking her head.

"Is everything all right?" he asked.

"I don't know and, frankly, I don't want to stick around and find out."

Wynn chuckled. "I don't, either," he said, rejoining the stream of traffic.

They were off on what she hoped would be a grand adventure in the land of Z.

Chapter Fifteen

"This is Zoe," K.O. said as her niece wrapped one arm around her leg. After a half-hour of instructions, Zelda was finally out the door, on her way to meet Zach at the hotel. The twins stood like miniature statues, dressed in jean coveralls and red polka-dot shirts, with their hair in pigtails. They each stared up at Wynn.

"No, I'm Zara."

K.O. narrowed her eyes, unsure whether to believe the child. The twins were identical and seemed to derive great satisfaction from fooling people, especially their parents.

"Zoe," K.O. challenged. "Tell the truth."

"I'm hungry."

"It'll be dinnertime soon," K.O. promised.

Zoe—and she felt sure it *was* Zoe—glared up at her. "I'm hungry *now*. I want to eat *now*." She punctuated her demand by stamping her foot. Her twin joined in, shouting that she, too, was hungry.

"I want dinner *now*," Zara insisted.

Wynn smiled knowingly. "Children shouldn't be forced

to eat on a schedule. If they're hungry, we should feed them no matter what the clock says."

Until then, the girls had barely acknowledged Wynn. All of a sudden, he was their best friend. Both beamed brilliant smiles in his direction, then marched over and stood next to him, as though aligning themselves with his theories.

"What would you like for dinner?" he asked, squatting down so he was at eye level with them.

"Hot dogs," Zoe said, and Zara agreed. The two Yorkies, Zero and Zorro, seemed to approve, because they barked loudly and then scampered into the kitchen.

"I'll check the refrigerator," K.O. told him. Not long ago, Zelda hadn't allowed her daughters anywhere near hot dogs. She considered them unhealthy, low-quality fare that was full of nitrates and other preservatives. But nothing was off limits since Zelda had read *The Free Child* and become a convert.

"I'll help you look," Zara volunteered and tearing into the kitchen, threw open the refrigerator door and peered inside.

Not wanting to be left out, Zoe dragged over a kitchen chair and climbed on top. She yanked open the freezer and started tossing frozen food onto the floor. Zero and Zorro scrambled to get out of the way of flying frozen peas and fish.

"There aren't any hot dogs," K.O. said after a few minutes. "Let's choose something else." After all, it was only four o'clock and she was afraid that if the girls ate too early, they'd be hungry again later in the evening.

"I *want* a hot dog," Zara shouted.

"Me, too," Zoe chimed in, as though eating wieners was a matter of eternal significance.

Wynn stood in the kitchen doorway. "I can run to the store."

K.O. couldn't believe her ears. She hated to see him cater to the whims of Zoe and Zara, but far be it from her to object. If he was willing to go to those lengths to get the twins the meal they wanted, she'd let him do it.

"Isn't that nice of Dr. Jeffries?" K.O. asked her nieces.

Both girls ignored her and Wynn.

K.O. followed him into the other room, where Wynn retrieved his jacket from the hall closet. "I'll be back soon," he said.

"I'll put together a salad and—"

"Let the girls decide if they want a salad," Wynn interrupted. "Given the option, children will choose a well-balanced diet on their own. We as adults shouldn't be making these decisions for them."

K.O. had broken down and bought a copy of *The Free Child* at a small bookstore that had recently opened on Blossom Street. She'd skimmed it last night, so she knew this advice was in the book, stated in exactly those words. She might not approve, but for tonight she was determined to follow his lead. So she kept her mouth shut. Not that it was easy.

While the girls were occupied, he planted a gentle kiss on her lips, smiled and then was out the door.

It was now three days since they'd been able to spend time together. With that one short kiss, a lovely warmth spread through her. She closed the door after him and was leaning against it when she noticed that the twins had turned to stare at her. "While we're waiting for Wynn to get back, would you like me to read you a story?" she asked. The salad discussion could wait.

The girls readily agreed, and the three of them settled

on the sofa. She was only a few pages into the book when both Zoe and Zara slumped over, asleep. Before Zelda left, she'd said the twins had been awake since five that morning, excited about Katherine's visit. Apparently they no longer took naps. This was something else Wynn had advised. Children would sleep when they needed to, according to him. Regimented naptimes stifled children's ability to understand their internal clocks. Well, Zoe's and Zara's clocks had obviously wound down—and K.O. was grateful.

The quiet was so blissful that she leaned her head back and rested her own eyes. The tranquility didn't last long, however. In less than fifteen minutes, Wynn was back from the store, carrying a plastic bag with wieners and fresh buns. The dogs barked frantically as he entered the house, waking both children.

"Here they are," he announced as if he brandished an Olympic gold medal.

Zara yawned. "I'm not hungry anymore."

"Me, neither," Zoe added.

It probably wasn't the most tactful thing to do, but K.O. smiled triumphantly.

"That's okay. We can wait until later," Wynn said, completely unfazed.

He really was good with the girls and seemed to enjoy spending time with them. While K.O. set the kitchen table and cleared away the clutter that had accumulated everywhere, Wynn sat down and talked to the twins. The girls showed him the Christmas tree and the stockings that hung over the fireplace and the nativity scene set up on the formal dining room table.

K.O. heard Zoe mention her imaginary horse named Blackie. Not to be outdone, Zara declared that *her* imaginary horse was named Brownie. Wynn listened to them seriously and even scooted over to make room for the horses on the sofa. K.O. was grateful that Wynn was sharing responsibility for the girls, whose constant demands quickly drained her.

"I'm hungry now," Zoe informed them half an hour later.

"I'll start the hot dogs," K.O. said, ready for dinner herself.

"I want pancakes."

"With syrup," Zara said. Zoe nodded.

K.O. looked at Wynn, who shrugged as if it was no big deal.

"Then pancakes it is," K.O. agreed. She'd let him cope with the sugar high. For the next ten minutes she was busy mixing batter and frying the pancakes. The twins wanted chocolate syrup and strawberry jam on top, with bananas and granola. Actually, it didn't taste nearly as bad as K.O. had feared.

According to her sister's instructions, the girls were to be given their medication with meals. After dinner, Zoe and Zara climbed down from their chairs. When K.O. asked them to take their plates to the sink, they complied without an argument or even a complaint.

"Time for your medicine," K.O. told them next. She removed two small bottles filled with pink antibiotic from the refrigerator.

The two girls raced about the kitchen, shrieking, with the dogs yapping at their heels. They seemed incapable of standing still.

"Girls," K.O. ordered sternly. "Take your medicine and then you can run around." The way they were dashing back and forth, it was difficult to see who was who.

Zara skidded to a stop and dutifully opened her mouth. Carefully measuring out the liquid, K.O. filled the spoon and popped it into the child's mouth. Immediately afterward, the twins took off in a frenzied race around the kitchen table.

"Zoe," K.O. said, holding the second bottle and a clean spoon and waiting for the mayhem to die down so she could dispense the correct dose to her other niece. "Your turn."

The twin appeared in front of her, mouth open. K.O. poured medicine onto the spoon. About to give it to Zoe, she hesitated. "You're not Zoe. You're Zara."

"I'm Zoe," she insisted. Although the girls were identical, K.O. could usually tell one from the other, partly by their personalities. Zara had the stronger, more dominant nature. "Are you sure?" she asked.

The little girl nodded vigorously. Uncertain, K.O. reluctantly gave her the medication. The twins continued to chase each other about the kitchen, weaving their way around and between Wynn and K.O. The dogs dashed after them, yapping madly.

Wynn asked, "Is everything all right?"

K.O. still held the empty spoon. "I have a horrible feeling I just gave two doses to the same girl."

"You can trust the twins to tell you the truth," Wynn pronounced. "Children instinctively know when it's important to tell the truth."

"Really?" K.O. couldn't help worrying.

"Of course. It's in the book," Wynn said as if quoting Scripture.

"You didn't feed Blackie and Brownie," Zara cried when K.O. tossed the leftover pancakes in the garbage.

"Then we must." Wynn proceeded to remove the cold pancakes and tear them into small pieces. Zero and Zorro leaped off the ground in an effort to snatch up the leftovers.

Zoe and Zara sat on the floor and fed the dogs and supposedly their imaginary pets, as well.

The yapping dogs were giving K.O. a headache. "How about if I turn on the television," she suggested, shouting to be heard above the racket made by the girls and the dogs.

The twins hollered their approval, but the show that flashed onto the screen was a Christmas cartoon featuring none other than Santa himself. Jolly old soul that he was, Santa laughed and loaded his sleigh while the girls watched with rapt attention. Knowing how her sister felt, K.O. figured this was probably the first time they'd seen Santa all season. K.O. glanced at Wynn, who was frowning back.

"Let's see what else is on," K.O. said quickly.

"I want to watch Santa," Zoe shouted.

"Me, too," Zara muttered.

Wynn sat on the sofa between them and wrapped his arms around their small shoulders. "This show is about a character called Santa Claus," he said in a solicitous voice.

Both girls were far too involved in the program to be easily distracted by adult conversation.

"Sometimes mommies and daddies like to make believe, and while they don't mean to lie, they can mislead their children," he went on.

Zoe briefly tore her gaze away from the television screen. "Like Santa, you mean?"

Wynn smiled. "Like Santa," he agreed.

"We know he's not real," Zoe informed them with all the wisdom of a five-year-old.

"Santa is really Mommy and Daddy," Zara explained. "*Everyone* knows that."

"They do?"

Both girls nodded.

Zoe's eyes turned serious. "We heard Mommy and

Daddy fighting about Santa and we almost told them it doesn't matter 'cause we already know."

"We like getting gifts from him, though," Zara told them.

"Yeah, I like Santa," Zoe added.

"But he's not real," Wynn said, sounding perfectly logical.

"Mommy's real," Zara argued. "And Daddy, too."

"Yes, but…" Wynn seemed determined to argue further, but stopped when he happened to glance at K.O. He held her gaze a moment before looking away.

K.O. did her best to keep quiet, but apparently Wynn realized how difficult that was, because he clammed up fast enough.

The next time she looked at the twins, Zara had slumped over to one side, eyes drooping. K.O. gently shook the little girl's shoulders but Zara didn't respond. Still fearing she might have given one twin a double dose of the antibiotic, she knelt down in front of the other child.

"Zoe," she asked, struggling to keep the panic out of her voice. "Did you get your medicine or did Zara swallow both doses?"

Zoe grinned and pantomimed zipping her mouth closed.

"Zoe," K.O. said again. "This is important. We can't play games when medicine is involved." So much for Wynn's theory that children instinctively knew when it was necessary to tell the truth.

"Zara likes the taste better'n me."

"Did you take your medicine or did Zara take it for you?" Wynn asked.

Zoe smiled and shook her head, indicating that she wasn't telling.

Zara snored, punctuating the conversation.

"Did you or did you not take your medicine?" Wynn demanded, nearly yelling.

Tears welled in Zoe's eyes. She buried her face in K.O.'s lap and refused to answer Wynn.

"This isn't a joke," he muttered, clearly losing his patience with the twins.

"Zoe," K.O. cautioned. "You heard Dr. Jeffries. It's important for us to know if you took your medication."

The little girl raised her head, then slowly nodded. "It tastes bad, but I swallowed it all down."

"Good." Relief flooded K.O. "Thank you for telling the truth."

"I don't like your friend," she said, sticking her tongue out at Wynn. "He yells."

"I only yelled because…you made me," Wynn countered. He marched to the far side of the room, and K.O. reflected that he didn't sound so calm and reasonable anymore.

"Why don't we all play a game?" she suggested.

Zara raised her head sleepily from the sofa edge. "Can we play Old Maid?" she asked, yawning.

"I want to play Candyland," Zoe mumbled.

"Why don't we play both?" K.O. said, and they did. In fact, they played for two hours straight, watched television and then drank hot chocolate.

"Shall we take a bath now?" K.O. asked, hoping that would tire the girls out enough to want to go to bed. She didn't know where they got their stamina, but her own was fading rapidly.

The twins were eager to do something altogether different and instantly raced out of the room.

Wynn looked like he could use a break—and he hadn't even seen them at their most challenging. All in all, the girls were exhibiting good behavior, or what passed for good in the regime of the Free Child.

"I'll run the bath water," K.O. told Wynn as he gathered up the cards and game pieces. Had she been on her own, K.O. would have insisted the twins pick up after themselves.

While the girls were occupied in their bedroom, she put on a Christmas CD she particularly liked and started the bath. When she glanced into the living room, she saw Wynn collapsed on the sofa, legs stretched out.

"It hasn't been so bad," he said, as though that was proof his theories were working well. "As soon as the twins are down, we can talk," he murmured, "about us..."

K.O. wasn't ready for that, feeling he should spend more time with the girls. She felt honor-bound to remind Wynn of what he'd written in his book. "Didn't you say that children know when they need sleep and we as adults should trust them to set their own schedules?"

He seemed about to argue with her, but then abruptly sat up and pointed across the room. "What's that?"

A naked dog strolled into the living room. Rather, a hairless dog.

"Zero? Zorro?" K.O. asked. "Oh, my goodness!" She dashed into the bathroom to discover Zara sitting on the floor with Wynn's electric shaver. A pile of brown-and-black dog hair littered the area.

"What happened?" Wynn cried, hard on her heels. His mouth fell open when he saw the girls intent on their task. They'd gone through his toiletries, which were spread across the countertop next to the sink. K.O. realized that the hum of the shaver had been concealed by the melodious strains of "Silent Night." "What are you doing?"

"We're giving haircuts," Zara announced. "Do you want one?"

Chapter Sixteen

Two hours later, at ten-thirty, both Zoe and Zara were in their beds and asleep. This was no small accomplishment. After half a dozen stories, the girls were finally down for the night. K.O. tiptoed out of the room and as quietly as possible closed the door. Wynn was just ahead of her and looked as exhausted as she felt.

Zero regarded K.O. forlornly from the hallway. The poor dog had been almost completely shaved. He stared up at her, hairless and shivering. Zorro still had half his hair. The Yorkshire terrier's left side had been sheared before K.O. managed to snatch the razor out of her niece's hand. Last winter Zelda had knit tiny dog sweaters, which K.O. found, and with Wynn's help slipped over the two terriers. At least they'd be warm, although neither dog seemed especially grateful.

K.O. sank down on the sofa beside Wynn, with the dogs nestled at their feet. Breathing out a long, deep sigh, she gazed up at the ceiling. Wynn was curiously quiet.

"I feel like going to bed myself," she murmured when she'd recovered enough energy to speak.

"What time are your sister and brother-in-law supposed to return?" Wynn asked with what seemed to require an extraordinary amount of effort.

"Zelda said they should be home by three."

"That late?"

K.O. couldn't keep the grin off her face. It was just as she'd hoped. She wouldn't have to argue about the problem with his Free Child theories, since he'd been able to witness for himself the havoc they caused.

Straightening, K.O. suggested they listen to some more music.

"That won't disturb them, will it?" he asked when she got up to put on another CD. Evidently he had no interest in anything that might wake the girls.

"I should hope not." She found the Christmas CD she'd given to Zelda two years earlier, and inserted it in the player. It featured a number of pop artists. Smiling over at Wynn, she lowered the volume. John Denver's voice reached softly into the room, singing "Joy to the World."

Wynn turned off the floor lamp, so the only illumination came from the Christmas-tree lights. The mood was cheerful and yet relaxed.

For the first time in days they were alone. The incident with Wynn's father and the demands of the twins were the last things on K.O.'s mind.

Wynn placed his arm across the back of the sofa and she sat close to him, resting her head against his shoulder. All they needed now was a glass of wine and a kiss or two. Romance swirled through the room with the music and Christmas lights. Wynn must've felt it, too, because he turned her in his arms. K.O. started to close her eyes, anticipating his kiss, when she caught a movement from the corner of her eye.

She gasped.

A mouse…a rodent ran across the floor.

Instantly alarmed, K.O. jerked away from Wynn.

He bolted upright. "What is it?"

"A mouse." She hated mice. "There," she cried, covering her mouth to stifle a scream. She pointed as the rodent scampered under the Christmas tree.

Wynn leaped to his feet. "I see it."

Apparently so did Zero, because he let out a yelp and headed right for the tree. Zorro followed.

K.O. brought both feet onto the sofa and hugged her knees. It was completely unreasonable—and so clichéd—to be terrified of a little mouse. But she was. While logic told her a mouse was harmless, that knowledge didn't help.

"You have to get it out of here," she whimpered as panic set in.

"I'll catch it," he shouted and dived under the Christmas tree, toppling it. The tree slammed against the floor, shattering several bulbs. Ornaments rolled in all directions. The dogs ran for cover. Fortunately the tree was still plugged in because it offered what little light was available.

Unable to watch, K.O. hid her eyes. She wondered what Wynn would do if he did manage to corner the rodent. The thought of him killing it right there in her sister's living room was intolerable.

"Don't kill it," she insisted and removed her hands from her eyes to find Wynn on his hands and knees, staring at her.

The mouse darted across the floor and raced under the sofa, where K.O. just happened to be sitting.

Zero and Zorro ran after it, yelping frantically.

K.O. screeched and scrambled to a standing position on

the sofa. Not knowing what else to do, she bounced from one cushion to the other.

Zero had buried his nose as far as it would go under the sofa. Zorro dashed back and forth on the carpet. As hard as she tried, K.O. couldn't keep still and began hopping up and down, crying out in abject terror. She didn't care if she woke the girls or not, there was a mouse directly beneath her feet…somewhere. For all she knew, it could have crawled into the sofa itself.

That thought made her jump from the middle of the sofa, over the armrest and onto the floor, narrowly missing Zero. The lamp fell when she landed, but she was able to catch it seconds before it crashed to the floor. As she righted the lamp, she flipped it on, provided a welcome circle of light.

Meanwhile, Barry Manilow crooned out "The Twelve Days of Christmas."

Still on all fours, Wynn crept across the carpet to the sofa, which he overturned. As it pitched onto its back, the mouse shot out.

Directly at K.O.

She screamed.

Zero yelped.

Zorro tore fearlessly after it.

K.O. screamed again and grabbed a basket in which Zelda kept her knitting. She emptied the basket and, more by instinct than anything else, flung it over the mouse, trapping him.

Wynn sat up with a shocked look. "You got him!"

Both dogs stood guard by the basket, sniffing at the edges. Zero scratched the carpet.

Zelda's yarn and needles were a tangled mess on the floor but seemed intact. Breathless, K.O. stared at the basket, not knowing what to do next. "It had a brown tail," she commented.

Wynn nodded. "I noticed that, too."

"I've never seen a mouse with a brown tail before."

"It's an African brown-tailed mouse," he said, sounding knowledgeable. "I saw a documentary on them."

"African mice are here in the States?" She wondered if Animal Control knew about this.

He nodded again. "So I gather."

"What do we do now?" Because Wynn seemed to know more about this sort of thing, she looked to him for the answer.

"Kill it," he said without a qualm.

Zero and Zorro obviously agreed, because they both growled and clawed at the carpet, asking for the opportunity to do it themselves.

"No way!" K.O. objected. She couldn't allow him to kill it. The terriers, either. Although mice terrified her, K.O. couldn't bear to hurt any of God's creatures. "All I want you to do is get that brown-tailed mouse out of here." As soon as Zelda returned, K.O. planned to suggest she call a pest control company to inspect the entire house. Although, if there were other mice around, she didn't want to know it....

"All right," Wynn muttered. "I'll take it outside and release it."

He got a newspaper and knelt down next to the dogs. Carefully, inch by inch, he slid the paper beneath the up-ended basket. When he'd finished that, he stood and carried the whole thing to the front door. Zero and Zorro followed, leaping up on their hind legs and barking wildly.

K.O. hurried to open first the door and then the screen. The cold air felt good against her heated face.

Wynn stepped onto the porch while K.O. held back the

dogs by closing the screen door. They both objected strenuously and braced their front paws against the door, watching Wynn's every movement.

K.O. turned her back as Wynn released the African brown-tailed mouse into the great unknown. She wished the critter a pleasant life outside.

"Is it gone?" she asked when Wynn came back into the house, careful to keep Zero and Zorro from escaping and racing after the varmint.

"It's gone, and I didn't even need to touch it," he assured her. He closed the door.

K.O. smiled up at him. "My hero," she whispered.

Wynn playfully flexed his muscles. "Anything else I can do for you, my fair damsel?"

Looping her arms around his neck, K.O. backed him up against the front door and rewarded him with a warm, moist kiss. Wynn wrapped his arms about her waist and half lifted her from the carpet.

"You *are* my hero," she whispered between kisses. "You saved me from that killer mouse."

"The African brown-tailed killer rat."

"It was a *rat?*"

"A small one," he murmured, and kissed her again before she could ask more questions.

"A baby rat?" That meant there must be parents around and possibly siblings, perhaps any number of other little rats. "What makes you think it was a rat?" she demanded, fast losing interest in kissing.

"He was fat. But perhaps he was just a fat mouse."

"Ah…"

"You're still grateful?"

"Very grateful, but—"

He kissed her again, then abruptly broke off the kiss. His eyes seemed to focus on something across the room.

K.O. tensed, afraid he'd seen another mouse. Or rat. Or rodent of some description.

It took genuine courage to glance over her shoulder, but she did it anyway. Fortunately she didn't see anything— other than an overturned Christmas tree, scattered furniture and general chaos brought about by the Great Brown-Tailed Mouse Hunt.

"The fishbowl has blue water," he said.

"Blue water?" K.O. dropped her arms and stared at the counter between the kitchen and the living room, where the fishbowl sat. Sure enough, the water was a deep blue.

Wynn walked across the room.

Before K.O. could ask what he was doing, Wynn pushed up his sweater sleeve and thrust his hand into the water. "Just as I thought," he muttered, retrieving a gold pen.

After she'd found the twins with Wynn's electric shaver, she realized, they'd opened his overnight case.

"This is a gold fountain pen," he told her, holding up the dripping pen. "As it happens, this is a *valuable* gold fountain pen."

"With blue ink," K.O. added. She didn't think it could be too valuable, since it was leaking.

She picked up the bowl with both hands and carried it into the kitchen, setting it in the sink. Scooping out the two goldfish, she put them in a temporary home—a coffee cup full of fresh, clean water—and refilled the bowl.

Wynn was pacing the kitchen floor behind her.

"Does your book say anything about situations like this?" she couldn't resist asking.

He glared at her and apparently that was all the answer he intended to give.

"Aunt Katherine?" one of the twins shouted. "Come quick." K.O. heard unmistakable panic in the little girl's voice.

Soon the two girls were both crying out.

Hurrying into the bedroom with Wynn right behind her, K.O. found Zoe and Zara weeping loudly.

"What's wrong?" she asked.

"Freddy's gone," Zoe wailed.

"Freddy?" she repeated. "Who's Freddy?"

"Our hamster," Zoe explained, pointing at what K.O. now recognized as a cage against the far wall. "He must've figured out how to open his cage."

A chill went through her. "Does Freddy have a brown tail and happen to be a little chubby?" she asked the girls.

Hope filled their eyes as they nodded eagerly.

K.O. scowled at Wynn. African brown-tailed mouse, indeed.

Chapter Seventeen

Thankfully, Wynn rescued poor Freddy, who was discovered shivering in a corner of the porch. The girls were relieved to have their hamster back, and neither mentioned the close call Freddy had encountered with certain death. After calming the twins, it took K.O. and Wynn an hour to clean up the living room. By then, they were both cranky and tired.

Saturday morning, Zoe and Zara decided on wieners for breakfast. Knowing Wynn would approve, K.O. cooked the hot dogs he'd purchased the night before. However, the unaccustomed meat didn't settle well in Zoe's tummy and she threw up on her breakfast plate. Zara insisted that all she wanted was orange juice poured over dry cereal. So that was what she got.

For the rest of the morning, Wynn remained pensive and remote. He helped her with the children but didn't want to talk. In fact, he seemed more than eager to get back to Blossom Street. When Zelda and Zach showed up that afternoon, he couldn't quite hide his relief. The twins hugged K.O. goodbye and Wynn, too.

While Wynn loaded the car, K.O. talked to Zelda about holiday plans. Zelda asked her to join the family for Christmas Eve dinner and church, but not Christmas Day, which they'd be spending with Zach's parents. K.O. didn't mind. She'd invite LaVonne to dinner at her place. Maybe she'd include Wynn and his father, too, despite the disastrous conclusion of the last social event she'd hosted for this same group. Still, when she had the chance, she'd discuss it with Wynn.

On the drive home, Wynn seemed especially quiet.

"The girls are a handful, aren't they?" she asked, hoping to start a conversation.

He nodded.

She smiled to herself, remembering Wynn's expression when Zoe announced that their hamster had escaped. Despite his reproachful silence, she laughed. "I promise not to mention that rare African brown-tailed mouse again, but I have to tell LaVonne."

"I never said it was rare."

"Oh, sorry, I thought you had." One look told her Wynn wasn't amused. "Come on, Wynn," she said, as they merged with the freeway traffic. "You have to admit it was a little ridiculous."

He didn't appear to be in the mood to admit anything. "Are you happy?" he asked.

"What do you mean?"

"You proved your point, didn't you?"

So that was the problem. "If you're referring to how the girls behaved then, yes, I suppose I did."

"You claimed that after your sister read my book, they changed into undisciplined hellions."

"Well…" Wasn't it obvious? "They're twins," she said, trying to sound conciliatory, "and as such they've always needed a lot of attention. Some of what happened on Friday evening might have happened without the influence of your child-rearing theories. Freddy would've escaped whether Zelda read your book or not."

"Very funny."

"I wasn't trying to be funny. Frankly, rushing to the store to buy hot dogs because that's what the girls wanted for dinner is over the top, in my opinion. I feel it teaches them to expect that their every whim must be met."

"I beg to differ. My getting the dinner they wanted showed them that I cared about their likes and dislikes."

"Two hours of sitting on the floor playing Old Maid said the same thing," she inserted.

"I let you put them to bed even though they clearly weren't ready for sleep."

"I beg to differ," she said, a bit more forcefully than she'd intended. "Zoe and Zara were both yawning when they came out of the bath. I asked them if they wanted to go to bed."

"What you asked," he said stiffly, "was if they were *ready* for bed."

"And the difference is?"

"Two hours of storytime while they wore us both out."

"What would you have done?" she asked.

His gaze didn't waver from the road. "I would've allowed them to play quietly in their room until they'd tired themselves out."

Quietly? He had to be joking. Wynn seemed to have conveniently forgotten that during the short time they were on their own, Zoe and Zara had gotten into his overnight bag. Thanks to their creative use of his personal things, the goldfish now had a bluish tint. The two Yorkies were nearly hairless. She could argue that because the girls considered themselves *free,* they didn't see anything wrong with opening his bag. The lack of boundaries created confusion and misunderstanding.

"Twins are not the norm," he challenged. "They encourage ill behavior in each other."

"However, before Zelda read your book, they were reasonably well-behaved children."

"Is that a fact?" He sounded as though he didn't believe her.

"Yes," she said swiftly. "Zoe and Zara were happy and respectful and kind. Some would even go so far as to say they were well-adjusted. Now they constantly demand their own way. They're unreasonable, selfish and difficult." She was only getting started and dragged in another breath. "Furthermore, it used to be a joy to spend time with them and now it's a chore. And if you must know, I blame you and that blasted book of yours." There, she'd said it.

A stark silence followed.

"You don't mince words, do you?"

"No…"

"I respect that. I wholeheartedly disagree, but I respect your right to state your opinion."

The tension in the car had just increased by about a thousand degrees.

"After this weekend, you still disagree?" She was astonished he'd actually said that, but then she supposed his ego was on the line.

"I'm not interested in arguing with you, Katherine."

She didn't want to argue with him, either. Still, she'd hoped the twins would convince him that while his theories might look good on paper, in reality they didn't work.

After Wynn exited the freeway, it was only a few short blocks to Blossom Street and the parking garage beneath their building. Wynn pulled into his assigned slot and turned off the engine.

Neither moved.

K.O. feared that the minute she opened the car door, it would be over, and she didn't want their relationship to end, not like this. Not now, with Christmas only nine days away.

She tried again. "I know we don't see eye to eye on everything—"

"No, we don't," he interrupted. "In many cases, it doesn't matter, but when it comes to my work, my livelihood, it does. Not only do you not accept my theories, you think they're ludicrous."

She opened her mouth to defend herself, then realized he was right. That was exactly what she thought.

"You've seen evidence that appears to contradict them and, therefore, you discount the years of research I've done in my field. The fact is, you don't respect my work."

Feeling wretched, she hung her head.

"I expected there to be areas in which we disagree, Katherine, but this is more than I can deal with. I'm sorry, but I think it would be best if we didn't see each other again."

If that was truly how he felt, then there was nothing left to say.

"I appreciate that you've been honest with me," he continued. "I'm sorry, Katherine—I know we both would've liked this to work, but we have too many differences."

She made an effort to smile. If she thought arguing with him would do any good, she would have. But the hard set of his jaw told her no amount of reasoning would reach him now. "Thank you for everything. Really, I mean that. You've made this Christmas the best."

He gave her a sad smile.

"Would it be all right—would you mind if I gave you a hug?" she asked. "To say goodbye?"

He stared at her for the longest moment, then slowly shook his head. "That wouldn't be a good idea," he whispered, opening the car door.

By the time K.O. was out of the vehicle, he'd already retrieved her overnight bag from the trunk.

She waited, but it soon became apparent that he had no intention of taking the elevator with her. It seemed he'd had about as much of her company as he could stand.

She stepped into the elevator with her bag and turned around. Before the doors closed, she saw Wynn leaning against the side of his car with his head down, looking dejected. K.O. understood the feeling.

It had been such a promising relationship. She'd never felt this drawn to a man, this attracted. If only she'd been able to keep her mouth shut—but, oh, no, not her. She'd wanted to prove her point, show him the error of his ways. She still believed he was wrong—well, mostly wrong—but now she felt petty and mean.

When the elevator stopped at the first floor, the doors slid open and K.O. got out. The first thing she did was collect her mail and her newspapers. She eyed the elevator, wondering if she'd ever see Wynn again, other than merely in passing, which would be painfully unavoidable.

After unpacking her overnight case and sorting through the mail, none of which interested her, she walked across the hall, hoping to talk to LaVonne.

Even after several long rings, LaVonne didn't answer her door. Perhaps she was doing errands.

Just as K.O. was about to walk away, her neighbor opened the door just a crack and peered out.

"LaVonne, it's me."

"Oh, hi," she said.

"Can I come in?" K.O. asked, wondering why LaVonne didn't immediately invite her inside. She'd never hesitated to ask her in before.

"Ah…now isn't really a good time."

"Oh." That was puzzling.

"How about tomorrow?" LaVonne suggested.

"Sure." K.O. nodded. "Is Tom back?" she asked.

"Tom?"

"Your cat."

"Oh, oh…that Tom. Yes, he came home this morning."

K.O. was pleased to hear that. She dredged up a smile. "I'll talk to you tomorrow, then."

"Yes," she agreed. "Tomorrow."

K.O. started across the hall, then abruptly turned back. "You might care to know that the Raisin Bran got it all wrong."

"I beg your pardon?" LaVonne asked, narrowing her gaze.

"I think you might've read the kitty litter wrong, too. But then again, that particular box accurately describes my love life."

LaVonne opened the door a fraction of an inch wider. "Do you mean to tell me you're no longer seeing Wynn?"

K.O. nodded. "Apparently we were both wrong in thinking Wynn was the man for me."

"He is," LaVonne said confidently.

K.O. sighed. "I wish he was. I genuinely like Wynn. When I first discovered he was the author of that loony book my sister read…" Realizing what she'd just said, K.O. began again. "When I discovered he wrote the book she'd read, I had my doubts."

"It *is* a loony book," LaVonne said.

"I should never have told him how I felt."

"You were honest."

"Yes, but I was rude and hurtful, too." She shook her head mournfully. "We disagree on just about every aspect of child-rearing. He doesn't want to see me again and I don't blame him."

LaVonne stared at her for an intense moment. "You're falling in love with him."

"No, I'm not," she said, hoping to make light of her feelings, but her neighbor was right. K.O. had known it the minute Wynn dived under the Christmas tree to save her from the not-so-rare African brown-tailed mouse. The minute he'd waved down the horse-drawn carriage and covered her knees with a lap robe and slipped his arm around her shoulders.

"Don't try to deny it," LaVonne said. "I don't really know what I saw in that Raisin Bran. Probably just raisins. But all along I've felt that Wynn's the man for you."

"I wish that was true," she said as she turned to go home. "But it's not."

As she opened her own door, she heard LaVonne talking. When she glanced back, she could hear her in a heated conversation with someone inside the condo. Unfortunately LaVonne was blocking the doorway, so K.O. couldn't see who it was.

"LaVonne?"

The door opened wider and out stepped Max Jeffries. "Hello, Katherine," he greeted her, grinning from ear to ear.

K.O. looked at her neighbor and then at Wynn's father. The last she'd heard, Max was planning to sue LaVonne for everything she had. Somehow, in the past twenty-four hours, he'd changed his mind.

"Max?" she said in an incredulous voice.

He grinned boyishly and placed his arm around La-Vonne's shoulders.

"You see," LaVonne said, blushing a fetching shade of red. "My psychic talents might be limited, but you're more talented than you knew."

Chapter Eighteen

K.O. was depressed. Even the fact that she'd been hired by Apple Blossom Books as their new publicist hadn't been enough to raise her spirits. She was scheduled to start work the day after New Year's and should've been thrilled. She was, only...nothing felt right without Wynn.

It was Christmas Eve and it should have been one of the happiest days of the year, but she felt like staying in bed. Her sister and family were expecting her later that afternoon, so K.O. knew she couldn't mope around the condo all day. She had things to do, food to buy, gifts to wrap, and she'd better get moving.

Putting on her coat and gloves, she walked out of her condo wearing a smile. She refused to let anyone know she was suffering from a broken heart.

"Katherine," LaVonne called the instant she saw her. She stood at the lobby mailbox as if she'd been there for hours, just waiting for K.O. "Merry Christmas!"

"Merry Christmas," K.O. returned a little too brightly. She managed a smile and with her shoulders squared, made her way to the door.

"Do you have any plans for Christmas?" her neighbor called after her.

K.O.'s mouth hurt from holding that smile for so long. She nodded. "I'm joining Zelda, Zach and the girls this evening, and then I thought I'd spend a quiet Christmas by myself." Needless to say, she hadn't issued any invitations, and she'd hardly seen LaVonne in days. Tomorrow she'd cook for herself. While doing errands this morning, she planned to purchase a small—very small—turkey. She refused to mope and feel lonely, not on Christmas Day.

"Have dinner with me," LaVonne said. "It'll just be me and the boys."

When K.O. hesitated, she added, "Tom, Phillip and Martin would love to see you. I'm cooking a turkey and all the fixings, and I'd be grateful for the company."

"Are you sure?"

"Of course I'm sure!"

K.O. didn't take long to consider her friend's invitation. "I'd love to, then. What would you like me to bring?"

"Dessert," LaVonne said promptly. "Something yummy and special for Christmas."

"All right." They agreed on a time and K.O. left, feeling better than she had in days. Just as she was about to step outside, she turned back.

"How's Max?" she asked, knowing her neighbor was on good terms with Wynn's father. Exactly how good those terms were remained to be seen. She wondered fleetingly what the Jeffrieses were doing for Christmas, then decided it was none of her business. Still, the afternoon K.O. had found Max in LaVonne's condo, she'd been shocked to say the least. Their brief conversation the following day hadn't been too enlightening but maybe over Christmas dinner

LaVonne would tell her what had happened—and what was happening now.

Flustered, LaVonne lowered her eyes as she sorted through a stack of mail that seemed to be mostly Christmas cards. "He's completely recovered. And," she whispered, "he's apologized to Tom."

A sense of pleasure shot through K.O. at this...and at the way LaVonne blushed. Apparently this was one romance that held promise. Her own had fizzled out fast enough. She'd come to truly like Wynn. More than like... At the thought of him, an aching sensation pressed down on her. In retrospect, she wished she'd handled the situation differently. Because she couldn't resist, she had to ask, "Have you seen Wynn?"

Her friend nodded but the look in LaVonne's eyes told K.O. everything she dreaded.

"He's still angry, isn't he?"

LaVonne gave her a sad smile. "I'm sure everything will work out. I know what I saw in that Raisin Bran." She attempted a laugh.

"When you see him again, tell him..." She paused. "Tell him," she started again, then gave up. Wynn had made his feelings clear. He'd told her it would be best if they didn't see each other again, and he'd meant it. Nine days with no word told her he wasn't changing his mind. Well, she had her pride, too.

"What would you like me to tell him?" LaVonne asked.

"Nothing. It's not important."

"You could write him a letter," LaVonne suggested.

"Perhaps I will," K.O. said on her way out the door, but she knew she wouldn't. It was over.

Blossom Street seemed more alive than at any other time she could remember. A group of carolers performed at the corner, songbooks in their hands. An elderly gentleman rang a bell for charity outside the French Café, which was crowded with customers. Seeing how busy the place was, K.O. decided to purchase her Christmas dessert now, before they completely sold out.

After adding a donation to the pot as she entered the café, she stood in a long line. When her turn finally came to order, she saw that one of the bakers was helping at the counter. K.O. knew Alix Townsend or, at least, she'd talked to her often enough to know her by name.

"Merry Christmas, K.O.," Alix said.

"Merry Christmas to you, too." K.O. surveyed the sweet delicacies behind the glass counter. "I need something that says Christmas," she murmured. The decorated cookies were festive but didn't seem quite right. A pumpkin pie would work, but it wasn't really special.

"How about a small Bûche de Noël," Alix said. "It's a traditional French dessert—a fancy cake decorated with mocha cream frosting and shaped to look like a Yule log. I baked it myself from a special recipe of the owner's."

"Bûche de Noël," K.O. repeated. It sounded perfect.

"They're going fast," Alix pointed out.

"Sold," K.O. said as the young woman went to collect one from the refrigerated case. It was then that K.O. noticed Alix's engagement ring.

"Will there be anything else?" Alix asked, setting the pink box on the counter and tying it with string.

"That diamond's new, isn't it?"

Grinning, Alix examined her ring finger. "I got it last week. Jordan couldn't wait to give it to me."

"Congratulations," K.O. told her. "When's the wedding?"

Alix looked down at the diamond as if she could hardly take her eyes off it. "June."

"That's fabulous."

"I'm already talking to Susannah Nelson—she owns the flower shop across the street. Jacqueline, my friend, insists we hold the reception at the Country Club. If it was up to me, Jordan and I would just elope, but his family would never stand for that." She shrugged in a resigned way. "I love Jordan, and I don't care what I have to do, as long as I get to be his wife."

The words echoed in K.O.'s heart as she walked out of the French Café with a final "Merry Christmas." She didn't know Alix Townsend all that well, but she liked her. Alix was entirely without pretense. No one need doubt how she felt about any particular subject; she spoke her mind in a straightforward manner that left nothing to speculation.

K.O. passed Susannah's Garden, the flower shop, on her way to the bank. The owner and her husband stood out front, wishing everyone a Merry Christmas. As K.O. walked past, Susannah handed her a sprig of holly with bright red berries.

"Thank you—this is so nice," K.O. said, tucking the holly in her coat pocket. She loved the flower shop and the beauty it brought to the street.

"I want to let the neighborhood know how much I appreciate the support. I've only been in business since September and everyone's been so help ful."

"Here, have a cup of hot cider." Susannah's husband was handing out plastic cups from a small table set up beside him. "I'm Joe," he said.

"Hello, Joe. I'm Katherine O'Connor."

Susannah slid one arm around her husband's waist and gazed up at him with such adoration it was painful for K.O. to watch. Everywhere she turned, people were happy and in love. A knot formed in her throat. Putting on a happy, carefree face was getting harder by the minute.

Just then the door to A Good Yarn opened and out came Lydia Goetz and a man K.O. assumed must be her husband. They were accompanied by a young boy, obviously their son. Lydia paused when she saw K.O.

Lydia was well-known on the street.

"Were you planning to stop in here?" she asked, and cast a quick glance at her husband. "Brad convinced me to close early today. I already sent my sister home, but if you need yarn, I'd be happy to get it for you. In fact, you could even pay me later." She looked at her husband again, as if to make sure he didn't object to the delay. "It wouldn't take more than a few minutes. I know what it's like to run out of yarn when you only need one ball to finish a project."

"No, no, that's fine," K.O. said. She'd always wanted to learn to knit and now that LaVonne was taking a class, maybe she'd join, too.

"Merry Christmas!" Lydia tucked her arm in her husband's.

"Merry Christmas," K.O. returned. Soon they hurried down the street, with the boy trotting ahead.

Transfixed, K.O. stood there unmoving. The lump that had formed in her throat grew huge. The whole world was in love, and she'd let the opportunity of her life slip away. She'd let Wynn go with barely a token protest, and that was wrong. If she believed in their love, she needed to fight for it, instead of pretending everything was fine without him. Because it wasn't. In fact, she was downright miserable, and it was time she admitted it.

She knew what she had to do. Afraid that if she didn't act quickly, she'd lose her nerve, K.O. ran back across the street and into her own building. Marching to the elevator, she punched the button and waited.

She wasn't even sure what she'd tell Wynn; she'd figure that out when she saw him. But seeing him was a necessity. She couldn't spend another minute like this. She'd made a terrible mistake, and so had he. If there was any chance of salvaging this relationship, she had to try.

Her heart seemed to be pounding at twice its normal rate as she rode the elevator up to Wynn's penthouse condominium. She'd only been inside once, and then briefly.

By the time she reached his front door, she was so dizzy she'd become light-headed. That didn't deter her from ringing the buzzer and waiting for what felt like an eternity.

Only it wasn't Wynn who opened the door. It was Max.

"Katherine," he said, obviously surprised to find her at his son's door. "Come in."

"Is Wynn available?" she asked, as winded as if she'd climbed the stairs instead of taking the elevator. Talking to Wynn—*now*—had assumed a sense of urgency.

Wynn stepped into the foyer and frowned when he saw her. "Katherine?" She could see the question in his eyes.

"Merry Christmas," Max said. He didn't seem inclined to leave.

"Could we talk?" she asked. "Privately?" She was terrified he'd tell her that everything had already been said, so she rushed to add, "Really, this will only take a moment and then I'll leave."

Wynn glanced at his father, who took the hint and reluctantly left the entryway.

K.O. remained standing there, clutching her purse with one hand and the pink box with the other. "I was out at the French Café and I talked to Alix."

"Alix?"

"She's one of the bakers and a friend of Lydia's—and Lydia's the lady who owns A Good Yarn. But that's not important. What *is* important is that Alix received an engagement ring for Christmas. She's so happy and in love, and Lydia is, too, and Susannah from the flower shop and just about everyone on the street. It's so full of Christmas out there, and all at once it came to me that…that I couldn't let this Christmas pass with things between us the way they are." She stopped to take a deep breath.

"Katherine, I—"

"Please let me finish, otherwise I don't know if I'll have the courage to continue."

He motioned for her to speak.

"I'm so sorry, Wynn, for everything. For wanting to be right and then subjecting you to Zoe and Zara. Their behavior *did* change after Zelda read your book and while I can't say I agree with everything you—"

"This is an apology?" he asked, raising his eyebrows.

"I'm trying. I'm sincerely trying. Please hear me out."

He crossed his arms and looked away. In fact, he seemed to find something behind her utterly fascinating.

This wasn't the time to lose her courage. She went on, speaking quickly, so quickly that the words practically ran together. "Basically, I wanted to tell you it was rude of me to assume I knew more than you on the subject of children. It was presumptuous and self-righteous. I was trying to prove how wrong you were…are, and that I was right. To be honest, I don't know what's right or wrong. All I know is how much I miss you and how much it hurts that you're out of my life."

"I'm the one who's been presumptuous and self-righteous," Wynn said. "You *are* right, Katherine, about almost everything. It hasn't been easy for me to accept that, let alone face it."

"Oh, for heaven's sake, aren't you two going to kiss and make up?" Max demanded, coming back into the foyer. Apparently he'd been standing in the living room, out of sight, and had listened in on every word. "Wynn, if you let this woman walk away, then you're a fool. An even bigger fool than you know."

"I—I..." Wynn stuttered.

"You've been in love with her for weeks." Max shook his head as if this was more than obvious.

Wynn pinned his father with a fierce glare.

"You love me?" K.O. asked, her voice rising to a squeak. "Because I'm in love with you, too."

A light flickered in his eyes at her confession. "Katherine, I appreciate your coming. However, this is serious and it's something we both need to think over. It's too important—we can't allow ourselves to get caught up in emotions that are part of the holidays. We'll talk after Christmas, all right?"

"I can't do that," she cried.

"Good for you," Max shouted, encouraging her. "I'm going to phone LaVonne. This calls for champagne."

"What does?" Wynn asked.

"Us," she explained. "You and me. I love you, Wynn, and I can't bear the thought that I won't see you again. It's tearing me up. I don't *need* time to think about us. I already know how I feel, and if what your father says is true, you know how you feel about me."

"Well, I do need to think," he insisted. "I haven't figured out what I'm going to do yet, because I can't continue promoting a book whose theories I can no longer wholly support. Let me deal with that first."

"No," she said. "Love should come first." She stared into his eyes. "Love changes everything, Wynn." Then, because it was impossible to hold back for another second, she put down her purse and the Yule log and threw her arms around him.

Wynn was stiff and unbending, and then his arms circled her, too. "Are you always this stubborn?" he asked.

"Yes. Sometimes even more than this. Ask Zelda."

Wynn kissed her. His arms tightened around her, as if he found it hard to believe she was actually there in his embrace.

"That's the way to handle it," Max said from somewhere behind them.

Wynn and K.O. ignored him.

"He's been a real pain these last few days," Max went on. "But this should improve matters."

Wynn broke off the kiss and held her gaze. "We'll probably never agree on everything."

"Probably."

"I can be just as stubborn as you."

"That's questionable," she said with a laugh.

His lips found hers again, as if he couldn't bear not to kiss her. Each kiss required a bit more time and became a bit more involved.

"I don't believe in long courtships," he murmured, his eyes still closed.

"I don't, either," she said. "And I'm going to want children."

He hesitated.

"We don't need all the answers right this minute, do we, Dr. Jeffries?"

"About Santa—"

She interrupted him, cutting off any argument by kissing him. What resistance there was didn't last.

"I was about to suggest we could bring Santa out from beneath that sleigh," he whispered, his eyes briefly fluttering open.

"Really?" This was more than she'd dared hope.

"Really."

She'd been more than willing to forgo Santa as long as she had Wynn. But Santa *and* Wynn was better yet.

"No hamsters, though," he said firmly.

"Named Freddy," she added.

Wynn chuckled. "Or anything else."

The doorbell chimed and Max hurried to answer it, ushering LaVonne inside. The instant she saw Wynn and K.O. in each other's arms, she clapped with delight. "Didn't I tell you everything would work out?" she asked Max.

"You did, indeed."

LaVonne nodded sagely. "I think I may have psychic powers, after all. I saw it all plain as day in the leaves of my poinsettia," she proclaimed. "Just before Max called, two of them fell to the ground—together."

Despite herself, K.O. laughed. Until a few minutes ago, her love life had virtually disappeared. Now there was hope, real hope for her and Wynn to learn from each other and as LaVonne's prophecy—real or imagined—implied, grow together instead of apart.

"Champagne, anyone?" Max asked, bringing out a bottle.

Wynn still held K.O. and she wasn't objecting. "I need to hire you," he whispered close to her ear.

"Hire me?"

"I'm kind of late with my Christmas letter this year and I wondered if I could convince you to write one for me."

"Of course. It's on the house." With his arms around

her waist, she leaned back and looked up at him. "Is there anything in particular you'd like me to say?"

"Oh, yes. You can write about the success of my first published book—and explain that there'll be a retraction in the next edition." He winked. "Or, if you prefer, you could call it a compromise."

K.O. smiled.

"And then I want you to tell my family and friends that I'm working on a new book that'll be called *The Happy Child,* and it'll be about creating appropriate boundaries within the Free Child system of parenting."

K.O. rewarded him with a lengthy kiss that left her knees weak. Fortunately, he had a firm hold on her, and she on him.

"You can also mention the fact that there's going to be a wedding in the family."

"Two weddings," Max inserted as he handed LaVonne a champagne glass.

"Two?" LaVonne echoed shyly.

Max nodded, filling three more glasses. "Wynn and K.O.'s isn't the only romance that started out rocky. The way I figure it, if I can win Tom over, his mistress shouldn't be far behind."

"Oh, Max!"

"Is there anything else you'd like me to say in your Christmas letter?" K.O. asked Wynn.

"Oh, yes, there's plenty more, but I think we'll leave it for the next Christmas letter and then the one after that." He brought K.O. close once more and hugged her tight.

She loved being in his arms—and in his life. Next year's Christmas letter would be from both of them. It would be all about how happy they were…and every word would be true.

* * * * *

CALL ME MRS. MIRACLE

To
Dan and Sally Wigutow
and
Caroline Moore
in appreciation for bringing
Mrs. Miracle
to life

Chapter One

NEED A NEW LIFE? GOD TAKES TRADE-INS.

—MRS. MIRACLE

Jake Finley waited impatiently to be ushered into his father's executive office—the office that would one day be his. The thought of eventually stepping into J. R. Finley's shoes excited him. Even though he'd slowly been working his way through the ranks, he'd be the first to admit he still had a lot to learn. However, he was willing to do whatever it took to prove himself.

Finley's was the last of the family-owned department stores in New York City. His great-grandfather had begun the small mercantile on East 34th Street more than seventy years earlier. In the decades since, succeeding Finleys had opened branches in the other boroughs and then in nearby towns. Eventually the chain had spread up and down the East Coast.

"Your father will see you now," Mrs. Coffey said. Dora Coffey had served as J.R.'s executive assistant for at least twenty-five years and knew as much about the company as Jake did—maybe more. He hoped that when the time came she'd stay on, although she had to be close to retirement age.

"Thank you." He walked into the large office with its panoramic view of the Manhattan skyline. He'd lived in the city all his life, but this view never failed to stir him, never failed to lift his heart. No place on earth was more enchanting than New York in December. He could see a light snow drifting down, and the city appeared even more magical through that delicate veil.

Jacob R. Finley, however, wasn't looking at the view. His gaze remained focused on the computer screen. And his frown told Jake everything he needed to know.

He cleared his throat, intending to catch J.R.'s attention, although he suspected that his father was well aware of his presence. "You asked to see me?" he said. Now that he was here, he had a fairly good idea what had initiated this summons. Jake had hoped it wouldn't happen quite so soon, but he should've guessed Mike Scott would go running to his father at the first opportunity. Unfortunately, Jake hadn't had enough time to prove that he was right— and Mike was wrong.

"How many of those SuperRobot toys did you order?" J.R. demanded, getting straight to the point. His father had never been one to lead gently into a subject. "Intellytron," he added scornfully.

"Also known as Telly," Jake said in a mild voice.

"How many?"

"Five hundred." As if J.R. didn't know.

"What?"

Jake struggled not to flinch at his father's angry tone,

which was something he rarely heard. They had a good relationship, but until now, Jake hadn't defied one of his father's experienced buyers.

"For how many stores?"

"Just here."

J.R.'s brow relaxed, but only slightly. "Do you realize those things retail for two hundred and fifty dollars apiece?"

J.R. knew the answer to that as well as Jake did. "Yes."

His father stood and walked over to the window, pacing back and forth with long, vigorous strides. Although in his early sixties, J.R. was in excellent shape. Tall and lean, like Jake himself, he had dark hair streaked with gray and his features were well-defined. No one could doubt that they were father and son. J.R. whirled around, hands linked behind him. "Did you clear the order with...anyone?"

Jake was as straightforward as his father. "No."

"Any particular reason you went over Scott's head?"

Jake had a very good reason. "We discussed it. He didn't agree, but I felt this was the right thing to do." Mike Scott had wanted to bring a maximum of fifty robots into the Manhattan location. Jake had tried to persuade him, but Mike wasn't interested in listening to speculation or taking what he saw as a risk—one that had the potential of leaving them with a huge overstock. He relied on cold, hard figures and years of purchasing experience. When their discussion was over, Mike still refused to go against what he considered his own better judgment. Jake continued to argue, presenting internet research and what his gut was telling him about this toy. When he'd finished, Mike Scott had countered with a list of reasons why fifty units per store would be adequate. *More* than adequate, in his opinion. While

Jake couldn't disagree with the other man's logic, he had a strong hunch that the much larger order was worth the risk.

"You *felt* it was right?" his father repeated in a scathing voice. "Mike Scott told me we'd be fortunate to sell fifty in each store, yet you, with your vast experience of two months in the toy department, decided the Manhattan store needed ten times that number."

Jake didn't have anything to add.

"I don't suppose you happened to notice that there's been a downturn in the economy? Parents don't *have* two hundred and fifty bucks for a toy. Not when a lot of families are pinching pennies."

"You made me manager of the toy department." Jake wasn't stupid or reckless. "I'm convinced we'll sell those robots before Christmas." As manager, it was his responsibility—and his right—to order as he deemed fit. And if that meant overriding a buyer's decision—well, he could live with that.

"You think you can sell *all* five hundred of those robots?" Skepticism weighted each word. "In two weeks?"

"Yes." Jake had to work hard to maintain his air of confidence. Still he held firm.

His father took a moment to consider Jake's answer, walking a full circle around his desk as he did. "As of this morning, how many units have you sold?"

That was an uncomfortable question and Jake glanced down at the floor. "Three."

"Three." J.R. shook his head and stalked to the far side of the room, then back again as if debating how to address the situation. "So what you're saying is that our storeroom has four hundred and ninety-seven expensive SuperRobots clogging it up?"

"They're going to sell, Dad."

"It hasn't happened yet, though, has it?"

"No, but I believe the robot's going to be the hottest toy of the season. I've done the research—this is the toy kids are talking about."

"Maybe, but let me remind you, *kids* aren't our customers. Their parents are. Which is why no one else in the industry shares your opinion."

"I know it's a risk, Dad, but it's a calculated one. Have faith."

His father snorted harshly at the word *faith*. "My faith died along with your mother and sister," he snapped.

Involuntarily Jake's eyes sought out the photograph of his mother and sister. Both had been killed in a freak car accident on Christmas Eve twenty-one years ago. Neither Jake nor his father had celebrated Christmas since that tragic night. Ironically, the holiday season was what kept Finley's in the black financially. Without the three-month Christmas shopping craze, the department-store chain would be out of business.

Because of the accident, Jake and his father ignored anything to do with Christmas in their personal lives. Every December twenty-fourth, soon after the store closed, the two of them got on a plane and flew to Saint John in the Virgin Islands. From the time Jake was twelve, there hadn't been a Christmas tree or presents or anything else that would remind him of the holiday. Except, of course, at the store...

"Trust me in this, Dad," Jake pleaded. "Telly the Super-Robot will be the biggest seller of the season, and pretty soon Finley's will be the only store in Manhattan where people can find them."

His father reached for a pen and rolled it between his fingers as he mulled over Jake's words. "I put you in charge of the toy department because I thought it would be a valuable experience for you. One day you'll sit in this chair. The fate of the company will rest in your hands."

His father wasn't telling him anything Jake didn't already know.

"If the toy department doesn't show a profit because you went over Mike Scott's head, then you'll have a lot to answer for." He locked eyes with Jake. "Do I make myself clear?"

Jake nodded. If the toy department reported a loss as a result of his judgment, his father would question Jake's readiness to take over the company.

"Got it," Jake assured his father.

"Good. I want a report on the sale of that robot every week until Christmas."

"You'll have it," Jake promised. He turned to leave.

"I hope you're right about this toy, son," J.R. said as Jake opened the office door. "You've taken a big risk. I hope it pays off."

He wasn't the only one. Still, Jake believed. He'd counted on having proof that the robots were selling by the time his father learned what he'd done. Black Friday, the day after Thanksgiving, which was generally the biggest shopping day of the year, had been a major disappointment. He'd fantasized watching the robots fly off the shelves.

It hadn't happened.

Although they'd been prominently displayed, just one of the expensive toys had sold. He supposed his father had a point; in a faltering economy, people were evaluating their Christmas budgets, so toys, especially expensive ones, had taken a hit. Children might want the robots but it was their parents who did the buying.

Jake's head throbbed as he made his way to the toy department. In his rush to get to the store that morning, he'd skipped his usual stop at a nearby Starbucks. He needed his caffeine fix.

"Welcome to Finley's. May I be of assistance?" an older woman asked him. The store badge pinned prominently on her neat gray cardigan told him her name was Mrs. Emily Miracle. Her smile was cheerful and engaging. She must be the new sales assistant Human Resources had been promising him—but she simply wouldn't do. Good grief, what were they thinking up in HR? Sales in the toy department could be brisk, demanding hours of standing, not to mention dealing with cranky kids and short-tempered parents. He needed someone young. Energetic.

"What can I show you?" the woman asked.

Jake blinked, taken aback by her question. "I beg your pardon?"

"Are you shopping for one of your children?"

"Well, no. I—"

She didn't allow him to finish and steered him toward the center aisle. "We have an excellent selection of toys for any age group. If you're looking for suggestions, I'd be more than happy to help."

She seemed completely oblivious to the fact that he was the department manager—and therefore her boss. "Excuse me, Mrs...." He glanced at her name tag a second time. "Mrs. Miracle."

"Actually, it's Merkle."

"The badge says Miracle."

"Right," she said, looking a bit chagrined. "HR made a mistake, but I don't mind. You can call me Mrs. Miracle."

Speaking of miracles... If ever Jake needed one, it was now. Those robots *had* to sell. His entire future with the company could depend on this toy.

"I'd be more than happy to assist you," Mrs. Miracle said again, breaking into his thoughts.

"I'm Jake Finley."

"Pleased to meet you. Do you have a son or a daughter?" she asked.

"This is *Finley's* Department Store," he said pointedly.

Apparently this new employee had yet to make the connection, which left Jake wondering exactly where HR found their seasonal help. There had to be someone more capable than this woman.

"Finley," Mrs. Miracle repeated slowly. "Jacob Robert is your father, then?"

"Yes," he said, frowning. Only family and close friends knew his father's middle name.

Her eyes brightened, and a smile slid into place. "Ahh," she said knowingly.

"You're acquainted with my father?" That could explain why she'd been hired. Maybe she had some connection to his family he knew nothing about.

"No, no, not directly, but I *have* heard a great deal about him."

So had half the population on the East Coast. "I'm the manager here in the toy department," he told her. He clipped on his badge as he spoke, realizing he'd stuck it in his pocket. The badge said simply "Manager," without including his name, since his policy was to be as anonymous as possible, to be known by his role, not his relationship to the owner.

"The manager. Yes," she said, nodding happily. "This works out beautifully."

"What does?" Her comments struck him as odd.

"Oh, nothing," she returned with the same smile.

She certainly looked pleased with herself, although Jake

couldn't imagine why. He doubted she'd last a week. He'd see about getting her transferred to a more suitable department for someone her age. Oh, he'd be subtle about it. He had no desire to risk a discrimination suit.

Jake examined the robot display, hoping that while he'd been gone another one might have sold. But if that was the case, he didn't see any evidence of it.

"Have you had your morning coffee?" Mrs. Miracle asked.

"No," he muttered. His head throbbed, reminding him of his craving for caffeine.

"It seems quiet here at the moment. Why don't you take your break?" she suggested. "The other sales associate and I can handle anything that comes along."

Jake hesitated.

"Go on," she urged. "Everyone needs their morning coffee."

"You go," he said. He was, after all, the department manager, so he should be the last to leave.

"Oh, heavens, no. I just finished a cup." Looking around, she gestured toward the empty aisles. "It's slow right now but it's sure to pick up later, don't you think?"

She was right. In another half hour or so, he might not get a chance. His gaze rested on the robots and he pointed in their direction. "Do what you can to interest shoppers in those."

"Telly the SuperRobot?" she said. Not waiting for his reply, she added, "You won't have any worries there. They're going to be the hottest item this Christmas."

Jake felt a surge of excitement. "You heard that?"

"No..." she answered thoughtfully.

"Then you must've seen a news report." Jake had been waiting for exactly this kind of confirmation. He'd played a hunch, taken a chance, and in his heart of hearts felt it had been a good decision. But he had four hundred and ninety-seven of these robots on his hands. If his projections didn't pan out, it would take a long time—like maybe forever—to live it down.

"Coffee," Mrs. Miracle said, without explaining why she was so sure of the robot's success.

Jake checked his watch, then nodded. "I'll be back soon."

"Take whatever time you need."

Jake thanked her and hurriedly left, stopping by HR on his way out. The head of the department, Gloria Palmer, glanced up when Jake entered the office. "I've got a new woman on the floor this morning. Emily Miracle," he said.

Gloria frowned. "Miracle?" She tapped some keys on her computer and looked back at Jake. "I don't show anyone with that name working in your department."

Jake remembered that Emily Miracle had said there'd been an error on her name tag. He rubbed his hand across his forehead, momentarily closing his eyes as he tried to remember the name she'd mentioned. "It starts with an *M*—McKinsey, Merk, something like that."

Gloria's phone rang and she reached for it, holding it between her shoulder and ear as her fingers flew across the keyboard. She tried to divide her attention between Jake and the person on the line. Catching Jake's eye, she motioned toward the computer screen, shrugged and shook her head.

Jake raised his hand and mouthed, "I'll catch you later."

Gloria nodded and returned her attention to the caller. Clearly she had more pressing issues to attend to just then. Jake would seek her out later that afternoon and suggest Mrs. Miracle be switched to another department. A less demanding one.

As he rushed out the door onto Thirty-Fourth and headed

into the still-falling snow, he decided it would be only fair to give the older woman a chance. If she managed to sell one of the robots while he collected his morning cup of java, he'd consider keeping her. And if she managed to sell *two,* she'd be living up to her name!

Chapter Two

IF GOD IS YOUR COPILOT, TRADE PLACES.

—MRS. MIRACLE

Friday morning, and Holly Larson was right on schedule—even a few minutes ahead. This was a vast improvement over the past two months, ever since her eight-year-old nephew, Gabe, had come to live with her. It'd taken effort on both their parts to make this arrangement work. Mickey, Holly's brother, had been called up by the National Guard and sent to Afghanistan for the next fifteen months. He was a widower, and with her parents doing volunteer medical work in Haiti, the only option for Gabe was to move in with Holly, who lived in a small Brooklyn apartment. Fortunately, she'd been able to turn her minuscule home office into a bedroom for Gabe.

They were doing okay, but it hadn't been easy. Never

having spent much time with children Gabe's age, the biggest adjustment had been Holly's—in her opinion, anyway.

Gabe might not agree, however. He didn't think sundried tomatoes with fresh mozzarella cheese was a special dinner. He turned up his nose and refused even one bite. So she was learning. Boxed macaroni and cheese suited him just fine, although she couldn't tolerate the stuff. At least it was cheap. Adding food for a growing boy to her already strained budget had been a challenge. Mickey, who was the manager of a large grocery store in his civilian life, sent what he could but he had his own financial difficulties; she knew he was still paying off his wife's medical bills and funeral expenses. And he had a mortgage to maintain on his Trenton, New Jersey, home. Poor Gabe. The little boy had lost his mother when he was an infant. Now his father was gone, too. Holly considered herself a poor replacement for either parent, let alone both, although she was giving it her best shot.

Since she had a few minutes to spare before she was due at the office, she hurried into Starbucks to reward herself with her favorite latte. It'd been two weeks since she'd had one. A hot, freshly brewed latte was an extravagance these days, so she only bought them occasionally.

Getting Gabe to school and then hurrying to the office was as difficult as collecting him from the after-school facility at the end of the day. Lindy Lee, her boss, hadn't taken kindly to Holly's rushing out the instant the clock struck five. But the child-care center at Gabe's school charged by the minute when she was late. *By the minute.*

Stepping out of the cold into the warmth of the coffee shop, Holly breathed in the pungent scent of fresh coffee. A cheery evergreen swag was draped across the display case. She dared not look because she had a weakness for cranberry scones. She missed her morning ritual of a latte and a scone almost as much as she did her independence. But giving it up was a small sacrifice if it meant she could help her brother and Gabe. Not only that, she'd come to adore her young nephew and, despite everything, knew she'd miss him when her brother returned.

The line moved quickly, and she placed her order for a skinny latte with vanilla flavoring. The man behind her ordered a large coffee. He smiled at her and Holly smiled back. She'd seen him in this Starbucks before, although they'd never spoken.

"Merry Christmas," she said.

"Same to you."

The girl at the cash register told Holly her total and she opened her purse to pay. That was when she remembered— she'd given the last of her cash to Gabe for lunch money. It seemed ridiculous to use a credit card for such a small amount, but she didn't have any choice. She took out her card and handed it to the barista. The young woman slid it through the machine, then leaned forward and whispered, "It's been declined."

Hot embarrassment reddened her face. She'd maxed out her card the month before but thought her payment would've been credited by now. Scrambling, she searched for coins in the bottom of her purse. It didn't take her long to realize she didn't have nearly enough change to cover the latte. "I have a debit card in here someplace," she muttered, grabbing her card case again.

"Excuse me." The good-looking man behind her pulled his wallet from his hip pocket.

"I'm… I'm sorry," she whispered, unable to meet his eyes. This was embarrassing, humiliating, downright mortifying.

"Allow me to pay for your latte," he said.

Holly sent him a shocked look. "You don't need to do that."

The woman standing behind him frowned impatiently at Holly. "If I'm going to get to work on time, he does."

"Oh, sorry."

Not waiting for her to agree, the stranger stepped forward and paid for both her latte and his coffee.

"Thank you," she said in a low, strangled voice.

"I'll consider it my good deed for the day."

"I'll pay for your coffee the next time I see you."

He grinned. "You've got a deal." He moved down to the end of the counter, where she went to wait for her latte. "I'm Jake Finley."

"Holly Larson." She extended her hand.

"Holly," he repeated.

"People assume I was born around Christmas but I wasn't. Actually, I was born in June and named after my mother's favorite aunt," she said. She didn't know why she'd blurted out such ridiculous information. Perhaps because she still felt embarrassed and was trying to disguise her chagrin with conversation. "I do love Christmas, though, don't you?"

"Not particularly." Frowning, he glanced at his watch. "I've got to get back to work."

"Oh, sure. Thank you again." He'd been thoughtful and generous.

"See you soon," Jake said as he turned toward the door.

"I owe you," she said. "I won't forget."

He smiled at her. "I hope I'll run into you again."

"That would be great." She meant it, and next time she'd make sure she had enough cash to treat him. She felt a glow of pleasure as Jake left Starbucks.

Holly stopped to calculate—it'd been more than three months since her last date. That was pitiful! Three months. Nuns had a more active social life than she did.

Her last relationship had been with Bill Carter. For a while it had seemed promising. As a divorced father, Bill was protective and caring toward his young son. Holly had only met Billy once. Unfortunately, the trip to the Central Park Zoo hadn't gone well. Billy had been whiny and overtired, and Bill had seemed to want *her* to deal with the boy. She'd tried but Billy didn't know her and she didn't know him, and the entire outing had been strained and uncomfortable. Holly had tried—unsuccessfully—to make the trip as much fun as possible. Shortly thereafter, Bill called to tell her their relationship wasn't "working" for him. He'd made a point of letting her know he was interested in finding someone more "suitable" for his son because he didn't feel she'd make a good mother. His words had stung.

Holly hadn't argued. Really, how could she? Her one experience with Billy had been a disaster. Then, just a month after Bill's heartless comment, Gabe had entered her life. These days she was more inclined to agree with Bill's assessment of her parenting skills. She didn't seem to have what it took to raise a child, which deeply concerned her.

Things were getting easier with Gabe, but progress had been slow, and it didn't help that her nephew seemed to sense her unease. She had a lot to learn about being an effective and nurturing parent.

Dating Bill had been enjoyable enough, but there'd never been much chemistry between them, so not seeing him wasn't a huge loss. She categorized it as more of a disappointment. A letdown. His parting words, however, had left her with doubts and regrets.

Carrying her latte, Holly walked the three blocks to the office. She actually arrived a minute early. Working as an assistant to a fashion designer sounded glamorous but it wasn't. She didn't get to take home designer purses for a fraction of their retail price—except for the knockoff versions she could buy on the street—or acquire fashion-model hand-me-downs.

She was paid a pittance and had become the go-to person for practically everyone on staff, and that added up to at least forty people. Her boss, Lindy Lee, was often unreasonable. Unfortunately, most of the time it was Holly's job to make sure that whatever Lindy wanted actually happened. Lindy wasn't much older than Holly, but she was well connected in the fashion world and had quickly risen to the top. Because her work as a designer of upscale women's sportswear was in high demand, Lindy Lee frequently worked under impossible deadlines. One thing was certain; she had no tolerance for the fact that Holly now had to stick to her official nine-to-five schedule, which meant her job as Lindy Lee's assistant might be in jeopardy. She'd explained the situation with Gabe, but her boss didn't care about Holly's problems at home.

Rushing to her desk, Holly set the latte down, shrugged off her coat and readied herself for the day. She was responsible for decorating the office for Christmas, and so far, there just hadn't been time. On Saturday she'd bring Gabe into the office and the two of them would get it done. That meant her own apartment would have to wait, but…oh, well.

Despite her boss's complaints about one thing or another, Holly's smile stayed in place all morning. A kind deed by a virtual stranger buffered her from four hours of commands, criticism and complaints.

Jack…no, Jake. He'd said his name was Jake, and he was

cute, too. Maybe *handsome* was a more accurate description. Classically handsome, like those 1940s movie stars in the old films she loved. Tall, nicely trimmed dark hair, broad shoulders, expressive eyes and…probably married. She'd been too shocked by his generosity to see whether he had a wedding band. Yeah, he was probably taken. Par for the course, she thought a little glumly. Holly was thirty, but being single at that age wasn't uncommon among her friends. Her parents seemed more worried about it than she was.

Most of her girlfriends didn't even *think* about settling down until after they turned thirty. Holly knew she wanted a husband and eventually a family. What she hadn't expected was becoming a sole parent to Gabe. This time with her nephew was like a dress rehearsal for being a mother, her friends told her. Unfortunately, there weren't any lines to memorize and the script changed almost every day.

At lunch she heated her Cup-a-Soup in the microwave and logged on to the internet to check for messages from Mickey. Her brother kept in touch with Gabe every day and sent her a quick note whenever he could. Sure enough, there was an email waiting for her.

From: "Lieutenant Mickey Larson" <larsonmichael@goarmy.com>
To: "Holly Larson" <hollylarson@msm.com>
Sent: December 10
Subject: Gabe's email

Hi, sis,
Gabe's last note to me was hilarious. What's this about you making him put down the toilet seat? He thinks girls should do it themselves. This is what happens when men live together. The seat's perpetually up.

Has he told you what he wants for Christmas yet? He generally mentions a toy before now, but he's been suspiciously quiet about it this year. Let me know when he drops his hints.

I wish I could be with you both, but that's out of the question. Next year for sure.

I know it's been rough on you having to fit Gabe into your apartment and your life, but I have no idea what I would've done without you.

By the way, I heard from Mom and Dad. The dental clinic Dad set up is going well. Who'd have guessed our parents would be doing volunteer work after retirement? They send their love…but now that I think about it, you got the same email as me, didn't you? They both sound happy but really busy. Mom was concerned about you taking Gabe, but she seems reassured now.

Well, I better get some shut-eye. Not to worry—I reminded Gabe that when he's staying at a house with a woman living in it, the correct thing to do is put down the toilet seat.

Check in with you later.

Thank you again for everything.

Love,

Mickey

Holly read the message twice, then sent him a note. She'd always been close to her brother and admired him for picking up the pieces of his life after Sally died of a rare blood disease. Gabe hadn't even been a year old. Holly had a lot more respect for the demands of parenthood—and especially single parenthood—now that Gabe lived with her.

At five o'clock, she was out the door. Lindy Lee threw her an evil look, which Holly pretended not to see. She caught the subway and had to stand, holding tight to one of the poles, for the whole rush-hour ride into Brooklyn.

As she was lurched and jolted on the train, her mind wandered back to Mickey's email. Gabe hadn't said anything about Christmas to her, either. And yet he had to know that the holidays were almost upon them; all the decorations in the neighborhood and the ads on TV made it hard to miss. For the first time in his life, Gabe wouldn't be spending Christmas with his father and grandparents. This year, there'd be just the two of them. Maybe he'd rather not celebrate until his father came home, she thought. That didn't seem right, though. Holly was determined to make this the best Christmas possible.

Not once had Gabe told her what he wanted. She wondered whether she should ask him, maybe encourage him to write Santa a letter—did he still believe in Santa?—or try to guess what he might like. Her other question was what she could buy on a limited income. A toy? She knew next to nothing about toys, especially the kind that would intrigue an eight-year-old boy. She felt besieged by even more insecurities.

She stepped off the subway, climbed the stairs to the street and hurried to Gabe's school, which housed the after-hours activity program set up for working parents. At least it wasn't snowing anymore. Which was a good thing, since she'd forgotten to make Gabe wear his boots that morning.

What happened the first day she'd gone to collect Gabe still made her cringe. She'd been thirty-two minutes late. The financial penalty was steep and cut into her carefully planned budget, but that didn't bother her nearly as much as the look on Gabe's face.

He must have assumed she'd abandoned him. His haunted expression brought her to the edge of tears every time she thought about it. That was the same night she'd prepared her favorite dinner for him—another disaster.

Now she knew better and kept an unending supply of hot dogs—God help them both—plus boxes of macaroni and cheese. He'd deign to eat carrot sticks and bananas, but those were his only concessions, no matter how much she talked about balanced nutrition. He found it hilarious to claim that the relish he slathered on his hot dogs was a "vegetable."

She waited by the row of hooks, each marked with a child's name. Gabe ran over the instant he saw her, his face bright with excitement. "I made a new friend!"

"That's great." Thankfully Gabe appeared to have adjusted well to his new school and teacher.

"Billy!" he called. "Come and meet my aunt Holly."

Holly's smile froze. This wasn't just any Billy. It was Bill Carter, Junior, son of the man who'd broken up with her three months earlier.

"Hello, Billy," she said, wondering if he'd recognize her.

The boy gazed up at her quizzically. Apparently he didn't. Or maybe he did remember her but wasn't sure when they'd met. Either way, Holly was relieved.

"Can I go over to Billy's house?" Gabe asked. The two boys linked arms like long-lost brothers.

"Ah, when?" she hedged. Seeing Bill again would be difficult. Holly wasn't eager to talk to the man who'd dumped her—especially considering why. It would be uncomfortable for both of them.

"I want him to come tonight," Billy said. "My dad's making sloppy joes. And we've got marshmallow ice cream for dessert."

"Well..." Her meals could hardly compete with that—not if you were an eight-year-old boy. Personally, Holly couldn't think of a less appetizing combination.

Before she could come up with a response, Gabe tugged at her sleeve. "Billy doesn't have a mom, either," he told her.

"I have a mom," Billy countered, "only she doesn't live with us anymore."

"My mother's in heaven with the angels," Gabe said. "I live with my dad, too, 'cept he's in Afghanistan now."

"So that's why you're staying with your aunt Holly." Billy nodded.

"Yeah." Gabe reached for his jacket and backpack.

"I'm sorry, Billy," she finally managed to say, "but Gabe and I already have plans for tonight."

Gabe whirled around. "We do?"

"We're going shopping," she said, thinking on her feet.

Gabe scowled and crossed his arms. "I hate shopping."

"You won't this time," she promised and helped him put on his winter jacket, along with his hat and mitts.

"Yes, I will," Gabe insisted, his head lowered.

"You and Billy can have a playdate later," she said, forcing herself to speak cheerfully.

"When?" Billy asked, unwilling to let the matter drop.

"How about next week?" She'd call or email Bill so it wouldn't come as a big shock when she showed up on his doorstep.

"Okay," Billy agreed.

"That suit you?" Holly asked Gabe. She wanted to leave *now,* just in case Bill was picking up his son today. She recalled that their housekeeper usually did this—but why take chances? Bill was the very last person she wanted to see.

Gabe shrugged, unhappy with the compromise. He let her take his hand as they left the school, but as soon as they were outdoors, he promptly snatched it away.

"Where are we going shopping?" he asked, still pouting as they headed in the opposite direction of her apartment building. The streetlights glowed and she saw Christmas decorations in apartment windows—wreaths, small potted trees and strings of colored lights. So far Holly hadn't done anything. Perhaps this weekend she'd find time to put up their tree—after she'd finished decorating the office, of course.

"I thought we'd go see Santa this evening," Holly announced.

"Santa?" He raised his head and eyed her speculatively.

"Would you like that?"

Gabe seemed to need a moment to consider the question. "I guess."

Holly assumed he was past the age of believing in Santa but wasn't quite ready to admit it, for fear of losing out on extra gifts. Still, she didn't feel she could ask him. "I want you to hold my hand while we're on the subway, okay?"

"Okay," he said in a grumpy voice.

They'd go to Finley's, she decided. She knew for sure that the store had a Santa. Besides, she wanted to look at the windows with their festive scenes and moving parts. Even in his current mood, Gabe would enjoy them, Holly thought. And so would she.

Chapter Three

It was the second Friday in December and the streets were crowded with shoppers and tourists. As they left the subway, Holly kept a close watch on Gabe, terrified of becoming separated. She heaved a sigh of relief when they reached Finley's Department Store. The big display windows in the front of the fourteen-story structure were cleverly decorated. One showed a Santa's workshop scene, including animated elves wielding hammers and saws. Another was a mirrored pond that had teddy bears skating around and around. Still another, the window closest to the doors, featured a huge Christmas tree, circled by a toy train running on its own miniature track. The boxcars were filled with gaily wrapped gifts.

With the crowds pressing against them, Gabe and Holly

moved from window to window, stopping at the final one. "Isn't that a great train set?" she asked.

Gabe nodded.

"Would you like one of those for Christmas?" she murmured. "You could ask Santa."

Gabe glanced up at her. "There's something else I want more."

"Okay, you can tell Santa that," she said.

They headed into the store, and had difficulty getting through the revolving doors, crushed in with other shoppers. "Can we go home and have dinner when we're done seeing Santa?" Gabe asked.

"Of course. What would you like?"

If he said hot dogs or macaroni and cheese Holly promised herself she wouldn't scream.

"Mashed potatoes with gravy and meat loaf with lots of ketchup."

That would take a certain amount of effort but was definitely something she could do. "You got it."

Gabe cast her one of his rare smiles, and Holly placed her hand on his shoulder. This was progress.

The ground floor of Finley's was crammed. The men's department was to the right and the cosmetics and perfume counters directly ahead. Holly inched her way forward, Gabe close by her side.

"We need to get to the escalator," she told him, steering the boy in that direction. She hoped that once they got up to the third floor, the crowds would have thinned out, at least a little.

"Okay." He voluntarily slipped his hand in hers.

More progress. Visiting Santa had clearly been a stroke of genius on her part.

Her guess about the crowds was accurate. When they

reached the third floor Holly felt she could breathe again. If it wasn't for Gabe, she wouldn't come within ten miles of Thirty-Fourth on a Friday night in December.

"Santa's over there," Gabe said, pointing.

The kid obviously had Santa Claus radar. Several spry elves in green tights and pointy hats surrounded the jolly old man in the red suit. This guy was good, too. His full white beard was real. He must've just gotten off break because he wore a huge smile.

The visit to Santa was free but for an extra twenty dollars, she could buy a picture. They'd stopped at an ATM on their way to the subway and she'd gotten cash. Although she couldn't help feeling a twinge at spending the money, a photo of Gabe with Santa would be the perfect Christmas gift for Mickey.

The line moved quickly. Gabe seemed excited and happy, chattering away about this and that, and his mood infected Holly. She hadn't felt much like Christmas until now. Classic carols rang through the store and soon Holly was humming along.

When it was Gabe's turn, he hopped onto Santa's knee as if the two of them were old friends.

"Hello there, young man," Santa said, adding a "Ho, ho, ho."

"Hello." Gabe looked him square in the eyes.

"And what would you like Santa to bring you?" the jolly old fellow inquired.

Her nephew didn't hesitate. "All I want for Christmas is Telly the SuperRobot."

What in heaven's name was that? A robot? Even without checking, Holly knew this wasn't going to be a cheap toy. A train set—a small one—she could manage, but an electronic toy was probably out of her price range.

"Very well, young man, Santa will see what he can do. Anything else you're interested in?"

"A train set," Gabe said, his eyes serious. "But I *really* want Intellytron."

"Intellytron," Holly muttered to herself.

Santa gestured at the camera. "Now smile big for me, and your mom can collect the photograph in five minutes."

"Okay." Gabe gave Santa a huge smile, then slid off his knee so the next child in line could have a turn. It took Holly a moment to realize that Gabe hadn't corrected Santa about who she was.

Holly went around to the counter behind Santa's chair to wait for the photograph, accompanied by Gabe.

"I don't know where Santa will find one of those robots," she said, trying to get as much information as she could.

"All the stores have them," Gabe assured her. "Billy wants an Intellytron, too."

So she could blame Billy for this sudden desire. But since this was the only toy Gabe wanted, she'd do her best to make sure that Intellytron the SuperRobot would be wrapped and under the tree Christmas morning.

"Maybe I should see what this robot friend of yours looks like," she suggested. A huge sign pointing to the toy department was strategically placed near Santa's residence. This, Holly felt certain, was no coincidence.

"Toys are this way," Gabe said, leading her by the hand.

Holly dutifully followed. "What if they don't have the robot?" she asked.

"They will," he said with sublime confidence.

"But what if they don't?"

Gabe frowned and then tilted his chin at a thoughtful angle. "Can Santa bring my dad home?"

Holly's heart sank. "Not this year, sweetheart."

"Then all I really want is my robot."

She'd been afraid of that.

They entered the toy department and were met by a grandmotherly woman with a name badge that identified her as Mrs. Emily Miracle.

"Why, hello there," the woman greeted Gabe with a smile.

Gabe immediately smiled back at her. "Hello."

"I see you've been to visit Santa." She nodded at the photo Holly was holding.

"Yup," Gabe said happily. "He was nice."

"Did you tell Santa what you want for Christmas?"

"Intellytron the SuperRobot," he replied.

"Telly is a wonderful toy. Let me show you one."

"Please," Holly said, hoping against hope that the robot was reasonably priced. If fate was truly with her, it would also be on sale.

Mrs. Miracle took them to a display on the other side of the department, directly across from the elevator. The robots would be the first toys seen by those stepping off. She wondered why they weren't by the escalator, but then it dawned on her. Mothers with young children usually came up via elevator. The manager of this department was no dummy.

"Look!" Gabe said, his eyes huge. "It's Telly! He's here. I told you he would be. Isn't he the best *ever?*"

"Would you like to see how he works?" the grandmotherly saleswoman asked.

"Yes, please."

Holly was impressed by Gabe's politeness, which she'd never seen to quite this degree. Well, it was December, and this was the one toy he wanted more than any other. The saleswoman took down the display model and started to demonstrate it when a male voice caught Holly's attention.

"Hello again."

She turned to face Jake, the man she'd met in Starbucks that morning. For a moment she couldn't speak. Eventually she croaked out a subdued hello.

He looked curiously at Gabe. "Your son?"

"My nephew," she said, recovering her voice. "Gabe's living with me for the next year while his father's in Afghanistan."

"Nephew," he repeated, and his eyes sparked with renewed interest.

"I brought Gabe here to visit Santa and he said that what he wants for Christmas is Intellytron the SuperRobot."

"An excellent choice. Would you like me to wrap one for you now?"

"Ah…" Holly paused. "I need to know how much they are first." Just looking at the toy told her she wasn't getting off cheap.

"Two hundred and fifty dollars."

Holly's hand flew to her heart. "*How* much?"

"Two hundred and fifty dollars."

"Oh." She swallowed. "Will there be a sale on these later? A big sale?"

Jake shook his head. "I doubt it."

"Oh," she said again.

Jake seemed disappointed, too.

Holly bit her lip. This was the only gift Gabe had requested. He'd indicated mild interest in a train set, but that was more at her instigation. Watching his eyes light up as the robot maneuvered itself down the aisle filled her with a sense of delight. He loved this toy and it would mean so much to him. "I get my Christmas bonus at the end of next week. Will you still have the robot then?" Never mind that Lindy Lee might be less than generous this year....

"We should have plenty," Jake told her.

"Thank goodness," Holly said gratefully.

"We've sold a number today, but I brought in a large supply so you shouldn't have anything to worry about."

"Wonderful." She could hardly wait for Gabe to unwrap this special gift Christmas morning. Tonight, the spirit of Christmas had finally begun to take root in her own heart. Seeing the joy of the season in Gabe's eyes helped her accept that this year would be different but could still be good. Although she and Gabe were separated from their family, she intended to make it a Christmas the two of them would always remember.

"I want to thank you again for buying my latte this morning," she said to Jake. She was about to suggest she pay him back, because she had the cash now, but hesitated, hoping for the opportunity to return the favor and spend more time with him.

"Like I said, it was my good deed for the day."

"Do you often purchase a complete stranger a cup of coffee?"

"You're the first."

She laughed. "Then I'm doubly honored."

"Aunt Holly, did you see? Did you see Telly move?" Gabe asked, dashing to her side. "He can talk, too!"

She'd been so involved in chatting with Jake that she'd missed most of the demonstration. Other children had come over to the aisle, drawn by the robot's activities; in fact, a small crowd had formed to watch. Several boys Gabe's age were tugging at their parents' arms.

"We'll have to see what Santa brings," Holly told him.

"He'll bring me Telly, won't he?"

Holly shrugged, pretending nonchalance. "We'll have to wait and see."

"How many days until Christmas?" Gabe asked eagerly.

"Today's the tenth, so…fifteen days."

"That long?" He dragged out the words as if he could barely hang on all those weeks.

"The time will fly by, Gabe. I promise."

"Excuse me," Jake said as he turned to answer a customer's question. Her query was about the price of the robot, and the woman had nearly the same reaction as Holly. Two hundred and fifty dollars! A lot of money for a toy. Still, in Gabe's case it would be worth it.

Mrs. Miracle brought out the display robot to demonstrate again, and Gabe and a second youngster watched with rapt attention. The older woman was a marvel, a natural with children.

"So, you're the manager here," Holly said once Jake was free.

He nodded. "How'd you guess?" he asked with a grin.

"Your badge, among other things." She smiled back at him. "I was just thinking how smart you were to place Santa next to the toy section."

"That wasn't my idea," Jake said. "Santa's been in that location for years."

"What about the Intellytron display across from the elevator?"

"Now that *was* my idea."

"I thought as much."

Jake seemed pleased that she'd noticed. "I'm hoping it really takes off."

"Well, if Gabe's interest is any indication, I'm sure it will."

He seemed to appreciate her vote of confidence.

"Look!" Gabe said, grabbing Holly's hand. He pointed to a couple who were removing a boxed unit of Intellytron from the display. "My robot will still be here by Christmas, won't he?"

"Absolutely," she assured him.

Jake winked at her as Mrs. Miracle led the young couple toward the cash register.

"Hiring Mrs. Miracle was a smart move, too," she said.

"Oh, I can't really take credit for that," Jake responded.

"Well, you're lucky, then. She's exactly right for the toy department. It's like having someone's grandmother here. She's helping parents fulfill all their children's Christmas wishes."

Jake glanced at the older woman, then slowly nodded. "I guess so," he said, sounding a bit uncertain.

"Haven't you seen the way kids immediately take to her?" Holly asked.

"Not only can't I take credit for her being here, it's actually a mistake."

"A mistake," Holly echoed. "You're joking! She's *perfect*. It wouldn't surprise me if you sold out the whole toy department with her working here."

"Really?" He said this as if Holly had given him something to think about.

"I love her name, too. Mrs. Miracle—it has such a nice Christmas sound."

"That's a mistake, as well. Her name's not really Miracle. HR spelled it wrong on her badge, and I asked that it be corrected."

"Oh, let her keep the badge," Holly urged. "Mrs. Miracle. It couldn't be more appropriate."

Jake nodded again. "Perhaps you're right."

Mrs. Miracle finished the sale and joined them. "Very nice meeting you, Gabe and Holly," she said warmly.

Holly didn't remember giving the older woman her name. Gabe must have mentioned it.

"You, too, Emily," she said.

"Oh, please," she said with a charming smile. "Just call me Mrs. Miracle."

"Okay," Gabe piped up. "We will."

Chapter Four

LEAD ME NOT INTO TEMPTATION.
I CAN FIND THE WAY MYSELF.

—J. R. FINLEY

"I thought we'd bake cookies today," Holly said on Saturday morning as Gabe sat at the kitchen counter eating his breakfast cereal. When he didn't think she was looking, he picked up the bowl and slurped what was left of his milk.

"Cookies?" Gabe said, frowning. "Can't we just buy them?"

"We could," Holly answered, "but I figured it would be fun to bake them ourselves."

Gabe didn't seem convinced. "Dad and I always got ours at the store. We never had to *work* to get them."

"But it's fun," Holly insisted, unwilling to give up quite so easily. "You can roll out the dough. I even have special cookie cutters. After the cookies are baked and they've cooled down, we can frost and decorate them." She'd hoped this Christmas tradition would appeal to Gabe.

He slid down from his chair and carried his bowl to the dishwasher. "Can I go on the computer?"

"Sure." Holly made an effort to hide her disappointment. She'd really hoped the two of them would bond while they were baking Christmas cookies. Later, she intended to go into the office and put up decorations—with Gabe's help. She wanted that to be fun for him, too.

Gabe moved to the alcove between the kitchen and small living room with its sofa and television. Holly was astonished at how adept the eight-year-old was on the computer. While he logged on, she brought out the eggs and flour and the rest of the ingredients for sugar cookies and set them on the kitchen counter.

Gabe obviously didn't realize she could see the computer screen from her position. She was pleased that he was writing his father a note.

From: "Gabe Larson" <gabelarson@msm.com>
To: "Lieutenant Mickey Larson" <larsonmichael@goarmy.com>
Sent: December 11
Subject: Cookies

Hi, Dad,
Guess what? Aunt Holly wants me to bake cookies. Doesn't she know I'm a BOY? Boys don't bake cookies. It's bad enough that I have to put the toilet seat down for her. I hope you get home soon because I'm afraid she's going to turn me into a girl!
Gabe

Holly tried to conceal her smile. "Would you like to go into the city this afternoon?" she asked as she added the butter she'd cubed to the sugar in the mixing bowl.

Gabe turned around to look at her. "You aren't going to make me go shopping, are you?"

"No. I'll take you to my office. Wouldn't you like that?"

"Yes," he said halfheartedly.

"I have to put up a few decorations. You can help me."

"Okay." Again he showed a decided lack of enthusiasm.

"The Rockefeller Center Christmas tree is up," she told him next.

Now that caught his interest. "Can we go ice-skating?"

"Ah…" Holly had never gone skating. "Maybe another time, okay?"

Gabe shrugged. "Okay. I bet Billy and his dad will take me."

The kid had no idea how much that comment irritated her. However, Holly knew she had to be an adult about it. She hadn't phoned Bill to discuss the fact that his son and her nephew were friends. She would, though, in order to arrange a playdate for the two boys.

"I thought we'd leave after lunch," she said, resuming their original conversation.

"Okay." Gabe returned to the computer and was soon involved in a game featuring beasts in some alien kingdom. Whatever it was held his attention for the next ten minutes.

Using the electric mixer, Holly blended the sugar, butter and eggs and was about to add the dry ingredients when Gabe climbed up on the stool beside her.

"I've never seen anyone make cookies before," he said.

"You can watch if you want." She made an effort to sound matter-of-fact, not revealing how pleased she was at his interest.

"When we go into the city, would it be all right if we went to Finley's?" he asked.

Holly looked up. "I suppose so. Any particular reason?"

He stared at her as if it should be obvious. "I want to see Telly. He can do all kinds of tricks and stuff, and maybe Mrs. Miracle will be there."

"Oh."

"Mrs. Miracle said I could stop by anytime I want and she'd let me work the controls. She said they don't normally let kids play with the toys but she'd make an exception." He drew in a deep breath. "What's an 'exception'?"

"It means she'll allow you to do it even though other people can't."

"That's what I thought." He leaned forward and braced his elbows on the counter, nodding solemnly at this evidence of his elevated status—at least in Mrs. Miracle's view.

As soon as the dough was mixed, Holly covered it with plastic wrap and put it inside the refrigerator to chill. When she'd finished, she cleaned off the kitchen counter. "You want to lick the beaters?" she asked.

Gabe straightened and looked skeptically at the mixer. "You can do that?"

"Sure. That's one of the best parts of baking cookies."

"Okay."

She handed him one beater and took the second herself.

Gabe's eyes widened after his first lick. "Hey, this tastes *good*."

"Told you," she said with a smug smile.

"Why can't we just eat the dough? Why ruin cookies by baking 'em?"

"Well, they're not cookies unless you bake them."

"Oh."

Her response seemed to satisfy him.

"I'm going to roll the dough out in a few minutes. Would you help me decide which cookie cutters to use?"

"I guess." Gabe didn't display a lot of enthusiasm at the request.

Holly stood on tiptoe to take down the plastic bag she kept on the upper kitchen shelf. "Your grandma Larson gave these to me last year. When your dad and I were your age, we used to make sugar cookies."

Gabe sat up straighter. "You mean my dad baked cookies?"

"Every Christmas. After we decorated them, we chose special people to give them to."

Gabe was always interested in learning facts about Mickey. Every night he asked Holly to tell him a story about his father as a boy. She'd run out of stories, but it didn't matter; Gabe liked hearing them again and again.

"You gave the cookies to special people? Like who?"

"Well..." Holly had to think about that. "Once I brought a plate of cookies to my Sunday school teacher and one year—" she paused and smiled "—I was twelve and had a crush on a boy in my class, so I brought the cookies to school for him."

"Who'd my dad give the cookies to?"

"I don't remember. You'll have to ask him."

"I will." Gabe propped his chin on one hand. "Can I take a plate of cookies to Mrs. Miracle?"

Holly was about to tell him that would be a wonderful idea, then hesitated. "The problem is, if I baked the cookies and decorated them, they'd be from me and not from you."

Gabe frowned. "I could help with cutting them out and stuff. You won't tell anyone, will you?"

"Not if you don't want me to."

"I don't want any of my friends to think I'm a sissy."

She crossed her heart. "I promise not to say a word."

"Okay, then, I'll do it." Gabe dug into the bag of cookie

cutters and made his selections, removing the Christmas tree, the star and several others. Then, as if a thought had suddenly struck him, he pointed at her apron. "I don't have to put on one of those, do I?"

"You don't like my apron?"

"They're okay for girls, but not boys."

"You don't have to wear one if you'd rather not."

He shook his head adamantly.

"But you might get flour on your clothes, and your friends would guess you were baking." This was a clever argument, if she did say so herself.

Gabe nibbled on his lower lip, apparently undecided. "Then I'll change clothes. I'm not wearing any girlie apron."

"That's fine," Holly said, grinning.

The rest of the morning was spent baking and decorating cookies. Once he got started, Gabe appeared to enjoy himself. He frosted the Christmas tree with green icing and sprinkled red sugar over it.

Then, with a sideways glance at Holly, he promptly ate the cookie. She let him assume she hadn't noticed.

"Who are you giving your cookies to?" Gabe asked.

Actually, Holly hadn't thought about it. "I'm not sure." A heartbeat later, the decision was made. "Jake."

"The man in the toy department at Finley's?"

Holly nodded. "He did something kind for me on Friday. He bought my coffee."

Gabe cocked his head. "Is he your boyfriend?"

"Oh, no. But he's very nice and I want to repay him." She got two plastic plates and, together, they arranged the cookies. Holly bundled each plate in green-tinted cellophane wrap and added silver bows for a festive look.

"You ready to head into town?" she asked.

Gabe raced into his bedroom for his coat, hat and mittens. "I'm ready."

"Me, too." The truth was, Holly felt excited about seeing Jake again. Of course, there was always the possibility that he wouldn't be working today—but she had to admit she hoped he was. Her reaction surprised her; since Bill had broken off their relationship she'd been reluctant to even consider dating someone new.

Meeting Jake had been an unexpected bonus. He'd been so— She stopped abruptly. Here she was, doing it again. Jake had paid for her coffee. He was obviously a generous man... or he might've been in a rush to get back to the store. Either way, he'd been kind to her. But that didn't mean he was *attracted* to her. In reality it meant nada. Zilch. Zip. Gazing down at the plate of cookies, Holly felt she might be pushing this too far.

"Aunt Holly?"

She looked at her nephew, who was staring quizzically at her. "Is something wrong?" he asked.

"Oh, sorry... No, nothing's wrong. I was just thinking maybe I should give these cookies to someone else."

"How come?"

"I... I don't know."

"Give them to Jake," Gabe said without a second's doubt. "Didn't you say he bought your coffee?"

"He did." Gabe was right. The cookies were simply a way of thanking him. That was all. She was returning a kindness. With her quandary settled, they walked over to the subway station.

When they arrived at Finley's, the streets and the store were even more crowded than they'd been the night before. Again Holly kept a close eye on her nephew. She'd made a contingency plan—if they did happen to get separated, they were to meet in the toy department by the robots.

They rode up on the escalator, after braving the cosmetics aisles, with staff handing out perfume samples. Gabe held his nose, but Holly was delighted to accept several tiny vials of perfume. When they finally reached the toy department, it was far busier than it had been the previous evening. Both Gabe and Holly studied the display of robots. There did seem to be fewer of the large boxes, but Jake had assured her there'd be plenty left by the time she received her Christmas bonus. She sincerely hoped that was true.

The moment Gabe saw Mrs. Miracle, he rushed to her side. "We made you sugar cookies," he said, giving her the plate.

"Oh, my, these are lovely." The grandmotherly woman smiled. "They look good enough to eat."

"You *are* supposed to eat them," Gabe said with a giggle.

"And I will." She bent down and hugged the boy. "Thank you so much."

Gabe whispered, "Don't tell anyone, but I helped Aunt Holly make them."

Holly was standing close enough to hear him and exchanged a smile with Mrs. Miracle.

"You should be proud of that," Mrs. Miracle said as she led him toward the Intellytron display, holding the plate of cookies aloft. "Lots of men cook. You should have your aunt Holly turn on the Food Network so you see for yourself."

"Men bake cookies?"

"Oh, my, yes," she told him. "Now that you're here, why don't we go and show these other children how to work this special robot. You can be my assistant."

"Can I?" Wide-eyed, Gabe looked at Holly for permission.

She nodded, and Mrs. Miracle and Gabe went to the other side of the toy department. Holly noticed that Jake was busy with customers, so she wandered down a randomly chosen aisle, examining the Barbie dolls and all their accoutrements. She felt a bit foolish carrying a plate of decorated cookies.

As soon as he was free, Jake made a beeline toward her. "Hi," he said. "I didn't expect to see you again so soon."

"Hi." Looking away, she tried to explain the reason for her visit. "Gabe wanted to check out his robot again. After that, we're going to my office and then Rockefeller Center to see the Christmas tree…but we decided to come here first." The words tumbled out so quickly she wondered if he'd understood a thing she'd said.

He glanced at the cookies.

"These are for you," she said, shoving the plate in his direction. "Sugar cookies. In appreciation for my latte."

"Homemade sugar cookies," he murmured as if he'd never seen anything like them before.

He continued to stare at the plate for an awkward moment. Holly was afraid she'd committed a social faux pas.

"My mother used to bake sugar cookies every Christmas," Jake finally said. His eyes narrowed, and the memory seemed to bring him pain.

Holly had the absurd notion that she should apologize.

"I remember the star and the bell." He spoke in a low voice, as though transported through the years. "Oh, and look, that one's a reindeer, and of course the Christmas tree with the little cinnamon candies as ornaments."

"Gabe actually decorated that one," she said.

He looked up and his smile banished all doubt. "Thank you, Holly."

"You're welcome, Jake."

"Excuse me." A woman spoke from behind Holly. "Is there someone here who could show me the electronic games?"

Jake seemed reluctant to leave her, and Holly was loath to see him go. "I'll be happy to help you," he said. He set the cookies behind the counter and escorted the woman to another section of the department.

Holly moved to the area where Gabe and Mrs. Miracle were demonstrating Intellytron. A small crowd had gathered, and Gabe's face shone with happiness as he put the robot through its paces. In all the weeks her nephew had lived with her, she'd never seen him so excited, so fully engaged. She knew Gabe wanted this toy for Christmas; what Holly hadn't understood until this very second was just how much it meant to him.

Regardless of the cost, Holly intended to get her nephew that robot.

Holiday Sugar Cookies

(from *Debbie Macomber's Cedar Cove Cookbook*)

This foolproof sugar cookie recipe makes a sturdy, sweet treat that's a perfect gift or a great addition to a holiday cookie platter.

2 cups (4 sticks) unsalted butter, at room temperature
2 cups brown sugar
2 large eggs
2 teaspoons vanilla extract or grated lemon peel
6 cups all-purpose flour, plus extra for rolling
2 teaspoons baking powder
1 teaspoon salt

1. In a large bowl with electric mixer on medium speed, cream butter and sugar until light and fluffy. Add eggs and vanilla; beat until combined.

2. In a separate bowl, combine flour, baking powder and salt. Reduce mixer speed to low; beat in flour mixture just until combined. Shape dough into two disks; wrap and refrigerate at least 2 hours or up to overnight.

3. Preheat oven to 350°F. Line baking sheets with parchment paper. Remove 1 dough disk from the refrigerator. Cut disk in half; cover remaining half. On a lightly floured surface with floured rolling pin, roll dough ¼-inch thick. Using cookie cutters, cut dough into as many cookies as possible; reserve trimmings for rerolling.

4. Place cookies on prepared sheets about 1 inch apart. Bake 10 to 12 minutes (depending on the size of cookies) until pale gold. Transfer to wire rack to cool. Repeat with remaining dough and rerolled scraps.

Tip: Decorate baked cookies with prepared frosting or sprinkle unbaked cookies with colored sugars before putting them in the oven.

Makes about 48 cookies.

Chapter Five

PEOPLE ARE LIKE TEA BAGS—YOU HAVE TO DROP
THEM IN HOT WATER BEFORE YOU KNOW HOW
STRONG THEY ARE.

—MRS. MIRACLE

"Sugar cookies," Jake said to himself. A rush of memories warmed him. Memories of his mother and sister at Christmas. Spicy scents in the air—cinnamon and ginger and cloves. Those sensory memories had been so deeply buried, he'd all but forgotten them.

"We sold three of the SuperRobots this afternoon," Mrs. Miracle said, breaking into his thoughts.

Just three? Jake felt a sense of dread. He'd need to sell a lot more than three a day to unload the five hundred robots he'd ordered. He checked the computer, which instantly gave him the total number sold since Black Friday. When he saw the screen, his heart sank down to his shoes. This wasn't good. Not good at all. Jake had made a bold decision, hoping to prove himself to his father, and he was about to fall flat on his face.

"I'll be leaving for the night," Mrs. Miracle announced. "Karen—" the other sales associate "—is already gone."

He glanced at his watch. Five after nine. "By all means. You've put in a full day."

"So have you."

As the owner's son, Jake was expected to stay late. He wouldn't ask anything of his staff that he wasn't willing to do himself. That had been drilled into him by his father, who lived by the same rules.

"It's a lovely night for a walk in the park, don't you think?" the older woman said wistfully.

Jake lived directly across from Central Park. He often jogged through the grounds during the summer months, but winter was a different story.

Mrs. Miracle patted him on the back. "I appreciate that you let me stay here in the toy department," she said.

Jake turned to look at her. He hadn't said anything to the older woman about getting her transferred. He couldn't imagine HR had, either. He wondered how she'd found out about his sudden decision to keep her with him. Actually, it'd been Holly's comment about having a grandmotherly figure around that had influenced him. That, and Emily's obvious rapport with children.

"Good night, Mrs. Miracle," he said.

"Good night, Mr. Finley. Oh, and I don't think you need to worry about that robot," she said. "It's going to do very well. Mark my words."

Now it appeared the woman was a mind reader, too.

"I hope you're right," he murmured.

"I am," she said, reaching for her purse. "And remember,

this is a lovely evening for a stroll through the park. It's an excellent way to clear your head of worries."

Again, she'd caught him unawares. Jake had no idea he could be so easily read. Good thing he didn't play high-stakes poker. That thought amused him as he finished up for the day and left the store.

He was grateful not to run into his father because J.R. would certainly question him about those robots. No doubt his father already knew the dismal truth; the click of a computer key would show him everything.

When Jake reached his apartment, he was hungry and restless. He unwrapped the plate of cookies and quickly ate two. If this wasn't his mother's recipe, then it was a very similar one. They tasted the same as the cookies he recalled from his childhood.

Standing by the picture window that overlooked the park, he remembered the Christmas his mother and sister had been killed. The shock and pain of it seemed as fresh now as it'd been all those years ago. No wonder his father still refused to celebrate the holiday. Jake couldn't, either.

When he looked out, he noticed how brightly lit the park was. Horse-drawn carriages clattered past, and although he couldn't hear the clopping of the horses' hooves, it sounded in his mind as clearly as if he'd been out on the street. He suddenly saw himself with his parents and his sister, all huddled under a blanket in a carriage. The horse had been named Silver, he remembered, and the snow had drifted softly down. That was almost twenty-one years ago, the winter they'd died, and he hadn't taken a carriage ride since.

Mrs. Miracle had suggested he go for a walk that evening. An odd idea, he thought, especially after a long day spent dealing with harried shoppers. The last thing he'd normally want to do was spend even more time on his feet. And yet he felt irresistibly attracted to the park. The cheerful lights, the elegant carriages, the man on the corner selling roasted chestnuts, drew him like a kid to a Christmas tree.

None of this made any sense. He was exhausted, doubting himself and his judgment, entangled in memories he'd rather ignore. Perhaps a swift walk would chase away the demons that hounded him.

Putting on his coat, he wrapped the cashmere scarf around his neck. George, the building doorman, opened the front door and, hunching his shoulders against the wind, Jake hurried across the street.

"Aunt Holly, can we buy hot chestnuts?"

The young boy's voice immediately caught Jake's attention. He turned abruptly and came face-to-face with Holly Larson. The fourth time in less than twenty-four hours.

"Jake!"

"Holly."

They stared at each other, both apparently too shocked to speak.

She found her voice first. "What are you doing here?"

He pointed to the apartment building on the other side of the street. "I live over there. What are you doing here this late?"

"How late *is* it?"

He checked his watch. "Twenty to ten."

"Ten!" she cried. "You've got to be kidding. I had no idea it was so late. Hurry up, Gabe, it's time we got to the subway."

"Can we buy some chestnuts first?" he asked, gazing longingly at the vendor's cart.

"Not now. Come on, we have to go."

"I've never had roasted chestnuts before," the boy complained.

"Neither have I," Jake said, although that wasn't strictly true, and stepped up to the vendor. "Three, please."

"Jake, you shouldn't."

"Oh, come on, it'll be fun." He paid for the chestnuts, then handed bags to Holly and Gabe.

"I'm not sure how we got this far north," Holly said, walking close to his side as the three of them strolled down the street, eating chestnuts. "Gabe wanted to see the carriages in the park."

"Lindy told me about them." Gabe spoke with his mouth full. "Lindy Lee."

"Lindy Lee's my boss," Holly explained. "The designer."

Jake knew who she was, impressed that Holly worked for such a respected industry name.

"We went into Holly's office to decorate for Christmas, and Lindy was there and she let me put up stuff around her desk. That's when she told me about the horses in the park," Gabe said.

"Did you go for a ride?" Jake asked.

Gabe shook his head sadly. "Aunt Holly said it costs a lot of money."

"It is expensive," Jake agreed. "But sometimes you can make a deal with the driver. Do you want me to try?"

"Yeah!" Gabe said excitedly. "I've never been in a carriage before—not even once."

"Jake, no," Holly whispered, and laid a restraining hand on his arm. "I should get him home and in bed."

"Aunt Holly, *please!*" The eight-year-old's plaintive cry rang out. "It's Saturday."

"You're turning down a carriage ride?" Jake asked. He saw the dreamy look that came over Holly as a carriage rolled past—a white carriage drawn by a midnight-black horse. "Have you ever been on one?"

"No…"

"Then that settles it. The three of us are going." Several carriages had lined up along the street. Jake walked over to the first one and asked his price, which he willingly paid. All that talk about negotiating had been just that—talk. This was the perfect end to a magical day. Magical because of a plate of silly sugar cookies. Magical because of Holly and Gabe. Magical because of Christmas, reluctant though he was to admit it.

He helped Holly up into the carriage. When she was seated, he lifted Gabe so the boy could climb aboard, too. Finally he hoisted himself onto the bench across from Holly and Gabe. They shared a thick fuzzy blanket.

"This is great," Gabe exclaimed. "I can hardly wait to tell my dad."

Holly smiled delightedly. "I'm surprised he's still awake," she said. "We've been on the go for hours."

"There's nothing like seeing Christmas through the eyes of a child, is there?"

"Nothing."

"Reminds me of when I was a kid…"

The carriage moved into Central Park and, even at this hour, the place was alive with activity.

"Oh, look, Gabe," Holly said, pointing at the carousel. She wrapped her arm around the boy, who snuggled closer. "We'll go on the carousel this spring."

He nodded sleepily. The ride lasted about thirty minutes, and by the time they returned to the park entrance, Gabe's eyes had drifted shut.

"I was afraid this would happen," Holly whispered.

"We'll go to my apartment, and I'll contact a car service to get you home."

Holly shook her head. "I…appreciate that, but we'll take the subway."

"Nonsense," Jake said.

"Jake, I can't afford a car service."

"It's on me."

"No." She shook her head again. "I can't let you do that."

"You can and you will. If I hadn't insisted on the carriage ride, you'd have been home by now."

She looked as if she wanted to argue more but changed her mind. "Then I'll graciously accept and say thank-you. It's been a magical evening."

Magical. The same word he'd used himself. He leaped down, helped her and Gabe out, then carried Gabe across the street. The doorman held the door for them.

"Evening, Mr. Finley."

"Evening, George."

Holly followed him onto the elevator. When they reached the tenth floor and the doors glided open, he led the way down the hall to his apartment. He had to shift the boy in his arms to get his key in the lock.

Once inside Holly looked around her, eyes wide. By New York standards, his apartment was huge. His father had lived in it for fifteen years before moving to a different place. This apartment had suited Jake, so he'd taken it over.

"I see you're like me. I haven't had time to decorate for Christmas, either," she finally said. "I was so late getting the office done that I had to come in on a Saturday to do it."

"I don't decorate for the holidays," he said without explaining the reasons. He knew he probably sounded a little brusque; he hadn't meant to.

"I suppose you get enough of that working for the store."

He nodded, again avoiding an explanation. He laid a sleeping Gabe on the sofa.

"I'll see how long we'll have to wait for a car," he said. The number was on speed dial; he used it often, since he didn't own a car himself. In midtown Manhattan car ownership could be more of a liability than a benefit. He watched Holly walk over to the picture window and gaze outside. Apparently she found the scene as mesmerizing as he had earlier. Although he made every effort to ignore Christmas, it stared back at him from the street, the city, the park. New York was always intensely alive but never more so than in December.

The call connected with the dispatcher. "How may I help you?"

Jake identified himself and gave his account number and address, and was assured a car would be there in fifteen minutes.

"I'll ride with you," Jake told her when he'd hung up the phone.

His offer appeared to surprise her. "You don't need to do that."

"True, but I'd like to," he said with a smile.

She smiled shyly back. "I'd like it, too." Walking away from the window, she sighed. "I don't understand why, but I feel like I've known you for ages."

"I feel the same way."

"Was it only yesterday morning that you paid for my latte?"

"You were a damsel in distress."

"And you were my knight in shining armor," she said warmly. "You're still in character this evening."

He sensed that she wanted to change the subject because she turned away from him, resting her gaze on something across the room. "You know, you have the ideal spot for a Christmas tree in that corner," she said.

"I haven't celebrated Christmas in more than twenty years," Jake blurted out, shocking himself even more than Holly.

"I beg your pardon?"

Jake went back into the kitchen and found that his throat had gone dry and his hands sweaty. He never talked about his mother and sister. Not with anyone. Including his father.

"You don't believe in Christmas?" she asked, trailing after him. "What about Hanukkah?"

"Neither." He'd dug himself into a hole and the only way out was to explain. "My mother and sister were killed on Christmas Eve twenty-one years ago. A freak car accident that happened in the middle of a snowstorm, when two taxis collided."

"Oh, Jake. I'm so sorry."

"Dad and I agreed to forget about Christmas from that point forward."

Holly moved to his side. She didn't say a word and he was grateful. When people learned of the tragedy—almost always from someone other than him—they rarely knew what to say or how to react. It was an uncomfortable situation and still painful; he usually mumbled some remark about how long ago the accident had been and then tried to put it out of his mind. But he *couldn't,* any more than his father could.

Holly slid her arms around him and simply laid her head against his chest. For a moment, Jake stood unmoving as she held him. Then he placed his own arms around her. It felt as though she was an anchor, securing him in an unsteady sea. He needed her. *Wanted* her. Before he fully realized what he was doing, he lifted her head and lowered his mouth to hers.

The kiss was filled with urgency and need. She slipped

her arms around his neck, and her touch had a powerful effect on him.

He tangled his fingers in her dark shoulder-length hair and brought his mouth to hers a second time. Soon they were so involved in each other that it took him far longer than it should to hear the ringing of his phone.

He broke away in order to answer; as he suspected, the car was downstairs, waiting. When he told Holly, she immediately put on her coat. Gabe continued to sleep as Jake scooped him up, holding the boy carefully in both arms.

George opened the lobby door for them. Holly slid into the vehicle first, and then as Jake started to hand her the boy, he noticed a movement on the other side of the street.

"Jake?" Holly called from the car. "Please, there's no need for you to come. You've been so kind already."

"I want to see you safely home," he said as he stared across the street. For just an instant—it must have been his imagination—he was sure he'd seen Emily Merkle, better known as Mrs. Miracle.

Chapter Six

FORBIDDEN FRUIT CREATES MANY JAMS.

—MRS. MIRACLE

The phone rang just as Holly and Gabe walked into the apartment after church the next morning. For one wild second Holly thought it might be Jake.

Or rather, *hoped* it was Jake.

Although she'd been dead on her feet by the time they got to Brooklyn, she couldn't sleep. She'd lain awake for hours, thinking about the kisses they'd shared, replaying every minute of their time together. All of this was so unexpected and yet so welcome. Jake was—

"Hello," she said, sounding breathless with anticipation.

"What's this I hear about you turning my son into a girl?"

"Mickey!" Her brother's voice was as clear as if he were in the next room. He tried to phone on a regular basis, but it wasn't easy. The most reliable form of communication had proved to be email.

"So you're baking cookies with my son, are you?" he teased.

"We had a blast." Gabe was leaping up and down, eager to speak to his father. "Here, I'll let Gabe tell you about it himself." She passed the phone to her nephew, who immediately grabbed it.

"Dad! Dad, guess what? I went to Aunt Holly's office to help her decorate and then she took me to see the big tree at Rockefeller Center and we watched the skaters and had hot chocolate and then we walked to Central Park and had hot dogs for dinner, and, oh, we went to see Mrs. Miracle. I helped Aunt Holly roll out cookies and…" He paused for breath.

Evidently Mickey took the opportunity to ask a few questions, because Gabe nodded a couple of times.

"Mrs. Miracle is the lady in the toy department at Finley's," he said.

He was silent for a few seconds.

"She's really nice," Gabe continued. "She reminds me of Grandma Larson. I gave her a plate of cookies, and Aunt Holly gave cookies to Jake." Silence again, followed by "He's Aunt Holly's new boyfriend and he's really, really nice."

"Maybe I should talk to your father now," Holly inserted, wishing Gabe hadn't been so quick to mention Jake's name.

Gabe clutched the receiver in both hands and turned his back, unwilling to relinquish the phone.

"Jake took us on a carriage ride in Central Park and then…" Gabe stopped talking for a few seconds. "I don't know what happened after that 'cause I fell asleep."

Mickey was asking something else, and although Holly strained to hear what it was, she couldn't.

Whatever his question, Gabe responded by glancing at Holly, grinning widely and saying, "Oh, yeah."

"Are you two talking about me?" she demanded, half laughing and half annoyed.

She was ignored. Apparently Gabe felt there was a lot to tell his father, because he cupped his hand around the mouthpiece and whispered loudly, "I think they *kissed*."

"Gabe!" she protested. If she wanted her brother to know this, she'd tell him herself.

"Okay," Gabe said, nodding. He held out the phone to her. "Dad wants to talk to you."

Holly took it from him and glared down at her nephew.

"So I hear you've found a new love interest," Mickey said in the same tone he'd used to tease her when they were teenagers.

"Oh, stop. Jake and I hardly know each other."

"How'd you meet?"

"At Starbucks. Mickey, please, it's nothing. I only met him on Friday." It felt longer than two days, but this was far too soon to even suggest they were in a relationship.

"Gabe doesn't seem to feel that's a problem."

"Okay, so I took Jake a plate of cookies like Gabe said— it was just a thank-you for buying me a coffee—and…and we happened to run into him last evening in Central Park. It's no big deal. He's a nice person and, well…like I said, we've just met."

"But it looks promising," her brother added.

Holly hated to acknowledge how true that was. Joy and anticipation had surged through her from the moment she and Jake kissed. Still, she was afraid to admit this to her brother—and, for that matter, afraid to admit it to herself. "It's too soon to say that yet."

"Ah, so you're still hung up on Bill?"

Was she? Holly didn't think so. If Bill had ended the relationship by telling her the chemistry just wasn't there, she could've accepted that. Instead, he'd left her with serious doubts regarding her parenting abilities.

"Is that it?" Mickey pressed.

"No," she said. "Not at all. Bill and I weren't really meant to be together. I think we both realized that early on, only neither of us was ready to be honest about it."

"Mmm." Mickey made a sound of agreement. "Things are going better with Gabe, aren't they?"

"Much better."

"Good."

"He's adjusting and so am I." This past week seemed to have been a turning point. They were more at ease with each other. Gabe had made new friends and was getting used to life without his father—and with her. She knew she insisted on rules Mickey didn't bother with—like making their beds every morning, drinking milk with breakfast and, of course, putting the toilet seat down. But Gabe hardly complained at all anymore.

"What was it he told Santa he wanted for Christmas?" Mickey asked.

"So he emailed you about the visit with Santa, did he?"

"Yup, he sent the email right after he got home. He seemed quite excited."

"It's Intellytron the SuperRobot."

At her reference to the toy, Gabe's eyes lit up and he nodded vigorously.

"We found them in Finley's Department Store. Mrs. Miracle, the woman Gabe mentioned, works there…and Jake does, too."

"Didn't Gabe tell me Jake's name is Finley?" Mickey

asked. "He said he heard Mrs. Miracle call him that—Mr. Finley. Is he related to the guy who owns the store?"

"Y-e-s." How dense could she be? Holly felt like slapping her forehead. She'd known his name was Finley from the beginning and it hadn't meant a thing to her. But now…now she realized Jake was probably related to the Finley family—was possibly even the owner's son. No wonder he could afford to live where he did. He hadn't given the price of the carriage ride or the car service a second thought, either.

She had the sudden, awful feeling that she was swimming in treacherous waters and there wasn't a life preserver in sight.

"Holly?"

"I… I think he must be." She'd been so caught up in her juvenile fantasies, based on the coincidence of their meetings, that she hadn't paid attention to anything else.

"You sound like this is shocking news."

"I hadn't put two and two together," she confessed.

"And now you're scared."

"I guess I am."

"Don't be. He puts his pants on one leg at a time like everyone else, if you'll pardon the cliché. He's just a guy."

"Right."

"You don't seem too sure of that."

Holly wasn't. A chill had overtaken her and she hugged herself with one arm. "I need to think about this."

"While you're thinking, tell me more about this robot that's got my son so excited."

"It's expensive."

"How…expensive?"

Holly heard the hesitation in her brother's voice. He had his own financial problems. "Don't worry—I've got it. This is on me."

"You're sure about that?"

"Positive." The Christmas bonus checks were due the following Friday. If all went well, hers should cover the price of the toy with enough left over for a really special Christmas dinner.

Christmas.

When she woke that morning, still warm under the covers, Holly's first thought had been of Jake. She'd had the craziest idea that…well, it was out of the question now.

What Jake had confided about his mother and sister had nearly broken her heart. The tragedy had not only robbed him of his mother and sibling, it had destroyed his pleasure in Christmas. Holly had hoped to change that, but the mere notion seemed ridiculous now. She'd actually planned to invite Jake to spend Christmas Day with her and Gabe. She knew now that he'd never accept. He was a Finley, after all, a man whose background was vastly different from her own.

Half-asleep, she'd pictured the three of them sitting around her table, a lovely golden-brown turkey with sage stuffing resting in the center. She'd imagined Christmas music playing and the tree lights blinking merrily, enhancing the celebratory mood. She couldn't believe she'd even considered such a thing, knowing what she did now.

"I have a Christmas surprise coming your way," Mickey said. "I'm just hoping it arrives in time for the holidays."

"It doesn't matter," she assured her brother, dragging her thoughts away from Jake. She focused on her brother and nephew—which was exactly what she intended to do from this point forward. She needed to forget this romantic fantasy she'd invented within a day of meeting Jake Finley.

"I can guarantee Gabe will like it and so will you," Mickey was saying.

Holly couldn't begin to guess what Mickey might have purchased in Afghanistan for Christmas, but then her brother had always been full of surprises. He'd probably ordered something over the internet, she decided.

"Mom and Dad mailed us a package, as well," she told him. "The box got here this week."

"From Haiti? What would they be sending?"

"I don't have a clue," she said. Once the tree was up she'd arrange the gifts underneath it.

"You're going to wait until Christmas morning, aren't you?" he asked. "Don't open anything before that."

"Of course we'll wait." Even as kids, they'd managed not to peek at their gifts.

Mickey laughed, then grew serious. "This won't be an ordinary Christmas, will it?"

Holly hadn't dwelled on not being with her parents. Her father, a retired dentist, and her mother, a retired nurse, had offered their services in a health clinic for twelve months after the devastating earthquake. They'd been happy about the idea of giving back, and Holly had been happy for them. This Christmas was supposed to be Mickey, Gabe and her for the holidays—and then Mickey's National Guard unit had been called up and he'd left to serve his country.

"It could be worse," she said, and her thoughts involuntarily went to Jake and his father, who refused to celebrate Christmas at all.

"Next year everything will be different," Mickey told her.

"Yes, it will," she agreed.

Her brother spoke to Gabe for a few more minutes and then said goodbye. Gabe was pensive after the conversation with his father and so was Holly, but for different reasons.

"How about toasted cheese sandwiches and tomato soup for lunch?" she suggested, hoping to lighten the mood.

"That was your dad's and my favorite Sunday lunch when we were growing up."

Gabe looked at her suspiciously. "What kind of cheese?"

Holly shrugged. "Regular cheese?" By that she meant the plastic-wrapped slices, Gabe's idea of cheese.

"You won't use any of that buffalo stuff, will you?"

She grinned. "Buffalo mozzarella. Nope, this is plain old sliced regular cheese in a package."

"Okay, as long as the soup comes from a can. That's the way Dad made it and that's how I like it."

"You got it," she said, and moved into the kitchen.

Gabe sat on a stool and watched her work, leaning his elbows on the kitchen counter. Holly wasn't fooled by his intent expression. He wasn't interested in spending time with her; he was keeping a close eye on their lunch in case she tried to slip in a foreign ingredient. After a moment he released a deep sigh.

"What's that about?" she asked.

"I miss my dad."

"I know you do, sweetheart. I miss him, too."

"And Grandma and Grandpa."

"And they miss us."

Gabe nodded. "It's not so bad living with you. I thought it was at first, but you're okay."

"Thanks." She hid a smile and set a piece of buttered bread on the heated griddle, then carefully placed a slice of processed cheese on top before adding the second piece of bread. She planned to have a plain cheese sandwich herself—one with *real* cheese.

Obviously satisfied that she was preparing his lunch according to his specifications, Gabe clambered off the stool. "Can we go to the movies this afternoon?"

"Maybe." She had to be careful with her entertainment

budget, especially since there were additional expenses coming up this month. "It might be better if we got a video."

"Can I invite a friend over?"

She hesitated a moment, afraid he might want to ask his new friend, Billy.

"Sure," she said. "How about Jonathan Krantz?" Jonathan was another eight-year-old who lived in the building, and Caroline, his mother, sometimes babysat for her.

That was acceptable to Gabe.

After lunch they walked down to the neighborhood video store, found a movie they could both agree on and then asked Jonathan to join them.

Holly did her best to pay attention to the movie; however, her mind had a will of its own. No matter how hard she tried, all she could think about was Jake. He didn't phone and that was just as well. She wasn't sure what she would've said if he had.

Then again, he hadn't asked for her phone number. Still, he could get it easily enough if he wanted....

Late Sunday night, after Gabe was asleep, Holly went on the computer and did a bit of research. Sure enough, Jake was related to the owner. Not only that, he was the son and heir.

Monday morning, Holly dropped Gabe off at school and took the subway into Manhattan. As she walked past Starbucks, she felt a twinge of longing—for more than just the coffee they served. This was where she'd met Jake. Jake Finley.

As she walked briskly past Starbucks, the door flew open and Jake Finley dashed out, calling her name.

Holly pretended not to hear.

"Holly!" he shouted, running after her. "Wait up!"

Chapter Seven

COINCIDENCE IS WHEN GOD CHOOSES
TO REMAIN ANONYMOUS.

—MRS. MIRACLE

"Wait up!" Jake called. Holly acted as if she hadn't heard him. Jake knew better. She was clearly upset about something, although he couldn't figure out what. His mind raced with possibilities, but he couldn't come up with a single one that made sense.

Finally she turned around.

Jake relaxed. Just seeing her again brought him a feeling of happiness he couldn't define. He barely knew Holly Larson, yet he hadn't been able to forget her. She was constantly in his thoughts, constantly with him, and perhaps the most puzzling of all was the *rightness* he felt in her presence. He couldn't think of any other way to describe it.

Jake had resisted the urge to contact her on Sunday,

afraid of coming on too strong. They'd seen quite a bit of each other in the past few days, seemingly thrown together by fate. Coincidence? He supposed so, and yet... It was as though a providential hand was behind all this. Admittedly that sounded fanciful, even melodramatic. Nevertheless, four chance meetings in quick succession was hard to explain.

With someone else, a different kind of woman, Jake might have suspected these meetings had been contrived, and certainly this morning's was pure manipulation on his part. He'd hoped to run into her casually. But he hadn't expected to see Holly walk directly past the coffee shop. He couldn't allow this opportunity to pass.

She looked up at him expectantly; she didn't say anything.

"Good morning," he said, unsure of her mood.

"Hi." She just missed making eye contact.

He felt her reluctance and frowned, unable to fathom what he might have done to upset her. "What's wrong?" he asked.

"Nothing."

"Then why won't you look at me?"

The question forced her to raise her eyes and meet his. She held his gaze for only a fraction of a second before glancing away.

The traffic light changed and, side by side, they crossed the street.

"I'd like to take you to dinner," he said. He'd decided that if he invited her out on a real date they could straighten out the problem, whatever it was.

"When?"

At least she hadn't turned him down flat. That was encouraging. "Whenever you say." He'd rearrange his schedule if necessary. "Tonight? Tomorrow? I'm free every evening. Or I can be." He wanted it understood that he wasn't involved with anyone else. In fact, he hadn't been in a serious relationship in years.

His primary goal for the past decade had been to learn the retail business from the ground up, and as a result his social life had suffered. He worked long hours and that had taken a toll on his relationships. After his last breakup, which was in… Jake had to stop and think. June, he remembered. Had it really been that long? At any rate, Judith had told him it was over before they'd really begun.

At the time he'd felt bad, but agreed it was probably for the best. Funny how easily he could let go of a woman with hardly a pause after just four weeks. Judith had been attractive, successful, intelligent, but there'd been no real connection between them. The thought of letting Holly walk out of his life was a completely different scenario, one that filled him with dread.

All he could think about on Sunday was when he'd see her again. His pride had influenced his decision not to call her; he didn't want her to know how important she'd become to him in such a short time. Despite that, he'd gone to Starbucks first thing this morning.

"Tonight?" she repeated, referring to his dinner invitation. "You mean this evening?"

"Sure," he said with a shrug. "I'm available Tuesday night if that's better for you."

She hesitated, as if considering his offer. "Thanks, but I don't have anyone to look after Gabe."

"I could bring us dinner." He wasn't willing to give up that quickly.

Her eyes narrowed. "Why are you trying so hard?"

"Why are you inventing excuses not to see me?"

He didn't understand her reluctance. Saturday, when he'd dropped her off at her Brooklyn apartment and kissed her good-night, she'd practically melted in his arms. Now she couldn't get away from him fast enough.

Holly stared down at the sidewalk. People hurried past them and around them. They stood like boulders in the middle of a fast-moving stream, neither of them moving, neither talking.

"I… I didn't know who you were," she eventually admitted. "Not until later."

"I told you my name's Jake Finley." He didn't pretend not to understand what she meant. This wasn't the first time his family name had intimidated someone. He just hadn't expected that sort of reaction from Holly. He'd assumed she knew, and that was part of her charm because it hadn't mattered to her.

"I know you did," she countered swiftly. "And I feel stupid for not connecting the dots."

He stiffened. "And my name bothers you?"

"Not really," she said, and her gaze locked with his before she slowly lowered her lashes. "I guess it does, but not for the reasons you're assuming."

"What exactly am I assuming?" he asked.

"That I'd use you."

"For what?" he demanded.

"Well, for one thing, that robot toy. We both know how badly Gabe wants it for Christmas and it's expensive and you might think I…"

"*What* would I think?" he asked forcefully when she didn't complete her sentence.

"That I'd want you to get me the toy."

"Would you ask me to do that?" If she did, he'd gladly purchase it—retail price—on her behalf.

"No. Never." Her eyes flared with the intensity of her response. She started to leave and Jake followed.

"Then it's a moot point." He began to walk, carefully matching his longer stride to her shorter one. "Under no circumstances will I purchase that toy for you. Agreed?"

"Agreed," she said.

"Anything else?"

Holly looked at him and then away. "I don't come from a powerful family or know famous people or—"

"Do you think I care?"

"No, but if you did, you'd be plain out of luck."

He smiled. "That's fine with me."

"Okay," she said, stopping abruptly. "Can you explain why you want to see me?"

Jake wished he had a logical response. He felt drawn to her in ways he hadn't with other women. "I can't say for sure, but deep down I feel that if we were to walk away from each other right now, I'd regret it."

"You do?" she asked softly, and pressed her hand to her heart. "Jake, I feel the same way. What's happening to us?"

He didn't have an answer. "I don't know." But he definitely felt it, and that feeling intensified with each meeting.

They started walking again. "So, can I see you tonight?" he asked. That was important, necessary.

Her face fell. "I wasn't making it up, about not having anyone to take care of Gabe. If you were serious about bringing us dinner…"

"I was."

Her face brightened. "Then that would work out perfectly."

"Do you like take-out Chinese?" he asked, thinking Gabe would enjoy it, as well.

"Love it."

"Me, too, but you'll have to use chopsticks."

"Okay, I'll give it a try."

"Great." Jake breathed easier. Everything was falling into place, just the way he'd hoped it would. He glanced at his watch and grimaced. He was late for work. He hoped Karen or Mrs. Miracle had covered for him.

Retreating now, taking two steps backward, he called out to Holly, "Six-thirty? At your place?"

She nodded eagerly. "Yes. And thank you, Jake, thank you so much."

He raised his hand. "See you tonight."

"Tonight," she echoed, and they both turned and hurried off to their respective jobs.

Jake's step was noticeably lighter as he rushed toward the department store. By the time he arrived, ten minutes later than usual, he was breathless. He'd just clocked in and headed for the elevator when his father stopped him, wearing a frown that told him J.R. wasn't happy.

"Are you keeping bankers' hours these days?"

"No," Jake told him. "I had an appointment." A slight stretch of the truth.

"I was looking for you."

"Any particular reason?" Jake asked. He'd bet his lunch break this sudden interest in the toy department had to do with those robots.

His father surprised him, however, with a completely different question. "I heard from HR that you requested a transfer for one of the seasonal staff...."

"Mrs. Miracle."

"Who? No, that wasn't the name."

"No, it's Merkle or Michaels or something like that. The name badge mistakenly says Miracle, and she insisted that's what we call her."

His father seemed confused, which was fine with Jake. He felt he was being rather clever to keep J.R.'s attention away from the robots.

J.R. ignored the comment. "You asked for this Mrs. Miracle or whoever she is to be transferred and then you changed your mind. Do I understand correctly?"

"Yes. After I made the initial request, I realized she was a good fit for the department—a grandmotherly figure who relates well to kids *and* parents. She adds exactly the right touch."

"I see," his father murmured. "Okay, whatever you decide is fine."

That was generous, seeing that *he* was the department head, Jake mused with more affection than sarcasm.

"While I have you, tell me, how are sales of that expensive robot going?"

Jake wasn't fooled. His father already knew the answer to that. "Sales are picking up. We sold a total of twenty-five over the weekend."

"Twenty-five," his father said slowly. "There're still a lot of robots left in the storeroom, though, aren't there?"

"Yes," Jake admitted.

"That's what I thought."

He made some additional remark Jake couldn't quite grasp, but it didn't sound like something he wanted to hear, anyway, so he didn't ask J.R. to repeat it.

As he entered the toy department, clipping on his "Manager" badge, Jake was glad to see Mrs. Miracle on duty.

"Good morning, Mr. Finley," she said, looking pleased with herself.

"Good morning. I apologize for being late—"

"No problem. I sold two Intellytrons this morning."

"Already?" This was encouraging news and improved his workday almost before it had started. "That's wonderful!"

"They seem to be catching on."

The phone rang just then, and Jake stepped behind the counter to answer. The woman at the other end of the line was looking for Intellytron and sighed with audible relief when Jake assured her he had plenty in stock. She asked that he hold one for her.

"I'll be happy to," Jake said. He found Mrs. Miracle watching him, smiling, when he ended the conversation. "I think you might be right," he said. "That was a woman calling about Intellytron. She sounded excited when I told her we've got them."

Mrs. Miracle rubbed her palms together. "I knew it." The morning lull was about to end; in another half hour, the store would explode with customers. Since toys were on the third floor, it took time for shoppers to drift up the escalators and elevators, so they still had a few minutes of relative peace. Jake decided to take advantage of it by questioning his rather unusual employee.

"I thought I saw you on Saturday night," he commented in a nonchalant voice, watching her closely.

"Me?" she asked.

Jake noted that she looked a bit sheepish. "Did you happen to take a walk around Central Park around ten or ten-thirty?"

"My heavens, no! After spending all day on my feet, the last thing I'd do is wander aimlessly around Central Park. At that time of night, no less." Her expression turned serious. "What makes you ask?"

"I could've sworn that was you I saw across from the park."

She laughed as though the question was ludicrous. "You're joking, aren't you?"

"No." Jake grew even more suspicious. Her nervous reaction seemed to imply that she wasn't being completely truthful. "Don't you remember? You suggested I take a stroll through the park."

"I said that?"

"You did," he insisted. He wasn't about to be dismissed quite this easily. "You said it would help clear my head."

"After a long day at work? My goodness, what was I thinking?"

Jake figured the question was rhetorical, so he didn't respond. "I met Holly Larson and her nephew there," he told her.

"My, that was a nice coincidence, wasn't it?"

"Very nice," he agreed.

"Are you seeing her again?" the older woman asked.

"Yes, as a matter of fact, I am." He didn't share any details. The less she knew about his personal life, the better. Mrs. Miracle might appear to be an innocent senior citizen, but he had his doubts. Not that he suspected anything underhanded or nefarious. She seemed... Jake couldn't come up with the right word. He liked Mrs. Miracle and she was an excellent employee, a natural saleswoman. And yet... He didn't really know much about her.

And what he did know didn't seem to add up.

Chapter Eight

ASPIRE TO INSPIRE BEFORE YOU EXPIRE.

—MRS. MIRACLE

Holly felt as if she was walking on air the rest of the way into the office. It didn't matter how rotten her day turned out to be; no one was going to ruin it after her conversation with Jake.

She'd spent a miserable Sunday and had worked herself into a state after she'd discovered Jake's position with the department store. Son and heir. Now, having talked to him, she realized her concerns were irrelevant. Okay, so his family was rich and influential; that didn't define him or say anything about the person he really was.

The question that, inevitably, kept going around and around in her mind was why someone like Jake Finley would be interested in *her*. The reality was that he could have his pick of women. To further complicate the situation, she was taking care of Gabe. Lots of men would see her nephew as an encumbrance. Apparently not Jake.

Holly was happy they'd gotten this settled. She felt reassured about his interest—and about the fact that he'd promised not to purchase the robot for her. Mickey had offered, too, but she knew he was financially strapped. Besides, getting Gabe this toy for Christmas—as *her* gift to him—was important to Holly.

She couldn't entirely explain why. Maybe because of Bill's implication that she wasn't good with kids. She had something to prove—if not to Bill or Mickey or even Jake, she had to prove it to herself. Nothing was going to keep her from making this the best possible Christmas for Gabe.

Holly entered her cubicle outside Lindy Lee's office and hung up her coat. She'd been surprised to find her boss in the office on Saturday afternoon and had tried to keep Gabe occupied so he wouldn't pester her. Unfortunately, Holly's efforts hadn't worked. She'd caught Gabe with Lindy Lee twice. One look made her suspect Lindy didn't really appreciate the intrusion. As soon as they'd finished putting up the decorations, Holly had dragged Gabe out with her. But this morning, as she looked around the office, she was pleased with her work. The bright red bulbs that hung outside her cubicle created an air of festivity. She couldn't help it—she started singing "Jingle Bells."

"Where is that file?" Lindy Lee shouted. She was obviously in her usual Monday-morning bad mood. Her employer was sorting through her in-basket, cursing impatiently under her breath.

Of course, Lindy Lee didn't mention *which* file she needed. But deciphering vague demands was all part and parcel of Holly's job. And fortunately she had a pretty good idea which one her boss required.

Walking into Lindy Lee's office, Holly reached across the top of the desk, picked up a file and handed it to her.

Lindy Lee growled something back, opened the file and then smiled. "Thank you."

"You're welcome," Holly said cheerfully.

The designer eyed her suspiciously. "What are *you* so happy about?" she asked.

"Nothing… I met up with a friend this morning, that's all."

"I take it this *friend* is a man."

Holly nodded. "A very special man."

"Honey, don't believe it." She laughed as though to say Holly had a lot to learn about the opposite sex. "Men will break your heart before breakfast and flush it down the toilet just for fun."

Holly didn't bother to explain about Jake. Lindy Lee's experience with men might be far more extensive than her own, but it was obviously different. Jake would never do anything to hurt her; she was sure of it. Besides, Lindy Lee socialized in different circles—Jake's circles, she realized with a start. Still, Holly couldn't make herself believe Jake was the kind of man who'd mislead her. Even though they'd known each other so briefly, every instinct she had told her she could trust him, and she did.

No irrational demand or bad temper was going to spoil her day, Holly decided. Because that evening she was seeing Jake.

Holly guessed wrong. Her day was ruined.

Early that afternoon she slipped back into her cubicle after delivering Lindy Lee's latest sketches to the tech department, where they'd be translated into patterns, which would then be sewn up as samples. Lindy was talking to the bookkeeper and apparently neither one noticed that she'd returned.

Holly hadn't intended to listen in on the conversation, but it would've been impossible not to with Lindy Lee's office door wide-open. In Holly's opinion, if Lindy wanted to keep the conversation private, then it was up to her to close the door.

"Christmas bonuses are due this Friday," Marsha, the bookkeeper, reminded their boss.

"Due." Lindy Lee pounced on the word. "Since when is a bonus *due?* It's my understanding that a bonus is exactly that—a bonus—an extra that's distributed at my discretion."

"Well, yes, but you've given us one every year since you went out on your own."

"That's because I could afford to."

"You've had a decent year," Marsha said calmly.

Holly wanted to stand and cheer. Marsha was right; profits were steady despite the economy. The staff had worked hard, although their employer took them for granted. Lindy Lee didn't appear to notice or value the team who backed her both personally and professionally. More times than she cared to count, Holly had dropped off and picked up Lindy's dry cleaning or run errands for her. She often went above and beyond anything listed in her job description.

Not once had she complained. The way Holly figured it, her main task was to give Lindy Lee the freedom to be creative and do what she did best and that was design clothes.

"A *decent* year, perhaps," Lindy Lee repeated. "But not a stellar one."

"True," Marsha agreed. "But you're holding your own in a terrible economy."

"All right, I'll reconsider." Lindy Lee walked over to the

window, her back to Holly. Not wanting to be caught listening, Holly quietly stood. There was plenty to do away from her desk—like filing. Clutching a sheaf of documents, she held her breath as she waited for Lindy's decision.

"Everyone gets the same bonus as last year," Lindy Lee said with a beleaguered sigh.

Holly released her breath.

"Everyone except Holly Larson."

Her heart seemed to stop.

"Why not Holly?" Marsha asked.

"She doesn't deserve it," Lindy Lee said flippantly. "She's out of the office at the stroke of five and she's been late for work a number of mornings, as well."

The bookkeeper was quick to defend Holly. "Yes, but she's looking after her nephew while her brother's in Afghanistan. This hasn't been easy for her, you know."

Lindy Lee whirled around and Holly moved from her line of vision in the nick of time. She flattened herself against the wall and continued to listen.

"Yes, yes, I met the boy this weekend. She brought him on Saturday when she came in to decorate."

"On her own time," Marsha said pointedly.

"True, but if she managed her time better, Holly could've done it earlier. As it is, the decorations are up much later than in previous years. If I was giving out bleeding-heart awards this Christmas, I'd make sure Holly got one. No, I won't change my mind," she snapped as Marsha began to protest. "A bonus is a bonus, and as far as I'm concerned Holly doesn't deserve one. It's about merit, you know, and going the extra mile, and she hasn't done that."

Holly gasped.

"But—"

"I've made my decision."

Marsha didn't argue further.

Holly didn't blame her. The bookkeeper had tried. Holly felt tears well up but blinked them away. She was a good employee; she worked hard. While Lindy Lee was correct—these days she *did* leave the office on time—there'd been many a night earlier in the year when she'd stayed late without being asked. She'd often gone that extra mile for her employer. Yet all Lindy seemed to remember was the past three months.

She felt sick to her stomach. So there'd be no bonus for her. Although the amount of money wasn't substantial— maybe five hundred dollars—it would've made all the difference. But somehow, she promised herself, she'd find a way to buy Gabe his special Christmas toy.

Even though she was distracted by her financial worries, Holly managed to enjoy dinner with Jake and Gabe that evening. Jake brought chopsticks along with their take-out Chinese—an order large enough to feed a family of eight. Several of the dishes were new to Holly. He'd chosen moo shu pork and shrimp in lobster sauce, plus barbecue pork, egg rolls, fried rice and almond fried chicken.

Gabe loved every minute of their time with Jake. As he so eloquently said, "It's nice being around a guy."

"I don't know," Jake commented as he slipped his arm around Holly's waist. "Women aren't so bad."

Gabe considered his comment carefully. "Aunt Holly's okay, I guess."

"You *guess,*" she sputtered. Using her chopsticks she removed the last bit of almond fried chicken from her nephew's plate.

"Hey, that was mine," Gabe cried.

"That's what you get for criticizing women," Holly told

him, and then, to prove her point, she reached for his fried dumpling, too. In retaliation, Gabe reached across for her egg roll, dropping it on the table.

Jake immediately retrieved it and stuck one end in his mouth. "Five-second rule," he said just before he bit down.

When they'd finished, they cleared the table and settled down in front of the television.

As Jake flipped through the channels, Gabe asked, "When are we gonna put up the Christmas tree?"

"This week," Holly told him. She'd need to budget carefully now that she wasn't going to get her bonus. The tree— she'd hoped to buy a real one—was an added expense she'd planned to cover with the extra money. This year she'd have to resort to the small artificial tree she'd stuck in the back of her coat closet.

The news that she wouldn't be receiving the bonus was devastating. Holly's first instinct had been to strike back. If everyone else was getting a bonus, it didn't seem fair that she wasn't. Still, Lindy Lee had a point. Holly hadn't been as dedicated to her job since Gabe came into her life. She had other responsibilities now.

That afternoon she'd toyed with the idea of looking for a new job. She could walk out—that would show Lindy Lee. Reason quickly asserted itself. She couldn't leave her job and survive financially. It could take her months to find a new one. And although this was an entry-level position, the chance to advance in the fashion world was an inducement she simply couldn't reject that easily. She'd made friends at the office, too. Friends like Marsha, who'd willingly defended her to their employer.

Besides, if she left her job, there'd be dozens who'd leap at the opportunity to take her place. No, Holly would swallow her disappointment and ride this out until Mickey returned. Next Christmas would be different.

"Can Jake help decorate the Christmas tree?" Gabe asked.

Jake was sitting next to her and Holly felt him tense. His face was pale, his expression shocked.

"Jake." Holly said his name softly and laid her hand on his forearm. "Are you okay?"

"Sure. Sorry, no decorating trees for me this year," he said in an offhand way.

"Why not?" Gabe pressed. "It's really fun. Aunt Holly said she'd make popcorn and we'd have cider. She has some ornaments from when she and my dad were kids. She won't let me see them until we put up the tree. It'll be lots of fun." His young face pleaded with Jake to reconsider.

Holly gently placed her hand on her nephew's shoulder. "Jake said another time," she reminded him. Jake hadn't participated in any of the usual Christmas traditions or activities in more than twenty years, ever since he'd lost his mother and sister.

"But there won't be another time," her nephew sulked. "I'll be with my dad next year."

"Jake's busy," Holly said, offering yet another excuse.

"Sorry to let you down, buddy," Jake told Gabe. "We'll do something else, all right?"

Gabe shrugged, his head hanging. "Okay."

"How about if I take you ice-skating at Rockefeller Center? Would you like that?"

"Wow!" In his excitement, Gabe propelled himself off the sofa and landed with a thud on the living room carpet. "I wanted to go skating last Saturday but Aunt Holly doesn't know how."

"She's a girl," Jake said in a stage whisper. Then he looked at her and grinned boyishly. "Frankly, I'm glad of it."

"As you should be," she returned under her breath.

"When can we go?" Gabe wasn't letting this opportunity slip through his fingers. He wanted to nail down the date as soon as possible. "I took skating lessons last winter," he said proudly.

Jake hesitated. "I'll need to get back to you once I see how everything goes at the store. It's the Christmas season, you know, so we might have to wait until the first week of the new year. How about Sunday the second?"

"That *long?*"

"Yes, but then I'll have more time to show you some classic moves. Deal?"

Gabe considered this compromise and finally nodded. "Deal." They clenched their fists and bumped them together to seal the bargain.

The three of them sat side by side and watched a rerun of *Everybody Loves Raymond* for the next half hour. Jake was beside her, his arm around her shoulders. Gabe sat to her left with his feet tucked beneath him.

When the program ended, Gabe turned to Jake. "Do you want me to leave the room so you can kiss my aunt Holly?"

"Gabe!" Holly's cheeks were warm with embarrassment.

"What makes you suggest that?" Jake asked the boy.

Gabe stood in the center of the room. "My dad emailed and said if you came to the apartment, I should dis-dis-creetly leave for a few minutes, only I don't know what that word means. I think it means you want to kiss Aunt Holly without me watching. Right?"

Jake nodded solemnly. "Something like that."

"I thought so. Okay, I'm going to go and get ready for

bed." He enunciated each word as if reading a line of dialogue from an unfamiliar play.

Jake winked at Holly. "Pucker up, sweetheart," he said, doing a recognizable imitation of Humphrey Bogart.

Holly rolled her eyes and clasped her hands prayerfully. "Ah, sweet romance."

As soon as the bedroom door closed, Jake pulled her into his arms. The kiss was everything she'd remembered and more. They kissed repeatedly until Gabe came back and stood in front of them. He cleared his throat.

"Should I go away again?" he asked.

"No, that's fine," Holly said. She had trouble speaking.

"Your timing is perfect," Jake assured the boy.

Jake left shortly after that, and once she'd let him out of the apartment, Holly leaned against the door, still a little breathless. Being with Jake was very nice, indeed, but she had something else on her mind at the moment—Intellytron the SuperRobot and how she was going to afford one before Christmas.

Chapter Nine

IT'S HARD TO STUMBLE WHEN YOU'RE
DOWN ON YOUR KNEES.
—SHIRLEY, GOODNESS AND MERCY,
FRIENDS OF MRS. MIRACLE

Holly gave the situation regarding Gabe and the robot careful thought during the sleepless night that followed their dinner. She'd asked Jake about it when Gabe was out of earshot.

"There are still plenty left," he'd told her.

"But they're selling, aren't they?"

"Yes, sales are picking up."

That was good for him but unsettling for her. If she couldn't afford to pay for the robot until closer to Christmas, then she'd need to make a small deposit and put one on layaway now. She didn't know if Finley's offered that option; not many stores did anymore. She'd have to check with Jake. She dared not take a chance that Intellytron would sell out before she had the cash.

While she was dead set against letting Jake purchase the robot for her, she hoped he'd be willing to put one aside, even if layaway wasn't a current practice at higher-end department stores. If she made their lunches, cut back on groceries and bought only what was absolutely necessary, she should be able to pay cash for the robot just before Christmas.

Tuesday morning she packed a hard-boiled egg and an apple for lunch. For Gabe she prepared a peanut butter and jelly sandwich, adding an apple for him, too, plus the last of the sugar cookies. Gabe hadn't been happy to take a packed lunch. He much preferred to buy his meal with his friends. But it was so much cheaper for him to bring it—and, at this point, necessary, although of course she couldn't tell him why. The leftover Chinese food figured into her money-saving calculations, too. It would make a great dinner.

On her lunch hour, after she'd eaten her apple and boiled egg, Holly hurried to Finley's to talk to Jake. She'd been uneasy from the moment she'd learned she wasn't getting a Christmas bonus. She wouldn't relax until she knew the SuperRobot would still be available the following week.

Unfortunately, Jake wasn't in the toy department.

"He's not here?" Holly asked Mrs. Miracle, unable to hide her disappointment.

"He's with his father just now," the older woman told her, and then frowned. "I do hope the meeting goes smoothly. It can be difficult to read the senior Mr. Finley sometimes. But I have faith that all will end well." Her eyes twinkled as she spoke.

Holly hoped she'd explain, and Mrs. Miracle obliged.

"In case you didn't hear, Jake went over the department

buyer's head when he ordered those extra robots," she confided, "and that's caused some difficulty with his father. J. R. Finley has a real stubborn streak."

Mrs. Miracle seemed very well-informed about the relationship between Jake and his father. "The robots are selling, though. Isn't that right?" she asked, again torn between pleasure at Jake's success and worry about laying her hands on one of the toys. The display appeared to be much smaller than last week.

"Thankfully, yes," Mrs. Miracle told her. "Jake took quite a risk, you know?"

Holly shook her head.

"Jake tried to talk Mike Scott into ordering more of the robots, but Mike refused to listen, so Jake did what he felt was best." Her expression sobered. "His father was not pleased, to put it mildly."

"But you said they're selling."

"Oh, yes. We sold another twenty-five over the weekend and double that on Monday." She nodded sagely. "I can only assume J.R. is feeling somewhat reassured."

"That's great." Holly meant it, but a shiver of dread went through her.

"Several of our competitors have already sold out," Mrs. Miracle said with a gleeful smile.

"That's terrific news." And it was—for Finley's. Parents searching for the toy would now flock to one of the few department stores in town with enough inventory to meet demand.

"How's Gabe?" Mrs. Miracle asked, changing the subject.

"He's doing fine." Holly chewed her lip, her thoughts still on the robot. "Seeing how well the robot's selling, would it be possible for me to set one aside on a layaway plan?"

The older woman's smile faded. "Oh, dear, the store doesn't have a layaway option. They haven't in years. Is that going to be a problem for you?"

Holly wasn't surprised that layaway was no longer offered, but she figured it was worth asking. Holly clutched her purse. "I... I don't know." Her mind spinning, she looked hopefully at the older woman. "Do you think you could hold one of the robots for me?" She hated to make that kind of request, but with her credit card temporarily out of commission and no layaway plan, she didn't have any other choice. The payment she'd made on her card would've been processed by now, but she didn't dare risk a purchase as big as this.

"Oh, dear, I'm really not sure."

"Could you ask Jake for me?" Holly inquired. She'd do it herself if he was there.

"Of course. I just don't think I could go against store policy, being seasonal staff and all."

"I wouldn't want you to do that, Mrs. Miracle."

"However, I'm positive Jake would be happy to help if he can." She leaned closer and lowered her voice. "He's rather sweet on you."

Sweet? That was a nice, old-fashioned word. "He's been wonderful to me and Gabe."

"So I understand. Didn't he bring you dinner last night?"

Holly wondered how Mrs. Miracle knew about that, unless Jake had mentioned it. No reason not to, she supposed. "Yes, and it was a lovely evening," she said. The only disappointment had come when Gabe asked him to help decorate the tree and Jake refused. The mere suggestion had distressed him. She hadn't realized that the trauma of those family deaths was as intense and painful as if the accident had just happened. If it was this traumatic for Jake, Holly could only imagine what it was like for his father.

"Did you know Jake and his father leave New York every Christmas Eve?" Mrs. Miracle whispered.

It was as if the older woman had been reading her mind. "I beg your pardon?"

"Jake and his father leave New York every Christmas Eve," she repeated.

Holly hadn't known this and wasn't sure what to say.

"Isn't that a shame?"

Holly shrugged. "Everyone deals with grief differently," she murmured. Her brother handled the loss of his wife with composure and resolve. That was his personality. Practical. Responsible. As he'd said himself, he couldn't fall apart; he had a boy to raise.

Sally had been sick for a long while, giving Mickey time to prepare for the inevitable—at least to the extent anyone can. He'd loved Sally and missed her terribly, especially in the beginning. Yet he'd gone on with his life, determined to be a good father.

Perhaps the difference was that for the Finleys, the deaths had come suddenly, without warning. The family had awakened the morning of Christmas Eve, excited about the holiday. There'd been no indication that by the end of the day tragedy would befall them. The shock, the grief, the complete unexpectedness of the accident, had remained an unhealed wound all these years.

"He needs you," Mrs. Miracle said.

"Me?" Holly responded with a short laugh. "We barely know each other."

"Really?"

"We met last week, remember?"

"Last week," she echoed, with that same twinkle in her eye. "But you like him, don't you?"

"Yes, I guess I do," Holly admitted.

"You should invite him for a home-cooked dinner."

Funny, Holly had been thinking exactly that. She'd wait, not wanting to appear too eager—although heaven knew that was how she felt. And of course there was the problem of her finances....

"I'd like to have Jake over," she began. "He—"

"Did I hear someone mention my name?" Jake said from behind her.

"Jake!" She turned to face him as his assistant moved away to help a young couple who'd approached the department. From the corner of her eye, Holly saw that the husband and wife Mrs. Miracle had greeted were pointing at the SuperRobot. Mrs. Miracle picked up a box and walked over to the cash register to ring up the sale.

"Holly?" Jake asked.

"I need to put Intellytron on layaway but Mrs. Miracle told me you don't do that," she said in a rush.

"Sorry, no. I thought you were going to use your Christmas bonus to purchase the robot this week."

"I'm not getting one," she blurted out. She was close to tears, which embarrassed her.

"Listen, I'll buy the robot for Gabe and—"

"No," she broke in. "We already talked about that, remember? I won't let you."

"Why not?"

"Because... I just won't. Let's leave it at that."

He frowned but reluctantly agreed. "Okay, if that's the way you want it."

"That's the way it has to be."

"At least let me hold one for you," Jake said before she could compose herself enough to ask.

"You can do that?"

Jake nodded. "Sure. I'll set one aside right away and put your name on it. I'll tell everyone on staff that it isn't to be sold. How does that sound?"

She closed her eyes as relief washed over her. "Thank you. That would be perfect."

"Are you all right now?" He placed his hand on her shoulder in a comforting gesture.

"I'm fine. I apologize if I seem unreasonable."

"I understand."

"You do?" Holly wasn't convinced she could explain it herself. She just knew she had to do this. For Gabe, for Mickey…and for herself. The robot had become more than a toy. It was a symbol of her commitment to her nephew and her desire to give him the Christmas he deserved.

She saw that the department was busy and she was keeping Jake from his customers. "I have to get back to the office," she said.

He grinned. "Next time maybe you could stay longer."

Holly smiled back. "Next time I will."

"I'll call you. You're in the phone directory?"

She nodded, hoping she'd hear from him soon. "See you, Jake."

"See you, Holly."

As she walked toward the elevator, Mrs. Miracle joined her. "Mr. Finley suggested I take my lunch hour now," she said as they stepped into the empty car together. "What I feel like having is fried chicken."

"Fried chicken," Holly echoed. "My mother, who was born and raised in the South, has a special family recipe but she hasn't made it in years. I can't even remember the last time we ate fried chicken." In this age of heart-healthy diets, her mother had focused on lean, low-carb meals.

"A special recipe?" Mrs. Miracle murmured. "I'll bet it was good."

"The best." Now that she thought about it, Holly figured she might have a copy in her kitchen. "Mom put together a book of family recipes for me when I left home. I wonder if she included that one." Fried chicken was the ultimate comfort food and would make a wonderful dinner when she invited Jake over—sometime in the new year.

"She probably did. That sounds just like her."

"You know my mother?" Holly asked, surprised.

"No…no, but having met you, I know she must be a very considerate woman, someone who cares about family and traditions."

What a lovely compliment. The kind words helped take the sting out of her employer's refusal to give Holly a Christmas bonus. Lindy Lee was a modern-day Scrooge as far as Holly was concerned.

That evening, as dinner heated in the microwave, Holly searched through her kitchen drawers for the notebook where her mother had written various recipes passed down through her family.

"What would you think of homemade fried chicken for Christmas?" Holly asked Gabe. It wasn't the traditional dinner but roast turkey with all the fixings was out of her budget now. If Gabe considered her fried chicken a success, she'd serve it again when Jake came over.

"I've had take-out chicken. Is that the same?"

"The same?" she repeated incredulously. "Not even close!"

"Then I've never had it." He shrugged. "If it's not frozen or out of a can Dad doesn't know how to make it," Gabe said. "Except for macaroni and cheese in the box." He sat down at the computer and logged on to the internet, preparing to send an email to his father, as he did every night. He hadn't typed more than a few words when he turned and looked at Holly. "What's for dinner tonight?"

"Leftover Chinese. You okay with that?"

"Sure." Gabe returned to the computer screen.

Ten minutes later, he asked, "Can you invite Jake for Christmas dinner?"

"He won't be able to come."

"Why not?"

"He's going away for Christmas."

Gabe was off the internet and playing one of his games, jerking the game stick left and right as he battled aliens. "Why?"

"You'll have to ask him."

"I will." Apparently he'd won the battle because he let go of the stick and faced her. "You're going to see him again, right? You want to, don't you?"

Even an eight-year-old boy could easily see through her. "I hope so."

"Me, too," Gabe said, then added, "Billy wants me to come over after school on Friday. I can go, can't I?" He regarded her hopefully.

The boys had obviously remained friends. "I'll clear it with his dad first." Holly had been meaning to talk to Bill before this. She'd make a point of doing it soon, although she wasn't looking forward to contacting him.

The good news was that she'd found the recipe in her mother's book.

Fried Chicken

(from *Debbie Macomber's Cedar Cove Cookbook*)

The key to crisp fried chicken is cooking at a high temperature. Stick a candy or deep-frying thermometer in the chicken as you fry to make sure the oil temperature remains between 250° and 300°F.

1 whole chicken (about 3 ½ pounds), cut into
10 pieces
1 quart buttermilk
2 tablespoons Tabasco or other hot sauce
2 cups all-purpose flour
Salt and pepper, to taste
2 large eggs
1 teaspoon baking powder
½ teaspoon baking soda
Vegetable oil or shortening

1. Rinse chicken. In a large bowl or resealable plastic bag, combine buttermilk and Tabasco. Add chicken pieces, turn to coat. Refrigerate, covered, for at least 8 hours and up to 16, turning the pieces occasionally. Remove chicken from buttermilk; shake off excess. Arrange in a single layer on large wire rack set over rimmed baking sheet. Refrigerate, uncovered, for 2 hours.

2. Measure flour into large shallow dish; whisk in some salt and pepper. In a medium bowl, beat eggs, baking powder and baking soda. Working in batches of 3, drop chicken pieces in flour and shake dish to coat. Shake excess flour from each piece. Using tongs, dip chicken pieces into egg mixture, turning to coat well and al-

lowing excess to drip off. Return chicken pieces to flour; coat again, shake off excess and set on wire rack.

3. Preheat oven to 200°F. Set oven rack to middle position. Set another wire rack over a rimmed baking sheet, and place in oven. Line a large plate with paper towels. Pour oil about ½ inch up the side of a large, heavy skillet. Place skillet over high heat; let pan warm until oil shimmers.

4. Place half of chicken, skin-side down, in hot oil. Reduce heat to medium and fry 8 minutes, until deep golden brown. Turn chicken pieces; cook an additional eight minutes, turning to fry evenly on all sides. Using tongs, transfer chicken to paper towel–lined plate. After draining, transfer chicken to wire rack in oven. Fry remaining chicken, transferring pieces to paper towel–lined plate to drain, then to wire rack in oven to keep warm.

Serves 4 to 6.

Chapter Ten

MAY YOU LIVE ALL THE DAYS OF YOUR LIFE.

—MRS. MIRACLE

Emily Merkle smiled to herself. This latest assignment was going well. She enjoyed the ones that took place during the Christmas season most of all. She hadn't expected the romance between Jake and Holly to develop quite this quickly, so that was a bonus. Those two were very good together—and good for each other.

She attached her name badge to her sweater and hung her purse in the employee locker, then headed up to the toy department. She'd grown fond of Jake Finley. He was a kindhearted young man, a bit reserved, to be sure, but willing to take a risk he believed in. The robots were one example of that, his pursuit of Holly another.

Walking toward the elevator, she saw J. R. Finley, who'd

just come into the hallway. He stopped, and his eyes automatically went to her badge.

"Mrs. Miracle," he said thoughtfully. He seemed to be mulling over where he'd heard it before.

"Mr. Finley," she said in the same thoughtful tone.

"To the best of my recollection, we don't have an employee here at Finley's named Miracle."

Emily was about to identify herself, but before she could, J.R. continued.

"I pride myself on knowing the name of every employee at the Thirty-Fourth Street Finley's. Including seasonal staff." He narrowed his eyes. "Just a minute. I remember my son mentioning you earlier."

"The name is Merkle," Emily told him. "Emily Merkle."

Finley shook his head. "Can't say I'm familiar with that name, either."

"If you check with HR, I'm sure—"

"You're working with my son in the toy department, aren't you?" he said abruptly.

Emily frowned. "Are you always this rude, or are you making an exception in my case?"

He blinked twice.

He was used to everyone kowtowing to him. Well, *she* wouldn't do it.

"I beg your pardon?"

Emily met his look boldly. "I was saying something, young man."

J.R.'s head reared back and he released a howl of laughter. "*Young* man? My dear woman, it's been a long time since anyone referred to me as young."

Compared to her, he was practically in diapers. "That's beside the point."

He seemed confused.

"As I was saying," Emily continued politely, "if you care to check with HR, you'll find that I was hired last week as seasonal help."

"Only last week?" J.R. smiled at her. "That explains it, then."

"It does, indeed." She started down the hallway and was surprised when J.R. kept pace with her.

"You *are* working with my son, correct?"

"Yes. The toy department is extremely busy this time of year, as you well know." She glanced pointedly at her watch, wanting him to realize she should be on the floor that very moment.

"My son made a huge error in judgment by ordering five hundred of those expensive robots."

She was puzzled by his willingness to discuss business—and family—matters with a short-term employee. But she couldn't let his comment go unchallenged. "You think so, do you?" she asked mildly.

He gave her a startled look, as if no one had dared question his opinion before. "I know so," he insisted.

Emily was curious as to why he felt Jake was wrong and he was right. "Please tell me why you're so convinced your son's about to fail."

"Good grief, woman—"

"Call me Mrs. Miracle."

"Fine, Mrs. Miracle. Do you realize exactly how many of these… Intellytromps he needs to sell by Christmas? That's less than two weeks from now. It'll never happen."

"They're Intelly*trons*."

"Tromps, trons, whatever. They won't sell. Mark my words. It would take a miracle." He grinned broadly, obviously thinking himself very clever.

"You called?" she said, and laughed.

J.R. apparently didn't like the fact that she'd responded to his joke with one of her own. Instead of laughing, he scowled.

"Never mind," she said with a sigh. "I just wish you had more faith in your son."

He quickly took offense. "My son is my concern."

"He *is* your concern," she agreed. "And your future. So it's time you trusted his judgment."

She'd really ruffled his feathers now. He grew red in the face and puffed up like an angry rooster, his chest expanding. "Now listen here. I won't have an employee talking to me as if I'm some messenger boy."

Emily stood her ground. "Someone needs to tell you the truth and it might as well be me."

"Is that so?"

He sounded like a third-grader exchanging insults on the playground.

"You need to give your son a bit of leeway to make his own mistakes instead of second-guessing all his decisions."

He opened and closed his mouth as if he couldn't speak fast enough to say what was on his mind. He thrust out one hand. "Your badge."

So he intended to fire her. "You don't want to do that," she told him calmly.

"I will not have an insubordinate employee working in my store!"

"I'm temporary help," she reminded him. "I'll be gone soon enough."

"I expect you gone *today*."

"Sorry, I'm afraid that would be impossible. You'll need to reconsider."

Once again he couldn't seem to speak. "Are...are you

refusing to leave the premises?" he finally managed to sputter.

"Jacob Robert, settle down. You've always had a problem with your temper, haven't you? Now, take a deep breath and listen to me. You do not want to fire me this close to Christmas."

"Are you threatening me?" he growled. "And how do you know my middle name?"

"Not in the least," she said, answering his first question and ignoring his second.

"I'm calling Security and having you escorted from the building. Your check will be mailed to you."

"Security?" The image of two beefy security guards lifting her by the arms and marching her outside was so comical it made Emily laugh.

That seemed to infuriate him even more. "Do you find this humorous?"

"Frankly, yes." She wouldn't lie; the man was insufferable. Oh, heavens, she did have her work cut out for her. "Now, if you'll excuse me, your son needs my help."

His jaw sagged as she scurried past him and walked quickly to the elevator.

As she suspected, the toy department was in chaos. Poor Jake was run ragged—thanks, in part, to his father, who'd taken too much pleasure in making her late for her shift. That man was about to meet his match. Emily Merkle was not going to let one overstuffed, pigheaded man stand in the way of her mission.

She'd been on the floor for thirty minutes or so when J.R. unexpectedly showed up. When he saw how busy the department was, he did a double take.

"Don't stand there gawking," Emily said as she marched past him, leading a customer to the cash register. Brenda and Karen, also on duty, were bustling around, answering questions, ringing up sales, demonstrating toys.

He stared at her blankly.

"Help," she told him. "We could use an extra pair of hands, in case you hadn't noticed."

"Ah…" He froze, as if he didn't know where to start.

"That couple over there," Emily said, pointing in the direction of the board games. "They have a three-year-old and a six-year-old and they're looking for suggestions. Give them a few."

"Ah…"

"Don't just stand there with your mouth hanging open," she ordered. "Get to work!"

To his credit, J.R. rolled up his sleeves and dug in. J. R. Finley might know the name of every employee in his store—with minor exceptions, of course—but he was in way over his head when it came to recommending board games. To *her* credit, Emily kept her mouth shut.

At four o'clock there was a slight lull. "Dad," Jake greeted his father. "What brings you down here?"

J.R. squinted at Emily but didn't answer.

"Whatever it was, I'm grateful." He turned to Emily. "How many Intellytrons did we sell this afternoon?"

"Sixteen."

"Fabulous!" Jake couldn't conceal his excitement.

His father, however, looked as though he needed to sit down, put up his feet and have a cup of hot tea. In Emily's view, it would do the man good to work the floor once in a while. He might actually learn something that way.

"I came to talk to you about this woman." J.R. stabbed a menacing finger at Emily.

"Ah, you mean Mrs. Miracle," Jake said fondly. "She's a wonder, isn't she?"

"She's a nuisance," J.R. snapped. "I want her fired."

Jake laughed, which was clearly the opposite reaction of what his father expected.

"This is not a joke."

"Yes, it is," Jake insisted. "Didn't you see what a madhouse this place was? It's like that every day now. I can't afford to lose Mrs. Miracle."

Emily sauntered over to J.R.'s side and whispered saucily, "Told you so."

He shook his finger. "I don't care if I have to work this department on my own," he yelled, "I will not tolerate insubordination."

"Excuse me, Dad, I've got another customer."

"I do, too," Emily said. "But you can keep standing there for a while. You make a nice fixture."

A kid of about five stepped in front of J.R. and stared up at him. "Is that a trick, mister?"

J.R. lowered his arms. "What, son?"

The boy was completely enthralled. "The way you get your cheeks to puff out like that."

Difficult though it was, Emily managed not to laugh. The boy was quite observant. J.R. had the puffing of cheeks down to an art form.

Jake finished with his customer and hurried back to his father. "Dad, I am *not* firing Mrs. Miracle."

"No, you're not. I am," J.R. said. "It will give me great pleasure to make sure she never works in this store again."

"What did she do that was so terrible?" Jake demanded.

"She insulted me and meddled in my personal affairs," his father burst out.

"How?" Jake asked, calm and collected. He was the perfect contrast to his father, who waved both arms wildly and spoke loudly enough to attract attention from every corner of the third floor.

When J.R. didn't answer, Jake shrugged and said, "Sorry, Dad, I need her."

Emily smiled ever so sweetly.

"She's out of here," J.R. roared, making a chopping motion with his arm. She thought he resembled an umpire signaling a strikeout.

Jake shook his head. "She's our best sales associate by a mile, so if she goes, we might as well close down the entire department. You wouldn't want that, would you, Dad?"

J.R. hesitated.

"And if we close the department, you won't have a chance to prove how wrong I was by ordering five hundred Intellytrons," he said, as if that should be sufficient inducement to keep her on staff.

Emily suspected J.R. wanted Jake to fall flat on his face over this robot. He'd pay a high price for being right—and, as a matter of fact, he was dead wrong. She'd seen for herself how popular the toy was. She'd hoped it would be and had done her best to sell it. However, after the past twenty-four hours, she didn't need to try very hard; the toy sold itself. Apparently, its sudden popularity had begun like so many trends, on the West Coast. Now, the moment someone heard that Finley's still had robots in stock, they dashed over. Then they couldn't whip out their credit cards fast enough.

"I'd better stay," Emily murmured to Jake. "As much as I'd like to walk away right now, I wouldn't give your father the satisfaction."

J.R. stomped his foot.

"Are you having a temper tantrum?" she asked sweetly.

Jake only laughed. "Dad, I think it might be best if you went back to your office now. Or you could go home."

"This is *my* store and I'll stay anywhere I darn well please."

Jake leaned closer to his father and whispered, "You're scaring off my customers."

"Oh, sorry."

"We want customers, don't we, Dad? Isn't that the whole idea?"

"Don't get smart with me," J.R. muttered.

"Yes, Dad." Jake winked at Emily, who winked back.

J.R. must have caught sight of what they were doing. "What's that about?"

"What?" Emily asked, again the picture of politeness.

"What?" Jake echoed.

Seeing that he'd forfeited even the pretense of control, J.R. sighed. "Forget it."

"I can stay on, then?" Emily asked the store owner.

"Why ask me? I seem to have lost complete control of this company to a man I no longer recognize—my son." With that he marched toward the elevator that would deliver him to his private office on the fourteenth floor.

Chapter Eleven

PEOPLE ARE FUNNY. THEY WANT THE FRONT OF THE BUS,
THE MIDDLE OF THE ROAD AND THE BACK OF THE CHURCH.

—MRS. MIRACLE

Holly knew she couldn't postpone calling Bill Carter, since the boys wanted to get together two days from now. It would be petty to allow her awkward relationship with Bill to stand in the way of her nephew being friends with his son.

The problem was how to approach him. She waited until Gabe was in bed on Wednesday night. Then she drew in a deep breath and looked up Bill's home number, which she'd made a point of erasing from her mind—and her phone. She hated feeling nervous about this. It was a courtesy call and nothing more.

Bill picked up on the fourth ring, when she was about

to hang up, almost relieved he hadn't answered. Then all of a sudden, she heard, "Hello."

"Bill, it's Holly."

"Do you realize what time it is?"

"Uh, yes… It's nine-thirty. Am I calling too late?"

He didn't respond immediately. "I know why you're calling and I—"

"You do?" So all this angst had been for nothing. She should've noticed earlier how silly she was being, how badly she'd overreacted.

"It's about Tiffany, isn't it?"

"No…who's Tiffany?"

"You mean you *don't* know?"

Obviously she didn't. "Sorry, I think we're talking at cross-purposes here. I don't know any Tiffany—well, other than the one I met through work. I'm calling about Billy."

"My son?"

He sounded both relieved and worried, which confused Holly. "Listen, can we start over?" she asked.

"It's too late for that."

Just how obtuse *was* the man? "I don't mean our relationship, Bill. I was referring to our conversation."

"Just tell me why you called," he said, with more than a hint of impatience.

"I'm trying to, but you keep interrupting me. This isn't an easy phone call for me and your attitude's not helping." If Bill was a decent human being, he should understand this was difficult and appreciate the courage it had taken her to contact him. The fact that he didn't angered her. "No wonder the two of us aren't dating anymore," she muttered.

"Okay, fine. But what's that got to do with my son?"

She sighed loudly. "Since you haven't worked it out for yourself, I'll tell you. Billy and Gabe have become friends."

"Yeah? So what?"

"Well, I—" Before she could answer his rudely phrased question, he broke in.

"Wait a minute," he said suspiciously. "How do you know my son's friends with this kid?"

The way he said it practically implied that Holly had been stalking his son. "That's the most ridiculous question I've ever heard! I know because Gabe's my nephew."

"So?"

"So Billy wants Gabe to come home with him after school on Friday."

"Fine. And this concerns you how?"

"I thought I should tell you we're related."

"That still doesn't explain why you're calling. Shouldn't Gabe's parents clear this with me? Not you."

Holly gritted her teeth at his offensive tone. What she'd ever seen in this man was completely lost on her now. At the moment, she was grateful he'd broken it off.

"I have custody of Gabe," she said calmly. She didn't feel like describing how that had come about; it was none of his business—and besides, she wanted to keep the conversation as short as possible.

"*You* have custody?"

The question grated on her nerves. "Yes, *me,* and it's working out very nicely, I might add."

"Ah…" Bill apparently hadn't figured out yet how to react.

Holly had no intention of allowing him to make any more derogatory comments about her mothering skills. She launched right into her question, not giving him a chance to say much of anything. "Is it still okay if Gabe comes to your house after school?"

"Uh, sure."

"Do you have the same housekeeper looking after Billy as before?"

The suspicious voice was back. "Why do you ask?"

"Because I don't want Gabe visiting Billy if there isn't any adult supervision." The after-school program only went until five-thirty, and Bill was often home much later than that, which meant the part-time housekeeper picked the boy up and then stayed at the apartment to supervise him.

"Oh, yeah, Mrs. Henry still looks after Billy from five-thirty to seven, except for the nights I have social engagements. Then she stays until I get home."

He seemed to delight in letting her know—in what he probably thought was a subtle fashion—that he'd started dating again. Well, she had social engagements, too, even if they mostly involved going out with friends, but was mature enough not to mention it. Let him think what he liked.

Holly waited a moment, hoping he'd realize how juvenile his reaction had been. "Talking civilly isn't so hard, is it?" she asked.

"No," he agreed.

"Great. Now that's settled, what time would you like me to pick Gabe up?"

"You'll pick him up?"

"Would you rather bring him back to my apartment?" That certainly made it easier for her. Maybe he didn't want Holly showing up at his house, but if so, she didn't care enough to be offended.

"I can do that," he said.

"Fine."

"Fine," he echoed.

"What time should I expect you?"

"Seven-thirty, I guess."

"I'll be here."

She was about to disconnect when Bill's soft chuckle caught her off guard. "So Gabe's your nephew, huh?"

"I already told you that."

"You did. His last name's Larson?"

"Yes, Gabe Larson." She didn't see the humor in this. "I apologize for calling so late, but I thought it would be best if you and I talked when Gabe was in bed."

"Did you think I'd refuse to let the two boys be friends?"

"I wasn't sure. Our last conversation wasn't very pleasant and, well, it seemed better to ask."

"I'm glad you did."

She was glad to hear that because he sure hadn't acted like it.

Holly met Jake for lunch on Thursday. He'd called her at the office that morning and suggested a nearby restaurant; thankfully he'd insisted on buying. She might've sounded a bit too eager to accept, because she was sick of making do with leftovers. By cutting back, packing lunches and not spending a penny more than necessary Holly had managed to save seventy-five dollars toward the robot. According to her calculations, she'd have the funds to make the purchase but it would be close. Every cent counted.

Jake had arrived at the restaurant before her and secured a booth. "Hi," he said with a smile when she slid in across from him.

"Hi. This is nice. Thanks so much." She reached for the menu and quickly scanned the day's specials. She was so hungry, Jake would be fortunate if she could limit her selection to one entrée. As it was, she ordered a cup of wild-mushroom soup, half a turkey sandwich with salad and a slice of apple pie à la mode for dessert.

Jake didn't seem to mind.

"That was delicious," she said as she sat back half an hour later and pressed her hands over her stomach. "I probably ate twice as much as any other woman you've ever gone out with."

"It's a relief to be with someone who isn't constantly worried about her weight."

"I do watch my calories but I've been doing without breakfast, and lunches have been pretty skimpy and—"

"No breakfast?"

"That's not entirely accurate. I have breakfast, sort of. Just not much."

"And the reason is?"

Holly wished she'd kept her mouth shut. She pretended not to hear his question and glanced at her watch instead. "Oh, it's almost one. I should get back to work."

"Holly." Jake wasn't easily distracted. "Answer the question."

Her shoulders sagged. "I really do need to go."

"You're going without breakfast to save money for the robot, aren't you?"

"Sorry, I have to run." She slid out of the booth and grabbed her coat and purse. "Oh, before I forget. Gabe wanted me to invite you to come and watch us decorate our Christmas tree tomorrow night, if you can. He'll be at a friend's place and won't get home until seven-thirty."

He hesitated, and Holly knew why. "I won't be able to leave the store until at least nine," he said.

"I let Gabe stay up until ten on Friday and Saturday nights."

He hesitated again. Holly hadn't forgotten his reaction when Gabe had first mentioned decorating for Christmas. She knew that, like his father, he ignored the holiday—apart from being surrounded by all that bright and shiny yuletide evidence at the store. Perhaps it was selfish of her, but she wanted to show him the joy of Christmas, prove that not all his Christmas memories were bad. She was convinced there must be happy remembrances, too, and she hoped to revive those so he could let go of the past. Holly held her breath as she waited for his response.

Jake stared into the distance for what seemed like a long time before he said, "Okay, I'll come."

Her breath whooshed out in relief and she gave him her brightest, happiest smile. "Thank you, Jake." She finished putting on her coat, hoping he understood how much she appreciated his decision.

"Can we do this again?" he asked. "It's been crazy in the toy department. Mrs. Miracle insisted I take my lunch break early—and she said I should invite you. I need to get back to work, but I wanted to see you."

"I wanted to see you, too."

They left the restaurant together and went their separate ways. Holly's spirits were high. She'd cleared the air with Bill as much as possible, and Gabe had been excited to learn he'd be able to go to his friend's house on Friday.

When she returned to work, she found her boss on the phone, talking in her usual emphatic manner. Despite the fact that Holly wouldn't be receiving a Christmas bonus, she'd tried not to let that influence her job performance.

As soon as Lindy Lee saw her, she waved one arm to get her attention.

Holly stepped into her employer's office. "You're back late from lunch," Lindy said as she slammed down the phone.

"I have an hour lunch," Holly reminded her. She rarely took that long and often ate at her desk. Taking the full time allotted her was the exception rather than the rule.

"It's one-fifteen," Lindy Lee said pointedly, tapping her index finger against her wristwatch.

"And I left the office at twelve-thirty. Technically I still have fifteen minutes." Holly could see that she might have said more than necessary and decided it would be best to stop while she was ahead. "Is there something you need me to do?" she asked.

Frowning, Lindy handed her a thick file folder. "I need you to get these sketches over to Design."

"Right away." She took the folder and hurried out of the office, catching the elevator to the sixth floor. As she entered the design department she caught sight of one of the models regularly hired by the company. Tiffani White was tall, slim and elegant and she possessed about as perfect a body as one could hope to have. She was a favorite of Lindy Lee's and no wonder. The model showed Lindy's creations to their peak potential.

Tiffani saw Holly and blinked, as if she had trouble placing her, which was odd. They'd spent a fair amount of time together, since Holly had been backstage at several runway events with her.

"Lindy Lee asked me to deliver these sketches," she said to the head of the technical department. She turned to Tiffani.

"Hi, Tiff," she said casually.

"Hi." The model smiled—a smile that didn't quite reach her eyes.

Holly smiled back, but there was something strange going on. Tiffani had always been friendly. They'd even had coffee together now and then. Once, nearly a year ago when she'd been dating Bill, they'd run into Tiffani and—

Just a minute!

Thoughts and memories collided inside Holly's head.

The conversation with Bill the night before played back in her mind. He'd made an unusual comment when they'd first spoken, mentioning the name Tiffany—or rather, Tiffani, with an *i*. The pieces were falling into place....

"Tiffani," Holly said. "I talked to Bill the other night."

"You did?"

"Yes, and your name came up."

The model brought one beautifully manicured hand to her mouth. "It did? Then you know?"

"Well, not everything."

"I wanted him to tell you before now, but Bill said it wasn't really any of your business. I told him that sometimes we see each other at work and it would make things better for me if you knew."

"So the two of you are...dating?"

"Actually we're...talking about marriage."

Marriage. Bill was planning to *marry* Tiffani? This didn't make sense. The model was about the least motherly woman Holly had ever met; she'd even told Holly she didn't like children. And she'd demonstrated it, too. They'd had a shoot earlier in the year with a couple of child models and Tiffani had been difficult and cranky all day. She'd made it clear that she didn't enjoy being around kids.

Holly wondered if Bill had any idea of the other woman's feelings. Probably not, she thought uncharitably. All he saw was Tiffani's perfect body and how good she looked on his arm.

In some ways, she had to concede, Bill and Tiffani were a good match. Bill had his own graphic design business and often hosted clients. Tiffani would do well entertaining, but Holly suspected she didn't have a lot to offer as a stepmother to Billy.

Yet that'd been the excuse Bill had used when he'd broken off *their* relationship.

That was exactly what it'd been. An excuse, and a convenient one. He'd wanted Holly out of his life and he didn't care how badly he hurt her to make that happen. Granted, the relationship would've ended anyway, but in the process of hastening its demise, he'd damaged her confidence—in herself and in her maternal instincts.

Bill Carter was a jerk, no question about it. Tiffani was welcome to him.

Chapter Twelve

BE YE FISHERS OF MEN. YOU CATCH 'EM
AND GOD'LL CLEAN 'EM.

—MRS. MIRACLE

"Can I go see Telly the robot after school?" Gabe asked as Holly walked him to school Monday morning.

"Not today," she said, stepping up her speed so she'd make it to work on time. The last thing she needed was to show up late. As it was, Gabe would get out of school at eleven-thirty this morning for winter break, and there was no after-school care today. Thankfully her neighbor Caroline Krantz had children of her own, including a son, Jonathan, who was Gabe's age, and Gabe enjoyed going there. Today, however, he obviously had a different agenda.

"But it's been so *long* since I saw him and I want—"

"I know. I'm sorry, Gabe. But Christmas will be here soon," she said, cutting him off.

"Do you think Santa's going to bring me my robot?"

"We won't find out until Christmas, will we?" she said, ushering him along. At the school, she bent down and kissed his cheek. "Remember, you're going to Mrs. Krantz's house with Jonathan after school."

"Yeah," he said, kicking at the sidewalk with the toe of his boot.

"Call me at the office when you get there, okay?"

"Okay."

Holly watched him walk into the building and then half ran to the subway station.

She was jostled by the crowd and once again had to stand, clutching the pole as she rode into the city. Her weekend had been everything she'd hoped for. Jake had stopped by on Friday night, arriving later than expected. She'd assembled the small artificial tree, which she'd bought years before; she would've preferred a real one but didn't want to spend the money this year. Then she'd draped it with lights, and she and Gabe had carefully arranged the ornaments. They were almost done by the time Jake came over, and Gabe insisted that he place the angel on top of the tree. Holly wasn't sure how he'd react to that request. At first he'd hesitated until she explained it was an honor and that it meant a lot to Gabe. Then he reluctantly set the angel on the tree.

Maybe it wasn't up to her to change—or try to change—his feelings about Christmas, but she hoped to coax him by creating new memories and by reminding him of happy ones from his own childhood.

On Friday, after school and his playdate with Billy, Gabe had been exhausted by ten o'clock. Holly tucked him in, and then she and Jake had cuddled and kissed in front of the television. She couldn't remember what TV program they'd started to watch because they were soon more focused on each other than on the TV.

Thinking about Friday night with Jake made her tingle with excitement and anticipation. Bill could have his Tiffani. Holly would rather be with Jake. Their relationship held such promise....

Unfortunately, Jake was so busy at the store on Saturday that a couple of quick phone calls had to suffice. On Sunday evening he came to the apartment, bringing a takeout pizza and a bottle of lovely, smooth merlot—the best wine she'd had in ages. Jake had been full of tales about the store, and especially how well Intellytron was now selling. Rumor had it that Finley's was the only place in Manhattan that had the robot available, and customers had flooded the store, many of them going straight from Santa's throne to the toy department. No one else had guessed that Intellytron would be one of the hottest retail trends of the season.

While Holly was thrilled for Jake, she was still concerned that there wouldn't be any left once she could afford to make the purchase. Jake had again assured her she didn't need to worry; he'd put one aside for Gabe. It was safely hidden away in the back of the storeroom, with a note that said it wasn't to be sold.

Holly dashed into the office just in time. She saw Lindy Lee glance at her watch but Holly knew she had three minutes to spare. While Lindy Lee might not appreciate her new work habits, she was well within the bounds of what was required. Before Gabe's advent into her life, she'd often arrived early and stayed late. That wasn't possible now, and she was paying the price for her earlier generosity, which Lindy Lee had quickly taken for granted. Still, she enjoyed her job and believed she was a credit to her employer, even if Lindy didn't agree.

"Good morning," she said to her boss, sounding more cheerful than she felt. Holly was determined not to allow Lindy Lee's attitude to affect her day.

At noon, Holly began to check her watch every few minutes. She kept her cell phone on her desk, ready to receive Gabe's call. He should be phoning any time now; school was out, and he'd be going home with Jonathan. At twelve-thirty Holly started to worry. Gabe should be at the Krantzes'. Why hadn't he called? She felt too anxious to eat the crackers and cheese she'd brought, too anxious to do anything productive. She'd give him until one-fifteen and then she'd call.

At one-thirteen, her cell phone chirped, and she recognized the Krantzes' number. Holly heaved a grateful sigh. "Hello," she said.

"Holly?" It was Caroline.

"Oh, hi. Did everything go as scheduled? Did Gabe and Jonathan walk home from school together?"

"Well, that's the reason I'm phoning. Gabe didn't come home with Jonathan."

A chill raced down her spine. "What do you mean?"

"He told Jonathan there was something he needed to do first, so Jonathan came home by himself. I... I feel really bad about this."

"Where is he?" Holly asked, struggling not to panic.

"That's just it. I don't know."

There was a huge knot in Holly's chest, and she found it difficult to breathe. How could she tell her brother that Gabe had gone missing?

Panicked thoughts surged through her mind. He'd been abducted, kidnapped, held for ransom. Or even worse, simply taken, never to be seen or heard from again.

"I'll call you if I hear anything," Caroline told her. "I'd

go look myself but I can't leave the children. If he's not here in an hour, we'll reassess, call the police. In the meantime, I'll phone some of the other kids' parents."

"Yes… Thank you." Holly disconnected the line, her cell phone clenched in her fist.

"Holly?" Lindy Lee asked, staring at her. "What's wrong?"

Holly didn't realize she'd bolted to her feet. She felt herself swaying and wondered if she was going to faint. "My—my nephew's missing."

"Missing," Lindy Lee repeated. "What do you mean, missing?"

"He didn't show up at the sitter's house after school."

Lindy Lee looked at her watch. "It's a bit early for him to be out of school, isn't it?"

"No, not today," she said, panic making her sound curt. She was torn by indecision. Her first inclination was to contact the police immediately, not to wait another hour as Caroline had suggested. They should start a neighborhood search. Ask questions.

She wondered crazily if she should get his picture to the authorities so they could place it on milk cartons all across America.

Her cell phone chirped again and she nearly dropped it in her rush to answer.

"Yes?" she blurted out.

"Holly, it's Jake."

"I don't have time to talk now. Gabe's missing and we've got to contact the police and get a search organized and—"

"Gabe's with me," Jake interrupted.

She sank into her chair, weak with relief. "He's with you?"

"Yes. He came into the city."

"On his own?" This was unbelievable!

"Yup."

"You mean to say he walked from school to the subway station, took the train and then walked to Finley's by *himself?*" It seemed almost impossible to comprehend. She held her head in one hand and leaned back in her chair, eyes closed. She remembered what he'd said that morning, about wanting to see the robot, but she'd had no idea he'd actually try to do it.

"Would you like to talk to him?" Jake was asking.

"Please."

"Aunt Holly?" Gabe's voice was small and meek.

"So," she said, releasing a long sigh. Although the urge to lambaste him was nearly overwhelming, she resisted. "You didn't walk home with Jonathan the way you were supposed to?"

"No."

"Can you tell me why?"

"Because…"

"Because *what?*"

"I wanted to see Intellytron again and you said we couldn't and I thought, well, I know you have to work and everything, but I could come by myself, so I did. I remembered to take the green line and then I walked from the subway station." Despite the fact that he was obviously in trouble, there was a hint of pride in his voice.

Gabe had traveled into the city on his own just to see his favorite toy. The possibility hadn't even occurred to her. Holly suppressed the urge to break into sobs.

"I'm coming to get you right this minute," she declared. "Stay with Jake and Mrs. Miracle, and I'll be there as soon as I can. Now put Jake back on the phone."

His voice, strong and clear, came through a moment later. "Holly, it's Jake."

"I'm on my way."

"He'll be fine until you get here," he said.

"Thank you, thank you so much." This time, the urge to weep nearly overcame her.

"Everything's fine. Relax."

"I'm trying." She closed her cell, then looked up to see her boss standing in front of her desk.

"I take it you've located the little scoundrel?"

Holly nodded. "He came into the city on his own. Would it be okay if I brought him to the office for the rest of the day?" Taking him back to Brooklyn would be time-consuming and Lindy Lee would no doubt dock her pay. Holly needed every penny of her next paycheck. "I promise he won't make a sound."

Lindy Lee considered the request, then slowly nodded. "I enjoyed meeting Gabe that Saturday.... I wouldn't mind seeing him again."

Lindy Lee wanted to see Gabe again? *This* was an interesting development, as well as an unexpected one. Her employer wasn't the motherly type—to put it mildly. Lindy Lee was all about Lindy Lee.

Grabbing her coat and purse, Holly rushed over to Finley's, calling Caroline Krantz en route. The store was crowded, and by the time she reached the third floor Holly felt as though she'd run a marathon. She saw Mrs. Miracle first, and the woman's eyes brightened the instant she noticed Holly.

"You don't have a thing to worry about, my dear. Gabe is perfectly safe with Jake."

"Aunt Holly!" Gabe raced to her side and Jake followed.

"You're in a lot of trouble, young man," she said sternly, hands on her hips.

Gabe hung his head. "I'm sorry," he whispered, his voice so low she could hardly hear it.

Customers thronged the toy department, several of them carrying the boxes that held the SuperRobot. A line had already formed at the customer service desk, and she noted that a couple of extra sales associates were out on the floor today. Everyone was busy.

"You'll have to come back to the office with me," Holly told Gabe. "I'm warning you it won't be nearly as much fun as it would've been with Jonathan and his mother."

"I know," he muttered. "Am I grounded?"

"We'll discuss that once we're home."

"Okay, but nothing happened...."

"You mean nothing other than the fact that you nearly gave me a heart attack."

Jake murmured a quick goodbye and started to leave to help a customer but Mrs. Miracle stopped him. "I'll take care of them," she said. "Besides, I believe there was something you wanted to ask Holly?"

"There was?" He looked surprised, wrinkling his brow as if he couldn't recall any such question.

"The Christmas party," Mrs. Miracle said under her breath. "You mentioned asking Holly to go with you."

Jake's mouth sagged open. "I'd thought about it, but I didn't realize I'd said it out loud." Now, instead of looking surprised, he seemed confused. "My father and I usually just make a token appearance."

"This year is different," the older woman insisted. "You need to be there for your staff. After all, the toy department's the busiest of the whole store at Christmastime.

And," she continued sagely, "I predict record sales this year. Your staff needs to know you appreciate them."

"But…"

"I can't go," Holly said, resolving the issue. "There's no one to watch Gabe."

"Oh, but there is, my dear," Mrs. Miracle told her.

Holly frowned. Finding someone to stay with Gabe had always been a problem. She didn't want to impose on Caroline any more than she already did, especially since her neighbor wouldn't take any payment. With Jake they'd managed to work around it, which was easy enough, since Jake had mostly come to her apartment.

"I'll be more than happy to stay with Gabe while the two of you attend the party," Mrs. Miracle said.

It was generous of her to offer, but Holly couldn't accept. She shook her head. "You should be at the party yourself, Mrs. Miracle."

"Oh, heavens, no. After a full day on my feet I'll look forward to sitting in that comfy blue chair of yours. The one your parents gave you."

Before she could question how Mrs. Miracle knew about her chair, Jake asked, "Would you like to go to the party with me?" His eyes met hers, and she found herself nodding.

"Yes," she whispered. "When is it?"

"Wednesday night, after the store closes."

"Wednesday," she repeated.

"I'll pick you up at nine-thirty. I know that's late but—"

"I'll be ready."

"I'll come over a bit earlier," Mrs. Miracle added. "The two of you will have a *lovely* evening." She spoke with the utmost confidence, as if no other outcome was possible.

Holly and Gabe left a few minutes later, and Jake walked

them to the elevator. "I'll see you Wednesday," he said as he pressed the button.

"Listen, Jake, you don't need to do this. I mean, it's fairly obvious you didn't intend to ask me and—"

"I'd really like it if you'd come to the party with me," he said, and she couldn't doubt his sincerity.

"Then I will," she murmured. "I'll look forward to it."

In the elevator, Holly remembered Mrs. Miracle's comment. The woman had never been to her apartment and yet somehow she knew about the chair her parents had given her. Furthermore, she seemed to know her address, too.

Oh, well. Gabe had probably told her. He obviously felt comfortable with the older woman and for that Holly could only be grateful.

Chapter Thirteen

CARS ARE NOT THE ONLY THING
RECALLED BY THEIR MAKER.

—MRS. MIRACLE

On Wednesday at nine-fifteen, Emily stood at Holly's door, her large purse draped over one arm and her knitting bag in the other hand. Holly answered, smiling in welcome. She absolutely sparkled. In her fancy black dress and high heels, her hair gathered up and held in place with a jeweled comb, she looked stunning.

"Mrs. Miracle, I can't thank you enough." Holly stepped aside so Emily could enter the apartment. "Tonight wouldn't be possible if not for you."

"The pleasure's all mine," she said. She put down her bags, then unwrapped the knitted scarf from around her neck and removed her heavy wool coat. Holly hung them in the hallway closet as Emily arranged her bags by the chair, prepared to settle down for the evening. The toy department had kept her busy all day and she was eager to get off her feet.

Holly followed her into the small living room. "I feel bad that you won't be attending the party."

"Oh, no, my dear." Emily dismissed her concern. "I'm not a party girl anymore." She chuckled at her own humor. "Besides, I intend to have a good visit here with my young friend Gabe."

"He's been pretty subdued since the episode on Monday. He's promised to be on his best behavior."

"Don't you worry. We'll have a grand time together." And they would.

"Hi, Mrs. Miracle."

She was surprised to see Jake standing on the other side of the room. He'd arrived early, she thought approvingly, and he looked quite debonair in his dark suit and red tie. She'd seen an improvement in his attitude toward Christmas, mostly due to Holly and Gabe. And she had it on excellent authority that it would improve even more before the actual holiday.

"Gabe's on the computer," Holly said, pointing at the alcove between the living room and kitchen. "He's had his dinner and he can stay up until ten tonight."

Gabe twisted around and waved.

Emily waved back. "I'll make sure he's in bed by ten."

Jake held Holly's coat and the young woman slipped her arms into the sleeves. "I appreciate your volunteering to watch Gabe," he said with a smile for Emily.

"As I told Holly, I'm delighted to do it." She walked over to where Gabe sat at the small desk and put her hand on his shoulder. "Now, you two go. Have fun."

Holly kissed the top of Gabe's head. "Be good."

"I will," the boy said without taking his eyes from the screen.

Holly and Jake left, and Emily had to grin as she glanced over Gabe's shoulder at the message he was emailing his father.

From: "Gabe Larson" <gabelarson@msm.com>
To: "Lieutenant Mickey Larson" <larsonmichael@goarmy.com>
Sent: December 22
Subject: Me and Aunt Holly

Hi, Dad,
I made Aunt Holly cry. Instead of going to Jonathan's house like I was supposed to, I went to see the robot. I was afraid the store would run out before Santa got my Intellytron. Aunt Holly came and picked me up and when we were outside she started to cry. When I asked her why she was crying she said it was because she was happy I was safe.

Are you mad at me? I wish Aunt Holly had gotten mad instead of crying. I felt awful inside and got a tummy ache. She took me back to her office and made me sit quiet all afternoon. But that was okay because I knew I didn't do the right thing. Her boss is real pretty. I don't think she's around kids much because she talked to me like I was in kindergarten or something. I think she's nice, though.

You said you had a gift coming for me for Christmas. It isn't here yet. I know I was bad, so you don't have to send it if you don't want. I'm sorry I made Aunt Holly cry.
Love,
Gabe

Emily sank down in the big comfortable chair, rested her feet on the matching ottoman and took out her knitting. She turned on the television and had just finished the first row when Gabe joined her. He didn't say anything for a long time, but Emily could see his mind working.

After a while he said, "My dad's going to be mad at me."

"It was brave of you to tell him you did something you weren't supposed to," she murmured.

Gabe looked away. "I told him he doesn't need to send me anything for Christmas. He said there was a special gift on the way but it hasn't come. He probably won't send it now."

"Don't be so sure." She pulled on the skein of yarn as she continued knitting.

"What if Santa finds out what I did?" His face crumpled in a frown. "Do you think maybe he won't bring me the robot 'cause I went to Finley's by myself and I didn't tell anyone where I was going?"

"Well, now, that remains to be seen, doesn't it?"

Gabe climbed onto the sofa and rested his head against the arm. "I didn't think Aunt Holly would be so worried when I didn't go to Jonathan's house after school. She got all weird."

"Weird?"

"Yeah. When we were still at her office, all of a sudden she put her arms around my neck and hugged me really hard. Isn't that weird?"

Emily shrugged but didn't answer. "Are you ready for Christmas?" she asked instead.

Gabe nodded. "I made Aunt Holly an origami purse. A Japanese lady came to my school and showed us how to fold them. She said they were purses, but it looks more like a wallet to me, all flat and skinny." He sighed dejectedly. "I wrapped it up but you can't really see where the wrapping stops and the gift starts."

"I bet Holly will really like the purse because you made it yourself," Emily said with an encouraging smile.

"I made my dad a gift, too. But Aunt Holly and I mailed off his Christmas present a long time ago. They take days and days to get to Afghanistan so we had to go shopping before Thanksgiving and wrap up stuff for my dad. Oh, we mailed him the picture of me and Santa, too. And I made him a key ring. And I sent him nuts. My dad likes cashews. I've never seen a cashew in the shell, have you?"

"Why, yes, as a matter of fact I have," she said conversationally.

Gabe sat up. "What do they look like?"

"Well, a cashew is a rather unusual nut. My goodness, God was so creative with that one. Did you know the cashew is both a fruit *and* a nut?"

"It is?"

"The fruit part looks like a small apple and it has a big stem."

The boy's eyes were wide with curiosity.

"The stem part is the nut, the cashew," she explained.

"Wow."

"And they're delicious," she said. "Good for you, too," she couldn't resist adding.

"What are you doing for Christmas?" Gabe asked.

"I've been invited to a party, a big one with lots of celebrating. I'll be with my friends Shirley, Goodness—"

"Goodness? That's a funny name."

"Yes, you're right. Anyway, the party preparations have already begun. It won't be long now."

"Oh." Gabe looked disappointed.

"Why the sad face?"

"I was going to ask you to come here for Christmas."

Emily was touched by his invitation. "I know you'll have a wonderful Christmas with Holly," she said.

"I invited Aunt Holly's boss, too."

She had to make an effort to hide her smile. This was all working out very nicely. Very nicely, indeed.

"Lindy didn't say she'd come for sure but she might." He paused. "She said to call her Lindy, not Ms. Lee like Aunt Holly said I should."

"Well, I hope she comes."

"Me, too. I think she's lonely."

"So do I," Emily agreed. The boy was very perceptive for his age, she thought.

"I asked her what she wants for Christmas and she said she didn't know. Can you *believe* that?"

In Emily's experience, many people walked through life completely unaware of what they wanted—or needed. "I brought along a book," she said, changing the subject. "Would you like to read it to me?" She'd put the children's book with its worn cover on the arm of her chair.

Gabe considered this. "I'm not in school now. Can you read it to me?"

"The way your dad used to when you were little?" she asked.

Gabe nodded eagerly. "I used to sit on his lap and he'd read me stories until I fell asleep." His face grew sad. "I miss my dad a lot."

"I know you do." Emily set aside her knitting. "Would you like to sit in my lap?"

"I'm too big for that," he insisted.

Emily could see that despite his words he was mulling it over. "You're not too big," she assured him.

Indecision showed on his face. Gabe wanted to snuggle

with her, yet he hesitated because he was eight now and eight was too old for such things.

"What book did you bring?" he asked.

"It's a special one your grandma Larson once read to your dad and your aunt Holly."

"Really? How'd you know that?"

"Oh, I just do. It's the Christmas story."

"I like when the angels came to announce the birth of Baby Jesus to the shepherds."

She closed her eyes for a moment. "It was the most glorious night," she said. "The sky was bright and clear and—"

"And the angels sang," Gabe finished enthusiastically. "Angels have beautiful voices, don't they?"

"Yes, they do," Emily confirmed. "They make music we know nothing about here on earth… I'm sure," she added quickly. "Glorious, heavenly music."

"They do?" He cocked his head to one side.

"You'll hear it yourself one day, many years from now."

"What about you? When will you hear it?"

"Soon," she told him. He climbed into her lap and she held him close. He really was a sweet boy and would become a fine young man like his father. He'd be a wonderful brother to his half brother and half sister, as well—but she was getting ahead of herself.

"Tell me more about the angels," Gabe implored. "Is my mom an angel now?"

"No, sweetheart. Humans don't become angels. They're completely separate beings, although both were created by God."

"How come you know so much about angels?"

"I read my Bible," she said, and he seemed to accept her explanation.

"I never knew my mom," he said somberly. "Dad has

pictures of her at the house. I look at her face and she smiles at me but I don't remember her."

"But you do understand that she loved you very much, right?"

"Dad said she did, and before she died she made him promise that he'd tell me every night how much she loved me."

"I know," she whispered.

"Do you think there are lots of angels in heaven?" Gabe asked.

"Oh, yes, and there are different kinds of angels, too."

"What kinds are there?"

"Well, they have a variety of different tasks. For instance, Gabriel came to Mary as a messenger. Other angels are warriors."

"When I get to heaven, I want to meet the warrior angels."

"And you shall."

"Do you think I was named after the angel Gabriel?" he asked.

Emily pressed her cheek against the top of his head, inhaling the clean, little-boy scent of his hair. "Now, that's something you'll need to ask your father when you see him."

"Okay, I will."

"Gabriel had one of the most important tasks ever assigned," Emily said. "He's the angel God sent to tell Mary about Baby Jesus."

He yawned. "Can people see angels?"

Emily's mouth quivered with a smile she couldn't quite suppress. "Oh, yes, but most people don't recognize them."

Gabe lifted his head. "How come?"

"Not all angels show their wings," she said.

"They don't?"

"No, some angels look like ordinary people."

"How come?"

"Well, sometimes God sends angels to earth. But if people saw their wings, they'd get all excited and they'd miss the lesson God wanted to teach them. That's why angels are often disguised."

"Are they always disguised?"

"No, some are invisible. Other times they look like ordinary people."

"Do angels only come to teach people a lesson?"

"No, they come to help, too."

Gabe yawned again. "How do angels help?"

"Oh, in too many ways to count."

He thought about that for a while, his eyelids beginning to droop.

"Are you ready for me to read you the story?" Emily asked.

"Sure." He rested his head against her shoulder as she opened the book. She read for a few minutes before she noticed that Gabe had fallen asleep. And she hadn't even gotten to the good part.

Chapter Fourteen

The Christmas party was well under way by the time Holly and Jake arrived. When they entered the gala event, the entire room seemed to go still. Holly kept her arm in Jake's, self-conscious about being the center of attention.

"Why's everyone looking at us?" she whispered.

Jake patted her hand reassuringly. "My father and I usually show up toward the end of the party, say a few words and then leave. No one expected me this early."

He'd mentioned that before. Still, she hadn't realized his arrival would cause such a stir. Jake immediately began to walk through the room, shaking hands and introducing Holly. At first she tried to keep track of the names, but soon gave up. She was deeply impressed by Jake's familiarity with the staff.

"How do you remember all their names?" she asked when she had a chance.

"I've worked with them in each department," he explained. "My father felt I needed to know the retail business from the mail room up."

"You started in the mail room?"

"I did, but don't for a minute consider the mail room unimportant. I made that mistake and quickly learned how vital it is."

"Your father is a wise man."

"He is," Jake said. "And a generous one, too. But he'd describe himself as *fair*. He's always recognized the value of hiring good people and keeping them happy. I believe it's why we've managed to hold on to the company despite several attempts to buy us out."

It went without saying that Jake intended to follow his father's tradition of treating employees with respect and compensating them generously.

Ninety minutes later Holly's head buzzed with names and faces. They sipped champagne and got supper from the buffet; the food was delicious. Numerous people commented happily on seeing Jake at the party.

His father appeared at about midnight and immediately sought out his son and Holly.

"So this is the young lady you've talked about," J. R. Finley said, slapping Jake jovially on the back.

"Dad, meet Holly Larson."

J.R. shook her hand. "I'm pleased to meet you, young lady. You've made a big impression on my son."

Holly glanced at Jake and smiled. "He's made a big impression on me."

J. R. Finley turned to his son. "When did you get here?"

"Before ten," Jake said.

His father frowned, then moved toward the microphone. As was apparently his practice, he gave a short talk, handed out dozens of awards and bonuses and promptly left.

The party wound down after J.R.'s speech. People started to leave, but almost every employee, singly and in groups, approached Jake to thank him for attending the party. Holly couldn't tell how their gratitude affected Jake, but it had a strong impact on her.

"They love you," she said when they went to collect their coats.

"They're family," Jake said simply.

She noticed that he didn't say Finley's employees were *like* family but that they *were* family. The difference was subtle but significant. J.R. had lost his wife and daughter and had turned to his friends and employees to fill the huge hole left by the loss of his loved ones. Jake had, too.

As they stepped outside, Holly was thrilled by the falling snow. "Jake, look!" She held out her hand to catch the soft flakes that floated down from the night sky. "It's just so beautiful!"

Jake wrapped his scarf more securely around his neck. "I can't believe you're so excited about a little snow."

"I love it…. It's so Christmassy."

He grinned and clasped her hand. "Do you want to go for a short walk?"

"I'd love to." It was cold, but even without boots or gloves or a hat, Holly felt warm, and more than that, *happy*.

"Where would you like to go?" Jake asked.

"Wherever you'd like to take me." Late though it was, she didn't want the night to end. Lindy Lee had never thrown a Christmas party for her staff. Maybe she'd talk to Lindy about planning one for next December; she could discuss the benefits—employee satisfaction and loyalty, which would lead to higher productivity. Those were the terms Lindy would respond to. Not appreciation or enjoyment or fun. Having worked with Lindy as long as she had, Holly suspected her employer wasn't a happy person. And she wasn't someone who cared about the pleasure of others.

"I thought this would be a miserable Christmas," Holly confessed, leaning close to Jake as they moved down the busy sidewalk. They weren't the only couple reveling in the falling snow.

"Why?" Jake asked. "Because of your brother?"

"Well, yes. It's also the first Christmas without my parents, and then Mickey got called up for Afghanistan so there's just Gabe and me."

"What changed?"

"A number of things, actually," she said. "Meeting you, of course."

"Thank you." He bent down and touched his lips to hers in the briefest of kisses.

"My attitude," she said. "I was worried that Gabe would resent living with me. For months we didn't really bond."

"You have now, though, haven't you?"

"Oh, yes. I didn't realize how much I loved him until he went missing the other day. I… I don't normally panic, but I did then."

Holly was still surprised by how accommodating her employer had been during and after that crisis. First Lindy Lee had allowed Gabe to come to the office and then she'd actually chatted with him. Holly didn't know what the two of them had talked about, but her employer had seemed almost pleasant afterward.

"Remember the other night when you and Gabe decorated your Christmas tree?" Jake asked.

"Of course."

"Gabe asked me about mine."

"Right." It'd been an awkward moment. Gabe had been full of questions. He couldn't understand why some people chose not to make Christmas part of their lives. No tree. No presents. No family dinner. The closest Jake and his father got to celebrating the holidays was their yearly sojourn to the Virgin Islands.

Holly knew this was his father's way of ignoring the holiday. Jake and J.R. left on Christmas Eve and didn't return until after New Year's.

She was sure they'd depart sooner if they could. The only reason they stayed in New York as long as they did was because of the business. The holiday season made their year financially. Without the last-quarter sales, many retailers would struggle to survive. Finley's Department Store was no different.

"You told Gabe you didn't put up a tree," Holly reminded him.

"I might've misled him."

"You have a tree?" After everything he'd said, that shocked her.

"You'll see." His stride was purposeful as they continued walking. She soon figured out where they were headed.

"I can't wait," she said with a laugh.

When they reached Rockefeller Center, they stood gazing up at the huge Christmas tree, bright with thousands of lights and gleaming decorations. Jake gestured toward it. "*That's* my Christmas tree," he said.

"Gabe's going to be jealous that I got to see it again—with you."

Music swirled all around them as Jake slipped his arm about her waist. "When I was young, I found it hard to give up the kind of Christmas I'd known when my mother and sister were alive. Dad refused to have anything to do with the holidays but I still wanted the tree and the gifts."

Holly hadn't fully grasped how difficult those years must've been for him.

"Dad said if I wanted a Christmas tree, I could pick one in the store and make it my own. Better yet, I could claim the one in Rockefeller Center and that's what I did."

Instinctively she knew Jake had never shared this information with anyone else.

"Well, you've got the biggest, most beautiful Christmas tree in the city," she said, leaning her head against his shoulder.

"I do," he murmured.

"Jake," she said carefully. "Would you consider having Christmas dinner with Gabe and me?"

He didn't answer, and she wondered if she'd crossed some invisible line by issuing the invitation. Nevertheless she had to ask.

"I know that would mean not joining your father when he leaves for the Caribbean, but you could fly out the next day, couldn't you?" Holly felt she needed to press the issue. If he was ever going to agree, it would be tonight, after he'd witnessed how much it meant to Finley's employees that he'd attended their party.

"I could fly out later," he said. "But then I'd be leaving my father alone on the saddest day of his life."

"I'd like to invite him, too."

Jake's smile was somber and poignant. "He'll never come, Holly. He hates anything to do with Christmas—outside of the business, anyway."

"Maybe so, but I'd still like to ask him." She wasn't sure why she couldn't simply drop this. It took audacity to invite two wealthy men to her small apartment, when their alternative was an elaborate meal in an exotic location.

She was embarrassed now. "I apologize, Jake. I don't know what made me think you'd want to give up the sunshine and warmth of a Caribbean island for dinner with me and Gabe."

"Don't say that! I want to be with you both."

"But you don't feel you can leave your father."

"That's true, but maybe it's time I started creating traditions of my own. I'd be honored to spend Christmas Day with the two of you," he said formally.

Holly felt tears spring to her eyes. "Thank you," she whispered.

She turned to face him. He smiled as she slid her hands up his chest and around his neck. Standing on the tips of her toes with a light snow falling down on them, she pressed her mouth to his.

Jake held her tight. Holly sensed that they'd crossed a barrier in their relationship and established a real commitment to each other.

"When I come, I'll bring the robot for Gabe and hide it under the tree so it'll be a real surprise."

"I'll give you the money on Friday—Christmas Eve."

Christmas Eve.

"Okay." She knew he'd rather not take it, but there was no question—she had every intention of paying.

Jake called his car service, and a limousine met them at Rockefeller Center fifteen minutes later. When he dropped her off at the apartment Mrs. Miracle was sound asleep, still in the blue chair. Jake helped her out to the car, then had the driver take her home. Holly was touched by his thoughtfulness.

Even after Jake had left, Holly had trouble falling asleep. Her mind whirled as she relived scenes and moments of what had been one of the most memorable evenings of her life. When the alarm woke her early Thursday morning, she couldn't get up and just dozed off again. She finally roused herself, horrified to discover that she was almost half an hour behind schedule.

She managed to drag herself out of bed, gulp down a cup of coffee and get Gabe up and dressed and over to the Krantzes'.

Filled with dread, Holly rushed to work. As she yanked off her coat, she heard her name being called. Breathless, she flew into Lindy Lee's office; as usual, Lindy looked pointedly at her watch.

Holly tried to apologize. "I'm sorry I'm late. I'll make up the twenty-five minutes, I promise."

Lindy Lee raised one eyebrow. "Make sure you do."

Holly stood waiting for the lecture that inevitably followed. To her astonishment, this time it didn't. "Thank you for understanding."

"See to it that this doesn't happen again," her employer said, dismissing Holly with a wave of her hand.

"It won't... I just couldn't seem to get moving this morning." Thinking she'd probably said too much already, she started to leave, then remembered her resolve to discuss a Christmas party with Lindy Lee.

Aware that Holly was lingering, Lindy Lee raised her head and frowned. "Was there something else?"

"Well, yes. Do you mind if I speak freely?"

"That depends on what you have to say." Lindy Lee held her pen poised over a sheet of paper.

"I was at the employees' party for Finley's Department Store last evening," she said, choosing her words carefully. "It was a wonderful event. The employees work together as a team and…and they feel such loyalty to the company. You could just tell. They feel valued, and I doubt there's anything they wouldn't do to help the company succeed."

"And your point is?" Lindy Lee said impatiently.

"My point is we all need to work as a team here, too, and it seemed to me that maybe we should have a Christmas party."

Lindy Lee leaned back in her chair and crossed her arms. "In a faltering economy, with flat sales and an uncertain future, you want me to throw a *Christmas party?*"

"It's…it's just an idea for next year," Holly said, and regretted making the suggestion. Still, she couldn't seem to stop. "The future is always uncertain, isn't it? And there'll always be ups and downs in the economy. But the one constant is the fact that as long as you're in business you'll have a staff, right? And you need them to be committed and—"

"I get it," Lindy Lee said dryly.

Holly waited.

And waited.

"Let me think about it," Lindy Lee finally mumbled.

She'd actually agreed to think about it. Now, this was progress—more progress than Holly had dared to expect.

Chapter Fifteen

THE BEST VITAMIN FOR A CHRISTIAN IS B1.

—MRS. MIRACLE

Jake Finley was in love. Logically, he knew, it was too soon to be so sure of his feelings, and yet he couldn't deny his heart. Love wasn't about logic. He'd been attracted to Holly from the moment he met her, but this was more than attraction. He felt...connected to Holly, absorbed in her. He thought about her constantly. Over the years he'd been in other relationships, but no woman had made him feel the way Holly did.

When he arrived at work Thursday morning, he went directly to his father's office. Dora Coffey seemed surprised to see him.

"Is my father in yet?" Jake asked her.

"Yes, he's been here for a couple of hours. You know your father—this store is his life."

"Does he have time to see me?" Jake asked next. "No meetings or conference calls?"

"He's free for a few minutes." She left her desk and announced Jake, who trailed behind her.

When Jake entered the office, his father stood. "Good morning, son. What can I do for you?" He gestured for Jake to take a seat, which he did, and settled back in his own chair.

Jake leaned forward, unsure where to start. He should've worked out what he was going to say before coming up here.

"I suppose you want to gloat." J.R. chuckled. "You were right about that robot. Hardly anyone else forecast this trend. I turned on the TV this morning and there was a story on Telly the SuperRobot. Hottest toy of the season, they said. Who would've guessed it? Not me, that's for sure."

"Not Mike Scott, either," Jake added, although he didn't fault the buyer.

"True enough. And yet Mike was the first to admit he didn't see this coming."

So Scott had mentioned it to J.R. but not to him. Still, it must've taken real humility to acknowledge that he'd been wrong.

"I'm proud of you, son," J.R. continued. "You went with your gut and you were right to do it."

Jake wondered what would've happened if Finley's had been stuck with four hundred leftover robots. Fortunately, however, he wouldn't have to find out.

"I checked inventory this morning, and we have less than twenty of the robots in stock."

Jake didn't need to point out the benefits of being the only store in the tristate area with *any* robots in stock. Having a supply—even a rapidly dwindling supply—of the season's most popular toy brought more shoppers into the store and created customer loyalty.

"They're selling fast. The entire quantity will be gone before Christmas."

"Good. Good," his father said. He grinned as he tilted back in his high leather chair. "Oh, I enjoyed meeting your lady friend last night."

"Holly enjoyed meeting you."

"She's special, isn't she?"

Jake was astonished that his father had immediately discerned his feelings for Holly. "Yes, but… What makes you say that?" He had to ask why it had been so obvious to his father.

J.R. didn't respond for a moment. Finally he said, "I recognized it from the way you looked at her. The way you looked at each other."

Jake nodded but didn't speak.

"I remember when I met your mother." There was a faraway expression in his eyes. "I think I fell in love with Helene as soon as I saw her. She was the daughter of one of my competitors and so beautiful I had trouble getting out a complete sentence. It's a wonder she ever agreed to that first date." He smiled at the memory.

So rarely did his father discuss his mother and sister that Jake kept quiet, afraid that any questions would distract J.R. He craved details, but knew he had to be cautious.

"I loved your mother more than life itself. I still do."

"I know," Jake said softly.

"She wasn't just beautiful," he murmured, and the same faraway look stole over him. "She had a heart unlike anyone I've ever known. Everyone came to her when they needed something, whether it was a kind word, a job, some advice. She never turned anyone away." His face, so often tense, relaxed as he sighed. "I felt that my world ended the day your mother and Kaitlyn died. Since then you've been my only reason for going on."

"Well, I hope your grandchildren will be another good reason," Jake teased, hoping to lighten the moment.

J.R. gave a hearty laugh. "They certainly will. So… I was right about you and Holly."

"It's too early to say for sure," Jake hedged. Confident though he was about his own feelings, he didn't want to speak for Holly. Not yet…

"But you *know.*"

"It looks…promising."

Slapping the top of his desk, J.R. laughed again. "I thought so. I'm happy for you, Jake."

"Thanks, Dad." But he doubted J.R. would be as happy when he found out what that meant, at least as far as Christmas was concerned.

"Oh, before I forget," J.R. said with exquisite timing. "Dora's ordered the plane tickets for Christmas Eve. We leave JFK at seven and land in Saint John around—"

"Dad, I'll need to change my ticket," Jake said, interrupting his father.

That brought J.R. up short. "Change your ticket? Why?"

"I'll join you on the twenty-sixth," Jake explained. "Holly invited me to spend Christmas Day with her and her nephew."

J.R.'s frown was back as he mulled over that statement. "You're going to do it?"

"Yes. I told her I would."

J.R. stood and walked to the window, turning his back to Jake. "I don't know what to say."

"Holly invited you, too."

"You told her it was out of the question, didn't you?"

More or less. "You'd be welcome if you chose to come."

Slowly J.R. turned around. "Well," he said with a sigh, "I suppose it was unrealistic of me not to realize times are changing." He paused. "I look forward to our vacation every year."

Jake had never thought of their trip to the Caribbean as a getaway. His father always brought work with him and they spent their week discussing trends, reading reports and forecasting budgets. It was business, not relaxation.

"You call it a *vacation?*" Jake asked, amused.

"Well, yes. What would you call it?" J.R. frowned in confusion.

Jake hesitated, then decided to tell the truth, even if his father wasn't ready to hear it. "I call it an escape from reality—but not from work. A vacation is supposed to be fun, a break, a chance to do nothing or else do something completely out of the ordinary. Not sit in a hotel room and do exactly the same thing you'd be doing here."

J.R.'s frown deepened.

"Admit it, Dad," Jake said. "You don't go to the islands to lounge on the beach or snorkel or take sightseeing trips. Far from it. You escape New York because you can't bear to be here over Christmas."

J.R. shook his head.

Jake wasn't willing to let it go. "From the time Mom and Kaitlyn died, you've done everything possible to pretend there's no Christmas.

"As a businessman you need the holidays to survive financially but if it wasn't for that, you'd ban anything to do with Christmas from your life—and mine."

J.R. glared at Jake. "I believe you've said enough."

"You need to accept that Christmas had nothing to do with the accident. It happened, and it changed both our lives forever, but it was a fluke, a twist of fate. I wish with everything in me that Mom and Kaitlyn had stayed home that afternoon, but the fact is, they didn't. They went out, and because their cab collided with another one, they were killed."

"Enough!" J.R. shouted.

Jake stood. "I didn't mean to upset you, Dad."

"If that's the case, then you've failed. I *am* upset."

Jake regretted that; nevertheless, he felt this had to be said. "I'm tired of running away on Christmas Eve. You can do it if you want, but I'm through."

"Fine. Spend the day with Holly if you prefer. It's not going to bother me."

"I wish you'd reconsider and join us."

J.R. tightened his lips. "No, thanks. You might think I'm hiding my head in the sand, but the truth is, I enjoy the islands."

Jake might have believed him if J.R. had walked along the beach even once or taken any pleasure in their surroundings. Instead, he worked from early morning to late evening, burying himself in his work in a desperate effort to ignore the time of year—the anniversary of his loss.

"Yes, Dad," Jake said rather than allow their discussion to escalate into a full-scale argument.

"You'll come the next day, then?"

Jake nodded. He'd make his own flight arrangements. They always stayed at the same four-star hotel, the same suite of rooms.

"Good."

Jake left the office and hurried down to the toy department. He was surprised to see Mrs. Miracle on the floor. According to the schedule she wasn't even supposed to be in. That was his decision; since she'd volunteered to watch Gabe, he'd given her the day off.

"I didn't expect to see you this morning," he said.

"Oh, I thought I'd come in and do a bit of shopping myself."

"I didn't realize you had grandchildren," he said. In fact, he knew next to nothing about Mrs. Miracle's personal life, including her address. He'd offered to have the driver take her home and she'd agreed, but only on the condition that he be dropped off first. For some reason, he had the impression that she lived close to the store....

"So how'd the meeting with your father go?" she asked, disregarding his remark about grandchildren.

"How did you know that's where I was?" Jake asked, peering at her suspiciously.

"I didn't, but you looked so concerned, I guessed it had to do with J.R."

"It went fine," he said, unwilling to reveal the details of his conversation with an employee, even if she'd become a special friend. He didn't plan to mention it to Holly, either. All he'd say was that he'd extended the dinner invitation to his father and J.R. had thanked her but sent his regrets.

"I'm worried about J.R.," Mrs. Miracle said, again surprising him.

"Why? He's in good health."

"Physically, yes, he's doing well for a man of his age."

"Then why are you worried?" Jake pressed.

Instead of answering, the older woman patted his back. "I'm leaving in a few minutes. Would you like me to wrap Gabe's robot before I go?"

"Ah, sure," he said.

"You *are* taking it with you when you go to Holly's for Christmas, aren't you?"

"Yes."

"Then I'll wrap it for you. I'll get some ribbon and nice paper from the gift-wrapping kiosk."

"Thank you," Jake said, still wondering what she'd meant about J.R.

The older woman disappeared, leaving Jake standing in the toy department scratching his head. He valued Mrs. Miracle as an employee and as a new friend, and yet every now and then she'd say something that totally confused him. How did she know so much about him and his father? Perhaps she'd met his parents years ago. Or...

Well, he couldn't waste time trying to figure it out now.

Jake was walking to the customer service counter when his cell phone rang. Holly. He answered immediately.

"Can you talk?" she asked. "I know it's probably insane at the store, but I had to tell you something."

"What is it? Everything okay?"

"It's my boss, Lindy Lee. Oh, Jake, I think I'm going to cry."

"What's wrong?" he asked, alarmed.

"Nothing. This is *good*. Lindy just called me into her office. I spoke with her this morning about a Christmas party. I saw what a great time your employees had. I thought it would help morale, so I mentioned it to Lindy Lee."

"She's going to have a party?"

"No, even better than that. I can have a real Christmas dinner now with a turkey and stuffing and all the extras like I originally planned. I... I'd decided to make fried chicken because I couldn't really afford anything else, and now I can prepare a traditional meal."

"You got your bonus?"

"Yes! And it's bigger than last year's, so I can pay for the robot now."

"That's fabulous news!"

"It is, Jake, it really is." She took a deep breath. "If you don't mind, I'd like to call your father and invite him personally."

Jake's smile faded. "I should tell you I already talked to Dad about joining us on Christmas Day."

"I hope he will."

"Don't count on it." Jake felt bad about discouraging her. "I think he'd like to, but he can't let go of his grief. He feels he'd dishonor the memory of my mother and sister if he celebrated Christmas. For him, their deaths and Christmas are all tied together."

"Oh, Jake, that's so sad."

"Yes…" He didn't say what he knew was obvious—that, until now, the same thing had been true of him.

"I'm looking forward to spending the day with you," Jake said, and he meant every word. "Can you meet me for lunch this afternoon?" he asked, not sure he could wait until Christmas to see her again.

When she agreed, he smiled, a smile so wide that several customers looked at him curiously…and smiled back.

Chapter Sixteen

HAPPIEST ARE THE PEOPLE WHO GIVE THE MOST
HAPPINESS TO OTHERS.

—MRS. MIRACLE

That same morning Lindy Lee called Holly into her office again. Saving the document she was working on, Holly grabbed a pad and pen and rushed inside. Gesturing toward the chair, Lindy invited her to sit. This was unusual in itself; Lindy Lee never went out of her way to make Holly comfortable. In fact, it was generally the opposite.

"I've given your suggestion some thought," she said crisply.

"You mean about the Christmas party for next year?"

Lindy Lee's eyes narrowed. "Of course I mean the Christmas party. I want you to organize one for tomorrow."

"*Tomorrow?* But—"

"No excuses. *You're* the one who asked for this."

"I'll need a budget," Holly said desperately. It was a little late to be organizing a party. Every caterer in New York would've been booked months ago. Finding a restaurant with an opening the day before Christmas would be hopeless. What was she thinking when she'd suggested the idea to Lindy Lee? Hadn't she emphasized that she was talking about the *following* year? Not this one? Holly hardly knew where to start.

Lindy Lee glared at her. "I'm aware that you'll require a budget. Please wait until I'm finished. You can ask your questions then."

"Okay, sorry." Holly wasn't sure how she was supposed to manage this on such short notice.

Lindy explained that she'd close the office at two, that she wanted festive decorations and Christmas music, and that attendance was mandatory. "You can bring your nephew if you like," she added, after setting a more than generous budget.

"In other words, the family of staff is included?"

"Good grief, no."

"But Gabe's family."

"He's adorable. He even—" Lindy Lee stopped abruptly.

Holly was in complete agreement about Gabe's cuteness, but it wouldn't go over well if Gabe was invited and no one else's children were. "The others might get upset," Holly said, broaching the subject cautiously. "I mean, if I bring Gabe and no other children are allowed, it might look bad."

Lindy Lee sat back and crossed her arms, frowning. "If we invite family, then the place will be overrun with the little darlings," she muttered sarcastically. She sighed. "*Should* we include them?"

Holly shook her head. "There are too many practical considerations. People with kids would have to go home and pick them up and… Well, I think it's too much trouble, so let's not."

"Okay," Lindy said with evident relief.

"I'll get right on this."

"You might invite Gabe to the office again," Lindy Lee shocked her by saying. "Maybe in the new year."

Holly wondered if she'd misunderstood. "You want me to bring Gabe into the office?"

"A half day perhaps," her boss said, amending her original thought.

"Okay." So Gabe had succeeded in charming Lindy Lee, something Holly had once considered impossible.

Lindy Lee turned back to her computer, effectively dismissing Holly. Head whirling with the difficulty of her assignment, Holly returned to her own desk. She immediately got a list of nearby restaurants and began making calls, all of which netted quick rejections. In fact, the people she spoke with nearly laughed her off the phone. By noon she was growing desperate and worried.

"How's it going?" Lindy Lee asked as she stepped out of her office to meet someone for lunch. "Don't answer. I can tell by the look on your face."

"If only we'd scheduled the party a bit sooner…"

"You shouldn't have waited until the last minute to spring it on me," she said, laying the blame squarely on Holly.

That seemed unfair and a little harsh, even for Lindy Lee.

"We could have our event here in the building," Lindy Lee suggested, apparently relenting. "The sixth floor has a big open space. Check with them and see if that's available."

"I'll do it right away."

"Good," Lindy said, and turned to leave.

"I'll make this party happen," Holly promised through gritted teeth.

"I'll hold you to that," Lindy Lee tossed over her shoulder on her way out the door.

As soon as she'd left, Holly called the sixth floor. As luck would have it, the only time available was the afternoon of Christmas Eve—exactly what she needed. That solved one problem, but there was still an equally large hurdle to jump. Finding a caterer.

Despite the urgency of this task, Holly kept her lunch date with Jake. These last days before Christmas made getting away for more than a few minutes difficult for him. Yet he managed with the help of his staff who, according to Jake, were determined to smooth the course of romance. Mrs. Miracle, God bless her, had spearheaded the effort.

Holly picked up a pastrami on rye at the deli and two coffees, and walked to Finley's; that was all they really had time for. Now that she'd been assured of her Christmas bonus, Holly had resumed the luxury of buying lunch. When she arrived at the store, white bag in hand, Jake was busy with a customer.

Mrs. Miracle saw her and came over to greet Holly. "My dear, what's wrong?"

Once again Holly was surprised at how readable she must be. "I'm on an impossible mission," she said.

"And what's that?" the older woman asked.

Holly explained. As soon as she'd finished, Mrs. Miracle smiled. "I believe I can help you."

"You can?" she asked excitedly.

"Yes, a friend of mine just opened a small restaurant in the Village. She's still getting herself established, but she'd certainly be capable of handling this party. What are you planning to serve? Sandwiches? Appetizers? Cookies? That sort of thing?"

"The party will be in the early afternoon, so small sandwiches and cookies would be perfect. It doesn't have to be elaborate." At this point she'd accept almost anything.

"I'll get you my friend's number."

"Yes, please, and, Mrs. Miracle, thank you so much."

"No problem, my dear. None whatsoever." The older woman beamed her a smile. "By the way, I've set up a table in the back of the storeroom for you and Jake to have your lunch."

"How thoughtful."

"You go on back and Jake'll be along any minute. Meanwhile, I'll get you that phone number."

"Thanks," she said again. "Could you tell me your friend's name?"

"It's Wendy," she said. "Now don't you worry about a thing, you hear?"

Feeling deeply relieved, Holly went to the storeroom. Sure enough, Mrs. Miracle had set up a card table, complete with a white tablecloth and a small poinsettia in the middle. Holly put down the sandwich, plus a couple of pickles and the two cups of coffee.

Jake came in a few minutes later, looking harassed. He kissed her, then took his place. "It's crazy out there," he said, slumping in his chair.

"I can tell." She noticed that the rest of the staff was diligently avoiding the storeroom, no doubt under orders from Mrs. Miracle.

He reached for his half of the massive sandwich. "I sold the last of the robots this morning."

"That's wonderful!"

"It is and it isn't," he said between bites. "I wish I'd ordered another hundred. We could've sold those, as well. Now we have to turn people away. I hate disappointing anyone."

"Is there any other store in town with inventory?"

"Nope, and believe me, I've checked. Another shipment is due in a week after Christmas but by then it'll be too late."

Holly hated to bring up the subject of Gabe's Intellytron, but she needed Jake's reassurance that the one he'd set aside hadn't been sold in the robot-buying frenzy. "You still have Gabe's, don't you?"

Still chewing on his sandwich, Jake nodded. "Mrs. Miracle wrapped it herself. It's sitting right over there." He pointed to a counter across from her. The large, brightly decorated package rested in one corner.

"I'm so grateful you did this for me," she told him. Meeting Jake had been one of the greatest blessings of the year—in so many ways.

"Thank Mrs. Miracle, too," he said. "She wasn't even supposed to be in today, but she ended up staying to help us out."

The few minutes they'd grabbed flew by much too quickly. Jake stood, kissed her again, and they left the storeroom together. As they stepped onto the floor, Mrs. Miracle handed her a slip of paper. "The name of the restaurant is Heavenly Delights and here's the number."

"Heavenly Delights," Holly repeated. "I'll give your friend a call as soon as I'm back at my desk."

"You do that."

Holly tucked the paper in her coat pocket and nearly danced all the way to the office. With a little help from Mrs. Miracle, she'd be able to pull off a miracle of her own—she'd organize this Christmas party, regardless of the difficulties and challenges.

Once at her desk, Holly reached for the phone and called the number Mrs. Miracle had written down for her.

"Hello." A woman answered on the third ring.

"Hello," Holly returned brightly. "Is this Wendy?"

"Yes. And you are?"

"I'm Holly Larson, and I'm phoning on behalf of Lindy Lee."

"Lindy Lee, the designer?" Wendy sounded impressed.

"Yes," Holly answered. "I know I'm probably calling at the worst time, but I felt I should contact you as soon as possible." She assumed the restaurant would be busy with the lunch crowd.

"No, no, this is fine."

"I was given your phone number by Emily Miracle."

"Who?"

"Oh, sorry. Her badge says Miracle, but that's a mistake. Rather than cause a fuss, she asked that we call her Mrs. Miracle, although that's not actually her name. I apologize, but I can't remember what it is. I'm so accustomed to calling her Mrs. Miracle." Holly hoped she wasn't rambling.

"Go on," Wendy urged without commenting on all the confusion about names.

"Long story short, she suggested I call you about catering Lindy Lee's Christmas party for her employees."

"She did?"

"Yes… She highly recommended you and the restaurant."

"What restaurant?"

"Heavenly Delights," Holly said. Wendy must own more than one. "The location in the Village."

"Heavenly Delights," Wendy gasped, then started to laugh. "Heavenly Delights?"

"Yes." Holly's spirits took a sharp dive; nevertheless, she forged ahead. "I'm wondering if you could work us into your schedule."

"Oh, dear."

Holly's spirits sank even further. "You can't do it?"

"I didn't say that."

Her emotions went from hopeful to disheartened and back again. "Then you could?"

"I… I don't know what to say." The woman seemed completely overwhelmed.

Yes, I can do it would certainly make Holly's day, but the words weren't immediately forthcoming.

"Unfortunately, the party's scheduled for tomorrow afternoon—Christmas Eve." Holly suspected that, by then, practically everyone in the restaurant business would be closing down and heading home to their families. As an incentive, she mentioned the amount she could offer. The catering would take up most of the budget, with a little left over for decorations.

"That sounds fair," Wendy said.

"Would you be able to accommodate us?" she asked hopefully. "We're talking about forty people, give or take."

"I…"

Holly closed her eyes, fearing the worst.

"I think I could. However, there's something you should know."

"What's that?"

"First, I can't imagine who this Mrs. Miracle is."

"As I said, that isn't her real name. But I can find out for you, if you like."

"No, it doesn't matter. What I wanted to tell you is that I don't have a restaurant."

"No restaurant?" Holly's mouth went dry.

"The thing is, I've been talking with my daughter about opening one. She's attending culinary school. I've been praying about it, too. However, a lot of problems stand in the way—one of which is money."

"Oh."

"When I applied for a loan, the bank officer asked me

what we intended to call the restaurant. Lucie and I have gone over dozens of names and nothing felt right. Our specialty would be desserts.... I like the name Heavenly Delights. If you don't mind, I'll borrow it."

"I... That's the name Mrs. Miracle gave me."

"Well, if *she* doesn't mind, we'll definitely use it." She paused. "Maybe I know her, but right now I can't figure out who she is."

"Um, so if you don't have a restaurant yet, you can't cater the event?"

"I can't," Wendy agreed. "But perhaps Lucie and her friends from culinary school could."

"Really?" Holly asked excitedly.

"Give me your number and I'll call her to see if we can make this happen."

"Great!"

Holly fidgeted until Wendy called back five minutes later. "We'll do it," Wendy told her. "Lucie talked to several of her colleagues and they're all interested. I can promise you'll *love* their menu. Lucie's already working on it."

"Fabulous. Thank you! Oh, thank you so much." Her relief was so great that she felt like weeping.

She disconnected just as Lindy returned from lunch.

"The party's all set," Holly said happily.

"Really?" She'd impressed Lindy Lee, which was no small feat.

"Christmas Eve from two to four."

Her employer nodded. "Good job, Holly."

Holly closed her eyes and basked in the glow of Lindy Lee's approval.

Chapter Seventeen

WE DON'T CHANGE GOD'S MESSAGE.
HIS MESSAGE CHANGES US.

—MRS. MIRACLE

Jake glanced at his watch and felt a surge of relief. Five-thirty on Christmas Eve; in half an hour, the store would close its doors for the season.

Finley's would open again on the twenty-sixth for the year-end frenzy. He felt good that toy sales for this quarter were twenty percent higher than the previous year. He attributed the boost in revenue to Intellytron the SuperRobot. Jake felt vindicated that his hunch had been proven right. He'd be proud to take these latest figures to his father. While the robot alone didn't explain the increase, the fact that it was available at Finley's had brought new customers into the store.

Holly was occupied with her boss and the Christmas

party, which she'd arranged for Lindy Lee at the last moment. The poor girl had worked herself into a nervous state to pull off the event, and Jake was confident that the afternoon had gone well. He knew Holly had obsessed over each and every detail.

No doubt exhausted, she'd go home to her Brooklyn apartment as soon as she was finished with the cleanup. Jake would come by later that evening to spend time with her and Gabe. The three of them would enjoy a quiet dinner and then attend Christmas Eve services at her church.

It felt strangely luxurious not to be rushing away from the city with his father, although Jake was saddened that he hadn't been able to convince J.R. to join them on Christmas Day.

His cell chirped, and even before he looked, Jake knew it was Holly.

"Hi," he said. "How'd the party go?"

"Great! Wonderful. Even Lindy Lee was pleased. The caterers did a fabulous job, above and beyond my expectations. Wendy told me that Heavenly Delights plans to specialize in desserts and they should. Everything was spectacular."

"I'm glad."

"Don't forget to bring over Gabe's gift tonight," she said in a tired voice. As he'd expected, Holly was worn-out.

"Sure thing."

"We'll hide it in my bedroom until he goes to sleep, and then we can put it under the tree. That way it'll be the first thing he sees Christmas morning."

"Sounds like a plan."

"I'll distract him when you arrive so you can shove it in my closet."

"Okay."

She hesitated. "Are you sure you can't talk your father into coming for Christmas dinner?"

"I don't think so, Holly. He isn't ready to give up his... vacation." He nearly choked on the word.

"Ask him again, would you?" she said softly.

"I will," he agreed with some reluctance, knowing it wouldn't have any effect.

"And thank Mrs. Miracle for me. She saved the day with this recommendation."

"Of course. Although I believe she's already left."

"She'll be back, won't she?"

"As seasonal help, she'll stay on until the end of January when we finish inventory." The older woman had been a real success in the department. She'd reassured parents and entertained their kids. If she was interested, Jake would like to offer her full-time employment.

He ended his conversation with Holly and went into the storeroom to pick up Gabe's robot.

He stopped short. The package that had lain on the counter, the package so beautifully wrapped by Mrs. Miracle, was missing.

Gone.

"Karen," Jake said, walking directly past a customer to confront one of the other sales associates. If this was a practical joke, he was not amused. "Where's the robot that was on the counter in the storeroom?" he demanded, ignoring the last-minute shopper she was assisting.

Karen blinked as though he was speaking in a foreign language. "I beg your pardon?"

"The wrapped gift in the storage room?" he repeated.

"I... I don't have a clue."

"You know what I'm talking about, don't you?"

Her face became flushed. "I'm not sure."

"It was wrapped and ready for delivery and now it's missing." Jake couldn't believe anyone would steal the robot. He knew his employees, and there wasn't a single one who was capable of such a deed. He'd stake his career on it.

"Did you ask John?"

"No." Jake quickly sought out the youngest sales associate. John had just finished with a customer and looked expectantly at Jake.

"The robot's missing," he said without preamble.

John stared back at him. "The one in the storeroom?"

"Are there any others in this department?" he snapped. If there were, he'd grab one and be done with it. However, no one knew better than Jake that there wasn't an Intellytron to be had.

"I saw it," Gail said, joining them.

Relief washed over Jake. Someone had moved it without telling him; that was obviously what had happened. The prospect of facing Holly and telling her he didn't have the robot didn't bear thinking about.

That morning, the moment she'd received her Christmas bonus, Holly had rushed over to Finley's to pay for the toy. Her face had been alight with happiness as she described how excited Gabe would be when he found his gift under the Christmas tree. That robot meant so much to the boy. If Jake didn't bring it as promised, Holly might not forgive him. He hoped that wouldn't happen, but the thought sent a chill through him nonetheless.

Frances, another sales associate, came over, too. "Mrs. Miracle had it," she said.

"When?"

"This morning," Frances explained. "She didn't mention it to you?"

"No." Jake shook his head. "What did she do with it?"

Frances stared down at the floor. "She sold it."

"*Sold* it?" Jake exploded. This had to be some kind of joke—didn't it? "How could she do that? It was already paid for by someone else." That robot belonged to Gabe Larson. She knew that as well as anyone.

"Why would she sell it?" he burst out again, completely bewildered.

"I… I don't know. You'll have to ask her," Frances said. "I'm so sorry, Mr. Finley. I'm sure there's a logical explanation."

There'd better be. Not that it would help now.

Sick at heart, Jake left the department and went up to his father's office. Dora had already gone home; the whole administrative floor was deserted. He didn't know what he'd tell Holly. He should've taken the robot to his apartment and kept it there. Then he could've been guaranteed that nothing like this would happen. Still, berating himself now wouldn't serve any useful purpose.

Preparing for his flight, J. R. Finley was busy stuffing paperwork in his computer case when Jake entered the office. J.R. looked up at him. "What's the matter with you? Did you decide to come with me, after all?"

"No. Have you decided to stay in New York?" Jake countered.

"You're kidding, right?"

Jake slumped into a chair and ran his fingers through his hair. "Gabe's robot is missing," he said quietly. "Emily Miracle, or whatever her name is, sold it."

"Mrs. Miracle?" J.R.'s face tightened and he waved his index finger at Jake. "I told you that woman was up to no good, butting into other people's business. She's a troublemaker. Didn't I tell you that?"

"Dad, stop it. She's a sweet grandmotherly woman."

"She's ruined a little boy's Christmas and you call that *sweet?*" He made a scoffing sound and resumed his task of collecting papers and shoving them into his case.

"Do you have any connections—someone who can locate a spare Intellytron at the last minute?" This was Jake's only hope.

Frowning, his father checked his watch. "I'll make some phone calls, but I can't promise anything."

Jake was grateful for whatever his father could do. "What about your flight?"

J.R. looked at his watch again and shrugged. "I'll catch a later one."

Jake started to remind his father that changing flights at this point might be difficult, but stopped himself. If J.R. was going to offer his assistance, Jake would be a fool to refuse.

"I'll shut down the department and meet you back here in twenty minutes," Jake said.

His father had picked up his phone and was punching out numbers. One thing Jake could be assured of—if there was a single Intellytron left in the tristate area, J.R. would locate it and have it delivered to Gabe.

He hurried back to the toy department and saw that the last-minute customers were being ushered out, bags in hand, and the day's sales tallied. The store was officially closed. His staff was waiting to exchange Christmas greetings with Jake so they could go home to their families.

"Is there anything we can do before we leave?" John asked, speaking for the others.

"No, thanks. You guys have been great. Merry Christmas, everyone!"

As soon as they'd left, he got Mrs. Miracle's contact information and called the phone number she'd given HR.

To his shock, a recorded voice message informed him that
the number was no longer in service. That wasn't the only
shock, either—she'd handed in her notice that afternoon.

He groaned. Mrs. Miracle was unreachable and had ab-
sconded with precious information regarding the robot—
like why she'd sold it and to whom.

Jake returned to his father's office to find him pacing the
floor with the receiver pressed to his ear. J.R. glanced in
Jake's direction, then quickly looked away. That tight-lipped
expression told Jake everything he needed to know—his
father hadn't been successful.

He waited until J.R. hung up the phone.

"No luck," Jake said, not bothering to phrase it in the
form of a question.

J.R. shook his head. "Everyone I talked to said as far
as they knew we're the only store in five states to have the
robot."

"*Had.* We sold out."

"Apparently there isn't another one to be found anywhere
till after Christmas."

Jake had expected that. A sick feeling attacked the pit
of his stomach as he sank into a chair and sighed loudly. "I
appreciate your help, Dad. Thanks for trying."

"I'm sorry I couldn't do more." J.R. nodded and placed a
consoling hand on Jake's shoulder. "I know how you feel."

Jake doubted that but he wasn't in the mood to argue.

"Holly's special," J.R. said. "I've known that since the
first time you mentioned her."

"She is." Jake was in full agreement there.

"If it'd been your mother who needed that thing, I
would've moved heaven and earth to make sure she got it."

He reconsidered. Maybe his father *did* know what he
was feeling. He'd done his utmost to keep Holly and Gabe

from being disappointed. Unfortunately, nothing he or J.R. did now would make any difference. It was simply too late.

"Every Intellytron in New York State and beyond is wrapped and under some youngster's tree," J.R. said.

Jake rubbed his face. "I'll come up with something to tell Holly and Gabe," he said, thinking out loud.

"Is there anything else the boy might like?" his father asked.

The only toy Gabe had referred to, at least in Jake's hearing, was the robot. He'd even risked Holly's wrath and traveled into the city on his own just to see it again and watch it in action.

"What about a train set?" his father suggested. "Every little boy wants a train set."

Jake had. He'd longed for one the Christmas his mother and sister had died. But there'd been no presents the next morning or any Christmas morning since the accident.

"He might," Jake said. "But—"

"Well, we have one of those."

Jake wondered what his father was talking about. As head of the toy department Jake was well aware of the inventory left in stock and there were no train sets. This season had been record-breaking in more ways than one; not only the robot but a number of other toys had sold out. The trains, a popular new doll, a couple of computer games… "Exactly where is there a train set?" he asked. "Unless you mean the one in the window…"

"Not the display train. A brand-new one. Except that it's twenty-one years old." J.R. swallowed visibly. "I have it," he said. "It's still wrapped in the original paper. Your mother bought it for you just before…" He didn't need to finish the sentence.

"Mom bought me the train set I wanted?" Jake asked, his voice hoarse with emotion.

J.R. grinned. "You were spoiled, young man. Your mother loved you deeply. And your little sister adored you."

A sense of loss hit him hard and for a moment that was all Jake could think about. "You kept the train set all these years?" he finally asked.

J.R. nodded solemnly. "I always meant to give it to you but I could never part with it. In a way, holding on to it was like…having your mother still with me. I could pretend it was Christmas Eve twenty-one years ago and she hadn't died. Don't worry, I didn't *actually* believe that, but I could indulge the fantasy of what Christmas should've been. That train set made the memory so real…."

"And you're willing to give it up for Gabe?"

"No" was his father's blunt reply. "I'm willing to give it up for *you*."

Jake smiled and whispered, "Thanks, Dad."

"You're welcome. Now we've got a bit of digging to do. I don't remember where I put that train set but I know it's somewhere in the condo. Or maybe the storage locker. Or…"

"Do we have time? Did you change your flight?"

"Flight?" J.R. repeated, then seemed to remember he was scheduled to fly out that evening. Shaking his head, he muttered, "It's fine. I'll catch one tomorrow if I have to."

Jake didn't want to pressure his father, but he'd promised Holly he'd invite J.R. to dinner at her apartment. Although he'd already tried once, he'd ask again. If he was going to disappoint her on one front, then the least he could do was surprise her on another.

"Since you're apparently staying over…" he began.

"Yes?"

"Have Christmas dinner with Holly and Gabe and me tomorrow afternoon. Will you do that, Dad?"

His father took a long moment to consider the invitation. Then, as if the words were difficult to say, he slowly whispered, "I believe I will. Something tells me your mother would want me to."

Chapter Eighteen

GOD ISN'T POLITICALLY CORRECT.
HE'S JUST CORRECT.

—MRS. MIRACLE

Holly set the phone down and forced herself to keep the smile on her face. Gabe's robot was missing. Because Gabe was in earshot, she couldn't ask Jake the questions that clamored in her mind. He'd said something about Mrs. Miracle, but Holly had been too disheartened to remember what followed.

Adding to her distress, Jake had said there was something he needed to do with his father, which meant he'd have to renege on dinner that night. In addition to the bad news about the missing robot, Jake had passed on some good news, too. Evidently his father had changed his plans and would be joining them on Christmas Day, after all, which delighted Holly and greatly encouraged her. She recognized that this was no small concession on J.R.'s part.

"Isn't Jake coming for dinner?" Gabe asked, looking up from his handheld video game. He lay on the sofa as he expertly manipulated the keys.

"I... No. Unfortunately, Jake has something else he has to do," Holly explained, doing her best to maintain an even voice. "Something really important," she emphasized.

Gabe frowned and sat up. "What's more important than Christmas Eve?"

Again Holly made an effort to pretend nothing was wrong. "We'll have to ask when we see him tomorrow," she said airily.

Her nephew slouched back onto the sofa. His downcast look prompted Holly to sit beside him. She felt as depressed as Gabe did, but was trying hard not to show it. In the larger scheme of life, these disappointments were minor. Nevertheless, she'd hoped to give Gabe a very special gift this year. And she'd hoped—so had Gabe—to spend Christmas Eve with Jake.

"Did Jake promise to come tomorrow?"

"He'll be here."

"But he said he'd come for dinner tonight, too—and he didn't."

"We'll have a wonderful time this evening, just the two of us." She slipped her arm around his small frame and squeezed gently.

Gabe didn't seem too sure of that. "Can I email my dad?"

"Of course." Holly would come up with ways to keep them both occupied until it was time to walk to church for the Christmas Eve service. They could watch a Christmas movie; Gabe might enjoy *The Bishop's Wife,* Holly's favorite, or *A Christmas Carol* with Alastair Sim as the ultimate Scrooge. Still cheering herself up, she headed into her kitchen to start frying the chicken, which had been marinating in buttermilk since six that morning. They'd have turkey tomorrow, but tonight she'd make the meal she associated with her mother…with comfort.

Gabe leaped up from the sofa and hurried into the kitchen. "Can we invite Mrs. Miracle for dinner?" he asked excitedly.

"Oh, Gabe, I wish we'd thought of that sooner."

"I like Mrs. Miracle."

"I like her, too." The older woman had never mentioned whether she had family in the area, which made Holly wonder if she was spending this evening by herself.

Gabe returned to writing his email. "Dad's surprise didn't come, did it?" he said in a pensive voice.

Holly suddenly realized it hadn't. This complicated everything. Not only wouldn't she be able to give her nephew the only toy he'd requested for Christmas, but the gift his father had mailed hadn't arrived, either.

"He might be mad at me for going into the city by myself," Gabe murmured.

"Oh, sweetie, I'm positive that's not it."

Before she could finish her reassurances, the doorbell chimed. Hoping, despite everything, that it was Jake, Holly answered the door, still wearing her apron. To her astonishment, Emily Miracle was standing in the hall.

"I hope you don't mind me dropping in unexpectedly like this."

"Mrs. Miracle! Mrs. Miracle!" Gabe rushed to the door. "We were just talking about you." He grabbed her free hand and tugged her into the apartment. "Can you stay for dinner? Aunt Holly's making fried chicken and there's corn and mashed potatoes and cake, too. You can stay, can't you? Jake said he was coming and now he can't."

"Oh, dear," Emily said, laughing softly. "I suppose I could. I came by to bring you my Christmas salad. It's a family favorite and I wanted to share it with you."

"That's so nice of you, Emily," Holly said, adding a place setting to the table. Her mood instantly lightened.

"Jake *said* he'd come," Gabe pouted.

"He's doing something important," Holly reminded her nephew.

"I'm sure he is," Emily said, giving Holly a covered ceramic bowl and removing her coat. "It isn't like Jake to cancel at the last moment without a good reason. He's a very responsible young man—in his personal life and in business, too. He'll do his father proud." She held out her hands for the bowl.

"You mean *does* his father proud," Holly corrected, passing it back. She had every confidence that Jake would one day step up to the helm at Finley's, but that was sometime in the future. Jake seemed to think it might take as long as five years, and he said that suited him fine.

"Yes, that's what I mean. I've enjoyed working with him this Christmas season." Emily made her way into the kitchen and put her salad in the refrigerator.

"Can you come to church with us?" Gabe asked, following her. "It's Christmas Eve, and there's a special program and singing, too."

"I'd like that very much, but unfortunately I already have other plans."

"We're grateful you could have dinner with us," Holly said. She waited until Gabe had left the room before she asked Emily about the robot.

"Do you have any idea what happened to the you-know-what Jake put aside?" She spoke guardedly because the apartment was small and she wanted to ensure that Gabe didn't hear anything that would upset him.

Mrs. Miracle was about to answer when he dashed into the kitchen again.

Grasping the situation, she immediately distracted him. "Do you want to help me fill the water glasses?" she asked.

"Okay," Gabe agreed.

Emily poured water into the pitcher, which she handed to Gabe. Holding it carefully, he walked over to the dining area, which was actually part of the living room. The older woman turned to Holly. "I think there was a misunderstanding between Jake and me," she said in a low voice. "I'll clear everything up as soon as I can."

"Please do," Holly whispered. She tried to recall her conversation with Jake. He seemed to imply that Emily had sold the robot to someone else. That didn't seem possible. She'd never do anything to hurt a little boy; Holly was convinced of it.

The fried chicken couldn't have been better; in fact, it was as good as when her mother had prepared this dish. Holly had wanted tonight's meal to be memorable for Gabe, and because Mrs. Miracle was with them, it was.

During dinner, Emily entertained them with story after story of various jobs she'd taken through the years. She'd certainly had her share of interesting experiences, working as a waitress, a nanny, a nurse and now a salesperson.

All too soon, it was time to get ready for church. Holly reluctantly stood up from the table.

"Everything was lovely," Mrs. Miracle told her with a smile of appreciation. "I've never had chicken that was more delicious." She carried her empty dessert plate to the kitchen sink. "And that coconut cake…"

"I liked the sauce best," Gabe chimed in, putting his plate in the sink, too.

"I loved the salad," Holly said, and was sincere. "I hope you'll give me the recipe."

"Of course. I'll be happy to write it out for you now if you'll get me some paper and a pen."

Holly tore a page from a notebook and grabbed Gabe's Santa pen; minutes later, Mrs. Miracle handed her the recipe with a flourish. "Here you go." Then she frowned at her watch. "Oh, my. I hate to run, but I'm afraid I must."

"No, no, don't worry," Holly assured her. "We have to leave for church, anyway. I'm just glad you could be with us this evening. It meant a lot to Gabe and me."

The older woman bent down and kissed the boy's cheek. "This is going to be a very special Christmas for you, young man. Just you wait. It's one you'll remember your whole life. Someday you'll tell your grandchildren about the best Christmas of your life."

"Do you really think so?" Gabe asked, eyes alight with happiness.

She reached for her coat and put it on before she hugged Holly goodbye. "It's going to be a special Christmas for you, as well, my dear."

Holly smiled politely. Maybe Mrs. Miracle was right, but it definitely hadn't started out that way.

Gabe woke at six o'clock Christmas morning. He knocked on Holly's bedroom door and shouted, "It's Christmas!" Apparently he suspected she might have forgotten.

Holly opened one eye. Still half-asleep, she sat up and stretched her arms above her head.

"Can we open our presents?" Gabe asked, leaping onto her bed.

"What about breakfast?" she said.

"I'm not hungry. You aren't, either, are you?" The question had a hopeful lilt, as though any thought of food would be equally irrelevant to her.

"I could eat," she said.

Gabe's face fell.

"I could eat...later," she amended.

His jubilant smile reappeared.

"Shall we see what Santa brought you?" she asked, tossing aside her covers. She threw on her housecoat and accompanied him into the living room, where the gifts beneath the small tree awaited their inspection.

Gabe fell to his knees and began rooting through the packages she'd set out the night before, after he'd gone to sleep. He must've known from the size of the wrapped boxes that the robot wasn't among them. He sat back on his heels. "Santa didn't get me Intellytron, did he?"

"I don't know, sweetie. I hear Santa sometimes makes late deliveries."

"He does?" Hope shone in his face. "When?"

"That I can't say." Rather than discuss the subject further, Holly hurried into the kitchen.

While she put on a pot of coffee, Gabe arranged the gifts in two small piles. Most of them had been mailed by Holly's parents, and Gabe's didn't take long to unwrap. He was wonderful, sweetly expressing gratitude and happiness with his few gifts. A number of times Holly had to wipe tears from her eyes.

"I hope you're not too disappointed," she said when she could speak. "I know how badly you wanted the robot—and I'm sure Santa has one for you but it might be a little late."

Gabe looked up from the new video game she'd purchased on her way home from work. "I bet I'll still get Intellytron. Mrs. Miracle said this was going to be my best Christmas ever, remember? And it wouldn't be without my robot." He jumped up and slid his arms around Holly's neck and gave her a tight hug.

She opened her gifts after that—a book from her parents, plus a calendar and a peasant-style blouse. And the origami purse from Gabe, which brought fresh tears to her eyes.

They had a leisurely breakfast of French toast and then, while Gabe played with his new video game, Holly got the turkey in the oven. The doorbell rang around eleven o'clock.

Jake and his father came in, carrying a large wrapped box between them. Holly's heartbeat accelerated. It must be Intellytron, although the box actually seemed too big.

"Merry Christmas," Jake said, and held her close. "Don't get excited—this isn't what you think it is," he whispered in her ear just before he kissed her.

"Merry Christmas, young man," J.R. said, and shook Gabe's hand.

"What's that?" Gabe asked, eyeing the box Jake had set on the carpet.

"Why don't you open it and see?" J.R. suggested.

Jake stood at Holly's side with his arm around her waist. "I'm sorry I had to cancel last night," he said in a low voice.

"It's fine, don't worry."

"Mrs. Miracle came over," Gabe said as he sat on the floor beside the box.

"Emily Miracle?" Jake frowned. "Did she happen to deliver something?" he asked, his eyes narrowing.

"She brought a Christmas salad for dinner," Gabe told him, tearing away the ribbon. He looked up. "We didn't eat it all. Do you want to taste it?" He wrinkled his nose. "For green stuff, it was pretty good."

"I wouldn't want to ruin my dinner," J.R. said, smiling down at him. "Go ahead, young man, and let 'er rip."

Gabe didn't need any encouragement. He tore away the wrapping paper. "It's a train set," he said. "That was the second thing on my Christmas list, after Intellytron. Can we set it up now?"

"I don't see why not," Jake told him and got down on his knees with Gabe. "I wanted one when I was around your age, too."

"Did you get one?" Gabe asked.

Jake looked at his father, who sat on the sofa, and nodded. "I certainly did, and it was the best train set money could buy."

Gabe took the engine out of the box. "Wow, this is heavy."

"Let's lay out the track first, shall we?"

Holly sat on the sofa next to Jake's father. "I'm so glad you could have dinner with us."

"I am, too." A pained look came over him and he gave a slight shake of his head. "I was sure I'd never want to celebrate Christmas again, but I've decided it's time I released the past and started to prepare for the future."

"The future?" she repeated uncertainly.

"Grandchildren," J.R. said with a sheepish grin. "I have the distinct feeling that my son has met the woman he's going to love as much as I loved his mother."

Embarrassed, Holly looked away. With all her heart she hoped she was that woman.

"Jake would be furious with me if he knew I'd said anything. It's too soon—I realize that. He probably isn't aware of how strongly he feels, but I know. I've seen my son with other women. He's in love with you, the same way I was in love with Helene."

Holly was about to make some excuse about dinner and return to the kitchen when the doorbell chimed again. Everyone looked at her as if she knew who it would be.

"I… I wonder who that is," she murmured, walking to the door.

"It could be Mrs. Miracle," Gabe said hopefully.

Only it wasn't.

Holly opened the apartment door to find her brother standing there in his army fatigues, wearing a smile of pure happiness. In his arms he held a large wrapped box.

"Mickey!" she screamed. He put down the box and hugged her fiercely.

"Dad!" Gabe flew off the floor as though jet-propelled and launched himself into his father's arms.

Eyes closed, Mickey held the boy for a long, long time.

Merry Christmas, Holly thought, tears slipping down her face. Just as Emily Miracle had predicted, this was destined to be the best Christmas of Gabe's life.

Baby Arugula Salad with Goat Cheese, Pecans and Pomegranate Seeds

(from Debbie Macomber's Cedar Cove Cookbook)

*This salad is a lively blend of sharp arugula,
tangy goat cheese,
mellow pecans and tart pomegranates. If you can't find
arugula, substitute any delicate salad green.*

1 small shallot, minced
3 tablespoons balsamic vinegar
1 teaspoon Dijon mustard
Salt and pepper, to taste
½ cup extra-virgin olive oil
10 to 12 cups baby arugula (about 10 ounces)
1 cup pomegranate seeds (from one pomegranate)
½ cup toasted pecans, chopped
1 cup crumbled goat cheese

5. In a measuring cup, whisk shallot, vinegar, mustard, salt and pepper until combined. Slowly pour oil in a stream until blended.

6. In a large serving bowl, combine arugula, pomegranate seeds and pecans. Add dressing; toss to coat. Top salad with cheese; toss once.

Tip: Extra-virgin olive oil, which comes from the first cold pressing of the olives, has a stronger, purer flavor than virgin olive oil. Since it is more expensive, most cooks prefer to use it only for salad and other uncooked dishes. Virgin olive oil is better for sautéing.

Serves 8.

Chapter Nineteen

Mickey stepped into the apartment, still holding Gabe, and extended his hand to Jake. "You must be Jake Finley."

"And you must be Holly's brother, Mickey."

"I am."

"What's in there?" Gabe asked, looking over his father's shoulder at the large box resting on the other side of the open door.

"That's a little something Santa asked me to deliver," Mickey told his son.

Gabe squirmed out of his arms and raced back into the hallway. He stared at Holly and his grin seemed to take up his whole face. "I think I know what it is," he declared before pushing the box inside. "Aunt Holly told me Santa sometimes makes deliveries late."

No one needed to encourage him to unwrap the gift this time. He tore into the wrapping paper, which flew in all directions. As soon as he saw the picture of Intellytron on the outside of the box, Gabe gave a shout of exhilaration.

"It's my robot! It's my robot!"

"Wherever did you find one?" J.R. asked Mickey. The older man stepped forward and extended his hand. "J. R. Finley," he said.

"He bought it at Finley's," Jake answered in a confused tone.

"Our department store?" J.R. sounded incredulous. "When?"

"My guess is that it was late on Christmas Eve." Again, Jake supplied the answer.

"And how do you know all this?" Holly had a few questions of her own.

"Because that's the gift wrap Mrs. Miracle used."

"But...who sold it to him?" J.R. appeared completely befuddled by this latest development.

"Mrs. Miracle," Jake and Holly murmured simultaneously.

"He's right," Mickey said as he sat on the couch next to his son, who remained on the floor. "I remember her name badge. Mrs. Miracle. We talked for a few minutes."

Thankfully, Gabe was too involved with his robot to listen.

"I had a chance to go into the city yesterday," Mickey told them.

"Wait." Holly held up her hand. "You've got some splainin' to do, Lieutenant Larson. Why are you in New York in the first place?"

Mickey laughed. "Don't tell me you don't want me here?"

"No, no, of course I do! But you might've said something."

"I couldn't."

"Security reasons?" Holly asked.

"No, just that I wasn't sure I'd get the leave I was hoping for. I've been sent back for specialized training—I'll be at Fort Dix for the next six weeks. I didn't want to say anything to Gabe yet, in case it fell through. I could tell from his emails that he was starting to adjust to life here with you. It would've been cruel to raise his hopes, only to have Uncle Sam dash them. Turns out I was on duty until nine this morning…so here I am. I thought I'd bring Gabe his Christmas surprise."

"You might've mentioned it to *me*," Holly said with more than a little consternation.

"True, but I had to take your poor track record with keeping secrets into consideration."

"I can keep a secret," she insisted.

"Oh, yeah? What about the time you told Candi Johnson I had a crush on her?"

"I was twelve years old!"

Jake chuckled and she sent him a stern look. If Mickey had asked her not to say anything about his possible visit, she wouldn't have uttered a word. Then it occurred to her that he'd hinted at it when he referred to the surprise he was sending Gabe. Fantastic, stupendous, *exhilarating* though this was, a Christmas visit was the last thing she'd expected.

"But why buy the robot?" Holly asked. "I told you I'd get it for Gabe."

"Yes, but you were going without lunches—"

"True," she interrupted, whispering so Gabe wouldn't hear. "Then Lindy Lee had a change of heart and decided to give me a Christmas bonus, after all."

Mickey shrugged. "You didn't say anything to me. Not that it matters because *I* wanted to get this for Gabe."

"I didn't tell you I received my bonus?"

"You've done enough for the two of us," Mickey told her, his eyes warm with appreciation. "I didn't want to burden you with the added expense of Christmas."

"Hey, Holly, that means Finley's owes you two hundred and fifty dollars," Jake said. "Plus tax. By the way, Mickey, did you tell Mrs. Miracle who you were?" he asked, approaching the two of them. He slipped his arm around Holly's waist and she casually leaned against him.

Mickey shook his head. "Should I have?"

Jake and Holly exchanged a glance, but it was Jake who voiced their question. "How did she know?"

"Know what?" Mickey asked.

"That it was you," Holly said.

"Look, Dad!" Gabe cried out.

Mickey turned his attention to the robot, who walked smartly toward him, stopped and asked in a tinny voice, "When…do…you…go…back…to… Afghanistan?"

Mickey's eyes widened. "How'd you make him say that?"

J.R., who'd been working with Gabe, grinned at Mickey. "I programmed him," Gabe announced proudly. "Mr. Finley helped, but he said I can do it on my own now that I know how."

"You managed to get the robot to do that already?"

"He does all kinds of cool tricks, Dad. Watch."

While Mickey and Gabe were engaged in programming the robot, Jake and Holly stepped into the kitchen.

"She *couldn't* have known Mickey was Gabe's father." Jake's face was clouded with doubt. "Could she?"

Holly didn't have an answer.

Jake continued, still frowning. "I tried to reach her, but the phone number she listed with HR wasn't in service."

"Then ask her when you see her again," Holly said. Jake had mentioned that, as seasonal help, Emily Miracle would be working until after inventory had been completed in January.

"I won't be able to," Jake told her. "When I went to HR for her personal information, I discovered that she'd handed in her notice. Christmas Eve was her last day."

"But…" Holly wanted to argue. Surely Mrs. Miracle would've said *something* at dinner the night before. Things didn't quite add up.… And yet, this wonderful woman had done so much to brighten their Christmas.

Before she could comment, the doorbell rang again. Holly chuckled, not even daring to guess who it might be *this* time. Her apartment was turning into Grand Central Station. If she had to guess, the last person to cross her mind would've been…

"Lindy!" Her employer's name shot out of Holly's mouth the second she opened the door.

Lindy Lee smiled hesitantly. "I hope I'm not intruding."

"You came, you came." Gabe bounded up from the floor and raced to Lindy Lee's side, taking her hand.

Lindy gave Holly an apologetic look. "Gabe invited me and since I, uh, didn't have any commitments, I thought I'd stop by for a few minutes and wish you all a merry Christmas." She glanced about the room. "I see you already have a houseful."

"I'm Gabe's father," Mickey said, stepping forward. "Holly's brother." He set his hands on Gabe's shoulders.

"She's the lady I wrote you about," Gabe said, twisting around and looking up at his father. "Isn't she pretty?"

"Yes, she is.…" Mickey seemed unable to take his eyes off Lindy Lee.

Holly wouldn't have believed it possible, but Lindy actually blushed.

"Thank you," the designer murmured.

"Make yourself at home," Holly said. "I was just about to serve some eggnog. Would you like a glass?"

"Are you sure it won't be any bother?"

"She's sure," Gabe said, dragging Lindy Lee toward the couch. "Here, sit next to my dad." He patted an empty space on the sofa. "Dad, you sit here."

Mickey smiled at Lindy Lee. "I guess we've got our orders."

"Yes, sir," Lindy joked, winking at Gabe.

"You know what she said to me, Dad?"

"What?"

"I said," Lindy Lee supplied, "that I need a little boy in my life. A little boy just like Gabe."

Holly wondered if she'd heard correctly. This woman who looked identical to her employer sounded nothing like the Lindy Lee she knew. Gone was the dictatorial, demanding tyrant who ran her fashion-design business with military precision. She'd either been taken over by aliens or Lindy Lee had a gentle side that she kept hidden and revealed only on rare occasions. Like Christmas...

An hour later, during a private moment in the kitchen, Jake gave Holly a gift—a cameo that had once belonged to his mother. He said J.R. had given it to him for this very purpose the night before. Holly was thrilled, honored, humbled. She held her breath as he put the cameo on its gold chain around her neck. Holly didn't have anything for him, but Jake said all he wanted was a kiss, and she was happy to comply.

Two hours after that, the small group gathered around the table laden with Christmas fare, including several bottles of exceptional wine brought by Jake and his father. Gabe sat between Mickey and Lindy Lee and chatted nonstop, while J.R. and Jake sat with Holly between them. They took turns saying grace, then took turns again, passing serving dishes to one another.

Amid the clinking of silverware on china and the animated conversation and laughter, Gabe's voice suddenly rose.

"Mrs. Miracle was right," he declared after his first bite of turkey. "This is the *best* Christmas ever."

Emily Merkle reached for her suitcase and started down the long road. Her job in New York was finished, and it had gone even better than she'd expected. Holly and Jake were falling in love. J.R. had more interest in anticipating the future than reliving the pain of the past. Mickey had met Lindy Lee, and Gabe had settled in nicely with his aunt Holly.

Emily hadn't walked far when she was joined by two others, a beautiful woman and a ten-year-old girl. Kaitlyn skipped gracefully at her mother's side, holding Helene's hand.

"All is well," Emily told the other woman. "J.R. and Jake will celebrate Christmas from now on. It was a big leap for J.R., but once the grandchildren arrive, he will lavish them with love."

"Jake will marry Holly?" she asked.

Emily nodded. "They'll have many years together."

"You chose well for my son."

Emily nodded in agreement. Jake and Holly were a good match and they'd bring out the best in each other.

The other woman smiled contentedly. "Thank you," she whispered.

"It was my pleasure," Emily told her.

And it truly was.

* * * * *

Get 4 FREE REWARDS!

We'll send you 2 FREE Books plus 2 FREE Mystery Gifts.

Both the **Romance** and **Suspense** collections feature compelling novels written by many of today's bestselling authors.

YES! Please send me 2 FREE novels from the Essential Romance or Essential Suspense Collection and my 2 FREE gifts (gifts are worth about $10 retail). After receiving them, if I don't wish to receive any more books, I can return the shipping statement marked "cancel." If I don't cancel, I will receive 4 brand-new novels every month and be billed just $7.24 each in the U.S. or $7.49 each in Canada. That's a savings of up to 28% off the cover price. It's quite a bargain! Shipping and handling is just 50¢ per book in the U.S. and $1.25 per book in Canada.* I understand that accepting the 2 free books and gifts places me under no obligation to buy anything. I can always return a shipment and cancel at any time. The free books and gifts are mine to keep no matter what I decide.

Choose one: ☐ **Essential Romance**   ☐ **Essential Suspense**
  (194/394 MDN GQ6M)   (191/391 MDN GQ6M)

Name (please print)

Address   Apt. #

City   State/Province   Zip/Postal Code

Email: Please check this box ☐ if you would like to receive newsletters and promotional emails from Harlequin Enterprises ULC and its affiliates. You can unsubscribe anytime.